Praise for
of Eri

LEARNIN

"I was completely taken with this novel and its hauntingly real descriptions of what it means to welcome a loved one home from war when big pieces of them have been punched out. . . . What makes this gem of a novel so special is that it isn't a book written for survivors or military audiences or any niche group; it is a universal and instructive tale of what it takes to dig down and find the good parts of a marriage, to fight not only for those you love but to be willing to make course corrections when life throws a curveball through your picture-perfect plans. . . . I dare anyone to read this book and not be fully absorbed and haunted by these two intricately drawn characters. . . . Celello has created a masterful mosaic of what PTSD can do to families."

—Lee Woodruff, *New York Times* bestselling author
of *Those We Love Most* and coauthor of *In an Instant*

"*Learning to Stay* is a compelling novel about a soldier who returns from Iraq a much different man than the one who first deployed and the wife poised between staying in this suddenly volatile relationship or forging ahead on her own. As an Army spouse, I am grateful for Erin Celello's dedication to revealing 'the hidden wounds of war' and how they impact our military and their families."

—Siobhan Fallon, author of *You Know When the Men Are Gone*

continued . . .

MIRACLE BEACH

"*Miracle Beach* gives the reader a vivid sense of the Pacific Northwest and the world of show jumping, but most importantly it shows how characters shattered by grief can put the pieces back together in an entirely new way. Erin Celello writes of loss and resilience with a sure, honest hand."

—Heidi Jon Schmidt, author of *The Harbormaster's Daughter*

"*Miracle Beach* ripples with surprising twists and turns. Erin Celello has a knack for writing characters that jolt the reader with the risks they take while also creating a satisfying sense of rightness. Love is here, grief, the beauty of place, suspense, and an ending that fits just right. Erin Celello has given us a fulfilling novel in *Miracle Beach*."

—Tina Welling, author of *Cowboys Never Cry* and *Fairy Tale Blues*

"*Miracle Beach* is a lyrical, surprising novel, set in a landscape as wild as memory. Erin Celello understands that the past is always present, and she takes that age-old truth and spins it into a story of secrets, sorrow, and second chances. A marvelous debut."

—Dean Bakopoulos, author of *My American Unhappiness*

"The skillfully portrayed, believably flawed heroine has to simultaneously come to grips with the upheaval of everything she knows and her tumultuous past. Celello gets to the heart of the human character, making this story one powerful read."   —*Romantic Times*

"Celello brings a fine sense of place to this earthy small town in Vancouver, Canada."   —*Publishers Weekly*

ALSO BY ERIN CELELLO

Miracle Beach

Learning to Stay

Erin Celello

NAL Accent
Published by New American Library,
a division of Penguin Group (USA) Inc.,
375 Hudson Street, New York, New York 10014, USA
Penguin Group (Canada), 90 Eglinton Avenue East, Suite 700, Toronto,
Ontario M4P 2Y3, Canada (a division of Pearson Penguin Canada Inc.)
Penguin Books Ltd., 80 Strand, London WC2R 0RL, England
Penguin Ireland, 25 St. Stephen's Green, Dublin 2,
Ireland (a division of Penguin Books Ltd.)
Penguin Group (Australia), 250 Camberwell Road, Camberwell,
Victoria 3124, Australia (a division of Pearson Australia Group Pty. Ltd.)
Penguin Books India Pvt. Ltd., 11 Community Centre,
Panchsheel Park, New Delhi - 110 017, India
Penguin Group (NZ), 67 Apollo Drive, Rosedale, Auckland 0632,
New Zealand (a division of Pearson New Zealand Ltd.)
Penguin Books (South Africa) (Pty.) Ltd., 24 Sturdee Avenue,
Rosebank, Johannesburg 2196, South Africa

Penguin Books Ltd., Registered Offices:
80 Strand, London WC2R 0RL, England

First published by NAL Accent, an imprint of New American Library,
a division of Penguin Group (USA) Inc.

First Printing, February 2013
1   3   5   7   9   10   8   6   4   2

 REGISTERED TRADEMARK—MARCA REGISTRADA

LIBRARY OF CONGRESS CATALOGING-IN-PUBLICATION DATA:

Celello, Erin.
Leaning to stay/Erin Celello.
p. cm.
ISBN 978-0-451-23697-5
1. Marriage—Fiction. 2. Iraq War, 2003–2011—Veterans—Fiction. 3. Human-animal
relationships—Fiction. 4. Domestic fiction. I. Title.
PS3603.E4L43 2013
813'.6—dc23   2012031699

Set in Minion Pro   •   Designed by Elke Sigal

Printed in the United States of America

PUBLISHER'S NOTE

This is a work of fiction. Names, characters, places, and incidents either are the product of
the author's imagination or are used fictitiously, and any resemblance to actual persons,
living or dead, business establishments, events, or locales is entirely coincidental.

The publisher does not have any control over and does not assume any responsibility
for author or third-party Web sites or their content.

For LLC and LSC,
who couldn't stay, and for ADO—
I'm so glad you did.

Prologue

This is how you survive a war.

Each morning as you wake, you run a hand over the cold space in the bed next to you. It's a simple touchstone, a reminder. You are here; your husband is not.

You sleep on his side of the bed now. Most mornings, your eyes are blurry and the text on your phone runs together when you check for a message from him. You have to squint, sometimes closing one eye or the other, scanning the e-mail that has come in overnight (mostly spam) to pick out the distinct peaks and valleys of your husband's name, Brad Sabatto, among it. If there is no new e-mail message, you reread some of the old ones. You have your favorites.

You make your own coffee, and because you're not a morning person like your husband, who is not here, sometimes you run late enough that the coffee doesn't get made. You brace yourself for the sludge in the law firm's kitchen that you'll have to drink until you can run out between appointments and get yourself a proper cup of joe.

You chitchat with your assistant and some of the other associates and say, "Fine," whenever anyone asks how you're holding up and how Brad is doing "over there." You spend much of your time doing math, trying to convert time zones, until the numbers break down and you can't remember whether you're ahead of Iraqi time or the other way around—whether your husband is in your past or you're in his. You spend too much time trying to decide which would be better.

You bring your phone into meetings and court appearances because it makes you feel better. You would worry less if he hadn't gone over there as infantry, as a grunt, but this is how things have played out. So you use personal e-mail far more than you're sure is allowed by the law firm's lengthy policies and procedures, and vow to be a better employee when your husband is stateside once again, and safe.

You don't know what it is that your husband is doing over there— what duties, thoughts, and dangers fill the minutes of his day. You can only imagine, and you are certain that the imagining is worse than knowing. But when you ask, he changes the subject. This happens often enough that, after a while, you stop asking. There's little sense in wasting the few moments you get to hear his voice on questions that won't be answered.

Because you aren't certain what, exactly, you should worry about, you try to stop yourself short of doing much active worrying. You tell yourself that he's smart and quick and strong and so are the guys around him. You tell yourself that the question is not *if* he comes home, but *when*—that he has a job to do over there and he's doing it, and you have your job to do here, and someday this will all seem like a tiny blip on the long timeline of your life.

Sometimes you even believe yourself.

But then there are times when the minutes of this damn deployment seem more like hours, the hours more like whole months to endure, and you wonder whether it's ever going to end. Once in a while you duck into the stairwell, prop the door open with your shoe so you can get back out, and have yourself a good little meltdown.

On those days you try to fill your time. You schedule lunches and drinks and sometimes dinners. You file motions and send letters to and on behalf of your clients and volunteer to write research memos for the partners. You answer e-mail and return voice mail. You become the world's best, most efficient, most hardworking attorney.

Most days, you drop off dry cleaning and pick it up. You sort the mail and pay bills and call the plumber when the bathroom sink won't stop dripping, and again, three days later, when water starts seeping through the wall next to the shower. You cancel a dentist appointment your husband made months ago, before any of this was the plan. You mow the lawn until it's covered in white, and then you scrape ice and shovel snow. You load and empty the dishwasher, scrub the tub, and wash sheets and clothes. Sometimes you fold them. Oftentimes you don't. Toward the end of some days, the responsibility of doing every last thing yourself, alone, weighs so heavy on you that you almost can't move.

You go to sleep, and wake up the next day, and then you do it all over again. Because there's no stopping this war. Soon enough you'll learn that. Soon enough you'll learn that sometimes you can fight and fight and never win. Because sometimes the war follows you home. And sometimes, it doesn't leave. It settles in and puts its feet up in your favorite recliner, nice and comfortable and oh-so-content to be there.

One

November 2004

"Turn that junk off, will you?" Darcy says, nodding at the television. "It's not good for you." Darcy's gurgling, wriggling ten-month-old daughter, Mia, is sitting naked on a blanket on the living room floor, fresh from her bath. Darcy bends down and rubs her nose against Mia's. The baby grabs a handful of Darcy's hair and Darcy pries it away. She adds, "For any of us."

Darcy's husband, Collin, became Brad's mentor when he fast-tracked for Officer Candidate School after enlisting. Now Collin is my husband's CO in Iraq. Here, Darcy is mine.

Anderson Cooper is promising an update on the war after the commercial break, complete with details about a roadside bombing in Anbar Province outside of Baghdad, where our husbands are stationed, but I listen to Darcy. Deep down, I know she's right. And it's rumored that our guys will be coming home soon anyway. Still, that OFF button is always heavy as a cinder block to move.

I watch Darcy pick up Mia—with her plump cheeks and impossi-

bly small pinkies and the little wisp of blond hair that tops her head—
and something inside me strains like a pulled muscle.

It's not true what they say about a biological clock. Nothing inside
me is ticking. Ticking suggests patience. What I have inside me is all
about pulsing and yearning and wandering the baby aisles of Target
for an hour when I went in only for deodorant, some highlighters,
and paper towels.

I trace a finger across Mia's velvet skin, Darcy smiles a half smile
at me, and Mia flails her chubby arms, now grabbing for Darcy's
glasses. "Soon, Elise," she says softly. She's used to this—to me, my
wistfulness around babies. With Brad in Iraq, every month I cross off
the calendar is one more without the promise of having my own.

Darcy's house feels like a home, unlike the house Brad and I
bought before he left. Ours has all the ambiance of an oversize college
dorm room, given the melding of our used and mismatched furniture. At Darcy's, the couches match the curtains, her well-worn
kitchen table expands to seat ten and often does on holidays, and a
ceramic heart that reads HAPPILY EVER AFTER hangs by a coiled wire
over the stove. Darcy is five years older than I am, and even though
she looks young, the years between us feel greater. She and Collin
have been married for more than a decade already. By comparison, I
discovered Brad's middle name only a few summers ago.

"Can you check the piccata?" Darcy's voice calls out as she carries
Mia down the hall to the nursery. Darcy likes to say that Mia found
her voice as soon as she came into the world and has elected to use it
fully every day, ever since. I can hear her jabbering to herself, which I
know she'll continue to do right up until the moment sleep overtakes
her. Darcy sits with her each night, in a rocking chair next to the crib,
and sings lullabies accented now and then by Mia until she quiets
down and her breathing slows. She's a funny baby. A great baby. The
kind of baby I am certain I'll never have, because not many women

do, and because, if my mom is to be believed, karma is definitely gunning for me with a little one as prickly and feisty as I was. Or still might be, now and again.

I walk to the stove, where a giant frying pan holds chicken breasts, broth, and tiny green olive–like things all gurgling at a low simmer. This is the other thing about Darcy's house—every Tuesday that I'm here, and the occasional morning or afternoon on the weekend, it always smells like the next meal isn't far off from being finished. At breakfast, muffins or scones. At lunch, bacon for BLTs. Tuesday dinners are wild cards, but always something delicious that I've never before heard of. Probably because my idea of dinner is salad—from a box—because even with something as basic as lettuce or noodles, I still need the premix and instructions spelled out for me on the back.

Darcy had been a teacher in the same middle school as her husband, Collin. But after Mia was born, Darcy stayed home. She started watching the Food Network as if it were her job, and threw herself into perfecting the recipes she saw. It didn't hurt, either, that the rattling of a grocery cart soothed Mia to sleep like a lullaby. Collin would come home each night to a feast after coaching sixth-grade basketball. Now that he—as well as Brad—has been deployed, I've become her tester, her audience, her calf to fatten.

I don't have the faintest idea what I am supposed to "check" with the chicken. Perhaps just that it's not burning? With the wooden spoon that was balanced on the pan, I scrape the bottom, turning up little brown flakes. Unsure whether that is what's supposed to happen, I turn down the heat a touch. Then I bring the spoon to my lips. The sauce glides smooth and buttery over them, but finishes in my mouth with a tang that makes my mouth pucker.

A car door slams in front of Darcy's house. It isn't altogether unusual for some of the other Guard wives to stop over now and then at night, looking for some way to stave off loneliness, a nightmare, a rumor run rampant on any number of social networks, or a bad newscast. Throughout Collin's years of service, from his time in the National Guard and the cadet program in college to serving as an officer in this most recent deployment, Darcy has collected a number of us, like a menagerie of strays. Many of us are from different eras of Collin's military career and don't know one another well, but we are all Darcy's. She found me standing at the edge of a gym before the send-off. I had to take a late lunch from work to be able to attend and was wearing a smart gray suit in a sea of camo and T-shirts, capris and tank tops, and gobs of kids—not belonging in more ways than one.

I walk to the front window and nudge the curtain aside with my elbow because I am still carrying the wooden spoon. A car I don't recognize—a dark nondescript sedan—is parked in front of Darcy's house. By the light of the streetlamp, I see two men in stiff dress greens get out. They stand at the end of the sidewalk, talking. My breath catches in my chest.

Usually, when Darcy tells me to turn off the news, she'll say, "You're not going to get anything but crazy from watching that box. Good news never comes from there and the really bad news will show up at your doorstep."

And here it was.

Like the goddamn ark, they always come aboard in twos.

I drop the spoon and it clatters at my feet. I step back from the window, breath spurting from my nose in gasps.

No no no no no, I think. The words in my head are a snare drum, pounding forceful and fast.

I push the curtain aside again. One officer is walking toward the door. The other stands at ease near the car.

I walk to the door. Instead of opening it, I press my forehead and nose against it, finding it soothingly cool. Here, on this side of the door, Darcy's entire world is intact. And on the other side it is breaking into shards so tiny and jagged, no amount of glue is going to be able to piece them back together. Then there's me, in between.

My left hand reaches for the doorknob. My right, braced on the frame, grazes a piece of paper taped there. It is Collin's packing list for Iraq, an index card with his chicken scratch in smudged pencil. I never paid it much attention before. Darcy liked having it up; I suppose, as a reminder of him. It's become a fixture at her house, blending into the scenery like the drying rack for Mia's bottles next to the sink or the faint stain of red wine near the fireplace where Jenny Levinson knocked over a glass with the stray sleeve of her oversize sweater. Now, Darcy will have to look at that list, written in Collin's hand, every time she leaves the house. Every time someone comes to the door. I think of taking it down, then decide it isn't my place to do something like that. Then I wonder what my place is, exactly, in a situation like this.

I worry for Darcy. I think that today, right now, in Mia's bedroom, might be the last time Darcy feels anything akin to happy, ever again. I imagine the loneliness that will burrow its way into her life now, following her around like an extra shadow.

I open the door.

"Mrs. Rutledge?"

"No," I say.

"Is she home?"

"Yes."

"Can you get her, ma'am? I need to speak with her."

"No. She's putting the baby down. We're about to eat dinner."

I say this as if he had asked if I wanted to buy some candy bars or maybe a new vacuum cleaner.

The officer pretends as though mine is a perfectly rational response. Which is to say, he doesn't flinch.

"Ma'am," he counters. It's a statement. Not an introduction, or a bridge, or a question. It says, "We've done this before; we're here to help; let's all try to deal with this the best we can."

"Darcy and Mia, they're happy right now," I plead, whispering. I think of Darcy in the dark, in Mia's room, and how right this minute, maybe she's thinking of Collin—about the last e-mail he sent her or when she'll receive another, about the things they'll do together when he comes back, about their upcoming anniversary and how she'll celebrate it alone. I know these thoughts, because they're mine, too.

And in her thoughts, right now, Collin is still alive on the other side of the world, going about his day. But out here he's lifeless—just a body. Maybe not even that any longer. He might not even be an identifiable whole now. A shudder runs through me.

The officer doesn't smile, but his stoicism radiates reassurance and something just shy of warmth. He raises his eyebrows and gestures toward the inside of the house, toward the living room. I nod and point toward the couch.

I close and lock the door behind him. Then I think of the other officer out by the car, in the November cold, and as if it makes some sort of difference, I flip the dead bolt open again.

The air fills with a charred smell. *Shit, the chicken*. I hadn't watched it. And now Darcy's dinner is ruined. Does it matter, though? Will she even be hungry? Is Darcy someone who eats when she's upset, or does she go into starvation mode? Should I order a pizza, just in case? For all of the intimate details I know about Darcy, this—how she grieves—is one that, until this moment, I have escaped having to know. I turn the burner off and think that already, I am a failure at picking up her pieces. She doesn't even know her whole world has crumbled and I'm already bumbling and stepping on the shards.

And then, a small, defeated sigh escapes from the hallway, where Darcy must have seen the man in full dress greens standing in her living room. And I wonder if I should have been the one to tell her, kneeling down in front of her in Mia's room instead of her coming out to this. I wonder if I did the right thing, letting him in at all.

She crumples right where the hallway opens into the living room. I get her up and over to the couch. The CNO doesn't offer to help, but perhaps he can't. I know there are strict rules about their interactions with us, though I've been careful not to learn what any of them are. He sits across from her, perched on the edge of his chair, one hand on each of his knees.

Darcy has wedged herself into the couch like a wounded animal, cornered. Her knees are folded to her chest, arms encircling them. She shakes her head side to side, slowly, as he talks.

"Ma'am, the Secretary of the Army has asked me to express his deep regret that your husband, Second Lieutenant Collin Rutledge, was killed in action in Iraq today," the officer says. "The secretary extends his deepest sympathy to you and your family in your loss." Darcy studies him in a way that, if I were he, would make me uncomfortable.

I watch Darcy watch the CNO. My head should be filled with concern for her. But right now my only thought is, *Thank God it wasn't Brad.* I know this news doesn't involve my husband because Collin had recently taken over for the Company XO, who had to leave the theater because of a death in the family, and Collin had spent his most recent days inside the wire at the Tactical Operations Center. After Collin was promoted and tucked safely inside the FOB, I spent a fair amount of time being bitter that my husband was still out patrolling Iraqi roads for bombs lying in wait to blow him up. And I try not to think this, but my mind overrules my better sensibilities: It's ironic, really, that Collin would end up being killed within the safety of the TOC, presumably from a mortar, while Brad is still out there, lumbering along in a Humvee. Waiting. Watching.

There is a long silence, and then Darcy raises her chin. It's a proud, defiant act. "Thank you," she says, almost inaudibly. "Thank you," she says again, and this time all of us hear her. "I know it's not easy, this part of your—job." She almost chokes on that last word, but she forces it out.

"Ma'am," the officer says, his voice husky with all he probably isn't at liberty to say.

"What happened?" Darcy asks. She pats the cushion next to her and gestures to me. I sit, and she reaches for my hand. A squawk sounds from the baby monitor and I feel Darcy tense, bracing to see if another cry will follow—if she'll have to add a fussy, overtired baby to this mix. The CNO pauses, noticing Darcy's averted attention. But seconds pass, and all is quiet down the hall. Darcy sighs and looks back toward the CNO.

"Lieutenant Rutledge was leading a patrol outside of Fallujah, ma'am. The convoy came across an improvised explosive device— an IED."

I am focused on the CNO's trembling hands. Then his words register. She blurts, "But he doesn't go on patrol."

They have the wrong guy. Oh Sweet Jesus, they have the wrong guy.

Though even as I think these words, I don't fully believe them. I hope, but I don't believe. This is the Army, after all, an outfit not prone to such mix-ups.

"The platoon leader was ill," the CNO says. "Lieutenant Rutledge subbed in for him."

I wonder if he should be telling Darcy this—that her husband, Mia's dad, isn't coming home because he was somewhere he shouldn't have been. And then, the CNO's words start to congeal into a chain of horrifically linked thoughts: Brad's squad leader was sick out the window of their Humvee the day before. Brad and Collin weren't ever supposed to be on duty together, but from the sound of it, they could have been today. Collin is dead. Brad could be.

I don't think I let the sound welling up inside me—a cry heavy with surprise and shock and fear—past my throat, my lips. But Darcy and the CNO's eyes train on me, and time seems to slow almost to the point of pausing. Until this second, I hadn't even entertained the possibility that Brad could be caught up in all this—the formality of dress greens and "ma'ams" and the Secretary of the Army's bullshit condolences.

"Were there other casualties?" Darcy asks, looking at me. My fist is in my mouth, fingers against my teeth.

"Several, ma'am."

"Oh God," I breathe.

"Several as in two others, or as in ten others?" Darcy asks.

"I don't have an exact number, ma'am."

"How in the hell can you not have an exact   " Darcy is winding up, getting ready to light into the CNO, but he ignores her.

"Do you have someone over there?" he asks me. He has turned his entire body toward me, waiting for my response.

I nod. "In that platoon."

"Husband?" he asks.

I nod again.

"Ma'am, I'm going to need you to go home and wait there, please. Right now."

I can't breathe. It feels as though the blood has drained from my face and my body. I half expect, as I look down, to see my heart lying right there on Darcy's nice cream carpeting. I think of the night I showed up, shaking and unable to get it together, on Darcy's doorstep. I made the mistake of watching the nightly news with Peter Jennings, and as he and the reporter calmly narrated B-roll of Blackwater agents being dragged from burning cars and beaten, I couldn't stop. Because that was exactly where Brad was—in that same city where the charred bodies of the Americans were hanged from a bridge while throngs of people not only stood by, but cheered as if they were at a goddamn street festival. I barely made it to the bathroom before I threw up my dinner. Then I drove straight to Darcy's.

"I can't do this," I said, without even saying hello, when she opened the door. That night, she rubbed my back as I hung my head between my legs and tried to breathe. "You can do this," she said. "You can and you will."

But she was wrong. I'm not cut out for this—for any of it. I don't know how. I don't want to know how.

I look at Darcy. She squeezes my hand. "You don't know anything for sure yet," she says.

"But what about you?"

"It's okay. I'll have my own team of these guys here before you're even home." She looks over at the CNO, who nods. He even manages not to frown. It's nearly a smile.

I don't know how she can be so composed, so *with* it, when I already feel myself breaking. Already feel broken. Because it's not okay. None of it. Not by a long shot.

"Staff Sergeant Gerlach came here with me. He'll drive you home, wait with you there," the CNO says. "One of us will deliver your vehicle if you leave a key with me."

I scan the room for my purse, my cell phone, my jacket, and locate them hanging on a spare dining room chair, pushed up against a wall. They all seem so far away, and it reminds me of one of those dreams in which I need to run but can't coordinate my limbs to move, as though they've just then tripled in size and weight. My brain knows what to do; my body, though, isn't willing.

I hand my keys to the CNO and Darcy takes me by the shoulders.

"The sooner you get home, the sooner you'll know," she says. She pulls me into a tight hug. I half expect to feel metal and wires beneath her skin.

Making my way down the front walk and toward the waiting Staff Sergeant Gerlach, I glance back. There's a warm glow seeping out into the night from the Rutledge's little bay window, and it betrays the scene unfolding inside. Even from my perch on the sidewalk, I can see Darcy standing in the middle of the living room, unmoved from where she hugged me, hands over her face, her body trembling.

Two

Staff Sergeant Gerlach so believes in the economy of words that by the time we drive the few miles from Darcy's east side bungalow to my house on Vilas Street, almost equidistant from each other on opposite sides of the glowing Capitol, we cover most of my questions: "When will I know?" (Not certain, ma'am); "Is there a chance he's still alive?" (Can't say, ma'am); "Could this be a mistake? Might it be another patrol, another unit, and you got some bad information?" (Highly unlikely, ma'am); "How does this work? Do you just drive me home and drop me off? How long will you stay?" (As long as you would like me to or need me to, ma'am).

I am better at solitude than most. Instead of finding company for the nights I'm alone—which have been many these days—I usually light a candle, put on some Amos Lee or Ellis Paul, and relax into it. Tonight, though, Brad's absence looms large in our house. The thought that he might not come back here has transformed the familiar and comfortable quiet dark into something heavy and sinister and booming loud. It yells to me that all the nights of my life to follow could look precisely like this one. But because it doesn't yell as loudly with him there, Staff Sergeant Gerlach stays when I ask him to.

Any military spouse knows how this works, because we've all heard the urban legends about a friend of a friend of a friend who has had to weather the notification process. We know they will notify you only at your registered residence, never by telephone, and not between the hours of midnight and six a.m. We know the notification officers have to race the clock to inform next of kin before the twenty-four-hour news cycle does, and what they used to have three weeks to accomplish now must be done in less than eight hours after confirmation of a casualty on the battlefield. We know that if there are outstanding notifications yet to be made, e-mail stops flowing in, temporarily blacked out by the military powers that be. We breathe easier when the Internet highways reopen. We no longer feel our hearts trying to beat right out of our chests. We are like visitors at a zoo. We feel for those who slog through hours in agony, awaiting any definitive news that will end the wait, but we are thankful, too, not to be them.

Or tonight, not to be me.

Sergeant Gerlach perches on a small part of a couch cushion, using only as much as is absolutely necessary, and when I hear a sound, or catch the briefest flash of lights in the street outside, I spring up to the window and watch. I wear a path from the window to the kitchen to check the time—10:13, 10:17, 10:20, 10:25, 10:32—and back to the couch. Staff Sergeant Gerlach's eyes follow me like a dutiful dog tracking the movements of its owner.

At 10:49 I decide this isn't working. I root in the closet until I find a hat and mittens and my down jacket. Staff Sergeant Gerlach has only a flimsy-thin trench coat with him, so I eye his slight frame and fish out a weather-appropriate jacket and hat that will cover it.

I cross from the front hall closet to where he sits and hold the jacket out to him. He eyes me, then the jacket, and then me again. It's a nondescript black ski coat, and I can tell what he is thinking:

Wearing this woman's dead husband's jacket when she finds out he's actually, officially dead could be all sorts of bad. So I tell him that it's mine—a necessary lie to prevent from freezing the person who is to keep me tethered to sanity tonight. He takes the coat from me.

I duck into the kitchen, dig to the back of the refrigerator for two bottles of Guinness, and gesture with my chin toward the front door. Staff Sergeant Gerlach follows my lead.

We settle shoulder to shoulder on the front stoop and the night hangs big and quiet around us. It hasn't yet snowed, but you can almost smell it on the air. It won't be long now.

I give thanks that the street is empty of cars. There's a faint sound of tires rolling down Park Street some blocks away, but, mercifully, none turn in our direction, saving my battered heart the trouble of leaping up into my throat at the possibility of one of those cars carrying clones of Staff Sergeant Gerlach from stopping in front of this house.

I offer him one of the beers. He declines. "On duty," he says. I ask him how long until he isn't on duty. "Midnight," he says.

"For twelve oh one," I say, setting the open beer on the step below us. "So that's the cutoff?" I take a sip of my own bottle. The stout slips over my lips, bitterly cold, and jolts me better than any shot of espresso might.

Staff Sergeant Gerlach nods.

"And they wait, then? Until morning?"

Staff Sergeant Gerlach nods again.

"No offense," I say, "but of all the idiotic things the military does, I think that takes the cake. Who is honestly supposed to magically stop worrying at precisely twelve oh one, turn in for a good night's sleep, and wake up at six a.m. to do it all over again? What idiots," I spit.

Staff Sergeant Gerlach holds his hands up in a conciliatory gesture.

"I know, I know," I say. "Don't shoot the messenger, right?"

"At least not this one, please, ma'am," he says.

I look askance at him and catch the faintest hint of a smile playing at the corner of his mouth.

"Did you just make a funny?" I ask.

He purses his lips as if pondering it, then nods.

"Are you *allowed* to do that?"

He shrugs.

I look at him again. Not straight on, but out of the corner of my eye. Staff Sergeant Gerlach has a face that might have been augmented by a good, shaggy mop of surfer hair had the Army allowed that sort of thing and if his own weren't more red than dirty blond. His face as a whole is mostly unremarkable: kind brown eyes, a perfectly fine nose, a chin that's neither particularly strong nor jutting. He smells of spearmint and aftershave.

I do this sometimes—compare my husband to what else is out there. It's a mental exercise, just to double-check. Just to make sure. I think if they're being deep-down honest, everyone does this now and then. I can't be alone. What's important is landing on the right side of the question: Would I marry him again—still?

Me? It's yes every time. It's always been yes. A hundred thousand times yes.

I know I shouldn't, but my mind jumps ahead—to jerking awake every morning with the realization that Brad isn't simply not with me, but he isn't anywhere anymore, fresh as the first minute I got the news. To replaying the last message he left me, knowing that that voice no longer exists in the world and that it can no longer make a sound. To packing up his clothes, contacting his friends with the news, throwing away (or keeping?) his toothbrush, cologne, hair goop. To having to go about my daily life again—preparing research memos, meeting with clients, going to court, grocery shopping, and pumping gas—all the time knowing that I'll never, ever talk to, touch, or see my husband again.

The sheer stress of it all pushes down on me, as if I were pulling twelve g's right here on my front steps. It alternately hurts and it aches, but it doesn't seem to ebb. My head throbs. My stomach spins. I try a deep breath and come up empty. Then another, and another. Before I know it, I'm gasping.

"Ma'am?" Staff Sergeant Gerlach places a hand on my shoulder, trying to turn me to look his way, but I can't move. "Ma'am," he says, gently shaking my shoulder. "Ma'am, hang your head between your knees. Right between your knees, ma'am."

I succumb to the little pressure he places on my back. I do as I'm told.

"That's it, ma'am," he says. "Just like that. Nice, slow breaths now."

I am not going to survive this: the waiting—and the everything that is to come after the waiting is over. I don't know why people don't actually cave in on themselves; I don't know why piles of rubble that used to be people who have lost someone they loved don't dot the sidewalks, living rooms, and kitchens of the world.

I look at the time. It is 11:11, a time Brad marks by holding both arms straight over his head. I mimic this memory. It's a reflex: hands straight up as if I were signaling a field goal.

"Make a wish," he always says when the clock reads all ones. And so I do: *Please bring him back to me. I don't care if he's missing a leg, or an ear. As long as he's with me.* At this moment, I'll do anything. I'll do whatever it takes.

"Ma'am?"

I shake my head, lower my hands, take a swig of beer.

·   ·   ·

The rest of the night passes like this:

My cell phone displays 11:42. Staff Sergeant Gerlach asks me what Brad is like. I appreciate that he uses the present tense. I have a hard time thinking of what to say, of untwining the slideshow of memories of Brad playing through my head, of how to describe his smells and sounds: the strong, manly mix of him after a workout; the sweet strawberry essence of his hair after a shower, regardless of the shampoo he uses; the tangy sour of his morning breath that I've never minded a bit; the grunt that he lets out when something amuses him; the hurried whisper of his breath in my ear that turns into a low, contented moan—almost indiscernible—when he comes. The way he snores like a cartoon character—his lips fluttering and flapping on the exhale; and how it drives me nuts that he keeps a stash of plastic picks with him at all times and digs at his teeth with them at the table; how he's the only man I've ever met who subscribes to and actually reads *The Economist* flap to flap; that he loves pizza and taking midnight walks to the Union Terrace just to dip his toes into Lake Mendota; that he always finds a dollar or some change to put in those covered coffee cans at cash registers—for someone stricken by cancer or a car accident, or to support the local animal shelter—and that he knows the homeless woman who used to wander the street in front of our old apartment by name (Helen) and always thinks to pick up her favorite sandwich (ham and cheese) for the next time he sees her.

These things are, to me, Brad. But there is so much more—so many intangibles. And so I fall back on generalities. I tell him that Brad is the kindest, smartest man I've ever met, equal parts patience and handsome, and that he's going to be a great dad. (Here I stumble over the tense—future simple or past conditional? I correct myself, settling on future conditional: "He would make a great dad.") I wonder how many times Staff Sergeant Gerlach has heard this exact same description from other wives. And I think, maybe none of our love stories are half as special as any of us think.

12:06. That's the time on my cell phone. I'm still watching for headlights, thinking that maybe there's a discrepancy between my time and the time on the dashboard of the car on its way to my house. But if there's an outfit that would likely sync every clock in its possession, it's the military. "So, that's it?" I ask Staff Sergeant Gerlach. Greg. He nods and without a word, prods me to my feet and gets me inside. We shed our coats in a pile, and I retire to the armchair by the front window to continue my lookout. But things outside are quiet and dark now, and I stare down the barrel of the night stretching between me and six a.m. and wonder if anyone has ever died from waiting, from not knowing. I decide I could very well be the first.

It's 12:16. I ask Staff Sergeant Gerlach, Greg, if there isn't someone—anyone—he could call. He shakes his head, tells me there are no strings to pull, calls me ma'am. I tell him that if I'm never called ma'am again as long as I live, it'll be far too soon. Then, all the wiles I honed through hours and hours of moot court and client negotiations exhausted, I try plain old-fashioned begging. "Please," I say, "can't you just do something?" He shakes his head and I tell him that he can go fuck himself—and the Secretary of the Army, too— while he's at it. I think I see him flinch, though I can't be sure.

It's 12:42. I put on Ellis Paul and turn off the lights. I lie with my back on the floor and my feet propped on Brad's recliner—a worn, brown leather monstrosity that he found at an antique store on Sherman Avenue and that looks like something my law firm might have been fond of in the 1920s. Staff Sergeant Gerlach, Greg, propped upright on the couch, has fallen asleep. I know this when I hear soft snoring behind me. I pull a blanket from the basket near the fireplace and float it over him.

It's 2:58. I will Brad to be alive. The patience to meditate has always eluded me, but this one time I perform like a lifelong yogi. My mind is a white sheet, billowing on a breeze of three words: "You are okay." My pulse slows, my eyes rest, and my muscles sag. My body is thankful for the release. I add yoga to the list of things I will gladly do if only Brad comes home.

It's 3:03. I try to imagine Brad not breathing, unable to smile that big smile of his, his lips singing "Come on Eileen" and changing all the lyrics to "Elise" when he wanted to talk me into anything. I try to imagine him as a body, instead of him. I'm trying to prepare myself for what's to come, for the shock of it. But even the preparing is too awful, and I retreat instead to a memory of Brad twirling a section of my hair around his finger. It's so real, I can almost feel the light tug, his finger grazing the skin of my scalp.

It's 3:36. I am caught in that shadowland between sleeping and waking, between not real and real, where someone is holding my hand. I press myself against the hand, and the body attached to it. But something is off. There's the cold metal of a watch where there shouldn't be, sharp angles of bone not there before. I open my eyes and start. "I'm sorry," Greg says. "You were crying out, in your sleep." My hand is warm where he holds it. I close my eyes and try to pretend that it's Brad's skin pressed to mine—his warmth flowing through my fingers, my palm, my pores.

It's 4:17. I'm on a roller coaster, but not one that goes around in circles. This one goes wherever I want it to. I am using the roller coaster to save Brad, who is stranded at the top of a mountain, and I am rocketing down a particularly hairy drop that's jostling me hard back and forth, back and forth, when a loud beeping sounds, and then suddenly it's not Brad I'm going to save but Staff Sergeant Gerlach I'm trying to get to. I come to, to Staff Sergeant Gerlach—Greg—shaking me and holding my cell phone, telling me to hurry up and answer it.

I croak hello. A voice at the other end asks if I am Mrs. Bradley Sabatto. I say what Granna drilled into me as a little girl was proper phone etiquette: "This is she," despite learning in college that it wasn't at all proper grammar. If this were any other time, on any other night, I'd let him know that I still have my own first name, thank you very much.

"Ma'am, my name is Lieutenant Colonel Nathan Spencer."

I hear a sharp intake of breath on the other end that I'm sure Lieutenant Colonel Spencer didn't intend. "I have some news about your husband," he says.

Three

Brad is not the only soldier in his convoy to survive. But he is the only one to walk away in one piece, more or less. He spends a few days in and out of surgery in Iraq, and he is transferred to Germany for further medical attention. The IED blast that killed Darcy's husband and six others has left Brad's body looking like a scrapyard of shrapnel, but since there are a mere handful of weeks before the rest of his unit leaves the theater, he will be coming home ahead of them.

I am not a religious person, nor am I a great mathematician, but over the past weeks, I have considered all the odds against my husband's safe return. After each calculation, I said little prayers of thanks. I say one more now for good measure, looking out over Madison's Capitol Square, the scene below bathed in afternoon sun like a picture plated in gold.

Brad enlisted after his best friend was killed in a helicopter crash in Afghanistan. Up until that afternoon, when he came home and told me he had spent the afternoon with a local Army recruiter instead of taking his GREs, we had our life planned. He was fresh back from studying in Oxford, and I was an associate at a local law firm. We had so much ahead of us. Good things. But the military came out of nowhere, a car running a red light, and T-boned those perfect plans of ours.

I told Brad it was fine—that we'd be fine; that he'd be fine. I played some version of what I thought a good military wife should be, because what else was I supposed to do? Tell him that his selfish, stupid, wholly unilateral decision meant, at best, one more year of postponing an addition to our family, and, at worst, reducing our twosome by half? No, I kept that to myself, where it festered and burned until I was almost glad when he deployed, because I didn't have to swallow it back down every time I laid eyes on him.

But right now, blanketed by the knowledge that my husband is alive and will soon be on his way home, I'm suddenly freed to feel proud of him like I could have—should have—been all along. Below my office window, on the sidewalks around the Capitol, a couple walks hand in hand. She's wearing a red peacoat and he has on a three-quarter-length wool dress coat with a smart plaid scarf draped around his neck. He says something to her, and she recoils in mock surprise or anger before he pulls her into him and wraps an arm around her, marching her forward and kissing her cheek. They're near enough to my window now that I can make out her earrings, glinting silver in the sun, and the wedding band on his left hand. Before I got the call that Brad was okay and that he'd be coming home, I would have turned away from the couple long before, unable to stomach the agony that comes from window-shopping for something you know you might never have.

But Lieutenant Colonel Spencer told me that Brad would be fine, and he'd be coming home "soon." It didn't matter that he couldn't pinpoint a precise date for me. The facts are these: My husband's return is imminent, and pretty soon, we'll be back in the club with that happy couple below. We'll walk those same sidewalks in the same way—leaning into each other because we want to be closer still, because we've always been drawn together like that. Because we have our whole lives ahead of us again. And I'll forget that the possibilities were anything but.

Since Lieutenant Colonel Spencer's call, I've developed an obsession with homecoming videos. I tell myself that I'll watch only one, but inevitably, I go on to the next—soldiers showing up in their kids' classrooms and spelling bees, at fast-food restaurants and during the opening ceremonies at sporting events—until too much time has passed. I picture how Brad's homecoming will play out. Will he surprise me at work? Or will he call en route so I can meet him at the airport, running the wrong way up the down escalator to get to him, to throw my arms around him and bury my head next to his? I imagine the relief that will course through me when I can finally touch him again, in the flesh. And in my mind, that river of relief is fed by tributaries of pride and desire. I feel a kinship with Penelope waiting for Odysseus, with the nurse in Times Square letting herself be kissed so passionately by a random passing sailor. Returning from war is an ancient, primitive ritual, and I imagine the marriage beds of the Greeks—and so many who followed them in history—burned red-hot the nights of those homecomings. In ancient wars, women felt defended and protected; the men who returned survived danger others couldn't and, in doing so, separated themselves from other men, elevated themselves toward the gods. There was, perhaps, no greater aphrodisiac. My inner feminist would hate to admit it, but things haven't changed all that much.

Today I sit in the litigation team's weekly status meeting, staring at my phone—at a video compilation with sound on mute but the looks on the faces in it unmistakable: joy, relief, release. In one after another, the soldier walks up to his or her family, and it's as if someone has pressed the PLAY button on their lives. When I look up, my eyes are watery and I start to scribble nonsense on a yellow legal pad until I'm certain they won't spill over.

I don't know when, exactly, Brad will be home. The military has given me a range of dates and the assurance that Brad will notify me before he leaves, or when he's en route and more certain of an arrival time. So, when I walk in our house, set down my workbag, and look up to see Brad standing in the kitchen, having just poured himself a glass of water, it's like seeing a ghost.

He is wearing jeans and a gray T-shirt, and both hang more loosely on him than I remember. Even though it's December here, he's tan and barefoot. There's an unspecific hardness to him, about him, as if his aura has developed corners and jagged edges. But he's Brad. And he's here.

I don't rush to Brad to wrap my arms around his neck or fit my lips and cheek into its crook. I don't scream or squeal. I don't do any of the things I imagined I would in this moment. Instead, I stand immobilized with big gobs of tears running down my face.

Brad comes to me, presses me to his chest like a child, and eventually, the flow slows and then stops. Feeling both silly and sluiced, I lift my head and bring my lips to Brad's cheek. I let them hover there. Not since our first kiss have I slowed to notice every little nuance about how this feels. It's said that distance makes the heart grow fonder, but no one mentions this: how the simple act of pressing your lips against the skin of a cheek—an act we take for granted starting shortly after infancy—can make your heart leap if you take the time to let it.

I close my eyes and my breathing falls in line with Brad's, the rise and fall of our chests, together, creating a nearly silent soundtrack to this moment.

We lie in bed and I shiver as Brad kisses me—neck, ears, forehead, collarbone. It's cold in our house because our furnace is on the fritz again, but it's more than that. It's all the thrill of the first time we made love, only without the worries of where our relationship is going, if it's going to last, if it's for real. I get to feel all this and know exactly where we've ended up. It's a high that leaves me tingling and shivering in every last cell of my body.

Afterward, I watch Brad sleep. I see him twitch and hear him mumble. I'm exhausted, but the grumbling of my stomach keeps me awake. I haven't eaten since that morning, and then only a packaged blueberry muffin from the firm's vending machine that tasted more like cellophane than blueberry. But the thought that Brad might up and disappear keeps me tethered to the bed.

Eventually my stomach and reasoning win out and I slip from our room, drawing Brad's T-shirt over my head as I go. I make myself a mayonnaise and cheese sandwich, a guilty pleasure I usually deny myself because it's artery-clogging unhealthy, and because Brad finds it disgusting. But tonight—tonight calls for a celebration. I even find one lonely Leinenkugel Berry Weiss, a remnant of summer, in the back of the refrigerator and crack it open. I stand over the sink, eating and sipping and looking out over our meager backyard, bathed in the light of a low-hanging moon.

And that's when I see him.

I press my face close to the kitchen window, fighting to see past my reflection and into the yard, where Brad, wearing only jeans, is walking toward the back fence. I can see shadows of scars that crisscross his back and shoulders, looking louder and angrier than Brad ever has been. Although it's been cold enough to snow, there's none on the ground; still, it's winter in Wisconsin and Brad is barefoot. I watch as he watches the fence, like a dog on high alert—body tensed, ready to spring on whatever might be lying in wait out there.

I didn't hear him leave, but I hear him come in and I meet him in the hallway. For the first time, I notice how far away Brad looks—as if his body was here and his mind, his thoughts, everything else inside of him were still stuck somewhere a million miles away. His eyes are black and empty, and when I ask him what he was doing, he says, "Just checking."

"For what?" I ask. "It's three in the morning, baby."

First he looks past me with those eyes, and then he walks past me and back to bed. "Just checking," he says once more, his voice trailing down the hallway in his wake.

Four

The next morning I wake to Brad looking at me. He is smiling and his eyes are filled with light. Late-morning sun streams through the window. I'm not sure exactly what time it is, and for the first time in so very long, I don't care. For the first time in what seems like an eternity, I don't reach first thing for my phone, for news from Brad. Because he's here. Right beside me. It seems almost too good to be true.

"Hey, beautiful," he whispers.

"Hey, yourself," I say.

We make love then. And where the night before was all about making up for the time lost between us, full of impatience and craving and insistence, this morning we are in no hurry. We are gentle with each other—meditative, studious even.

When the sun is full and bright and streaming in our bedroom window, I get up and make us coffee. I bring a mug for Brad and a mug for me back to bed. Then we huddle under the covers because, though it looks like a beautiful day, the thermometer suctioned to the outside of our kitchen window is hovering around twenty degrees. After so many months of wanting so badly to have Brad here to talk to, all of the thoughts and words I've stored up since he left seem to have become bottlenecked, not one of them able to make it through. Instead, I keep looking at him, trying to memorize his features in case he isn't really here after all—or for long.

"What?" he asks.

I shake my head. "I still can't believe it. That you're back."

"In the flesh," he says. And his lips curl into a smile, but the words don't.

We decide to venture out for brunch, to Mickey's Dairy Bar. It's one of our favorite places—a diner so popular with the college students because of the cheap prices and overabundant portions that the line almost always snakes out the door, even in winter.

"It's going to be a wait," I tell Brad.

He shrugs. "I've waited a lot longer for a lot less than a giant egg scramble with gravy. Plus you don't know how many times I dreamed about—ahh—"

Brad looks confused. "About?" I say.

"You know—going to that place."

"That place?"

"I forget what it's called."

It's the only place that Brad and I ever go for breakfast, and we go every Saturday morning. But he's been gone a long time, and he's only just gotten back. And in between, his mind has been on many other things. "Mickey's?" I say, hesitating, as if that might not be what Brad meant.

He nods. "Right, Mickey's."

"I'm going to take a shower," I say, placing my hands on either side of Brad's face and drawing him toward me until his lips graze mine. I was the one to kiss Brad first, the night we met, and he always said that he knew at that moment I was the girl for him—something about that kiss did it. Now and then I try to replicate it, to convince him all over again.

I was juggling two-too-many tables at the Vierling that night, when a man at a table full of men waved me down and asked me for the check while placing his hand in an area that wasn't quite my back and wasn't quite my ass. He was dark haired and handsome and arrogant in a way that I could tell didn't suit him. And when I finished my shift, he was waiting outside the back door, holding a cup of coffee that he said he had been drinking steadily since dinner because he wanted another chance to make a first impression. He walked me out into a night full of snow intent on making its way to the ground, silent and purposeful. Even now I remember the way the cottony quiet of each footfall on unshoveled sidewalks and unplowed streets made it feel as if we were the only two in the city; I remember the way everything looked impossibly white against the midnight. We talked about school and religion and politics as he walked me home, all the way to the end of Presque Isle Avenue, where I lived in a second-story flat in a student house, the only redeeming features of which were its proximity to the beach and the new porch the landlord had put on the year before. Brad was about to turn and walk away when I called him back and kissed him.

The next morning, he was at my stove in rumpled jeans and a gray T-shirt, humming a tune I couldn't quite place, as he tried to toss a pancake up and out of the pan instead of using a spatula to flip it. My Sunday *Times* was open to the Style section. The pancake landed with a splat on an unlit burner, uncooked side down. He noticed me standing there and said, "Pancakes over easy?" He smiled at me and I smiled at his dimples. I loved him already.

That was the start. All because of my hands on his cheeks, my lips on his. Those dimples. That attempt at pancakes. And here we are, having come full circle and now starting to get to know each other all over again. Or, at least it feels that way, because I feel a pitter-patter in my chest, a flip-flop in my stomach as I step into the shower and let the hot water run over me.

I remind myself to call Darcy when I get dressed. It's a call I've been putting off, and now, it's a call I don't quite know how to make. The difference in our lives has become nearly unfathomable. My husband has come home; hers did not. It is that simple, and that complicated. I feel thankful, seeing firsthand what my life might look like in a parallel dimension, and then I feel guilty for feeling thankful.

I stay in the shower until the water starts to run lukewarm. When I get out, Brad is standing by the sink, naked. He is looking at me intently. Not smiling.

"You're leering," I tell him. I laugh, trying to make it into a joke. But the way he's staring at me makes the little hairs on my arms and neck rise up. *It's Brad,* I tell myself. *It's just that he's been gone for a while. He just feels like a stranger.* I take a step back anyway.

Brad doesn't say anything. He steps to me and pulls me toward him. His hand is rough on my elbow and strong, like a vise grip.

"Babe, I've got to get dressed so we can go," I say, pulling away from him. "If we don't get there before noon, we'll never get a table."

"No," he says. "Now."

"What's with the 'Me Tarzan, you Jane' routine?" I say, still trying to joke. "Can't get enough of me, huh?" I wrench my arm from his grip and pat him on the chest and emit a thin, shaky laugh. But there's something bothersome about Brad's visage, infected with varying strains of blank and confused.

"This morning? Last night? Once in between for good measure?" I say. "Remember?"

He drops his hand from my elbow and backs away. "Yeah. Right. Of course," he says, though I'm not sure either one of us believes him just then.

Five

It's gotten dark enough outside that I have to turn the bedroom light on to find the pair of jeans I want. This also means we're running late. Again.

"Brad! We've got to go. Hurry up!" I cringe at the words coming from my mouth. I sound, if not like my mother, then very much like someone's. But Darcy is inexplicably holding her annual Christmas party this year just weeks after burying her husband, and I'm wary of how this is going to go. I want to be there early to help her—to keep an eye on her. I wanted to have arrived at her house a full hour ago.

"The top doesn't work," he says.

"What top?" I yell down the hall.

"I can't get the toothpaste to work."

I storm into the bathroom and grab the tube from him. It has a protective seal that needs to be peeled off before use, which I do before handing it back to him. True, it's a different brand than we usually buy, but my husband is a Rhodes scholar who specializes in Russian and spent the better part of last year operating complex machinery such as guns and rockets. "It works fine," I say. "Be smarter than what you're working on."

It's a phrase I've used a million times. It's an old habit, is all. But Brad looks instantly angry. "Were you always such a bitch?" he asks. "Or is that a new thing?"

We drive to Darcy's house in stony silence, and when we arrive, already there is nowhere to park. Though I can usually find a spot immediately in front of Darcy's house, tonight the street is packed and the only open space is more than two blocks away. While we walk, I try to talk myself out of being upset. I think back to all of the pamphlets and newsletter articles I've read on deployment and return, and remind myself that there's always an adjustment period. All those reunion videos—couples jumping into each other's arms, the hanging on to each other for dear life, the tears and kisses and more tears and then more kisses? That's real. But so is this—all that comes after the cameras stop rolling.

As we make our way up the front walk, I place a hand on Brad's back and let it linger there—a conciliatory gesture, though maybe one that is too subtle. Darcy flings the door open when we knock, as if she has been just behind it, waiting. Her house is warm with laughter and bodies. The skin on my fingers and cheeks smarts from the sudden change in temperature. Darcy hugs each of us and I hug her back, lingering. She has gotten thin. I can feel bones where pillows of flesh used to be. Brad and I shrug out of our jackets and hand them to Darcy.

"Drinks are in the kitchen," she says. "There's beer, wine, eggnog." She throws the "eggnog" in Brad's direction, given that he doesn't usually drink much and also loves her eggnog.

"Eggnog?" I say. "You made your eggnog?"

Darcy shrugs. "It's easy," she says. And although I believe that it's not a complicated recipe, this is her first holiday alone, so soon without Collin. Nothing is easy. Not even eggnog.

Beyond Darcy, I see that garland and colored lights have been strung over windows and doorways, and a decorated tree fills one corner of the living room. I know it was Darcy and Collin's tradition to select and cut down their own tree at one of the surrounding tree farms. They did this every year on the first weekend of December. Not wanting to call and broach a subject she'd rather avoid, I have been wondering what Darcy did this year. And now I picture Darcy with Mia in a sling, trudging around the tree farm and sipping hot cocoa while waiting for her tree to be wrapped and loaded, watching all the families—similar to the one she had only months before—come and go. Or worse, she might have driven to one of the many temporary Christmas tree sales posts that spring up in gas stations or grocery store parking lots in the weeks surrounding the holidays, paid forty dollars, and loaded and unloaded the tree herself, decorating it with only Mia's cooing to keep her company. My breath hitches in my throat. I cough hard to dislodge it, along with those pictures of Darcy stuck in my mind.

I circle my friend's shoulders with my arms and she puts her arm around my waist. Brad goes ahead into the kitchen while Darcy and I hang back, surveying the crowd. "You're crazy, you know that?" I say to her. She nods and I catch the faintest tremble pass over her lip just as she bites down on the bottom one. "But I love you anyway," I tell her.

"So I'm a charity case?" she asks, incredulous, but a hint of a smile playing at the corner of her mouth.

"Are you kidding? I'm the charity case. You know what we'd be eating tonight if it weren't for you? Canned soup and grilled cheese. That is, if I managed not to burn it."

"Which?"

"Both."

"It's almost impossible to burn soup," Darcy says.

I raise an eyebrow. "You really want to challenge me on kitchen disasters? I have an intimate knowledge of all things burnable."

"But you have so many other good qualities," she jokes. "Now go eat."

Darcy gives me a gentle push toward her kitchen table, which is overflowing with plates of stuffed mushrooms, mini quiches, baked cheeses and dips; vats of Swedish meatballs and garlic-sautéed shrimp; platters of bars and holiday cookies any bakery would be proud to serve. She has been cooking her way through the stages of grief and is, quite possibly, the first widow to have sent visitors home with food instead of the other way around. I pick up a mushroom and half expect to taste the bitter tang of mourning, the saltiness of tears in it right along with its usual earthy, savory flavors.

A quick scan of the faces in Darcy's living/dining room reveals that there are a lot of people here I don't know, or have met only briefly, and I'm reluctant to wade out into that sea of small talk. Throughout Collin's time in the Guard—a decade or so—Darcy has collected friends from a variety of different eras, and most of the crowd consists of people Darcy and Collin both worked with. From a quick survey of the room, it seems that, aside from some of the teachers, not many in attendance here know one another all that well. The party is missing that hum of constant conversation, and more handshakes than hugs are being exchanged. I get the sense that they're here for Darcy, and not really for the party.

"Is Mia at her grandma's?"

"She'll bring her by later on. They were all going shopping and then for dinner."

Just the mention of Mia makes me smile. I never thought it possible to love someone else's child so much. "I'm so glad I'll get to see her," I say. "But promise me you'll let me know if you need some help with her, too. I'll take her anytime, you know."

Darcy gives me a look. "And do what—prop her up in a file cabinet?"

"Ha, ha, ha," I say, deadpan. "Very funny." But Darcy has a point. Despite how close the two of us are, and despite my regular offers, Darcy has never asked me to watch Mia. But that's probably just as well, because as appealing as spending time with her sounds, once I'm into the thick of the week, something always comes up. Last year I billed somewhere around two thousand hours, and the only full day I took off was for Granna's funeral. I took the job at Early, Janssen, and Bradenton because I was promised a lot of client contact and because, since it was a smaller firm, I thought I was signing up for less of a corporate culture. Instead, I've landed in a small firm with a big-firm attitude. It's a place that demands the same hours as a big firm, but without any of the support, such as paralegal teams, an on-site mail room, messengers in an instant, or a team of reference librarians to find that one obscure statistic or case, which I could spend an afternoon or more searching for when I should be doing a million other things. It's a firm that also comes with the implicit understanding that although vacation or sick time—or weekends—might technically be part of the benefits package, you shouldn't actually take any of it—not if you want to be there for long.

Brad sidles up to us, and I can smell his drink before I see it: some sort of dark liquor—whiskey or brandy—cut with little more than a few ice cubes.

"Brad," I say under my breath. I shoot a glance down at the plastic tumbler he's holding.

"What?" he snaps.

"Nothing. It's just a little more drink than you usually have."

He eyes me, and his mouth sets in a thin, hard line.

"Maybe I have a different usual," he says.

I shrug, relinquishing any hope of not having to be the one to drive us home tonight. But Brad has been out of the country—in the Middle East—for nearly a year. Brad is home alive. And I can hear Mariah Carey's "All I Want for Christmas Is You" coming from the Sounds of the Season channel on Darcy's television. Driving us home is the least I can do.

"Go for it, then," I tell him. "You've earned it." I stretch up to kiss his cheek, but he turns at the last second, and my lips grace only air.

I do my best to mingle. I would rather we were here for dinner with just Darcy, but for her I will make the best of it. However, making the best of it mostly involves keeping an eye on Brad, because every time I look over at him, he is standing by himself. Some people come up to him. A few Guard people who seem to know him, or at least of him, give him a one-armed hug and tell him they're glad he's back. Those who don't know him shake his hand and thank him for his service. Every time someone touches him, I see Brad shrink back, then fight the urge by nodding and smiling, trying to cover it up.

Still others—friends and acquaintances alike—keep their distance from Brad, regarding him from afar. It would be a different scene if some of Brad's unit were here, but they're still over there, working to hand things off before they return in a week or two. Most of the guests are from other areas of Darcy and Collin's life— neighbors, family, and coworkers—who don't know quite what to say to Brad. Because it's not as if he's back from vacation or a work trip, and there are no easy questions to ask to keep the conversation going when someone has returned from war.

I'm surveying the room, trying to decide how much I should interfere on Brad's behalf, when Sondra Thompson catches my eye and waves tentatively at me. Sondra is one of Darcy's longtime crew, and though we've socialized only a handful of times, I've always liked her.

She's in sales of some sort—software or pharmaceuticals—and between her model-pretty looks and no-nonsense demeanor, I imagine her running circles around her male colleagues, and the poor saps she's selling anything to. My only complaint about Sondra is that I don't get to see her enough.

I wander over to her and she gives me a shoulder-to-shoulder hug. Sondra is tall, with impossibly smooth mocha skin, and an Afro and nails that are always manicured. No matter how great I might feel about my choice of outfit or rare good-hair day, one step into Sondra's orbit and I'm back to feeling painfully plain. But the most beautiful thing about Sondra is her ability to make each person around her feel like he's her very favorite person.

"I was hoping you'd be here," she says in a way that makes me fully believe her. Sondra's hand lingers on my shoulder for a moment longer than necessary, and she gives it an extra squeeze.

"Must be great to have him back," she says, nodding in Brad's direction.

"It really is," I say. "And you, too. How's Antony doing?"

Sondra's husband lost both arms to an IED and has been moving through the corridor of military medical facilities stretching from Germany to Washington, D.C., to, most recently, Minneapolis, for more than five months now. Sondra nods as if agreeing with something I said, as if I hadn't asked a question. After a few seconds she says, "He's finally in rehab. It's nice to be within driving distance of him."

Later, it will dawn on me that she hasn't actually answered the question I asked her. But I don't think about that now. Instead, I plow full-on ahead into how wonderful it must be to have him home, making all sorts of verbal faux pas that will make me cringe at some point in the future, like saying that I'm sure his injuries will require an adjustment but how nice it must be to know her husband is home for good, and safe.

"It's a relief," Sondra says. "That he's safe. You're right. It's a huge relief." She looks back over at Brad, who has positioned himself beside the sliding glass door and keeps looking from it to the front door and back again like a Secret Service agent anticipating trouble. "How is he doing?" she asks.

I nod and smile and shake my head, still hardly believing that across the room from me is Brad and that I don't need to fear the nightly news or a knock at my door any longer. I have spent so much time lately feeling terrible for Darcy, and for just a moment, standing here beside Sondra, I steep in the knowledge that that godforsaken desert decided to spit out each of our husbands. "He's great," I say. "Just great."

Sondra's smile is tinged with something I can't pinpoint. "I'm glad," she says. Then she takes my hand in hers. "Just promise me one thing: When it's not great, you let someone know. Me, or Darcy, or someone." She squeezes my hand and before she can let go, I take it from her.

I can't help but let my eyes narrow. My head cocks in surprise. She sees the unasked question in these movements. "It always gets hard, Elise," she says. "You think you'll be the only one. That your husband is the exception. At some point, though, it'll come for you, too."

"What will?"

A woman with severely bobbed red hair is approaching us. She probably doesn't know anyone else here and looks to have been orphaned by a previous conversation, hovering in our orbit and waiting. Sondra takes my hand, gives it one more squeeze, then releases it. "Don't be a stranger, okay?" she says, before fixing the red-haired woman with a toothy smile and excusing herself.

· · ·

A couple hours and twice that number of Jack and Cokes later, Brad drifts farther and farther away from me, and I relax in the knowledge that he's having a good time. Then I hear a woman, one of Darcy's former coworkers, whose name I believe is Cheri, talking to my husband.

"And after the whole kitchen is all done, after the contractors have cleaned up and left and the appliances are delivered and installed, I go to open the refrigerator and I can't even get my hand in. That's as far as it would open! Can you believe it? I was so angry. I mean, I had all of these groceries sitting on the counter and no way of getting them in the stupid refrigerator." She rolls her eyes and sighs. "It was just one headache after another. Don't ever do a remodel—buy new instead."

I hear this conversation for what it is: cocktail-party talk—a way to fill up time in a conversation. It's a story with themes so obvious that anyone can relate to them and conjure the appropriate incredulous response—anyone except Brad.

Cheri looks to him for his reaction, and for the briefest moment, his face is blank—perplexed, even. Then laughter erupts from somewhere deep inside him, with all the force of a volcanic eruption. He throws his head back and guffaws like he's front row at a comedy club, like a maniac. One by one, heads turn. I feel the burn of eyes staring at him. And at me.

"You call that a problem?" Brad laughs. "Cabinets and new refrigerators? Jesus Christ, that's a problem?" Then he leans in to Cheri and, like an older boy asking if a younger one wants to see a stash of stolen *Playboy* magazines, says, "You want to hear a real problem?"

Sensing that nothing good can come from this, I swoop in and grab Brad's arm, making sure he can see me as I do it, so as not to take him by surprise. "Babe, we need to get going," I say, trying to make my voice sound as light and sweet as spun sugar, though it will be quivering all over the place if I am forced to say much more. "Sorry, Cheri," I say, and I steer Brad toward the kitchen, where Darcy is preparing more appetizers.

"Gotta run!" I call to her. She comes out to hug me, and fortunately, only rubs Brad's arm.

"It's good to have you back," Darcy says to him, and for an instant, I think she's going to crumble. But she takes a deep breath and smiles. Brad fixes her with a blank stare. I don't know where he's gone, but he's no longer here. Collin is gone, and sometimes I think Brad is, too—just a different kind of gone. This is something I don't dare say out loud, though. Not to Darcy. Not even to myself.

"I'll give you a call tomorrow," I tell her.

When we get into the car, I suggest we should drive the long way home to take in the lights. This is something Brad has always loved doing, and a holiday tradition I have merely tolerated. I steer through Maple Bluff and ooh and aah at the decorations, pointing out the ones I find especially spectacular. Brad stares out the passenger side window. He doesn't seem to notice one house over any other.

I reach over and link my fingers with his.

"Brad?" I am afraid of what I'm about to ask, but I feel I have to, and so I plow ahead, giving scant thought to the words I'm saying before they tumble out. "When you asked Cheri if she wanted to know what a real problem was, you were talking about over there, weren't you?"

Brad doesn't look at me. His gaze is still fixed outside his car window and his face is stony. He nods.

"What were you going to tell her?" I ask him.

"Stop it, E.," he says.

"What was it like over there, babe?" I press. I am suddenly desperate to know what he knows. To understand the sort of life he's lived all these months away from me, from here. To have confirmed or denied that he saw the terrible things, or worse ones, that fill the news each night.

"Goddamn it, Elise. Drop it."

I've seen documentaries on the two world wars, Vietnam, Rwanda, and Kosovo. I've seen the cable news coverage of Iraq and Afghanistan. I know what the definition of atrocity is. But that was over there, and Brad is here. And I need him to share this with me. I need to feel close to him again. For him to feel that closeness, too. There's a huge hole in our life together, cut out of the last year by preschool scissors that left ragged edges and pieces strewn about. If we can arrange those pieces into a complete picture that we can both see, maybe then we can resume living this life we built together.

"There's nothing that happened that would make me think any different of you," I say. When he doesn't respond, I squeeze his hand and whisper, "You can tell me. It's okay."

Brad snatches back his hand, and when I look into his eyes, they are wild and brimming.

"Goddamn you," he says.

When I slow to a stop at the intersection of Sherman and Gorham, Brad opens his door and gets out.

"Brad!"

He looks at me before he slams the door. He shakes his head and jogs off.

Twice I roll down the window and call to him to get back in the car, but he ignores me. I resort to trailing him at a speed so slow, it's nearly idling. If it weren't for Brad's outfit—khakis and an untucked button-down shirt—you'd think he was out for a jog, his cadence is so steady and sure.

Outside the car windows, twinkling lights—some multicolored and some white—are blurred by the tears pooling in my eyes. It's a kaleidoscope of merriment meant for someone else this year.

When I'm certain that Brad is, in fact, headed home, I drive ahead of him. I'm able to start a fire and open a beer for each of us by the time he arrives. When he doesn't come inside, I meet him on the front porch.

I hold out a bottle to him. "This is a cold and very funny-looking olive branch," I tell him. He doesn't laugh, but he takes the bottle from me.

"Come inside," I say. "I have a fire going."

This is the way we've weathered many a Wisconsin winter—a crackling fire and just the two of us, talking, at the end of the day. It isn't regular or planned enough to be a routine, but they are the key moments—the day stretching out behind us like a race well run and our voices floating in the dark—that I will remember above any others.

Brad shakes his head and pats the space on the porch step next to him. "I'm tired of being hot. I'm tired of sweat. It's good to feel cold," he says.

I'm wearing only a long-sleeved shirt and a thin sweater, and the winter wind cuts straight through to my skin, but I sit down next to Brad. Tonight, we don't talk. We sit and sip, staring out at the street-lights coating the scene with an effulgence that makes it look as though it's been painted on canvas.

When the shivering my whole body is doing migrates to my teeth, Brad wraps an arm around my shoulders and pulls me close. I shut my eyes and breathe deeply, and as I do, I hear Sondra's words in my ears. But they're drowned out by Brad saying, "Team BE, babe. You and me," which is what we always called ourselves when things got rough—when we were down to the last twenty dollars in our checking account even as the monthly bills continued to roll in; when one of our former landlords gave us only two weeks' notice to find a new place to live in February, in a town where almost every rental is on an August-to-August cycle; or when Brad's father, Mert, told Brad that "real men join the Marines," instead of telling Brad that he was proud of him for enlisting in the Army.

"Promise?" I whisper, letting my head loll onto Brad's chest.

"Promise," he says.

Six

It is too early in the morning on the Friday after Christmas, and I am staring bleary-eyed at a breakfast of toast and over-easy eggs sprinkled with seasoning salt when Brad tells me he's going try to get into the University of Wisconsin-Madison's PhD program in Russian.

"It might be too late," I warn. If the UW's PhD programs are anything like its law school, they're sticklers for dates and deadlines, and not altogether good about accommodating requests or exceptions.

"Can't hurt to try," Brad says. His optimism is infectious. These past weeks he's been rattling around this house, drinking too much, sleeping when he should be awake, and pacing the fence line of our backyard when he should be sleeping. But this morning, he's up and showered and dressed. He's made me eggs. And now he wants to check out options directly related to his future. "You," I say, waving my fork in his direction, "are quite the guy. You know that?"

He's adjusting, and I'm adjusting. We're readjusting to life together. "So there," I'd like to say to Sondra. I take the bite of egg that is on my fork and set it on my plate; I get up from my seat at the table, and go around to his. I kiss him like I mean it, long and slow, feeling the softness of his lips—the velvety sensation, the distinct contours of them—against my own. The desire to feel them move from my lips to my neck to other parts of me that are now dressed for work rises up in me like an errant geyser, and I have to push it back down. Damn Judge Kresley and his penchant for scheduling eight a.m. hearings.

I stand up. "I'm going to miss you," I tell Brad, drawing back and holding his face between my hands. Darcy was scheduled to accompany Sondra to Minneapolis this weekend, but Mia has come down with the chicken pox and is all sorts of miserable, so I'm filling in.

Brad chucks my chin with curled fingers. "It's two nights, E.," he says. "No big thing. Anything for a mile, right?"

I smile at the memory—Brad cheering me on during my first, and only, marathon, the Whistlestop in far-northern Wisconsin that runs mostly along an old railroad grade. My GPS wristlet had quit working and so had my legs, and I had no idea how much farther I had to run when I saw Brad up ahead and told him I didn't think I could finish. "You can do anything for a mile," he said, and with that mantra stuck in my head, I ran. And ran. It was the longest mile of my life. After the race, I realized that it hadn't been one mile—it had been four—and I yelled at him: "You told me it was a mile!"

He shook his head. "Nope. That's what you wanted to hear. What I said was that you can do anything for a mile—and you did. I'm proud of you, E."

It was the way we signed off on our e-mail messages to each other during his deployment, and thinking back on each day that I woke up without him here over the past year, dwelling on having to spend two nights—not even a full forty-eight hours—apart seems ridiculous. Especially compared to what Sondra—or Darcy—has been facing.

"Anything for a mile," I repeat now, and I smile at my husband, full of thanks and contentment.

I get up and rinse my dish in the sink and load it into the dishwasher. I have exactly twenty minutes to make it to work, pick up the files I need, and get to court. I shoulder my workbag and an overnight bag. "Can you handle the recycling?" I ask Brad.

"Sure. At your service," he says, and I kiss him good-bye.

"See you Sunday," I say.

"See you Sunday."

I wonder if Sondra and I will have anything to talk about during the four-hour trip to Minneapolis, but I quickly realize I needn't have worried. Each of us has a conference call, and for the couple of hours in between we talk about work—about the challenges we've faced as career women, the shocking lack of competent bosses and managers in her field and mine, and the merits of our respective fantasy football teams.

"I've never met another woman who does fantasy football," she says. She's driving with one hand and twirling a piece of hair above her ear into submission. Outside the car windows, the bright afternoon sun seems to be fading by the second to a crisper, thinner, colder version of itself.

"It was cheaper and easier to learn than golf," I tell her. "Goes a long way with the guys in the office—especially the partners."

Sondra smiles and wags a finger in my direction. "You're a cagey one."

"That's not why you do it?"

Sondra shakes her head. "No, ma'am. I pretty much grew up on the bleachers of the Stick."

"The what?"

"Candlestick Park. In San Fran."

"You're from California?"

"Born and raised," Sondra says, and something in her demeanor changes, as if she's trying hard to remember something. Or someone. "That was a long time ago. Doesn't feel like it, but it was."

I get Sondra talking about her childhood and her family, mostly so I can avoid talking about my own. I couldn't have ever wished for better parents, but I've learned that something about being an orphan, even an adult orphan, tends to spark awkwardness in any conversation.

Sondra jumps on her conference call just as we're crossing through Hudson. I offer to drive, but she waves me off, and something about the fluid way in which she puts her hands-free headset on and connects the call makes me think that she's an old pro at having to drive and talk all at once. I'm not fluent enough in pharmaceuticalese to follow the conversation, and I let myself drift off into a dreamless, solid sleep.

When I wake, the sky is black and we're stopped in front of a behemoth building rising like a giant square moon at the end of a series of parking lots as big as football fields.

"Sorry I fell asleep," I say. I rub my eyes and shake my head as if to rattle loose the last remnants of sleep. "We're here?"

Sondra doesn't answer me. She's clutching the steering wheel and her forehead is pressed against it.

"Sondra?"

After a good long while, she speaks without lifting her head. "I don't think I can do this," she says.

I have no idea what she's talking about. Do what? We've come all this way to visit her husband. This isn't the first time she's seen him since he's been stateside. I don't see what the issue is. Darcy told me Sondra's family lived on the West Coast and she was tired of driving all this way by herself every weekend; she hadn't told me she was a flight risk.

"You mean you can't do it now?"

Sondra straightens up. She slaps her hands lightly against either side of her face and then runs them through her hair. She inhales and then exhales audibly. Then she shakes her head.

"I'm probably just tired. Let's check in. I'll come back in the morning."

"Okay," I say. "But isn't Antony expecting you?"

"I'll call and tell him we got a late start out of Madison." Sondra turns the key and the car's engine jumps to life, spitting warm air out the vents at us. I don't know how long we were stopped before I woke, and I don't realize until the heat hits me how chilled I am.

I just shrug, because what else am I supposed to do? My role here is clearly defined: copilot, banterer, judgment-free support. "Sure," I say. "Sounds good."

Sondra and I arrive at the Fisher House and find that the inn is nearly full, and that we'll need to share a room. It's homey enough not to feel like a hotel room, but strange enough to leave the impression I'm a guest in someone else's house. Our room has two full-size beds covered by blue and brown duvets and a brown love seat that folds out into another bed. As I begin to unpack, Sondra collapses onto the one farthest from the door and closes her eyes.

By the time I finish freshening up, my stomach is protesting that it's been fed only toast, eggs, and coffee all day. The smell of some indiscriminate food is wafting up from downstairs, which increases the insistent grumbling in my midsection.

"Want to go see what's cooking?" I ask Sondra.

She doesn't open her eyes. She has one hand laid across them like a 1940s starlet feigning fainting. "You go ahead," she says. "Scope things out for me. Maybe I'm coming down with something. I'm going to lie down for a bit."

"Okay," I say. I prop my suitcase against the end of the bed, pop it open, and since it doesn't look like we're venturing far tonight, swap my dress pants for jeans and my heels for slippers. I grab my workbag, turn on the desk light, and turn off the overhead lights on my way out the door.

Fisher House has a full kitchen where people who have better cooking skills than I do can fix their own meals, and where well-wishing volunteers keep the refrigerator stocked with prepared dishes for guests who are too inept, busy, or stressed to fend for themselves. I fall firmly into the second category. A board in the foyer informs me that tonight's selection is white chicken chili. This sounds as good as anything I could imagine.

The kitchen is illuminated only by under-cabinet lights. In the refrigerator I find a small portion of chili in a Tupperware container on the "free-for-all" shelf. When I put the container directly into the microwave instead of into a bowl, I think of how Brad would say that I'm upping my chances of dying of cancer, but at the moment my hunger exceeds my energy for worrying about future disasters. I want to eat and I want to sleep, and in between those two activities I still have a bit of work to do. If cutting out a step gets me closer to accomplishing all of those things, I'm willing to take the minute increased risk of getting sick down the road.

I eat standing up, like I often do at home. The chili goes down quickly and warms me from the inside out. Then I help myself to a Diet Coke and settle in the library to prepare a research memo one of the partners requested I turn in to him on Monday, as I was walking out the door this afternoon. I suspect it was punishment, made up on the spot, for the fact that I was leaving early on a Friday, but that only inspires me to work harder on it.

When I return to the room, Sondra is fully asleep, though she has changed into pajamas and tied her hair back with a scarf. It's been a whirlwind couple of weeks, chock-full of emotion and excitement and readjusting to new-old routines, and despite the nap I had in the car and the caffeine-laced Diet Coke I finished an hour ago, I am asleep, too, almost as soon as I crawl between the sheets.

In the morning, hallway noise and bright light streaming in through our room's window wake me. I look over, expecting to see Sondra still sleeping, but her bed is empty and the linens hardly look rumpled. She must have slept like the dead.

Apparently, so did I, because it's quarter to ten.

I assume Sondra has gone to see Antony, and I have plenty of work yet to keep me busy until she returns. I hurry off to the shower so I can get ready and finish my work before she gets back. I've never been to the Mall of America, and I've been hoping all along that we might go this afternoon. I'm not usually much of a shopper and I haven't yet asked Sondra, not wanting to be a bother or impose any constraints on her time, but something about that megamall fascinates me. For starters, how did they get a whole amusement park inside? And what kinds of people shop there? I'm intrigued by the potential people-watching.

I'm deep in thought about the feasibility of having whole stores dedicated only to baseball or trains or magnets—in Minnesota, of all places—when I see it: a note, handwritten, and next to it a printout of some sort, like a travel itinerary.

Elise—

I'm so sorry to do this, but I was right last night. I just can't go in there again. I'm done; I think I knew that all along, but I thought it would be different once I actually got here. It wasn't. I'll be on my way to California to visit my family for a while by the time you read this. I've purchased you a plane

ticket home tonight for your trouble, and I've prepaid your
cab fare to the airport. Please forgive me. I'm so sorry.
　—*Sondra*

I look at the printout. My flight leaves at five nineteen tonight. It's not even eleven o'clock yet. I try to call Brad to let him know there's been a change of plans, and I leave a message when his voice mail picks up. Then I call a cab.

Seven

The corridors of the Minneapolis VA Polytrauma Rehabilitation Center all look alike, awash in bland beiges, greens, and grays. The brain injury unit is quiet and many of the soldiers in it look like they don't have a thing wrong with them. Then I pass people missing limbs, hands, eyes—big chunks of their bodies that should otherwise be there and are now disguised with gauze. Some are in wheelchairs. Some are trying out new prostheses. Some sit and stare absently, off into a future that looks nothing like the one they were supposed to be living.

I walk and walk and walk—past physical therapy rooms as big as basketball courts and occupational therapy rooms with stairways to nowhere, kitchenettes, and brightly colored mats and giant exercise balls; past bustling nurses' stations; past the gift shop and snack counter; past patient rooms with the ambient sounds of daytime game shows and low moans. The walking feels good, as though I have a purpose.

And then a name on the board outside one of the rooms catches my eye: A. THOMPSON.

It could be Alex Thompson, or Andrew, or Austin. It's a ridiculously common name. Yet, somehow, even before I look in and see a bald, handsome man missing both his arms at the shoulders, I know this is Sondra's husband.

He is sitting in a chair by his bed, staring out the window. He turns and looks when I knock on the doorframe. He smiles as he gestures with his chin for me to come in, but his brow is knit.

"Antony?"

He nods.

"It's nice to meet you. I'm a friend of Sondra's. I'm Elise." I go to reach out my hand as I introduce myself. Thankfully, I stop my hand just in time and hook my fingers in my pocket to keep it there.

"Aw, yeah," Antony says, "of course. She mentioned you. Nice to meet you, too." He gives a definitive nod of his head—his new handshake.

I can't tell if he's telling the truth, or just trying to be nice. But I see instantly that this is the kind of guy Antony is. He wants to put people at ease.

"Come on in and have a seat," he says. I lower myself into a stiff plastic chair near the foot of his bed. "It's been boring around here lately. They cancelled my PT today, and I lost my roommate yesterday. It's nice to have a visitor."

I smile at Antony. I'm happy to break up his day. But I hadn't actually thought this through before I knocked on his door. Was that visitor remark a dig at Sondra? Does he know she's gone? Does he not? What am I supposed to tell him? How much?

But Antony's a talker, and he's off and running with conversation. I bet he can work the hell out of a cocktail party. We discuss our childhoods, why he loves the Army and Iraq, what he thinks is going to happen in Afghanistan, how Brad and I met, how Brad is doing, and what our plans are now that he's home. By the time I look up at the clock, almost two hours have gone by. I feel like I'm on a first date that's gone spectacularly well. So well, in fact, that I've almost forgotten that Sondra is well on her way to California by now and that I'm sitting here with her husband, whom she has abandoned.

"I should get going," I say, making a move to get up from my chair, "but thanks for a really nice visit."

"Thanks for dropping in," Antony says. "And don't be a stranger. Come on by again." He fixes me with a toothy grin.

"I'd like that," I tell him, though I'm not sure how that would work. If he were in Madison, I'd make sure to drop on by. But I doubt I'll be making the eight-hour round-trip to see him again.

I linger a moment, wondering whether I should say more, though I'm not sure what.

I'm nearly out the door when Antony calls after me, "If you see Sondra, tell her it's okay."

I turn toward him. I get the sense that she never told him she would be coming to visit in the first place. Maybe she knew this was how the trip would end. Maybe she didn't want to admit it, or hoped that if she just got herself here, inertia would take over and keep her from leaving.

"I'm sure she'll be by," I say.

He's smiling, but his eyes are as sad as a bloodhound's when he says, "Naw, she won't. That girl's as gone as the day is long. They amputate more than your injured parts in here, you know. But it's okay. You tell her that for me."

"I will," I say. I struggle for something to add. "Get well soon," doesn't quite do it. Neither does, "Take care."

"Be well, Antony," I say, finally. But when I do, his eyes are closed and his head is tipped back. Maybe he would signal or wave if he could. Maybe he wouldn't.

. . .

The sky is dark as my plane descends into Madison, the city spread out below like a fantastic model of itself, sparkling like a million tiny diamonds with the Capitol sitting like a crown jewel among them.

As the plane taxis to the gate, I power up my cell phone and try to call Brad again. I'd like a ride, but I'd also like to have dinner with my husband. There's a fantastic and affordable little bar–turned–Italian restaurant on the way from the airport to our house that would be the perfect place to reconnect with Brad and tell him about this surreal trip.

But his phone goes to voice mail—again, and again, and again, when I'm at the baggage claim, after I call for a cab, and as I'm on my way home in it. Weaving through the streets of Madison in the back of the cab, I feel like a tourist in the town I've called home for the past five years. By the time I hand over a twenty-dollar bill to my driver and tell him to keep the change, I'm fighting mad. I've been trying to call Brad since this morning, and he hasn't answered or returned any of my calls. He hasn't so much as sent a message in response.

By the time I walk into our darkened house, I'm irate.

Ever since I read Sondra's note this morning, the one constant thought I've had is that I can't wait to talk things over with Brad. All day, I imagined that he'd pick me up and that we'd stop off for a bite to eat on our way home. I'd tell Brad about Sondra, the note, and Antony, and he'd help me make sense of it all. We'd talk about how glad we were that we had dodged the proverbial bullet of those kinds of troubles. How glad we were to have our lives back to normal.

That's what we should be doing tonight. Instead, I'm alone, eating a peanut butter and banana sandwich and watching *Jeopardy!* I have just correctly guessed the eight-hundred-dollar question ("This ex-Cowboy joined Keith Jackson and Howard Cosell on the first *Monday Night Football* telecast"—"Who is Don Meredith, Alex?") when Brad walks in the door. His face is soft and sagging, his eyes unfocused, and he sways a bit when he takes off his jacket. When he turns back toward me, I see a gauze bandage covering the inside of his forearm.

"My God, Brad! What happened?"

He fixes me with a blank look. "What?"

"Your arm," I say.

He shrugs. "Got a tattoo."

He says this as though he is telling me he picked up a pack of gum from the gas station down the street, this man who used to say that a tattoo was an outward sign of a personality flaw. Brad broke up with a serious girlfriend in college, whom he loved, because she got a tiny hummingbird tattoo on the inside of her hip.

He cocks his head like a dog trying hard to understand, and says, "You're not supposed to be back until tomorrow."

"Change of plans," I say. My voice is measured but terse. I'm trying hard not to be as angry as I am. I keep telling myself that Brad didn't know I was coming home. But I'm tired and emotionally drained, and logic is no match for my emotions.

"Sondra left. She left her husband. She left me in Minneapolis." Saying those words aloud doesn't make them any more believable. "Who does something like that?"

Brad nods absently and walks to the kitchen. I stand where I am, waiting for him to come back out into the living room. I hear him take a pint glass from the cupboard and drop a handful of ice cubes from the freezer into it. Then I hear the glug-glug-glug of Jack Daniel's filling his glass, and as he tosses the jug into the recycling bin, the clatter of it falling to the floor. Even though I can't see it, I know it's because the bin is still jammed full.

"You didn't get the recycling out yesterday?" I call to him.

My tone is a little accusatory. Recycling day happens only once every two weeks, and even when I'm here alone, the too-small bin fills to capacity. With two of us under this roof, it's imperative that we don't miss a week. I'm disappointed, and maybe a little miffed. Brad is Mr. Dependable. When he says he's going to do something, it gets done. And this was the one, single thing he had to do.

Brad comes out to the dining room with the recycling bin. I expect him to keep going with it, to put it outside. Instead, he tosses it away from him, in my general direction. Cans and newspapers and bottles tumble out onto the floor. They land with a crash, and I jump.

"Happy?" he yells, and I jump again.

He starts to grab anything breakable—wine and beer and sparkling water bottles, empty jars of olives and maple syrup—and smashes them again, one by one against the hardwood like snap'n pop fireworks. When he's done, he goes back into the kitchen. I hear cabinets opening and closing. He returns with a box of cereal.

Brad opens the box and upends it, dumping the contents on the floor.

What is he doing? Has he lost his mind?

"March!" he barks at me. I startle.

"March!" he repeats, pointing to the pile of cereal.

My only thought is that I'm thankful I still have my boots on. I do as this man says—this man who has taken over my husband's body—because I do not know him, and I do not know what he'll do if I don't listen. I lift my knees, first one and then the other, crunching the cereal underfoot. A faint smile plays at the edge of Brad's lips at the sound.

I don't know how much time passes until I slow, and finally stop. He stands there, staring at me—glowering at me. And then he walks past me and out the front door, out into the night, leaving a trail of frigid winter air in his wake.

Not until the door slams shut do I feel the tears running down my cheeks. Our dining room floor is strewn with glass confetti. I fetch a plastic bag and begin disposing of the larger pieces; then I dig the vacuum out of the front hall closet and take care of the smaller shards and cereal crumbs.

I sit on the end of our bed and unzip my boots, bits of cereal falling from in between the treads. I swap my jeans and sweater for pajama pants and an old T-shirt, then climb into bed. And right before I turn out the light, I look up to see a woman staring back at me from the mirror above the dresser. Her hair is stringy and unkempt, her eyes red-rimmed. *Who are you?* I almost say the words out loud, though I know the answer: She is someone who is more than willing to pick up what has been broken.

Eight

In the hazy span between night and dawn, when the air is gray and the world outside is fully silent, I feel Brad crawl into bed next to me. I jump at his touch and then stiffen. Even before he speaks, I can smell his breath, sharp with the vapor of alcohol.

"I'm so glad you're home," he whispers into my neck. "I missed you."

I turn so I can see him. His eyes droop with lack of sleep and too much Jack. His face is puffy and unshaven.

"You missed me?"

He nuzzles into me. "Hmmm, yeah. Good trip?"

Does he not remember? Any of it?

"Brad," I say, choosing my words carefully, "I got home last night, remember?"

My heart is thudding in my chest, like an animal trying to escape its cage. Boom. Boom. Boom. I search his face for some flicker of recognition. Nothing registers.

"Sorry I was gone," he says. "I'll make it up to you tonight. Dinner out somewhere." And then his eyes close and almost instantly, he's snoring.

. . .

I dig my running clothes out from the bottom of the drawer, dress, and then carry my shoes to the living room to lace up. I can't remember the last time I ran. It was pre–Early, Janssen, and Bradenton, for sure. But it's too early to call Darcy, and I need to clear my head, or at least try.

I churn my legs, feeling the sweet burn in my thighs and my lungs that forces me to think of little else than this: one-two, one-two. Breathe in; breathe out. I run through campus, up State Street, and around the Capitol. I make a brief stop at work to get a drink of water and, because being warm feels good and I am willing to do anything that feels good right now, to avoid thinking about last night, I let myself into my office. I press the power button on my computer and while it's booting up, I stretch. I sift through my e-mail, triaging which messages I can answer quickly now and marking those that can wait for a more thorough response on Monday.

By the time I finish, it's close to noon and I'm famished. I choose a quicker, more direct route home. And with every step, a sense of dread grows in me like mold. How could Brad not remember last night? Was he that drunk? Will he even remember his promise to take me out tonight?

But when I return, there's a note on the snack bar:

Be back later. Dinner tonight, okay? I love you. —B.

I shower and then pull out my laptop to finish writing up a few memos and do a little research. At three o'clock, I finish all the work I can do without going back to the office for some files I need. My need—or desire—to talk to Darcy about what happened last night has disappeared. Brad had too much to drink, I've decided. I'll talk to him about it. Tonight.

But what do I do with myself now? I could clean the house, or just my closet. I could go shopping, though I hate shopping. None of those options sounds appealing.

I can't remember the last time I had my hair cut, though. I decide on this. And on the way home, I will buy new nail polish, eye shadow, and lip gloss in shades brighter than I might normally choose.

Why am I making such a big deal over this dinner? We'll likely end up at the brewpub near the square or the Indian restaurant just down from it, and neither requires fancy attire.

There hasn't often been a time in our shared history when money hasn't been tight—a trend that's continued. We bought our house, knowing that it needed some work, and anticipating that Brad would have gainful employment long before now, but our house seems bent on ambushing us. First the hot water heater went and then the washing machine, and lately there's been a spreading water stain on our bedroom ceiling, the result of an ice dam that I was too busy and too frightened to climb up on our roof and fix this winter. Add to that my college and law school loans having both come due in the past year, and our monthly budget looks like it's sprung a slow leak.

I half expect Brad to beg off dinner for this fact alone. He's the resident miser: clipping coupons, checking online for the cheapest gas in town before filling up, and preferring—always—to cook and eat in as opposed to going out to restaurants. I was always thankful that he couldn't see our bank account statements—a litany of take-out and fast-food places—while he was overseas.

Brad comes in just as I have put the finishing touches on my makeup and am admiring my newly trimmed hair, and he doesn't bother to remove his jacket. He walks over to me, wraps me in his arms, and rocks me back and forth. I can smell liquor on his breath, but in this moment, it's sexy in a "real men drink whiskey" sort of way. He otherwise seems fine, and I let myself fall into him. His embrace is so sure, so steady, so *him* that I wonder whether I might have imagined the events of last night.

Snow is falling steadily as Brad tells me to jump on the Beltline instead of heading up West Washington, toward the Capitol, where I expected we would end up tonight.

"Exit on Old Sauk Road," he says. "There's a new place I just heard about that I want to take you." Then he leans his head back and, I assume, falls asleep. He was discharged with a cabinet full of medications billed as antianxiety drugs or relaxants that knock him out in an instant. I'm charged with bittersweet emotions—sadness that he has to take pills before going out for dinner with me, happiness and relief that he's cognizant that he might need them and that he wants things to go well tonight enough to take them.

I am wholly unprepared when I walk into the restaurant Brad has chosen. It is awash in mahogany and leather, and I know without looking at a menu that this place is more expensive than any other we've ever dined at. It's the kind of place I'm used to going to with clients on the law firm's dime, but not with my husband on our own.

The waiter explains the restaurant's concept to us—small plates meant to share—and though I know we are at a pricey eatery, I'm still shocked when I look down to find that the small plates run anywhere from fifteen to thirty dollars apiece. I ask the waiter how many a table of two would normally order, and when he tells me five, I search Brad's face for some sort of reaction. There is none.

What there is, though, is a look of total and complete unease. He keeps glancing back over his shoulder. He is jumpy and his eyes are shifty. Beads of sweat have collected on his forehead. And as the waiter hits his stride in reciting that night's specials—something about "terrorized baby carrots"—(*Who makes this stuff up?* I make a note to ask Darcy if that's even a real thing, or just a way to make a hoity-toity place even hoitier)—Brad blurts, "Can we please move?" His tone leaves no real room for anything but an affirmative answer.

The waiter looks around the dining room and back at Brad. He's confused, and so am I. We're one of two couples in here, and the other is nowhere near us.

I furrow my brow as if to say, "What is going on?" but the waiter replies, "Absolutely, sir," and busies himself with collecting our menus. Brad, meanwhile, bolts for a table closest to the door.

"Babe, it's going to be cold here," I say. "How about over there?" I point to a table on the opposite side of the room and behind a half wall that would do wonders at stopping the draft coming from the restaurant's front entrance. But Brad either doesn't hear me or pretends not to. He sits down at the table he's chosen. I follow.

When the waiter comes back, I make awkward conversation with him, conscious of Brad's weird behavior. I'm sure he'll go home and gossip with his friends or roommate about us, but like any good server, he's pleasant and gracious now. I order drinks, then scan the menu for the cheapest items: bacon-wrapped pork tenderloin (fifteen dollars), crab cakes (sixteen dollars), sausage and mushroom flatbread (seventeen dollars), bone-in braised short ribs (eighteen dollars), and seared day boat scallops (twenty-six dollars). Brad's gaze darts frantically around the restaurant.

"Brad," I say, when the waiter has collected our menus and trotted off to put in our order, "this is going to be really expensive."

He waves me off. "It's fine," he says. "It's worth it. You're worth it."

Brad takes my hand and I notice, then, the tattoo I had forgotten about peeking out from under the cuff of his shirt.

"Can I see?" I ask, nodding down at it.

Brad looks at me. Studies me. Then he shrugs and rolls back his cuff and part of his shirt. Running down his left forearm, from the inside of his elbow to his wrist, is one word inked in ornate letters: *AWARIYAH*.

"What does it mean?" I ask.

He shrugs and pulls his shirt down over the letters—heavy, black, and still raw—on his arm. "Nothing. Just something we used to say over there," he says.

I nod, remembering the night of Darcy's party when I pushed too hard in trying to get Brad to talk. I decide to leave it be. Instead, I tell him what my past couple of days have been like—Sondra's unwillingness to go into the rehab center, how she fled with almost no forewarning, my visit with Antony, and my inability to tell him that his wife had up and left us both.

The waiter brings out our drinks, flatbread, and the scallops. I scoop up a scallop and toast point to place on Brad's plate, and I notice that his eyes have filled with tears. He shakes his head. "It's so unfair," he says, and before I ask him what he means, he places both hands on the table, palms down, smiles at me, and asks if we could maybe talk about something else.

"Tell me what you're up to at work," he says with a level of interest undeserving of a junior associate's duties.

"Oh God," I say. "We're racing to the basement on dreary subjects, huh? I could regale you with tales of municipal prosecutions, but you'd probably fall asleep at the table. Last week, though, I did get to argue a raze order on a ramshackle barn that was about to blow over with the next stiff wind. And this," I say, raising my glass of wine and tipping it toward Brad, "is why they pay me the big bucks."

Brad smiles and nods. "Ooh!" I say, remembering one interesting case I helped with, at least peripherally. "One of the partners is getting ready to argue a case before the state Supreme Court on behalf of these parents whose little girl died because they didn't get her the medical attention she needed, and he pulled me in to do the research."

I explain the case while more of our food arrives, then look to Brad, expecting him to ask me why parents would deny their child care—expecting him to engage me on where the moral, religious, and legal implications intersect, because that's what he would have done before. But his mind, I can tell, is elsewhere. I'm not sure if he even heard what I said. He is scanning the room; I try to follow, but I can't determine what he's looking for. Gusts of wind catch the outer door and rattle it, and, by extension, my husband. Brad picks up his Jack and Coke and downs what's left of it in one gulp. His skin looks cold and clammy, as though he's coming down with something.

"Do you mind if we go?" he asks.

I am about to point out that our last dish, the spare ribs, hasn't come yet, but there's something about the way Brad asks the question that stops me short of wondering why. And by the time I squeak out, "Okay," he has stood up and put his coat on.

It just takes time, I tell myself.

"I'll meet you in the car," he says. And before I can answer, like a ghost he's already gone. I pull out the emergency credit card to pay the outrageous tab and wait for the server to box the spare ribs.

It just takes time, I tell myself. *It's going to take some time.*

The restaurant is situated at the corner of an L-shaped strip mall, and the sidewalk that runs alongside it is covered with a light, fluffy snow. It's fallen faster than the business owners of the strip mall can shovel, and I hope that maybe Brad will see me and pull the car around. But none of the cars that I can see are even running; their headlights are all dark. So I pick my way down the sidewalk and then across the parking lot. I take choppy, deliberate steps, wary of falling in the cute but impractical heels I chose for this evening. Snow soaks my feet, wet and sharply cold, with every step, and I almost wish I hadn't bothered with the shoes. With the dressing up. With any of it.

Flakes continue to make their way to the ground, floating in the beam of my headlights like illuminated dust particles. The drive home feels like traveling by sleigh through the woods. Everything is quiet and coated in white—the trees, the guardrails, even the road.

We are one of the only cars in sight for mile after mile. Brad is jumpy and nervous, and I am lost in thought, trying to design the perfect sentence to ask him what is wrong, to help me understand what went on there at the restaurant to make him bolt. Is it something I should even ask? I don't understand what happened—what is happening to us. But Brad is like a human grenade, and I don't want to pull that pin. I am distracted and the car drifts right. The tires hit the rumble strips and Brad, jolted from his own private thoughts, screams, "What the fuck was that?"

I jerk the wheel hard to the left, back onto the road proper, and tell him it was nothing, but he is shaking, almost convulsing. His face is red, and he is gripping the door handle so hard that I can see it straining to come lose.

"You're going to get us killed," he spits out.

"I—I'm sorry. I just zoned out for a second there and—"

"Shut the fuck up and do your job," he says.

Brad has never talked like this to me before. Brad doesn't talk like this. He sounds like a superior giving orders to a subordinate who just endangered an entire platoon, not me—his wife. My breath hitches in my chest.

And then he is yelling at me again—yelling and grabbing for the steering wheel.

"Get over! Fucking get over! It's going to blow!"

I don't know what he's talking about, but my strength is no match for Brad's as he jerks the wheel hard to the left, toward the median. I brake instinctively and feel the wheels lock and start to slide. Everything outside of the car is a blur of white. Things inside the car are in sharp focus: Brad's face hard and angry; my hands slipping from the steering wheel; time slowing down. I have time to think, *Who are you?* and also, *I don't want to die like this.*

I close my eyes and brace myself—for the rumble of skidding off the road; the brief feeling of weightlessness as the grade of the median drops off below, and as we sail over it; the impact of hitting the opposite bank or the disorientation of rolling, wheels over roof. I wait. But it doesn't come. When I open my eyes, we are at a standstill. The car is pointing in exactly the wrong direction on the divided highway, but we are not moving and we have not died.

Brad is still yelling: "Go! Go! Fucking go!" And he is pointing straight ahead.

He wants me to drive in the direction he's gesturing—the wrong way up a four-lane highway. It seems any sort of movement will do. He's alternately yelling at me and glancing behind us at a full black garbage bag that someone dropped carelessly on the shoulder of the road.

My hands are shaking so badly, I can hardly steer the car into a U-turn. A little ways up the road, the garbage bag out of sight, I exit and then pull over. I put my forehead on the steering wheel and a sob wells up from somewhere so deep inside that I barely recognize it as mine. And then there is another anguished sound doing a two-part harmony with my own. I look over and see Brad curled against the passenger-side door. He is saying, "I'm so sorry. Oh God, I'm sorry."

My hands continue to shake and I can't steady them. I wonder how I'll be able to get us home. I look over at Brad. He is a ball of limbs—knees to forehead, elbows folded into hips, and his head tucked into the crook of his arms. "Make it stop," he says. I don't know what "it" is and I don't know what he's asking me to do, or if he's even asking this of me.

I'm scared of what might happen if I touch Brad—if he'll yell at me, or swing out and hit me. But I'm more scared of what might happen if I don't, and so I reach out and pull him to me. He resists at first, but soon his body slumps and his head leans heavily on my chest. I smooth his hair with my open palm. "I love you, Brad. You don't know how much I love you," I say. Then I shush him like a baby, rocking him the same way. "Shhh, now. It's okay. It's all right."

But I'm not sure, right then, that it is.

This late at night, with the whole world fast asleep, I still startle when a car drives by and slows at our intersection, fearful that it will stop. Fearful that men in dress greens will step out and deliver the news that I lived in fear of receiving, every hour, every day, for an entire year. Even now.

He is here, I tell myself. *He is here and he is safe.* But even with Brad sleeping in our bedroom instead of across an ocean in that sea of sand, those words hit the wrong pitch.

After this evening, adrenaline is still coursing through me, and after hours of staring at the ceiling, listening to Brad yell out in his dreams, I give up on sleep and sneak out to the living room with my laptop. The screen casts a ghostly glow reflected in the front window as I wait for the search engine to load.

Once it does, I type in the letters of the one word I know I shouldn't—the one word I know I should leave well enough alone: *awariyah.*

The answer pops up. Loosely translated from Arabic, it means "damaged goods." A lump the size of a lemon forms in my throat. My stomach constricts as if I've just been struck there. My hands start to shake. I have to clasp one with the other to steady them. I can't take my eyes off that word, the translation of those letters. Is this how he thinks of himself now? Enough to have the label permanently affixed to his skin? I feel ill. And profoundly sad. And frightened.

I think of Brad sobbing against me tonight, my shirt wet with his tears and his yelling at me the other night, "March!" over the cereal and shards of glass. I think of that summer only a few years ago that might as well be three whole lifetimes over, when the air-conditioning in our apartment broke during a heat streak so relentless people said even the elephants over at Vilas Zoo would hardly venture outdoors. Brad and I walked to the Union to dip our feet in Lake Mendota and sipped directly from the sweating pitcher of Spotted Cow between us while a group of skinny white college guys with dreadlocks who clearly equated volume with passion tried to rap their way through what I assumed was supposed to be a musical set. After the beer garden closed and the band mercifully stopped, we trekked back to our apartment, stripped the couch of its cushions, and placed them under the only window that opened. The light of the moon fell through it and onto us, both trying to sleep in the sweltering heat. I tossed and turned and at one point, found myself nose to nose with Brad, his eyes wide-open.

"E., if I roll over every morning for the rest of my life and you're not there, I couldn't live with myself," he whispered, out of nowhere. "I don't want to live without you."

"What are you talking about?"

"Making this official," he said.

And I remember, three days later, on a Wednesday afternoon, when I put on a white dress I had scavenged Aura Vintage for, and Brad wore a navy blue pin-striped suit. I didn't have parents to invite, and I didn't want Granna to feel she had to travel all the way from lower Michigan to be there, and Brad just had his brother and dad. During any given month he might or might not be talking to them because his dad could be a real son of a bitch, so it was only Brad and I and a judge at the Dane County Courthouse. Afterward, we splurged on lunch at the Ocean Grill and then walked to the Monona Terrace where we asked the Tai Chi instructor who had just finished her afternoon session if she would take our picture. That's the only photograph we have of our wedding day, and it now sits on a shelf across the room, but in it Brad's teeth are as big and white as Chiclets, and the water of Lake Monona in the background is as steely blue as my eyes, and my eyes—those eyes of mine are dancing.

Around me, our house is still and empty, dark, and quiet. I can barely make out that photo. I don't know whether I'd recognize us in it if I could.

I remember his words: "I don't want to live without you."

I look down at the illuminated computer screen, at the search results: *damaged goods.*

"I'm still here," I say out loud—to the night, to my quivering lip and rolling stomach, to my heart hammering in my chest and the metallic taste of fear coating my mouth, to this man who has come back, pretending to be my husband, and to my Brad who's still in there, somewhere. "I'm here and I'm not going anywhere."

It's a challenge, an edict, a flag with which I'm staking this ground.

Nine

As I roll into work at seven fifty-eight for an eight a.m. meeting, I vow, once again, to be more punctual. Being on time, after all, is a relatively low-level skill—one I should be able to master. One I should have mastered by this point in my life. And yet.

I get my jacket off, swap my boots for a pair of black heels I keep in the bottom drawer of my desk, and score a cup of sludge from the break room. Miraculously, I am only two minutes late for the meeting. Not so miraculously, I fail to pay attention to much of what is being discussed. My mind is churning through the events of yesterday, the night before, and all the days and weeks before that since Brad has been back, trying to sort out how much of his odd behavior is just plain old readjustment, and what might be cause for concern.

As it turns out, paying attention might have been a good idea.

"Elise, what are your thoughts on *Rowland*? What does Wisconsin case law say about its merits?" Susan asks me.

The normal me would have started rattling off pros and cons to taking the case and citing relevant or precedent-setting case law to support my final conclusion, because this is what I do best: I prepare more and know more than anyone else. I pride myself on being an encyclopedic font of knowledge for the partners, and I think that, like my law school profs, it's impossible for them not to appreciate some well-recited case law or an issue that's been researched from every possible angle. Obsessive, comprehensive knowledge of minutiae is in every good attorney's DNA. I learned early on to embrace that obsessiveness, to speak the language of my legal superiors.

But that was the old me. The new me, with a husband recently returned from war, has done the bare minimum in the past weeks and can't seem to follow a single thought from start to finish. All I can do is stare, gape-mouthed, back at Susan. Her own mouth is drawn into a tight, thin line.

"It's a slam dunk," a voice to my right says. "There's no way this is a wrongful death."

The voice belongs to Zach Newsome. He is a senior associate, whereas I am a junior associate. There are six of us on the litigation team at Early, Janssen, and Bradenton, LLC. Normally I'd be irritated at him for inserting himself into my moment, but today I'm all sorts of grateful.

Two of the non-equity partners, Mark Abuzzi and Connor Lax, flank Susan. To their right sit Crane Early and Gordon Janssen, finishing out the Early and Janssen part of Early, Janssen, and Bradenton.

"I don't know if I'd call it a slam dunk," Crane Early says. "A little boy died on our client's work site. They could get us on attractive nuisance."

While Crane continues to play devil's advocate, the others jump into the discussion like vultures and I look over at Zach and mouth, *Thank you.* He smiles and gives me a wink.

In the end, our team decides to take two personal injury cases in addition to *Rowland v. Champion Construction.* We'll be representing the company against the family of Nicky Rowland, an eleven-year-old boy who, along with a troop of his friends, snuck through a gap in some fencing surrounding a construction site outside the State Capitol one night and was crushed to death when a piece of metal fell on him.

"These sorts of cases are always tough, but I think we have a strong chance here if we play our cards right." Crane looks back and forth between Zach and me. "I'm expecting good things from you."

"You're giving us this case?" Zach asks.

"Well, Susan will be the lead, but I want you and Elise to do all the heavy lifting. We'll see where the chips fall if this thing goes to trial, which it probably will. Make sure to check in with Susan now and again, but it's yours for all practical purposes, at least for the time being. Questions?"

Both Zach and I shake our heads.

"Great," Crane says to us. "Expecting big things out of you two." Then he slaps his palms on the table and says to the rest of the group, "Okay, next week: same time, same place. Partners, hold back just a second. I'd like to discuss a couple things right quick."

Zach and I file out of the conference room and down the hall toward our offices, which are directly across from each other. He slaps me good-naturedly on the back.

"Think you're up for this one, Sabatto?"

"No more municipal prosecutions? You bet your ass." I look around me, then up at the ceiling. "This isn't heaven, is it?"

"It most certainly is not," Zach says. "Your first clue should be that there are still munies to try and that you've just been assigned more work, and not work *in place of* your other, more menial work."

"Ask me if I even care," I say. Although both Zach and I are early in our careers with the firm—almost four years for him and going on two for me—I can't help but feel that *Rowland* is an early test of our suitability for making partner.

Zach pats my backside with the file folders in his hand. "Just try to keep up, okay?" he says, flashing an impish smile at me. He's a shameless flirt, but he's an equal-opportunity flirt, so it's hard to feel truly flattered by him.

I scoff, "Don't get ahead of yourself, Newsome."

We agree to meet later that afternoon so that Zach can brief me on everything he has so far on the case and to come up with a game plan for discovery and beyond.

"Okay, then," I say. "On to death by e-mail." I've answered only the messages that I absolutely needed to reply to in the last couple of days instead of doing a clean sweep of my in-box, as I usually do on weekends. I make a mental note to ask Candace, our receptionist and office manager, to include me on today's lunch order.

I turn toward my office, but out of the corner of my eye, I catch Zach lingering—still looking at me. I stop and face him. One corner of his mouth is raised in a half smile.

"Whassup, buttercup?" I ask.

He waves me off. "Nothing," he says. "It's nothing." Then, as if reconsidering, he says, "So, I hear your guy is back, huh?"

I nod. "Got home a few weeks ago."

"That's great," Zach says, though the way he says "great" sounds as though he's trying to convince himself. "Congrats—or, whatever it is that you're supposed to say in this sort of situation."

"Thanks," I tell him. We stand awkwardly in the hallway a few seconds longer than we should. I search Zach's face for the source of this uncharacteristic awkwardness. He seems pensive, even sad. He meets my gaze and holds it, and his eyes startle me. I've never before noticed how piercing they are, like a swimming pool that's frozen over. As he stares back at me, something flutters deep inside. I feel my cheeks go hot, and I raise the manila folder I'm holding. "I should—ah—"

"Yeah," Zach says, not waiting for me to complete my sentence. "Me too. Absolutely. Catch you later."

We each beat a hasty retreat to our respective offices. When I reach mine, I close the door behind me and lean into it with my shoulders. I let my head fall back against it, close my eyes, and wonder, *What was that? What just happened?*

Ten

It's stress, I tell myself. *That's it. That's all.*

I have a million things to get done before my briefing with Zach later this afternoon, but I'm all nervous energy. I can't concentrate. I flit from one task to the next, not seeing any of them to completion. I pick up the phone and dial one of the only three numbers I know by heart. Darcy answers on the second ring.

"Meet me for coffee?" I ask, not bothering with pleasantries such as "Hello" or "How are you?"

"You, my friend, have impeccable timing," she says. "Mia just woke up from her nap, and I really, really need some liquid sleep. Give me fifteen minutes or so?"

"Great. See you then."

Ancora, the coffee shop where we always meet, is a mere stone's throw from my office, so I busy myself queuing up several e-mail responses to send automatically in the next hour—one to Susan, one to Zach, and a couple that require a "reply to all" to a swath of other members of the litigation team. I leave my coat and scarf hanging on the rack in the corner and disable my screen saver, making sure there are a variety of documents open on my desktop. If anyone comes looking for me, it will appear as though I have run to the restroom or for a refill on my coffee, as though they just missed me.

These are key precautions to take in a firm like Early, Janssen, and Bradenton, especially after being gone most of the previous Friday and landing a plum assignment for a junior associate. Although we're not the biggest, nor the best, firm in town, the attitude here seems to be that we'll never get there if we don't adopt the same culture. Here, there's not much differentiation between weekday and weekend, except for a relaxed dress code for the latter. Every day since I joined the firm, my life has revolved around sleeping, eating, and working—not necessarily in that order. And so, the junior associates all learn the same tricks, because there are, inevitably, dentist appointments to keep, car repairs to see to, the occasional cold or flu bug that knocks you flat, or sometimes, the overwhelming need to simply get out of the office—like now. The key is to create the illusion of being present.

Darcy, punctual to a fault, beats me to Ancora and has chosen a seat by the window. I'm thrilled to see Mia with her. That baby's coos and smiles always brighten my mood. I tell Mia this as I kiss her chubby cheeks.

"When are you going to quit trying to steal my kid and have your own?" Darcy asks. "It's been what, a month since Brad's been back?"

"Something like that," I say. Darcy's question would be offensive between lesser friends, but she has sat through enough of my laments over babies—or the lack thereof—in my life that it's a safe topic. "It's complicated, though."

I say this as I sip my coffee and Darcy blows on her tea and Mia babbles in her high chair while knocking her sippy cup to and fro. I don't say any more because I need to talk about me for once. I need to unload on Darcy all that's going on, all that's been going on for weeks now. I need someone to confide in. But I don't know how to say everything that's bouncing around in my head. And I'm hyperaware that, since Darcy's husband didn't come back and mine did, our friendship has grown uneven. The same rules that once governed it no longer apply.

In a nod to that unevenness, Darcy doesn't ask the follow-up question I'm hoping for, the only natural one to ask: "Why is that?" Instead, she rolls her eyes and, as if only half listening, says, "Well, are you at least trying?"

This question throws me. Despite wanting a baby more than anything in the world, despite thinking of little else besides trying for one as soon as Brad returned, I haven't felt I can broach the subject with him. And trying to do much more than talking about it has been difficult at best—between all of the readjustment hiccups and the fact that Brad is spending his nights sleeping on the floor next to our bed. But how do I complain to Darcy about this? Brad and I are separated by only a few feet. It's not a traditional arrangement, but it's not eternity, either.

"Depends what you mean by trying," I say.

"Do or do not," Darcy says in her best Yoda voice. "There is no try."

"Is it worth it?" I ask Darcy.

She looks at Mia. "You mean her? Is she worth it?"

I nod.

"Without a doubt the best thing I ever did," she says. "Even right now. Especially right now." Darcy's voice wavers. She stops and takes a deep breath. Then she exhales. "It'll be the best thing you've ever done, too." She smiles at me and pats my hand. The gesture is motherly, and nice.

"I hope so," I say.

Darcy raises an eyebrow.

I feel like a can of soda that someone has shaken. It's the result of the strain from the past weeks spent with this new version of Brad, and now that look from Zach—and the reaction it stirred in me. It's a pressure that has me straining against myself, ready to explode. I need to get it out, into the open.

Darcy reaches out and puts a hand over mine. "I know so," she says, her voice steady and certain now. "You're going to have it all." A cloud of sadness settles over her as she speaks those last few words. I realize too late, probably just as Darcy does, that she had it all, and she'll be settling for only a fraction of that vision. I realize, too, looking down at her hand resting on mine, Collin's wedding band floating below Darcy's on her ring finger, that I can't tell Darcy any of this. I can't confide in her—definitely not now. Maybe not ever.

I pick up Darcy's hand and examine it, turning it over and back. "You look like hell, Darce," I say, joking. "Why don't you let me take Mia tonight? Go for a power hour at the spa. Relax a little."

Darcy is a hard person to take care of. She's like a selectively permeable membrane, always doing for others but never taking any of that kindness in.

"The spa? Do I look like a spa kind of girl? I don't even know what I'd do there."

"Get a mani/pedi. Have your hair done. Get a massage. Meet someone for a drink. Do all of the above." I look at Darcy, who is staring me down, scowling. "Is that enough for one evening, or do you need additional suggestions?" I ask.

"You can be a real smart-ass when you want to be," she says.

I shrug. "It's starting to come back to me."

"I don't think it ever left." Darcy wads up her tea bag wrapper and napkin and places them in her empty cup. "I'll let you know," she says, standing up. Mia's patience for the high chair has waned and her sounds have shifted from babbling to little squawks. Though I've never actually heard her out-and-out cry, Darcy claims she will put on a full-volume performance if she's overtired.

She packs Mia's things and we hug good-bye before she picks Mia up out of her high chair.

"You call me," I say, wagging a finger at her.

Darcy nods. "I'll let you know," she says again, and we both know that she will likely spend tonight just as she's spent every other night since Mia was born—feeding and playing with her daughter, giving her a bath, singing her to sleep. Then she throws one arm around me in a hug.

"Thank you," she says.

There are tears in Darcy's eyes and she's looking wistful. I imagine her going home to where Collin's winter jackets still hang in their front hall closet, to where his shirts still lie folded in their dresser, and I wonder how I worked myself up to the point where I thought that my issues the past few days warranted the level of concern I've awarded them. I am lucky that Brad has come back, that he is alive; and although this phase of our relationship isn't an easy one, it's one that will pass. Standing here with Darcy, I see my situation for what it is: bumps in a road that will eventually be smoothed by time.

"You're welcome," I say, hugging her back. And when I step through the café doors and into the crisp winter wind coming full force off Lake Monona and barreling up the hill to King Street, I feel better. I feel settled.

Zach brings Susan in for our afternoon meeting, and any awkwardness between us has faded. Maybe I simply needed some fresh air, or maybe I imagined it all. Either way, the three of us settle into an easy rhythm, brainstorming various strategies that might work on *Rowland* and deciding who will be responsible for managing them. There is no small talk. Susan has been through the process of trying cases like this one many, many times before, and I get the distinct impression that she is going through these motions purely for our benefit.

As a result, we finish earlier than I anticipated we would. Susan asks Zach to stay behind, and I'm suddenly free to duck out of work, if not early, then at least at a reasonable hour—and without any potential for additional weird exchanges between me and Zach.

I decide to walk the mile or so home. The wind is less fierce than this afternoon, and the sky hangs black and clear overhead. As I walk, I breathe in through my nose, hold, and let my breath escape in one swift exhale from my mouth. It's the only thing I ever picked up from my attempt at yoga years before. I was always too impatient for the deliberateness, the slowness, that yoga demanded. But tonight, the breathing works just as well as holding some ridiculous pose. By the time I'm home, my muscles have loosened. My mind has slowed. I'm ready to go in search of that dark-haired, handsome guy from our wedding picture, because I know he's still in there, somewhere.

I turn the key in the lock and push our front door open. And I lose any semblance of calm I had the moment before.

Cupboards and drawers are hanging open, couch cushions are sprawled across the living room floor, and books have been pulled into heaps beneath the bookcases. It doesn't appear as if anything is missing. It's just been ransacked.

And then I see the mirrors.

One at the end of the hallway, one above our dresser in the bedroom, and another in the bathroom—all three are spidered with hundreds of breaks emanating from one single point of origin.

Scenarios start to pinball inside my head. Have we been robbed? Did Brad get into a fight with someone? With himself?

"Brad?" I call, tentatively at first, and then louder, until I'm yelling for him. "Brad! Babe? Brad!"

I search the house until I finally find him sitting on the back step, smoking. After his mom died of lung cancer, it used to take everything that he had not to lecture complete strangers on the inherent evil of cigarettes. Now he's up to a half a pack a day, as far as I can tell. His new habit concerns me, but it's a conversation for another time.

I sit down next to him. "Uh, babe?" I ask, not knowing how to broach the topic of the current condition of our house.

He looks at me as a stranger might.

"What happened?"

Brad shrugs, then asks, "What do you mean?" almost as an afterthought.

"To the house," I say. "It's been ransacked. Did someone break in?" I try to keep my voice even, to quell the panic rising from my chest. I can't decide which would be the better news: that we've been burglarized, or that Brad did this himself.

"Dunno," he says after a while. "Don't 'member." His words slur.

"Did you do all that?"

"I'll clean it up," he says. His voice is flat and almost inaudible.

I reach over and place a finger on his chin. I try to turn his head toward me, but he resists, staring straight out into the yard and the brittle cold settling in around us.

"Baby, did something happen? I don't understand."

Brad nods. He keeps nodding in place of talking. Finally, he says, "I tried to go and get a job."

"Well, that's good, babe. No?"

He shakes his head. "No one wanted me."

"Where did you apply?"

Brad shrugs. "I just walked. Bunch of different places. Gas stations, restaurants, stores on State Street. I'd tell them I just got back from Iraq, and they almost looked scared. One guy threw my paper in the trash when I left. I saw him through the front window. He looked at it and threw it right in the garbage." He flicks his cigarette angrily. Sparks scatter.

"It's a tough market," I say. "Rome wasn't built in a day. You only need one yes." I run out of clichéd platitudes. I can imagine how frustrating Brad's day must have been for him, but he took the initiative to go looking for a job. Inside me, a small ember of hope and positivity smolders.

There's one more thing I need to ask, though.

"Baby—the mirrors? What about the mirrors?"

Brad is quiet for a long time. A minute, maybe two or three. And right as I've given up on him responding to me in any real, meaningful way, right as I'm about to stand up and go inside, Brad says, "That guy looking at me? I didn't know him." He is sad when he says this, as if he's talking about an estranged friend, someone who let him down, betrayed his trust.

I take Brad's hand between both of mine. I run my fingers over it, the top first and then the palm, looking for cuts from where his fist might have struck the mirror. There are none. His skin is warm and chapped rough as usual. Its contours feel as they always have beneath my fingers. I know its ridges, its topography, like Braille. And I think, *This hand, this skin—at least these I know.*

Eleven

For all of my recent past—first at law school and then as the lowest totem on Early, Janssen, and Bradenton, LLC's pole—the measure of my success has been directly related to how much information I can cram into my brain, synthesize, and retain. I can't bake a cake or replace windshield wiper blades, and I don't have the first clue about how to balance a checkbook, but damn if I can't research the hell out of any issue thrown my way. I'm doubly lucky—not only am I good at research; I also like it. It relaxes me in a way not much else can. Some people exercise; others meditate or do yoga; still others drink up a snifter of scotch. I set myself adrift on a sea of information.

I should be doing any number of things right now—preparing discovery documents for *Rowland v. Champion Construction*, reviewing materials for a court appearance I have this afternoon, answering the glut of e-mail that floods my in-box around the clock. Instead, I am reading everything I can about deployments and reunions. And I am an island of calm, unadulterated efficiency—legal pad to my right filled with notes, my printer humming steadily with the reproduction of interesting or informative articles, five tabs open on my Internet browser so I can reference and cross-reference the resources. After last night, I have decided to stop waiting for the situation to take its course, to improve on its own. I am determined to help the process along—to fill in the gaps of all I don't yet know. Of all that isn't quite working for Brad and me. Of all that isn't quite making sense.

I am reading an article titled "Reuniting with Your Deployed Spouse" when I see two terms I have heard often, but never thought to apply to Brad. At the end of the article is a column headed by the words, *Post-Traumatic Stress Disorder* on the left, and *Traumatic Brain Injury* on the right. Under the headings are listed *Common Symptoms* of each, but from what I can tell, there is so much overlap that the lists could have been easily combined: trouble with memory or concentration; difficulty organizing and completing daily tasks; impulsive behavior; easily confused, irritated, or angered; changes in sexual activity; feeling anxious or jittery. *Check, check, and check.*

I switch back to a browser tab with an article titled "The Walking Wounded," about soldiers returning with the all too common brain injuries that are quickly becoming the *signature war wound*. I skimmed the article before, but not carefully. The term *brain injury* threw me, because Brad was home and fine—he was walking, talking, and for the most part, functioning. He didn't seem like someone with brain damage. He didn't have to have a piece of his skull removed to control the swelling of his brain like others in the article; he could carry on a conversation if he wanted to. I thought, until now, that he was irritable or distracted to the point of forgetting things because he was still getting used to life here. But as I reread, I think about how Brad was injured—in an IED explosion that probably sent his helmet ricocheting off the inside of the Humvee and his head off the inside of his helmet. I read a section that talks about the correlation between the length of time someone is unconscious and the severity of the brain injury, and I remember being told that it had taken Brad almost an hour to come to after the explosion. A picture starts to congeal in my mind—not of a man who is having the typical tough time adjusting to life stateside, to life outside of the military, but a very different one—of someone who is seriously wounded in more ways than one, even if those wounds aren't visible.

I rest my elbows on my desk and let my head relax into the palms of my hands. I don't want to see what I'm seeing: words like *brain injury* and *PTSD* and *incurable* in black and white on my computer screen; they lodge in my own brain like splinters. I want to believe that Brad will adjust and things will go back to normal for us. I know, now, that I've been fooling myself. I have been blindly, foolishly optimistic. Or, at times, simply blind and foolish.

But then, how could I not have been? I remember one night when Brad and I were unpacking boxes after we moved into our house, and I found the thesis he wrote at Oxford titled "Geopolitical Pluralism and the European Economy in the Post-Soviet World." I paged through it, struggling to understand even the abstract. It was humbling to think that the practice of putting my nose to the grindstone couldn't conjure smarts like Brad's, and I remember looking over at him as he sorted papers across the room, oblivious to the straight-up lust that a cursory read of a graduate thesis had kindled in me. He was easy on the eyes, sure. But that was never the thing that did it for me. It was always his smarts.

And one explosion—something that occurred in mere seconds—has undone all those years of learning. All of those hours studying and making connections. Of neurons and axons building bridges among synapses throughout his brain. It seems incomprehensible that one explosion could unravel the inner workings of Brad's head—his thoughts, his personality—so thoroughly. So completely. So quickly. Maybe that's why I never considered this possibility before—that Brad wasn't simply having a tough time adjusting, that he wasn't merely haunted by what he did or saw. Sure, I knew these things, PTSD and TBI and all other sorts of terrible letter combinations, existed. I knew that. But I thought they existed in other people's lives. Not ours.

I assumed that patience and time would be all the cure we'd need. That Brad would come around incrementally, day by day, until one morning we would wake up and be our old selves, together again. Now, I see how wrong I was. This is a problem much bigger than me. Than us.

In my line of work, solutions often come from working the phone, or if you can, working someone in person. Solutions come from asking for what you want, then negotiating, and once in a while, leveraging the possibility of an unpleasant end result for the other party if that other party does not acquiesce. Solutions are created, not found, as some are so fond of saying—from a policy of always standing firm, from not backing down.

But by three o'clock, I haven't taken a break and I haven't done a lick of billable work. I haven't eaten, and I haven't found one single answer to what I can do, or to what Brad should do. I started with Veterans Affairs and got passed around what seemed like the entire agency, until the umpteenth person told me I needed to call the National Guard first. The Guard told me to call the TMA—the TRICARE Management Activity office, which in turn told me to call the Guard. The person at the Guard—different from the first few people I talked to there—suggested I try the VA, since Brad's TRICARE was due to run out soon. The VA told me, probably so they didn't have to listen to me rant any longer, that they couldn't put Brad on a waiting list for services until his TRICARE ended. I threw a controlled fit, which I suspected led the man at the VA to offer putting me in contact with someone "high up" in Health Affairs at the office of the Assistant Secretary of Defense. They were certain he would be able to get me some answers. But the contact information I was given for the Health Affairs office was a general number, and I couldn't get past the automated menu because I didn't have a specific person's name to enter into the directory. Then I called the VA back, ready to beg.

"Listen," I say, "there's something really wrong with my husband. He needs help."

"If he's hurt, you should call 911, or take him to the emergency room," the woman from the VA says.

"He's not hurt. He was in Iraq and I think he has a traumatic brain injury. Maybe some issues from post-traumatic stress, too. He needs help. Mental help."

"Okay," the woman says. "We have a bit of a waiting list at the moment. I can get him in on June 23."

"Did you just say *June*?" I ask.

"Yes, June."

"But it's January," I say. "That's six months off."

"I know. I'm sorry. It's the best I can do. But your husband will have to call back and schedule it himself—you can't set up the appointment for him. Please tell him, too, that he'll need to provide proof that his injuries are service or combat related. I'd be happy to send you the requisite paperwork if that would make things easier."

My head spins. Isn't it enough that he was sent to Iraq—to a war zone? That he was injured there? What could Brad possibly give them—a casing from a bullet shot in his general direction? The pieces of shrapnel that hit him, some still lodged deep inside him—painful stowaways that he now has to live with? The request strikes me as utterly ridiculous, but I force myself to breathe deeply, to stay calm. I will help Brad track down whatever documentation he might need.

This is, after all, what law school trained me to do: figure out how to get the information I need and amass it to prove my case.

When I was a little girl—nine or ten at the most—my parents used to take me on vacation to a cabin up north located on some lake I don't recall the name of. I'm sure that if I went back now, that lake would look more like a pond, but from my little-kid vantage point, you could barely see the shore opposite our cabin and it might have been miles wide. So when, late one afternoon, as the sun was taking its time going down and sequins of gold and orange danced along the water's surface, my dad suggested we swim across, I thought he was insane. "*All* that way?" I asked him. I remember a playful smile tugged at the corners of his mouth. He looked so big, so grown-up, so *invincible* that day. I realize that I am older now, remembering him, than he was then.

"But what happens if we get out there and can't keep going?"

"You just keep swimming," he said, his tone turned serious. "One arm in front of the other. One kick after another. If you need to, you flip over and float on your back to rest. Then you keep going. You'll get there."

And we did. I dragged myself up on the opposite shore, as elated and spent as a triumphant conqueror. "See?" my father said, gently chucking me in the arm as we reclined in the hot summer sun, grass tickling our backs and legs and arms.

"One arm in front of the other," I agreed. And then, in a whisper, as if I'd divined some universal secret, I said, "Just keep swimming."

It became a motto of sorts for me. After my parents died. Then on those long, lonely nights in Marquette, where I hardly made a friend because of carrying a course overload and working almost full-time to pay my way. Then throughout law school. And now.

Keep swimming. Anything for a mile.

You're mixing metaphors, my inner critic scoffs.

Seriously? I want to tell her. We're seriously going to worry about mixed metaphors right now?

"Actually," I say into the phone, "moving my husband to the top of the waiting list would make things easier. You know, click, click, click, and done!"

The woman from the VA doesn't bite. Not surprisingly, my humor has a negligible effect. "I have some spousal support groups I can set you up with," she says. "If you could give me—"

I can't take any more. I disconnect the call while she's still talking.

So now it is after three o'clock in the afternoon and I have ended up precisely where I started. If I were doing this for my job, I would ask to talk to supervisors and I might threaten a long list of legal actions that I could take. But in that position, as an attorney representing a client's best interests, I would have some sort of authority. I would have the benefit of bravado and bluster, because at the end of the day it's my job, not my life.

Our life.

But as me, I can't exactly threaten to sue the military. I am not unique. I am one of hundreds of thousands of wives or parents or veterans themselves, having to crawl blindfolded through this arcane, unreasonably massive, nonsensical system.

Brad is not on my health insurance and I can't enroll him until the fall. Paying out-of-pocket for physical and mental therapy could cost us tens of thousands of dollars, if my estimates are correct, and that's money we just don't have. Now the VA can't see him for almost six months.

I am not only beyond frustrated; I am out of ideas.

I'm also, apparently, out of time.

Zach pokes his head in my door. I didn't hear him knock if he did.

"You almost ready?" he asks.

I look up at him, and my face must be as blank as my head, because he says, "To review? *Rowland*? With Bradenton?"

I keep staring at him. I have no clue what he's talking about. "Didn't we do that yesterday?"

He shakes his head. "I sent you an e-mail about it last night, after you left—remember? She wanted us to come up with a detailed timeline for the case and run it by her today?"

None of this sounds familiar to me. Of course it wouldn't, since I haven't so much as read through most of my e-mail today.

"Jesus Christ, Sabatto, we're going in to discuss a full game plan with her in twenty minutes, and you haven't prepared anything? What the hell have you been doing in here?"

"I—I—"

I'm usually a champ at thinking on my feet. An exasperated judge told me last year that I could talk a dog off a meat truck. But there is no getting around the fact that I can't bill one single minute of my time today.

Zach walks around to my side of the desk and I try to close the windows on my computer—not one of them having to do with Early, Janssen, and Bradenton or its clients. He looks at the open browser windows, and then at me, and then he sighs and walks out, slamming my office door behind him.

I lean my head against the back of my chair. The former business consultant on my moot court team was fond of saying that when you have too many priorities, you have no priorities. I assert that the same goes for worries. I close my eyes, and instead of thinking about Zach or *Rowland* or the VA hospital or a husband I can't seem to help, I think about that lake from my childhood until I can almost inhale the smell of pine, moist and heavy, and the faint musty-crisp scent of the lake. I picture myself in the water with my dad. I feel it, cold against my legs, my abdomen, my clavicle, my scalp. I feel it move through my hands as I pull my way across, arm over arm.

I gather my file on *Rowland* and a fresh legal pad, and start down the hall to this meeting I'm not prepared for, but my thoughts still aren't on *Rowland*. They're on Brad, and that little girl I used to be.

It feels as though I'm only treading water. And right now, I can't see the other side. But I vow to figure out how to tow both of us to shore.

Twelve

Soft yellow light spills from windows that I pass by as I plod my way home in the dark. It is late and I'm exhausted. I switch my workbag from one shoulder to the other every block or so, trying to alleviate the day's stress that has pooled in my trapezius. Every window holds enviable scenes—families sitting down to dinner, or cleaning up from just having eaten; a mom helping a young boy with his homework, and then a few more doors down, two kids—a boy and a girl—chasing each other around the living room with glowing light sabers; and on the block after that, a couple sitting in front of a fire, reading. Her legs are tossed over his lap and covered by a blanket. His hand rubs her knee absentmindedly. Every house, every window, backlit by butter, is a showcase of a life I'd like to have.

I wish I weren't so reluctant to see what was right in front of me this whole time. Brad and I are so off track that right about now, I wish I were anyone but me.

But I am me, and Brad is Brad. I hear my mother's voice in my head: "You get what you get and you don't throw a fit."

Tears spring to my eyes at the thought of my mom. God, I miss her. Movies and books always focus on graduations, weddings, births of children and other big moments when daughters pine for their deceased mothers. But they get it wrong. Would it be great to have my mom around for those high points? Sure. But times like these are when I feel her absence most acutely, when I'm being hollowed out, breath by breath, by longing.

For an entire year after my mother died, her wireless carrier failed to shut down her voice mail and at times like this, when all I wanted was to hear her voice, I'd call her number again and again just to listen to the recording. One night—a Thursday in March—a man's voice answered and gruffly told me that I had the wrong number before hanging up on me. Still, I've kept her name and number listed in my contacts and in my address book. I sorted through and gave away her skirts and sweaters and shoes, but I can't seem to part with those ten digits.

I have that same longing to call her now. To ask her what she'd do if she were me. What would she do if the man she married wasn't the man she was married to, and might never be again?

I shift my bag again at the intersection of West Washington and Park streets. The passing traffic forms a homophony of hum and slush loud enough to pause my internal monologue. I roll my head back and forth, stretching the taut muscles of my neck and shoulders. The light for the crosswalk changes to the white outline of a person, and as I step off the curb, I'm reminded of crossing a street like this one with Brad only days after he returned, and I shudder.

Had I not been by his side, he would have walked straight out into four lanes of heavy traffic on one of Madison's busiest thoroughfares without so much as glancing in either direction, or at the walk signal, which at that moment was a steady, glaring orange hand. Without thinking, I grabbed him by the collar and yanked back, hard. Brad whirled toward me and I stepped back, holding my hands above my head. Brad caught himself, midlunge, and we both stood there, staring at each other, wide-eyed.

"I take it they don't have crosswalks over there?" I joked, and I chalked up the incident to Brad's being inattentive or still trying to get his bearings. Now I realize it had nothing to do with Brad's being distracted or out of sorts. The signals most kindergartners know— man for *walk* and hand for *stop*—mean nothing to Brad's scrambled brain.

I call to Brad as I slip off my shoes and hang my coat on the rack just inside our front door. Glassy-eyed and stone-faced, he stumbles out of the hallway. I tell myself I've probably woken him from a nap, but the steadily evaporating jug of Jack Daniel's, which has become a fixture on our kitchen counter, could be to blame. I've been adding water to it, little by little, and though I know this is much like shoveling in the middle of a blizzard, it's the only thing I've been able to think to do.

"Hey there, handsome," I say, and I flash him a lopsided and impish grin. It's late and I'm tired. I'm not feeling the least bit amorous, and Brad is looking, in a word, rough; but this little household of ours needs a shot in the arm of positivity, of normalcy. When I was a few blocks from home, a voice in my head told me to start trying—really trying—to break this cycle we seem to have found ourselves in. Maybe it was my mom speaking to me, maybe not. But it's good guidance. If I treat Brad more like I used to—like my husband, my lover—and less like a problem child, maybe he'll respond in kind.

Only he doesn't respond. At all. *Keep trying. Keep at it until he does,* I tell myself.

I fish from my bag the pile of papers I printed at the office and spread them out on the table: brightly colored graphs and charts, bulleted lists of symptoms and treatment options, and the forms that the woman from the VA e-mailed me late this afternoon for Brad to fill out.

"What's all this?" he asks.

I bite my lower lip and take a deep breath. "Can we sit and talk for a minute?"

Brad nods and pulls up a chair. He turns to the papers on the table. As I struggle for the words I want—no, need—to say, his rifling of the papers becomes more forceful and frantic.

"I decided to do a little research, and—"

"What the fuck is this, Elise?" Brad interrupts me. He's holding up a page with "Signs of Traumatic Brain Injury" printed in bold red across the top. The corner is crinkled where he's closed his fist around it.

I open my mouth, but speech doesn't materialize. Brad's face is twisted into a scowl. His eyes are dark and narrow and brimming with rage.

"You think I'm fucking brain damaged? Is that it?"

"N-no," I stammer. "I didn't say that, babe. It's an injury. Traumatic brain injury and post-traumatic stress disorder are common—"

"I don't have a fucking disorder. What the fuck is all this?"

One of the things I have most loved about my husband is his introspective streak. He is always the first one to think through the decisions he makes, to evaluate how and why he is making them, and what those decisions mean or what they say about him. When we were moving into our house, I found a notebook he had been using as a journal, and the first few pages were missives on what he should do for a career under headings such as *Things I'm Good at*, *Things That Interest Me*, and *Weaknesses/Obstacles*. That streak is either gone, or so deeply buried, it might as well be.

I try a different tack. "Brad, this isn't anything to get worked up over. Seriously. There're so many people dealing with stuff like this that the VA said there's a pretty long waiting list. So that's the bad news."

"You called the *VA*? About *me*?"

I nod. "All this stuff—the nightmares and forgetting things and—your, um, reactions to things—they can help you with all of that. You just need to call this woman I spoke to and—"

With one sweep of his arm, Brad clears the table of every last piece of paper. They rustle to the ground like wounded birds.

"Fuck you, Elise," he says, and I wince. "You think this is easy, coming back here? Just because I'm not my cheery old self all the time doesn't mean there's something fucking *wrong* with me. I sure as hell don't have a disorder and I'm not fucking brain damaged."

"I didn't say you were. I just thought—"

Brad stands up; his chair teeters briefly on the rear two legs and then flops over backward.

"You didn't fucking think. You stupid, stupid bitch."

"I was just trying to help," I whisper.

He leans over, his face inches from my own, his arms on either side of me—one on my chair back and one on the table. My eyes squeeze shut, but I can feel his breath hot on my face.

"I don't *need* your *fucking* help," he says. His voice, his words, are all spittle and snarl. "You think you're so perfect—take a look in the fucking mirror for once."

He slaps the table hard with one hand and I feel a jolt as he kicks the leg of the chair I'm sitting on. When I open my eyes, I see the front door being pulled shut from the outside.

"They're all broken," I say.

Thirteen

Starting the following Monday, we have a full slate of depositions for *Rowland v. Champion Construction*, which Susan has put Zach and me fully in charge of. She has another pressing matter and won't be able to attend. As such, today is a big day. To mark it, I'm wearing my best, most serious suit: a charcoal gray pantsuit with only the faintest of cream pinstripes. I step out of my car and directly into a puddle, soaking my shoe and pant leg past the cuff.

We get situated in one of a long line of nondescript conference/ballrooms at a nondescript hotel at the edge of town—a location mutually agreed upon by the Rowlands' counsel and us. Zach and I face off against their attorneys. It's a power play, and they have the advantage in more ways than one. Not only is a cadre of lawyers sitting across from us, but a child is dead, and he died on our client's construction site. Any defendant in the wrongful death of a child knows that it's an uphill grind. Our goal is to avoid a trial, because there's hardly a jury on record that can get past anything bad happening to a child, regardless of the facts of the case. If one were to bug jury deliberations, I'd place money that the words, "They were just being kids," or some variation thereof, would be uttered repeatedly. It's never the kid's fault. And though sometimes blame should fall squarely on the parents, they're carrying enough grief and guilt already. So someone has to pay. And in this case, it could be our client.

The Rowlands' counsel has set up these depositions, which means that all of the witnesses will be of their choosing. In a couple of weeks, we'll reconvene for another round. We're planning to depose Mr. and Mrs. Rowland—a firefighter and kindergarten teacher, respectively. We'll try to poke holes in their motives for suing Champion and question their parenting. We'll have to ask the Rowlands why they allowed ten-year-old Nicky to play unsupervised, and blocks from their home, at nearly nine p.m., and we'll ask the boys he was with whose idea it was to climb into the construction site. We will try to assign blame to anyone except our client, and my stomach churns just thinking about those lines of questioning. I try to put it as far from my mind as I can. There's plenty today to command my attention.

The Rowlands' counsel opens with Officer Topher Frenty, a member of the Capitol Police who was on duty the night Nicky Rowland and his friends climbed into the construction site. Officer Frenty sits at the head of the table. He is a large man with a ruddy, honest face, like an overgrown Wisconsin farm boy, and looks considerably less commanding than a person wearing a law enforcement uniform often does. In fact, he almost looks frightened.

I sit next to Zach, jotting notes on a legal pad and once in a while writing down and showing him a follow-up question he should ask. The hotel conference room is frigid, and the coffee, which tastes like instant, is watery and doing little to warm me. I make a mental note to add additional layers of clothing for tomorrow's session.

The clock on the wall inches toward the noon hour, and finally, it's our turn to take a swing at the witness. Zach launches in, reminding me of a tennis ball machine, firing question after question at poor Frenty: "How long have you been with the Capitol Police? What did you do before that time? Ever had any issues with gambling? With booze? Ever had a reprimand while in the course of your employment?" It's a staccato, frenetic pace, with Zach moving on to the next question almost before Frenty has a chance to fully answer the one preceding it. Then Zach pauses to write something on the legal pad in front of him, takes a gulp of water, and looks up at Frenty. He doesn't say a word, and the mood in the room shifts. Frenty starts to fidget, and so do I. What does Zach know that the Rowlands' attorneys don't? I look down at the word he scribbled at the top of his legal pad, underlined three times. It reads *pause*.

I have to stifle a laugh. Zach doesn't know anything. He's giving a performance.

Zach is turned out in his professional best today, too: a navy blue suit, white shirt, and red tie—the POTUS, State of the Union look. He even broke out his Yale cuff links—something I've seen him do only once before. This is something I like about Zach. He's not in-your-face showy and arrogant on a daily basis—only when it really counts.

Zach asks Frenty if the hole in the fence that Nicky Rowland climbed through was noticeable.

"Oh yeah," Frenty says. "For sure."

Zach nods pensively, as if Frenty has just provided a particularly thoughtful answer—one warranting full consideration and understanding before he continues on to the next.

"And you saw it every day, right? How many times a day?" Zach asks him.

Officer Frenty scratches his chin and twists his mouth, thinking. "Over the three weeks, probably ten, twelve times, I'd say. Almost every day I was on duty."

Zach takes a moment to write something down on the pad of paper in front of him, which as far as I can tell is a whole mangled mess of chicken scratch. I couldn't read it even if it were directly in front of me. I hope Zach is the type of person who isn't easily confused by his own penmanship.

"What are we talking about here? A hole how big?" Zach asks.

I look sideways at him, my eyebrows arched in warning. When Zach doesn't notice, I take his pad from him and scribble in all caps at the top, *DON'T DO THIS!* Does he really want to establish a record of how big our client's potential negligence was?

Zach shakes his head at me and crosses out my letters with two quick lines. Then he leans back in his chair and drops an arm onto the back of mine. I work to keep my face expressionless, while inside I'm seething. If he's not going to take my advice seriously, why am I here?

He looks up at Frenty. "Sorry, Officer," he says, turning on the charm. "Pardon the interruption. Go ahead. Show me how big that hole was."

Officer Frenty smiles back at Zach and then stretches his arms out in front of him, holding them a little more than shoulder-width apart. "Maybe about this wide at the base."

"Can you say how big, in your estimation, that is—so the court reporter can get it down?"

"Oh, sure," Frenty says by way of apology. "Four feet, I'd say."

"That's a pretty big hole, then," Zach says. "So it comes undone at the corner and it rolls up. Would that be right?"

Frenty nods.

"I'm sorry," Zach says. "If you agree, you'll have to say so, so they can get it on the transcript." He gestures toward the court reporter, her fingers suspended above her keyboard.

"That's right," Frenty says.

Zach looks down at his legal pad. He flips the top sheet up, then the second, scanning the pages as though looking for something. Then he lowers them and takes time to note something else on his legal pad. When I look over, I see his pen making squiggly lines with the occasional loop—nonsense that only looks like writing.

"So . . . ," Zach says, making that one word sound like its own sentence. He sets his pen down and gives Officer Frenty his full attention once again. "You see this hole—a rather big hole, from what you're describing—and the situation concerns you, right? And you were so concerned that you reported it to someone?"

Frenty has started to perspire. Despite the conference room's chilly temperature, beads of sweat appear on his brow. He takes out a handkerchief to wipe them. "No," he says, and his voice squeaks.

"No?" Zach asks. "You must've talked to my client, then? Expressed your concerns to the project manager, a foreman—anyone?"

Frenty's head hangs. "No," he says.

I laugh inwardly and recline in my chair. Zach continues to grill Frenty, and it's clear he knows exactly what he's doing. He doesn't need a running commentary or any help from me. I keep an ear on their ongoing exchange, but I busy myself generating rebuttals to the witness they've called this afternoon—Champion Construction's lobbyist.

I hear the conference room door open behind me, and I see the faces on the opposite side of the table from me look away from Zach. The looks are quizzical, not welcoming, and so I turn to see what they're seeing.

Two police officers have entered the room.

"Gentlemen," the opposing counsel says, "we're almost done with Officer Frenty here. Just a few more minutes, please."

But the officers don't move. One of them is staring at me. "Elise Sabatto?" he says.

I nod. I wonder, for a brief moment, how he knew it was me. But then I look around and realize that I'm the only woman in the room.

"Can you come with us, please?"

I shake my head. "Can't this wait? We're almost done."

"I'm afraid not, ma'am."

I look at Zach, and in answer to his raised eyebrows, turn my hands over and raise them—a halfhearted shrug—as if to say, "I don't have a clue," because I honestly don't.

"Go ahead," Zach whispers. "I've got this."

"Thanks," I tell him. I leave my pen atop my legal pad, and the rest of my things—my bag and coat—hanging on the chair. I can't imagine that whatever the officers want will take long. I wonder which of my other clients absconded with his kid across state lines or has landed in the clink for yet another DUI.

I'm still running through that mental list of clients when I step out into the hallway. The officers are waiting for me. "Ma'am, you're going to need to come with us," says the younger officer who hadn't spoken previously.

"I thought that's what I was doing," I say. "Here I am."

He shakes his head. "Down to the station."

"I'm in the middle of depositions," I say. "Unless someone committed a murder, whoever needs my legal advice will just have to wait until I'm done here."

"Ma'am," the older officer says, "it's your husband. And we're here because he tried to."

Fourteen

Zach's face goes wooden when I tell him I have to leave. Wooden and red. Even the tips of his ears turn crimson.

"You can't," he says. "We have Anduzzi up next."

Carlo Anduzzi is Champion Construction's lobbyist. He's been my pet project—mine to ensure that we know everything the Rowlands' counsel knows about him and more. I've gone over every client he's represented, every meeting he's taken with legislators and the governor, every move he's made for the past five years. The only thing I don't know is if he prefers boxers or briefs. Given enough time, I'm sure I could ferret that out, too.

"I have to," I say. "Just trust me on this, please. Get them to take an early lunch. I'll be back in time for Anduzzi. I promise."

Zach gives me a look. The opposing counsel clears his throat.

"Something we should know about?" he asks. I shoot him the same look Zach just gave me and shake my head.

"I promise," I say in a hurried whisper, twining my middle and index fingers and tapping them on my chest, over my heart. "Early lunch. I'll be back."

I grab my coat and bag from the chair, and at the last minute, remember my legal pad with all my musings on questions and strategies for Anduzzi, and swipe that from the table as well. I scurry out of the room before Zach can get another word out of me. My head is swimming, and I don't trust myself not to tell him what's going on. Besides, "My husband was just picked up for attempted murder," doesn't exactly roll off the tongue.

The officers, Noble (older) and Karlson (younger), take turns peppering me with questions as we drive toward the police station: "Has your husband ever exhibited any violent tendencies toward anyone?"; "Has he ever threatened to hurt you or anyone else?"; "Have you noticed a change in his behavior recently?"; "Is there anything that might have happened in the past couple of weeks that could have triggered violent tendencies in him?"

I stare out the window. I think of all the strange things Brad has said and done since he's been back—his inability to open a tube of toothpaste, his tendency to charge through crosswalks without looking, the way he patrols our backyard at night. And then there are the outbursts, the most recent of which happened at our kitchen table late last week when he kicked my chair.

But I don't know exactly what happened yet. I don't know much of anything, save for what Officers Noble and Karlson have told me. Plus, my husband has a real, diagnosable disorder, whether he wants to admit it or not.

"Ma'am?"

"No," I say, choosing to answer only the last question. "No, I honestly can't think of anything." And that's not technically lying.

I still think there has to be a misunderstanding. In fact, there's a battle raging between what I know to be reality, which is that Brad has been picked up for attempted murder, and what I want to believe, which is that this has to do with a wayward client. I am a rational person who loves logic so much that it borders on obsession. Yet I can't seem to come down on the side of reason no matter the mental gymnastics I do.

We get to the station, and the police sit me down at an empty desk and continue to question me.

"I want to see my husband," I say in response to every question, stonewalling. I cross my arms for added effect.

"Ma'am, we need to finish talking to you first. We'll let you see him in a bit. Plus, he's meeting with his attorney."

"*I'm* his attorney," I say.

The two officers look at each other, unsure how to proceed. I'm guessing it's not every day that a suspect's wife wants to represent him. I'm pretty sure they haven't ever had this particular wrench thrown in their plans.

"But he has an attorney," one of them says.

"A public defender?" I ask. They nod. "Well, tell the public defender that his services aren't needed."

"Ma'am, I'm not sure we can do that."

"Am I a party to the crime?" I ask.

They shake their heads, perfectly synchronized.

"And am I a suspect in any way?"

More synchronized shaking.

"Then, according to Wisconsin state statute, you not only can do that; you're required to." I have no idea if this is completely true in this particular situation, and I couldn't quote the statute to them if my life depended on it, but something in my tone carries enough confidence to convince them I'm right.

"I'll relay the message," the younger one says, turning and walking away.

I smile at Officer Noble, who looks like someone just called checkmate on him in a few quick moves. I pull out my legal pad. "Maybe we can start with a quick briefing on what happened?" I say in the most friendly, agreeable tone I can muster.

Apparently, what happened is this: Sometime around when Zach and I were swearing in Topher Fenty for his deposition, my husband wandered into the home of seventy-nine-year-old Margie Valhalla, helped himself to a lunch of cold stew, and brandished a gun at the woman when she came home. He yelled, "Qeff Mahallak!" at her again and again until she crouched on the floor, covering her head with her hands.

It doesn't sound exactly like attempted murder to me. But it doesn't sound like my husband, either. For starters, he's never owned a gun and I have no idea where he got one—or why.

Do I even know this man? I wonder; then I shake the thought loose from my head. *It's a misunderstanding—you'll see.*

When they take me in to see Brad, he's sitting slump-shouldered in only a T-shirt and jeans, in a bare room slightly larger than a closet. His hair is disheveled, sprouts of it poking up every which way, and his eyes are red-rimmed. Those eyes lock on mine, and I'm not sure I've ever seen a look so pleading.

I want to wrap my arms around him, to tell him I'm going to fix it. But empty promises aren't a good Band-Aid for this situation; besides, I don't want to cross any ethical, professional, or legal lines—actual or perceived. Or, at least, not any more than those I might already have tripped over.

So I sit, hands clasped, while a police officer different from either of the two who were sent to fetch me questions Brad, writing down anything of importance and details I need to look into later.

"Let's go back to the beginning," the officer says. "Just tell me what you remember about today, from the time you woke up until now. What did you do? Who did you see? What shows did you watch?"

"I told you—I don't remember," Brad says wearily, not combatively.

Somehow I knew he was going to say that.

I've gotten used to this quirk of Brad's. Something will trigger him and send him spiraling into an alternate reality of sand and scalding sun and gunfire as common as birds chirping are here. Afterward, he rarely remembers any of it. Brad has already lost whole minutes, even hours, of his life this way.

"Come on. Give me anything," the officer says. "Why did you go into that house?"

Brad runs his hands over his face and through his hair. It's still sticking up, but all in the same direction. "I don't remember," he says.

"You went into an old woman's house, with a gun, and waited for her to get home. Why? What were you going to do?"

"I don't *remember*." Brad's voice cracks. I'm not sure if the officer hears it, but I do.

"I'm going to ask you one more time," the officer says. His face is as red as Zach's was when I told him I was leaving in the middle of Frenty's deposition.

And then I remember: Zach. The deposition. *Shit.*

I pull out my phone. It's nearly two o'clock and I have six missed calls. Anduzzi is scheduled for two o'clock. *Shit, shit, shit.*

I send Zach an e-mail: *Almost done. There in 20. Stall!* Then I ask the officer questioning Brad if I may talk to him outside. He holds up his index finger and continues with the question he was asking Brad. "What were you doing in that house?"

"Outside?" I ask the officer again.

This time he relents. In the hallway, I tell him that Brad is an Iraq vet only recently returned from active duty.

"I don't care if he's the goddamn president of the United States," he says. "He tried to kill an old lady when she walked into her own home. Does that sound like acceptable behavior to you?"

"Come on," I say. "We both know he didn't try to kill her. Anyway, Brad has . . . issues that he's struggling with right now. From being over there. I know my husband, and I know that he didn't set out to hurt that woman. He needs help."

"Then get him some." His tone is snotty—a sneer.

"You don't think I'm trying? Do you have any idea what kind of support these guys receive when they get back?"

The officer is staring me down. He shakes his head.

"I'll give you an idea: If they're still useful, if they can go back over to that godforsaken sandbox, the military fixes them up, good as new. Or, almost. Good enough, anyway." My voice starts rising and I make no effort to lower it. "But if they can't, if the soldier's medically discharged? Then they don't even get a new set of steak knives for their trouble. For having their lives turned upside down and then inside out. You know what a benefits specialist with the VA told me the other day? That they'd be happy to treat Brad if we can just establish that his 'difficulties' are related to his service. So I asked her what types of 'proof' would be acceptable—documents? Affidavits from guys he served with, or maybe one from his platoon commander? Oh, wait. Never mind. He was blown to bits in the same incident that left Brad like this." I point toward the examination room behind us.

The officer is no longer looking at me. Instead, he stares mostly at his shoes, with the occasional glance past me, down the hall.

"My husband's brain is so garbled that he can barely hold a single thought for any length of time, which makes holding down a job almost impossible. And because he can't get a job, he can't get insurance, which he needs because his TRICARE runs out in a handful of months and the waiting list to get him in to see someone about all this is nearly twice that long. My insurance won't cover him until our enrollment period starts, and even then they probably won't because he has so many preexisting conditions, I'm sure they'd run out of room on the fucking form trying to list them all. He's a good person, a kind person, who risked his life—*willingly*—for this country while you and your buddies were playing grab-ass and slugging down beers and high-fiving one another during Packers games on Sunday afternoons. So maybe you can go ahead and spare me the lectures on responsibility and good citizenship, okay?"

I fish my phone from my pocket and check the time. It is ten after two. "Shit," I mutter.

I hand the officer a business card. "I need to go back to work," I say. "I'll be back later. In the meantime, I'd appreciate your letting me know about the bond requirements for my husband."

I don't give him a chance to respond. I turn and walk down the hall, my heels click-click-clicking on the worn linoleum. When I come to the room where Brad is still sitting, head in his hands, I duck inside and kneel down next to him.

"Babe," I say, resting a hand on his knee, "I'm going to get this all straightened out. Just hold tight. And don't answer any questions from anyone until I'm here with you. Okay?"

He nods his head. "Okay," he says meekly.

"Repeat it to me," I say.

"Quit treating me like a little kid, E.," he says. There's a flash of anger in his face, but then it's gone and he's back to looking broken. "Please," he adds.

"I'm sorry," I say to him. "I'm so sorry, love. I'm going to fix this, okay?"

I want to kiss him, to press my forehead against his, to do any of the millions of things I so badly want to do right then to comfort him, to show him that everything is going to be all right. Instead, I trace a finger down his face and caress his cheek. Then, I pull on my coat and grab my notepad and bag, and I march out the door, making it all the way to the street in front of the police station before I realize that I don't have a way back to the hotel—not in time to make Anduzzi's deposition—and I sit down on the curb, press my forehead to my knees, and cry.

Fifteen

For three days I work on getting the charges against Brad dropped.

I think about him every minute of every hour of each of these few days, while he's sitting in jail. Part of me rails against the injustice: training someone to do whatever it takes to defend himself and his country, systematically turning him into a machine that can kill someone as easily as letting out a sneeze, and then locking him up when, fresh from combat, he doesn't immediately mesh with the nice, neat society we have going back home.

The other part of me is relieved. For now, there's someone else watching Brad. There's someone else responsible for him.

Zach walks into my office as I'm poring over books of Wisconsin criminal law statutes instead of files for *Rowland*. He shakes his head in disgust and closes my office door behind him. Then he sits down in one of the two client chairs opposite mine.

"Okay," he says. "Talk."

"What?" I ask. I know what he wants. And in truth, the very least I can do is explain. But I don't want anyone here to know. I want to get everything with Brad sorted out and go back to being the rising star of an attorney that I was up until a few months ago. I don't want the partners to think less of me. I don't want to answer questions such as "How are things going?" that always carry the double meaning, "Can we depend on you again yet?" Most of all, I don't want to pull Zach into the mosh pit of my personal life. Is it because I like having this one place, this one person with whom I still feel like my old self? Is it because I want him to think that I'm smarter and more capable than I feel right now? Maybe both.

"Tell me what's going on," he demands.

The thing is, I'm fresh out of confidants. In the past I've always confided in Brad first, then Darcy. Between the two of them and Granna, my life was full enough to not require expanding my circle of friends. Now none of them is an option.

But Zach is. Don't always think the worst of people. He might surprise you.

I bite my lip and look up at Zach. I don't know how to begin telling him, where to start.

"Sabatto, I covered your ass the other day. I had to call Susan in to help on Anduzzi when they wouldn't reschedule. I told her your dog got hit by a car and was hanging on by a thread, and that Soldier Boy wasn't around, so you had to rush to the vet."

"I don't have a dog," I say.

"That's what Susan said. I told her you just got one. You might want to think about actually doing that now, just in case she does a spot check."

See? a voice inside says.

I venture a laugh. "Maybe I could just say that it didn't work out?"

"That works, too," Zach says. "Get some used toys and a bed at least."

I give him a salute. "Roger that."

"So," Zach says, reaching for one of the books open in front of me and flipping to the front cover, "what is all this?"

I sigh. I've tried so hard for so long to keep these two worlds—my work and personal life—as far apart as possible. I don't have framed personal photographs in my office, only my diplomas and some generic artwork. I don't often wear a ring to work, and never to court, and I almost never reference my husband, since these things are only reminders to the partners that I have a personal life—and even worse, that I might someday soon choose to have children. Yet here those worlds are, colliding.

"Brad got in a bit of trouble," I say.

"What kind of trouble?"

I take a deep breath. "Attempted murder," I say, wincing. But when I look up, Zach hasn't run from the room. He's still sitting across from me, and although shock has registered on his face, it's not judgment. "Well, at least, that's what they're charging him with," I add.

"Jesus, Sabatto. What the hell?"

I tell him what I know: that Brad was sitting on seventy-nine-year-old Margie Valhalla's couch while eating her homemade beef stew and watching daytime television; that he threatened her in Arabic and with a gun when she came in her own front door.

"That's not attempted murder," Zach says.

"I know. But Omar won't drop the charges."

"Would you if you were him?" Zach asks. "That guy from Marshall is all over him right now."

Jason Omar, the prosecuting attorney, is up for reelection in the fall, and predictably, his opponent is accusing him of giving out too many wrist slaps and not enough maximum sentences. As a double whammy, Brad landed Judge Fletcher Smith, who is also up for reelection and who, coincidentally, set his bail at an astronomical fifty thousand dollars.

"It's ridiculous," I say. With every word, I'm starting to feel better—lighter, freer. "At the most, it's aggravated assault or assault with a deadly weapon. But Omar's standing by this bogus charge. In addition to B and E."

Zach is quiet. I can tell he's thinking. Then his face lights up. He leans back in the chair and throws his feet up on my desk. "Sabatto, my dear, you're going about this all wrong," he says.

"Oh?"

"Get out of attorney mode. Think like a regular person for once. Like a human being."

"I don't know how," I say. I mean to say that I don't know how not to think like an attorney, not that I don't know how to be a human being.

"Omar is disgracing a decorated veteran," Zach says. "I assume Brad got a Purple Heart, given his injuries? Right?"

I nod, a little perplexed by how Zach knows this. I was shocked when I found the medal stuffed unceremoniously in Brad's rucksack, the ribbon wrinkled and soggy. I always imagined Purple Hearts being awarded in grand ceremonies at the White House. Turns out it's more common to have someone with a box of medals make bedside presentations in the hospital, which I guess is a step up from former wars, when they were given out on the spot, often in the heat of battle.

"Instead of going after hardened criminals, Omar's targeting someone who almost died for this country. Leak that to the press. Play the political game. Play hardball."

"I don't know, Zach."

"What's there not to know? That's the way he's playing this. It's his career, but it's your life. You're more than justified."

I chew on my lip, considering. Zach is right. This isn't just another case that's landed on my desk.

"Wait," Zach says, tipping his chair forward until it's resting on all four legs again. "What did you say the woman's name was?"

"Margie Valhalla. Why?"

Zach leans forward across my desk. "I don't know. It sounds familiar. Like, really familiar. Have you done a search on her?"

"CCAP," I say.

"No, Sabatto. She's seventy-nine. What sort of sordid criminal history do you think she's hiding—armed robbery with knitting needles? Jesus. Do a real search. A search engine search."

I shake my head. The thought hadn't even occurred to me.

Zach nods in the direction of my computer screen. "Google her," he says. "I think you might find something interesting, if I remember correctly."

"Like what?" I ask, typing in Margie's name in quotation marks. The first item to appear is an obituary for a Vincent Valhalla, killed in action in Basrah, Iraq, in 2003. I read this information to Zach.

"By friendly fire, right?" he asks.

I nod.

Zach does a fist pump into the air, eminently pleased with himself. "I told you I remembered that name—it struck me as extra tragic because he was on his fourth tour or something, and that's the way he goes," Zach says. He shakes his head, clicking his tongue on the roof of his mouth. The sound of it makes my skin itch. "Vinnie Valhalla. There's your ticket."

I am not making whatever mental leap Zach would like me to. I tell him as much.

"The woman your guy nearly caused to have a heart attack is a Gold Star Mother, Sabatto. Get to her. Chances are she won't want to see another young soldier locked up. It's worth a try, right?"

"Yeah, absolutely," I say.

"I'll leave you alone for the rest of today," Zach says, getting up. "And I'll run interference with Susan. But get this done—today. Tomorrow I need you back on my team, okay?"

"Absolutely," I say.

Zach smiles at me—a genuine smile—and tiny starbursts of happiness and goodwill light up inside me.

People are good. Life is good. It's going to be okay.

Zach swings my office door open, and I call to him: "Zach?"

He pauses and turns around.

"Thank you. So much."

"Don't mention it," Zach says, and he leaves, closing the door softly behind him.

I spend the rest of the afternoon figuring out how to use the information Zach has led me to, trying not to think like an attorney. At my wits' end and needing a break, I pick up a copy of *On Wisconsin* magazine. I page absentmindedly through the articles. There's one on a UW-Madison graduate making it big nationally as a mentalist, another featuring cutting edge research happening at the university's Center for Sleep Medicine and Research, and another on the unbelievable lengths that recent graduates have to go to in order to gain a toehold in the workplace that makes me both shudder and offer up a small modicum of thanks that I graduated from college back when jobs and graduate school slots were easier to come by. They're all interesting articles, but none of them holds my attention.

Think, a voice in my head implores. *C'mon, Sabatto. You have a few hours, tops.*

Then I happen on a picture of a slump-shouldered woman in a sun hat walking through a barbed-wire-encased prison entrance under the headline, OPENING THE DOOR TO FORGIVENESS. The caption reads, "Jackie Millar brings an open mind and the capacity to forgive as she arrives at the Stanley Correctional Institution for her thirteenth annual meeting with one of the offenders who injured her while committing a violent crime." The rest of the article goes on to detail the UW-Madison law school's Restorative Justice Project, and I want to palm my forehead for not thinking of this sooner.

From memory, I dial Jason Omar's number. He answers on the first ring.

"Jason, it's Elise Sabatto, from Early, Janssen." Poor Bradenton. Everyone always leaves her off—too many syllables.

"Hey, Elise," he says. "What can I do for you?"

"I was wondering if I could swing by this afternoon."

Across the phone lines, I can almost hear the gears working and then clicking into place in Jason's head. "This is about your husband?"

"It is."

"Sorry, Elise. I'm booked all week."

"Come on, Prosecutor. Ten minutes. I'll come to you."

"Sorry. Call Janet, my assistant. She'll get you a slot next week. Nice talking to you, though. You have a good one," Jason Omar says, and hangs up.

Zach has given me one afternoon—which could be viewed as either one whole afternoon or only one afternoon—to slack on *Rowland* and take care of things with Brad. So I do the only thing I can in this situation: I gather my things and make a beeline for Jason Omar's office on the opposite side of Capitol Square.

I wait for more than an hour before Jason sticks his head out of his office and sees me.

"Elise Sabatto," he says in a singsong, but not altogether friendly voice.

I try out my sweetest smile on him.

He sighs. "You have ten minutes," he says.

"I'll take five."

When Jason sits down, his head looks disembodied, floating above stacks of file folders that rise from his desk like miniature skyscrapers. I can't imagine being him. Just the sight of all those files, stacks of organized chaos, gives me heart palpitations. And they're not even my responsibility.

I shake it off, though, and launch in: "Here's the deal, Prosecutor. I get that you're up against a tough primary challenge and you can't exactly walk away from this one. But from the looks of it, you're literally up to your neck in work, and this could be a tough sell—a decorated Iraq veteran who so far hasn't been able to get the services he needs and has coming to him."

Jason Omar nods along as I talk, seemingly not taking issue with anything I've said so far.

"So what's your pitch?" he asks.

"Have you heard about the Restorative Justice Project at UW-Madison?"

"Somewhat," he says. "Vaguely."

"It brings assailants and victims together. It's not perfect for every situation, but I think it might work here."

"And why is that?"

"You have a veteran of the Iraq war and a Gold Star Mother whose son was killed by friendly fire. Instead of wreaking more havoc on both their lives, you bring them together to talk. As Brad's counsel, I'll agree to whatever charges Mrs. Valhalla feels are fair and appropriate after that meeting."

"I don't know," Jason says. He leans back in his chair and taps a pen against his knuckles.

"The media would eat this up," I say, then add for effect, "either way," and wait for Jason to process what I'm saying. The good prosecutor's eyes narrow and harden—and I know he understands.

"It's a story that tugs at the heartstrings," I continue. "Plus, you get to take a completely unnecessary case off your load and distinguish yourself from Mr. Tough on Crime—you get to be tough on crime *and* reasonable. A real outside-the-box thinker and leader.

Voters will eat that up, too." I'm not sure I believe myself. Single voters are reflective and compassionate. But the electorate as a whole? Anything less than whole hog as far as sentencing goes tends to be completely unacceptable.

"I'm concerned with the law, Ms. Sabatto, not this race," Jason says.

I stifle a laugh. Jason Omar is a good prosecutor, but he's a born politician, a terrible liar, and from what I can tell, he could probably make a competition out of running the bathwater.

"Can't hurt; might help," I tell him. "I'll put it in writing right here and now. Just say the word."

He leans back in his chair and crosses his arms across his chest. "I'll call Mrs. Valhalla," he says. "And if she agrees—*if*—I'll think about it."

I know that this is as good an offer as I'm going to get. So I stand, thank Jason Omar for his time, and hope for the best.

Sixteen

The next morning, Jason Omar calls with the news that Margie Valhalla has agreed to a mediated meeting and will consider the charges afterward. The following Monday we all gather in a conference room at the Dane County Courthouse.

A uniformed officer escorts my husband in. Brad looks thin, but he's freshly shaven and dressed in normal clothes. I pushed hard for that—no handcuffs, no jumpsuit. Details can make a world of difference. He sits next to me. Across the table are Margie and Jason Omar. Margie is five-foot-nothing and probably one hundred pounds soaking wet. She's wearing black slacks and a red wool crepe jacket over a white turtleneck dotted with tiny red hearts. She has on glasses that take up three-quarters of her face and a red beaded necklace. She looks like everyone's favorite grandmother.

The mediator, a sweater-set-wearing, nondescript woman in her mid-fifties, if I had to guess, sits at the head of the table. I feel as if we've all been summoned to the principal's office in grade school, though with slightly higher stakes than having recess privileges revoked.

The mediator asks both Margie and Brad to introduce themselves to each other. Then she explains how the session will work: First, Margie will give her version of events; then Brad will provide his. Afterward, there will be an opportunity for discussion and questions.

"Well," Margie starts, her voice shaking, "I guess I was just surprised, is all, to find someone in my house." She is still holding her purse on her lap and is currently clutching the bag to her like a treasured stuffed animal.

"Can you walk us through what you remember happened?" the mediator asks.

Margie nods vigorously. "I opened my front door, and he was on the couch." She takes time to point at Brad. "Then he jumped up, and the bowl in his hands fell on the floor—it broke. It was one of my favorites. I ate my cream of wheat out of it every morning. But it broke, and then he started yelling some sort of nonsense at me."

"Were you scared?" the mediator asks. "Can you tell us what was going through your mind? How you felt?"

"Well, of course I was scared!" Margie says. "He had a *gun*, you know."

"Yes," the mediator says. "So what did you do?"

"I hit the deck," Margie says. "Stop and drop—no roll."

"And what about now?" the mediator asks. "Do you feel safe in your home?"

"I don't feel all that unsafe," Margie says. "But I do make certain to lock my door now."

"What questions do you have for Mr. Sabatto, Mrs. Valhalla?" the mediator asks.

Margie studies my husband, but her expression is not hard or angry. It's contemplative, searching.

"Why were you in my house?" she asks Brad. She is calm and she radiates kindness. I half expect her to offer him a homemade chocolate chip cookie and warm milk.

"Ma'am, I wish I remembered," he says. "I do." I've instructed Brad to work in his service, to acknowledge the issues he's encountered since returning. And to apologize. Apologize a hell of a lot, I told him.

"I have these spells," Brad continues. "They started a while after I got back. Sometimes I look around me—once, I was wandering around the UW business school—and I can't remember how I got there. I have no memories of walking there. Since I've been back, I just show up places all of a sudden, like I apparated to them."

"Apparated?" Margie Valhalla says.

"Sorry, ma'am. It's a Harry Potter reference."

"Oh," Margie says. "I've been meaning to read those. They're good?"

"They're excellent," Brad says.

"I think my grandson would like them. He's nine."

"He definitely would, ma'am."

"So you didn't want to hurt me?" Margie asks.

"No, ma'am. Never. Promise. I don't remember being in your house. I don't know why I would've been there."

Margie Valhalla studies my husband. "You know," she says after a while, "I had a son. He served over there. Four tours. He didn't come back."

I didn't tell Brad this ahead of time, and when he tears up, I'm glad I chose not to. It sounds cold and calculating, but my duty as Brad's attorney is to boost his chances of not having to spend one additional day in jail, or God forbid, prison, than he absolutely has to. If I have to manipulate the flow of information to achieve that result, so be it.

Plus, I wanted them to have as authentic a conversation as possible, and in all honesty, I wasn't convinced he'd remember even if I had told him about Margie's son.

"I'm so sorry, ma'am. So sorry," Brad says. His voice is thick with emotion.

"He was a little older than you," Margie continues. "What happened to him, it was a waste. And not just because our own bullets got him. If it hadn't been ours, it would have been theirs, or one of those blasted bombs. He kept going back. He kept going back because he didn't know how to be here anymore. He grew up here. It was his home. And you know what he told me?" She looks at Brad, who shakes his head. He is hanging on her words. "He told me that this—his *home*, where I lived and his wife and their two boys lived—felt like a foreign country to him. He said to me, 'Ma, I don't know the rules here anymore; I don't fit in. I can't stay.' And I couldn't fix him. Try as I might, he couldn't be fixed. He would've died no matter what. It was just a matter of time."

I am looking across the table at Margie Valhalla, but out of the corner of my eye I can see Brad's shoulders shaking. He is crying silently. He knows.

"That's how you feel, too?" Margie's voice is soft and gentle, like a warm breeze.

Brad nods. He studies the table. He nods again.

Margie leans across the table and pats Brad's hand. She turns and looks at Jason Omar, who is seated to her right. "He's been through enough," she says. "He's given enough." Then she looks me dead in the eye and says, "We all have."

Margie Valhalla rolls her chair back, grips the edge of the table with one hand, and pulls herself to her feet. "I'd like to be done now," she says tiredly. This might go down on record as the shortest restorative justice session ever, but no one is going to press a seventy-nine-year-old lady into staying longer.

Instead of exiting out the door behind her, though, Margie Valhalla walks around the mediator to the opposite side of the table where Brad and I are seated. When she reaches Brad, she takes his hands in hers and whispers to him, "You be a good boy now, okay?"

Brad bites his lip and nods. "I'm trying, ma'am," he says.

"I know," Margie says. She brings his hands to her lips. "I know you are. You just keep on doing that." Then, squeezing both his hands, she looks at Brad and smiles sadly. She puts her coat on and slings her purse over her arm, and on her way past him, Margie stops and places a hand on Brad's shoulder and lets it rest there, as if she's going to say something else to him. Instead, she pats it twice and continues toward the door.

I turn to Brad, wanting to share an intimate, celebratory moment with him. One look at my husband, though, and I realize those sentiments are misplaced. His hands rest on the tabletop and his head rests in his hands, as though it's become too heavy for him to lift. His shoulders are rounded into a slouch. His breathing comes out quick and shallow. There is nothing to celebrate here. Not for any of us.

That afternoon, while I am in my car en route to the office, Jason Omar calls to tell me that Margie Valhalla has advocated dropping all charges against Brad.

"With the stipulation that you get him some help," Jason says. "Understand?"

"I'm trying," I say.

"Do better than that. If I come across Brad's name again, I'm throwing the book at him."

"There won't be a next time," I say. "Thank you."

"Counselor?" Jason asks.

"Uh-huh."

"I know this couldn't have been easy for you. You do good work. That firm is lucky to have you. So is your husband."

My breath hitches and a sob wells up out of nowhere. I take a deep breath, swallowing it back down. A few kind words and I'm choking on emotion like a dog on a chicken bone.

"Thank you," I squeak, right before I hear the click of the call disconnecting.

Perhaps it's not the words. Perhaps it's the acknowledgment behind them. During the restorative justice session, I saw a moment pass between Margie and Brad when his eyes brightened and he seemed, if not his old self, then at least one far removed from the person he'd been since his return. A small intense flame of jealousy sprang up in me and I thought, *Why can't he respond to me like that?* She was a complete stranger. A stranger who formed a stronger bond with my husband in an hour than I had been able to establish in months.

He's needed someone to understand him; I've only been trying to fix him.

I see that now—the transformative power of being understood. Maybe all I've been needing is for someone, anyone, to say, "You know, you got dealt a bad hand. It sucks. But keep up the good work," because at this moment, it's as though I've been floating like a boat with limp, deflated sails, at the mercy of the wind and weather. And Jason Omar's kind words might as well have been a full-on gale.

The radio is playing a catchy tune that was the anthem of last summer, overplayed by pop radio DJs everywhere. Every time I heard it then, I rushed to change the station. It was too upbeat, too happy, too carefree for how I felt, with a husband halfway around the world enmeshed in a war with few clear objectives. But today, Jason Omar's recalled words ring in my ears. "That firm is lucky to have you. So is your husband."

Today, when I reach for the radio, it's to turn the volume up, and I start to sing along.

Seventeen

It takes time for Jason Omar to prepare and file a nolle prosequi, and to find a judge to enter it on the record, so I have to wait until my lunch break the next day to pick Brad up from jail. He looks tired and sallow, and he stares out the passenger side window as we drive away.

"Everything okay, babe?" I ask him. Okay is relative these days.

He shrugs. I reach for his hand and squeeze it. "We'll forget this ever happened," I say. "It's going to be fine."

"I know," he says.

"Then what's wrong?" I turn down the volume on the radio.

"Because I have forgotten it," he says. "But I still did it. I scared that poor woman to death. Maybe I was going to shoot her. I have no fucking clue if I was going to shoot her or not. And I don't remember a goddamn thing. Who does something like that and doesn't remember?"

I squeeze his hand again. "It's going to get better." I am all rainbows and unicorns these days since pulling off the improbable, if not impossible: confiding in Zach to great success, orchestrating a deal that gets my husband off an alleged attempted-murder rap, with upsides for everyone else involved, and getting back to business on *Rowland*—all in a matter of days.

Brad shakes his head. He's quiet for more than three blocks.

"I'm hungry," he says eventually.

"We don't have anything to eat at home—sorry." I give Brad a sheepish look. Grocery shopping is something I tend to avoid at all costs. I realize it's a necessity, but I also hate it. Usually, my feelings toward going to the store outweigh the fact that I know I need to. Left to my own devices, I've eaten corn or green beans straight from the can for dinner just to avoid grocery shopping. "We can stop on the way home and grab some sandwich fixings," I offer.

Brad doesn't object, so I overshoot the turn to our house and pull into the Copps down the street.

"Why don't you come in with me?" I suggest. "So we get what you really want." But that's only part of it. I feel better when I can keep my eye on Brad—when I can gauge the slightest of shifts in his mood or change in his carriage, all subtle clues as to what I can expect to happen next.

Brad acquiesces. He trudges behind me like a dutiful dog, and the sight of him reflected in the store's automatic doors just before they slide apart steals my breath. Slump-shouldered, his face drawn, he is the picture of a man broken.

The grocery store is nearly empty, and I think that if I made it a habit to do my shopping at this time of day instead of after work or on Sunday afternoons, I might actually be inclined to come more often. No one has parked a grocery cart in the middle of the aisle. No one has tried to run me over. We sail through the store. It's food-shopping nirvana, or the closest thing to it.

As the lone cashier on duty rings up our items—Black Forest ham, bread, mayonnaise, tomatoes, two frozen pizzas, microwave dinners that were on sale (five for ten dollars), toilet paper, shampoo, and apples—a mother with a young boy steps in line behind Brad. Freckled and mop-headed, the boy is maybe four years old. He makes me want to know what Brad looked like at his age. He is playing with a balloon his mother probably agreed to give him as a way to avoid a toddler-size meltdown and get through her errands. I wonder whether she knows how lucky she is to have this child in her charge, to get to spend afternoons with him. My desire to go up to him and cuddle him and tousle his hair, to pretend he's mine if only for a second, is so strong that I keep my hands on the counter. *Bend your fingers around this ledge,* I think to myself. *Watch them so they stay right there.*

Later, I won't remember hearing the balloon pop. I will only remember swiping my debit card through the kiosk when I hear Brad yell, "Incoming!" and I am being slammed into the hard floor, teeth first. I feel my lower lip go hot, as if a branding iron is being pressed to it, and I fear that my tooth has gone right through. I lie still for a moment, listening to Brad's breath, heavy in my ear. I run my tongue over each of my teeth, checking for sharp edges that shouldn't be there. Thankfully, there are none. I can't afford an afternoon off for dental repair right now, or the dental repair itself.

The little boy is wailing and his mother has backed him away from us, near a trough of candy bars, two for a dollar, sitting in the middle of the store's main aisleway. I wiggle free of Brad and stand up. He is still prone on the floor, looking up at me, his face frozen in a mask of shock and horror. I hear the cashier call for a cleanup on checkout twelve—gloves needed—as I bend down to Brad and offer him a hand. My lip is already swelling and I can hardly talk, so I motion for him to come on already and get up. I see the blood on the floor where I was lying and realize it's coming from me, from my lip. Much too late, I hold a hand against my chin to prevent blood from dripping onto my suit.

Brad struggles to his feet. He isn't wearing a jacket, and I can clearly see a giant wet spot spreading on his jeans from his nether regions. My husband has just wet himself.

He sees me looking at him. He sees me register what has happened. And then he runs.

I yell for him to stop, but he keeps going. The cashier hands me a wad of tissues, which I hold to my bleeding mouth. Then she tells me to "have a nice day" as she holds out our grocery bags. I imagine that she says this so many times each day, it's become rote for her—a habit or a tick she couldn't control if she wanted to. I take the bags from her, struggling to loop them all onto one arm so I can hold the tissue to my mouth with the other, and I can't help but roll my eyes.

By the time I make it to the car, Brad is nowhere to be found. I throw the grocery bags in the backseat and pace the parking lot, calling his name. There's no response.

I drive first around to the back of the store, and then toward home. I don't see any sign of Brad. Then I double back to the grocery store and drive in the opposite direction. No Brad. I double back once again and take a left on Wingra Drive, thinking maybe Brad is wandering the bike path that runs alongside it. When I get to the Arboretum, I turn around and retrace the route. I know there's not much chance he could have gotten so far as to actually walk into the Arb, and even if he had, I'd never be able to track him by car. Too many trails wind their way through the nature preserve. So I steer through all of the neighborhoods he might be picking his way through instead. But Brad is nowhere to be found. It's as though he's up and vanished.

The sky has turned cold and angry, as winter skies tend to do, when I pull into our driveway. I hope that Brad is sitting on the front steps waiting, or safe and warm inside our little bungalow. He is neither.

Not knowing what else to do, and where to look, I try calling him. Mere seconds later I hear his phone ringing. I trace it to the kitchen counter, where it has been this entire time.

Without taking my jacket off, I move to the couch and lie back, running my hands through my hair. It feels greasy and tangled, and I try to think of the last time I washed it—the last time I took a proper shower, which means time to wash and shave all the parts that need either in one session. I can't remember. And now, I have lost my husband.

Images of Brad walking into a random house that looks something like ours, of waving a gun at another Margie Valhalla, flash through my head like silent movies—none with happy endings. But I have no idea where else to look, or what else to do. And so I sit, paralyzed by inaction and indecision, and rub my temples.

With a start, I remember that the gun Brad waved at Margie Valhalla, discreetly handed to me when he was released into my care this afternoon, is stowed in my purse. Or, I think it is.

Please let it still be there. Please, please, please.

I walk to the kitchen, unaware that I'm holding my breath until I spot the handgun in the bottom of my bag. I let myself exhale. *Now what?*

Maybe I will try to sell it, or pawn it—whatever it is one does with a gun. I want it out of my house. I want it far, far away from both Brad and me. But it's late and selling it is not currently an option. So I wander our house, looking for a good hiding spot until I can get rid of it for good. I finally settle on a bank of shoe boxes containing all of my summer work shoes, taped shut and stacked two deep, on a shelf at the very tip-top of my closet. I pick a box, deposit the gun, retape it, and place it in the middle of the rear row. I curse myself for still not having gotten a fireproof lockbox for our valuables—something that's been on my to-do list for more than a year now, ever since we purchased this house. But this will work for now.

I close my closet door and sit down on our bed. My husband has attacked an old woman. He's disappeared over a popped balloon.

And now I'm hiding a gun from him. This feels like someone else's reality. Not mine. And acknowledging these points doesn't make them any more real. Above the dresser in front of me is a mirror with spidered glass. Versions of me—some complete, some reflecting only my hair, or half my face, or a slice of my neck—are reflected back.

I ask myself: If I had known that my marriage would turn out like this, knowing that there's no playbook for this kind of life, no instruction manual, and no truly right choice in sight—knowing all this, would I have signed on anyway?

"I don't know." I watch hundreds of different parts of my mouth say those words. "I honestly don't know."

Eighteen

I am in my office, but I am not present. I am just taking up space. I call Brad's phone every few minutes even though I know that phone is still on our kitchen counter, where it was when I left for work. Brad didn't come home last night, and he wasn't there when I woke up this morning. Every time I call, I hope that this time I'll hear his voice on the other end. I know better. But that doesn't mean I can't blindly hope.

At almost seven p.m., I look up the outside temperature: twenty-two degrees. Then I look up the number for the Madison police station. A man's voice answers on the third ring. I tell him I need to report my husband missing.

"Okay, ma'am," he says. "I can help you with that. How long has he been missing?"

"Since late yesterday afternoon," I say.

"So what makes you think he's missing?"

I tell the police officer about the incident at the grocery store, about Brad's military service, and about my suspicions regarding his yet-undiagnosed TBI and PTSD. The officer asks me for a physical description of Brad: height, weight, distinguishing characteristics, and what he was wearing.

"Okay," the officer says. "If he comes back between now and noon tomorrow, call us at this number to let us know."

"Why noon?" I ask.

"We can't start looking for him until then, ma'am."

"You—what? Are you serious?"

"I'm afraid so, ma'am."

"But it's twenty degrees out. He could freeze out there."

"You said he has a brain injury," the officer says. "Is he severely impaired?"

"What do you mean?"

"Does he know who he is? Where he lives? Can he ask for directions if he gets turned around?"

"Yes, of course, but—"

"Is he in danger of hurting himself or others?"

I think of Margie Valhalla and I know I should tell him yes. But I hear Jason Omar telling me that Brad has exactly one strike, which he's already used. Putting out an all-points bulletin saying that Brad could be armed and dangerous isn't something I imagine the good prosecutor will look kindly on.

"No," I say. My voice wavers.

"Ma'am, I know this is scary," the officer says, "but trust me, this happens, and it almost always turns out just fine. Most of the time the person just went for a long walk or bellied up to some bar their loved ones never thought to look in. They usually come back on home when they're ready. If we haven't heard from you by noon tomorrow, we'll start looking for him, okay?"

"That's the best you can do?" I ask.

"That's the best I can do," he says. "I'm sorry."

"Me too." I thank him even though I don't mean it, and I shove the phone into the receiver.

"What did that phone ever do to you?" a voice asks from the

doorway—Zach's voice. I manage a smile in response to his tired joke.

"How's it going?" he asks.

"Fine," I lie.

"I got pulled into a thing with Crane Early this afternoon and he's a hard guy to say no to. Can we meet first thing tomorrow and go over all this?"

"Sure, no problem," I say. The night stretches ahead of me, long and dark and marked by thick file folders that need to be reviewed and a seemingly endless stream of memos needing to be written.

"Big plans tonight with Soldier Boy?"

"Huh?" I ask.

"You know, lovers' day? Hallmark holiday designed to make all singletons feel like crap?"

With all that's been going on, I didn't realize what day it is.

Always on Valentine's Day, Brad would send me a bouquet of tulips (because roses were cliché) and have dinner waiting by the time I arrived home. Before Brad, I'd never thought much about Valentine's Day; it had been an occasion for other people to celebrate. But Brad would pull out all the stops, turning February into a month to look forward to instead of just four more weeks in the middle of the hardest part of winter. He hated to waste what little extra money we had dining out on a night he liked to call *Amateur Hour*, so he would cook, creating homemade pasta one year, a Moroccan stew the next, and last year, only weeks before he was deployed, he made the best beef Wellington I've ever tasted.

"We're not really that type," I say to Zach. What I don't say is that I have no idea where my husband is and that if I hadn't remembered it was February 14, Brad was doubly unlikely to.

Zach looks boyishly handsome standing in my office doorway, his hair expertly messed and falling in little waves toward his eyes, his shirt unbuttoned at the neck, no tie. Was he heading out for the night? On a date? Without warning, a hot flame of jealousy ignites in me.

Stop, I tell myself. *Just stop.*

But confiding in Zach came so easily the other day, and I feel a pull to tell him more. To have someone else know about Brad's mood swings, the way he grabs my arm so hard it bruises sometimes, or the night he ordered me around like one of his subordinates—pouring cereal all over our dining room floor and telling me to march on it. To share the weight of all that's happened. Of everything that continues to happen. I want someone else to shoulder the guilt I feel when I think of Brad, home all day alone, aimless and bored and who knows what else, and because so much of the time I feel worse when I'm there with him. I want Zach to tell me that I'm not the flimsy shell of a wife and a half-rate attorney that I feel I am most days.

"Okay, Sabatto. Well, have a good one anyway. See you tomorrow."

"You too," I say, and I watch him leave. I will him to turn around. Or to grab a couple of beers from the refrigerator and bring them back to my office, so we can sit here, alone together on this lovers' holiday, and watch the sky grow dark and the Capitol dome grow bright against it.

I turn my attention back to the computer screen. I click on files and start typing nonsense in an open, unaddressed e-mail to make it look like he interrupted the important work I was doing. When I look up, he's lingering in the doorway.

I raise my eyebrows at him as if to ask, "Can I help you?"

"Everything okay?" he asks. His body is in the hallway, but he's leaning back inside my office.

Tell him.

"Why?" I ask.

Tell him.

He shrugs. "Just checking."

No, I tell myself. *I'm not going to ruin both of our nights.*

"Everything's fine," I say. I smile for added effect.

Zach opens his mouth as though he's going to say something else, and then closes it as if he's thought better of the idea. He slaps his hand twice on the doorframe and nods. "Okay, then," he says. "Later, Sabatto."

"Later," I say, but he's already gone.

It takes time to gather the files I need to continue working tonight, and it's late by the time I start home. Normally, I'd worry about leaving Brad alone so long. It's always there, that worry—sitting in my stomach like a swallowed peach pit, a calcified organ. Who knows, though, if he's home tonight? Who knows if he's planning on coming home? I want to look for him. I should look for him. But I hardly know where to begin a search. With all the bars, meandering streets, parks, and bike paths in this town, he could be anywhere.

It is well past ten o'clock by the time I get home. Even in the dark, I can tell that the house is spotless. It smells like an unholy marriage between Pine-Sol and the vanilla candles scattered throughout the living room, dining room, and kitchen, their light flickering against the walls. The table is set with two place mats. On one is a plate covered with tinfoil, with silverware perfectly arranged on a cloth napkin I forgot we owned. Brad is not around.

I hang my jacket on the closet door and kick off my heels. Then I walk over to the table and sit down. A note, scrawled in Brad's handwriting, is propped against a water glass: *Dinner for you. I tried to wait up. I'm sorry.*

I lift the tinfoil and find a BLT with toasted bread, cut on the diagonal. Alongside it is a congealed mound of macaroni and cheese. It is as far from beef Wellington as a meal could get. I stifle a hitch of breath and pinch the bridge of my nose hard between my thumb and forefinger.

I think about how I spent my afternoon and early evening and I think about how Brad must have spent his. I wonder when he came home. I think about him scouring the kitchen to make a meal like he used to and finding only these ingredients, and making do anyway because maybe he wouldn't—couldn't—go back to the store.

The sandwich is soggy and the macaroni cold. I could easily remedy both of these in the microwave, but I don't. It wouldn't feel right. Eating this dinner is a penance of sorts.

I swallow the last bite, get up, and pile the silverware and crumpled ball of tinfoil on top of my plate. When I lift it, I find something underneath: a red envelope with a large, shakily written *E* smack dab in the center. I sit back down.

Inside the envelope is a card. On the front of the card are two yellow lab puppies, each holding one side of a red paper heart printed with the words "I love you." Inside, Brad has written, *Happy Valentine's Day. I'm sorry for being such a burden. Don't ever forget that you're my world. I love you. —B.*

I don't have a card to give him in return.

It is a cheap, cheesy card that's popular at gas stations and grocery stores, the kind of card you'd never find gracing the aisles of Hallmark. I want to run out and frame it.

I clear the table, blow out the candles, and tuck the card into my workbag. It will go on my desk as a reminder. Even though I have hours of work left to do tonight, I turn out the lights as I move down the hall toward the bedroom I share with Brad.

He is sleeping in a tangle of blankets on the floor next to the bed. His body swims in strips of blue-black light pouring in through the slatted blinds.

I whisper, "Brad," to see if he's awake. He almost always is. Sometimes he answers. Sometimes he doesn't. Tonight, though, there isn't a part of him that stirs at my voice. Maybe he's asleep after all.

His sleep is precious. It doesn't come easily to him these days. But I want to wake him, to have him crawl into bed next to me and hold me until we both fall asleep. I want to seduce him in the middle of the night, like I used to do when I woke up and couldn't fall back to sleep; to feel his body pressed up against me in the morning, strong and solid like a fortress wall. I want us to fall back into those familiar rhythms of touch that we perfected beyond words the past handful of years. I need to feel Brad's skin on mine, the weight of his body next to me. But Brad needs to be on the floor.

I hang an arm over the edge of the bed, next to my husband, to bridge the distance between us. It is an olive branch, a life ring I'm throwing to him. And when I wake in the morning, he has grabbed hold. My fingers are interlaced with his, and I wait until the absolute last minute to unweave them so I can ready myself for work. When I kiss him good-bye, careful not to startle him awake, I can still feel the heat of his skin pressed against mine, and I carry it with me. I carry it out into the snow and cold, still burning warm.

Nineteen

Most of the day, it's all I can do to keep my mind on work. I zone out during meetings, in the middle of writing e-mail, and while I'm waiting in line for a midafternoon jolt of caffeine. Forgotten are the grocery store incident and the long hours that followed when Brad went missing. Now, I have a hard time thinking of much else besides Brad's hand in mine this morning, the dinner he made last night, the way things might be starting to turn around. Finally.

Wind whips my hair across my face as I make my way back to the office, the steaming cup in my hand feeling like the only warm thing in the world at the moment. Winters in Wisconsin are largely manageable—until March rolls around. By then, you're always bone-weary from the biting air, the ice, and the unrelenting, day-in and day-out bundling and unbundling required to go anywhere. It hits you suddenly: One moment you're nicely settled in the groove of winter, and the very next you feel like you might actually lose your mind if you have to scrape your windshield or deice your locks one more damn time. It always gets old. And when it does, Wisconsinites flee for pastures that, if not greener, at least see the sun on a regular basis.

When I first heard Brad was coming home, I let myself daydream about taking a quick vacation with him somewhere, like we used to do—just pack a cooler with sodas and sandwiches and head due south, stopping only when we could get out of the car without donning a jacket. One year we drove to Louisville, Kentucky; another to Nashville. After the incident on the Beltline, I stopped thinking that driving any significant distance with Brad would be a prudent move. And after the incidents with Margie Valhalla and the balloon, I stopped hoping that we might ever take a vacation together again. I let myself hunker down into survival mode—one day to the next. But then there was last night, and this morning. And now I'm thinking that a getaway might be just the thing.

I have only half an hour before Zach and I are set to meet to review *Rowland v. Champion*, and I should be returning calls to a couple of new clients who were arrested for their second and fourth DUIs, respectively, last night, but before I know it, I'm so deep into Coast to Coast Travel's Web site that I can almost feel the sand between my toes.

I click through pictures of impossibly blue water and resorts nestled into linen white beaches, drinks in bright shades of pinks, greens, and yellows held by couples smiling at each other as if knowing a secret I'm not privy to. I think of sitting at a wooden table overlooking the ocean with Brad, a hot breeze drying the salty water on our skin as we share that same look. I'm enthralled by the transformative promise of it all—the sea, the sand, the glasses filled with red fruity goodness and topped with little paper umbrellas.

I'm enthralled by the lack of anything to worry about in a place like that.

Everything is included—the airfare, the food, the drinks— everything. Three nights and four days. And all for less than my monthly law school loan payment.

There are two voices arguing in my head. The first repeats, "You can't afford this," while the other points out that we have a credit card with an unused, sizable limit for "emergencies," and that my husband was gone for an entire year, during which he nearly died. We deserve a vacation. With all that's happened to us, doesn't the need for a break from our life rank right along with food, water, and shelter on Maslow's hierarchy of needs?

Then a third voice enters the conversation. The imaginary law firm partner says only one word in response: "No."

If I ask to take this time off right now, I'll be looked upon as a flake. As someone not worthy of the gift of *Rowland v. Champion Construction* that's been bestowed upon me. As someone not fit for partner and hardly fit for basic employment at Early, Janssen, and Bradenton. It matters little that when Brad was deployed, I did nothing but work—weekends, holidays, my birthday. I gave this firm my everything, and I squeezed blood from a stone doing it. But right now, we need me to keep my job more than we need a vacation.

I close the browser on my computer, the promise and lure of sand and sea and golden tans disappearing like a dream upon waking, as if they hadn't really existed. Outside my window, the sky has turned the color of a chalkboard, leaving not even a hint of sunlight to struggle through. A fierce March wind howls and kicks up the fine dusting of snow that's fallen since I returned from my coffee run.

A new e-mail flashes in the status bar on my computer. It's Zach, asking me to swing by his office. I type, *Will do—be right there*, and hit "send." I gather the files and notes I need for *Rowland* and head to Zach's office.

Zach wears shoes that look expensive and stylish. Expensive and stylish and foreign—as if he zipped on over to Rome to have them custom made. He has matching pairs in light and dark brown, black, navy blue, light beige, and a reddish brown. When I enter his office, he is on the phone. His chair is reclined and the reddish brown shoes are perched neatly on the edge of his desk. He uses the instep of one to scratch the top of his opposite foot and motions me in.

"Well, that's what you get for rooting against U-Dub: a busted bracket."

Zach is smiling and he winks at me. Then he holds up one finger to tell me he won't be much longer.

"Ha, ha ha. You're a funny one, Ricardo. Well, we'll see, I guess. I just don't see how UConn pulls this off, but if they do, I owe you a beer."

I gather that Zach is talking to Ricardo Welsh, a fellow up-and-coming litigator at Fitz and Simmons, one of Madison's premier firms, and I gather that UW-Madison—"U-Dub"—must be in the NCAA Sweet Sixteen. That's the extent of my basketball knowledge, and frankly, I'm proud that I know even this much.

There is more chuckling from Zach, and he says, "Sure thing, Counselor. Yup, you too," before leaning in to hang up the phone. Then he reclines again and brings a hand to his chin, resting it thoughtfully on his knuckles.

"What?" I ask, uncomfortable with the silence and with the look Zach is giving me.

He waves me off. "Nothing. I was just thinking that—eh—never mind. Anyway, good night last night?"

That meal. The card. Brad's skin on mine. I shrug. "Worked late, went home, worked some more," I say.

Zach nods, a knowing expression on his face. He seems pleased with this answer. A smile plays at the edge of his mouth.

"So," he says, "what can I do you for?"

I raise an eyebrow. "You wanted to see me?" I pat the files and legal pads I've brought with me. I'm pleased with both my self-control and preparedness. I feel like my old self. It feels good.

"Ahh, yes," Zach says. "Actually, I have a proposal for you."

"Oh?"

"I was talking with Bradenton this morning. She's on her way out to San Fran to do some discovery on *Bridge Global*—well, anyway, she had some ideas on tactics for our case that I'd like to go over with you."

There's something in the way he says "our case" that makes my body flush with pride. I'm reminded again what an opportunity this project is for a junior associate like me.

I knit my forehead. "Okay, shoot," I say. Since when does he need a proposal to discuss *Rowland*?

Zach looks at his watch and scowls. "See, the problem is that I have to be in court in fifteen minutes. So I wanted to see if you were free for dinner. Magnus at six thirty. Reservations are under my name."

My head snaps up in surprise. Not because I've long dreamed of eating at Magnus—a gourmet South American eatery where Brad and I once sheepishly ordered only drinks after seeing the menu prices and had to retreat home for sandwiches after—but because of Zach's presumption that I would be free tonight, that I will be more than happy to drop anything else I have going on and have dinner with him. And because it sounds suspiciously like a date.

On its face, this proposal of Zach's is reasonable. He will be in court until dinnertime, and he needs to eat. It's been pitched as a working meal. But there's something in Zach's demeanor, his self-assured delivery, the fact that he didn't put this in an e-mail but instead wanted to ask me face-to-face, which makes me think otherwise.

"You're going to expense dinner at Magnus? Do you really think that's the best use of the client's resources, Mr. Newsome?" I ask, calling his bluff. If our clients were the Rowlands instead of the state's largest construction company, there would be no way to stick them with the bill for an unnecessary three-hundred-dollar meal and still sleep at night.

I rub my hands together, feeling remnants of velvety warmth from Brad's skin early this morning. When I think of finally getting to try Magnus, the person I picture seated across from me is my husband.

"I have a lot to do tonight," I say. "How about we meet first thing in the morning over breakfast? Your pick."

Zach thinks for a minute, pursing his lips. Then he says, "Sure. I'll e-mail you a time and place. Do you have anything in the morning?"

"I'm free until nine o'clock."

"Sounds good," he says. He checks his watch and whistles. "Okay, you. Get on out of here. I've got a hot date with Judge Roselyn."

"Mañana," I call over my shoulder on the way out of his office.

This morning the streets and snowbanks and trees were covered with a grimy, dingy gray, but thanks to the thin sheen of snow that fell throughout the afternoon, it all looks crisp and new under the streetlights' glow.

I stop at Capitol Foods on my way home and pick up two chicken breasts, Parmesan and mozzarella cheese, sun-dried tomatoes, kalamata olives, and penne pasta—ingredients for the one "fancy" dish I know how to make, basically because I made it up and it's a recipe that consists of cutting everything into pieces, sautéing it, and then tossing it all with the pasta and cheese. At the last minute I add a bottle of Chianti. I resisted the urge to send us on a vacation we can't afford, and I declined dinner with a colleague at a place we also can't afford. A good bottle of wine is a reasonable splurge, and I'm feeling sentimental and a little celebratory after Brad's effort with dinner last night. I'm looking forward to actually enjoying a meal with him tonight. Would it be nice to sit across from him at Magnus? Sure. But these days I feel blessed to be sitting across from him at home.

I lug the groceries and my workbag up our front steps. Something about the lighting, the time of night, reminds me of the evening Sergeant Gerlach sat here beside me. And with that memory come all of the heavy, horrible feelings that washed over me then. My breath sticks on its way up my throat, and I'm rooted in place, if only for a second, by what tonight might look like if that night had turned out differently.

It's okay, though. It's all okay now, I remind myself. We've come out the other side. Again I think of waking up this morning, Brad's hand in mine, and smile as I turn the key in the lock.

The minute I open the front door, though, I can tell something is off. Everything in my range of sight is fine. Things are where they're supposed to be. But the atmosphere, the mood of the place, isn't right.

I call out for Brad, but there is no answer.

The light above the kitchen sink is on, but the rest of the house is dark. I set the groceries down on the counter next to a half-empty jug of Jack Daniel's, cap off. Next to that is Brad's cell phone. When I pick it up, it's either off or out of batteries.

I call Brad's name as I make my way down the hallway, nearly tripping over his rucksack, which is slumped against one wall, the top gaping open. There's no answer.

The door to our room is cracked open, and through it escapes a sliver of moonlight. I ease the door open slowly, quietly, so as not to wake a sleeping Brad. But I needn't worry. When I look in, there is a stack of folded blankets on the floor where I expect Brad to be and our bed is neatly made—all square corners and covers pulled taught as if over a drum.

Once again, I don't know where my husband is, or how long he will be gone this time. My previous gusto for creating a special night leaks out of me like air from a balloon, replaced by a sudden exhaustion that makes me sag.

I pad to the bathroom and turn the tub faucet as far as it will go, then let it run hot while I return to our room and undress. In the few moments I've been out of the bathroom, it has already filled with steam. I switch the lever to direct the water to the showerhead and step in, my skin gloriously assaulted with thousands of tiny red-hot pinpricks.

When I go to close the shower curtain behind me, I see it. I rub my eyes at first, but the words are still there, etched by steam on the new bathroom mirror: *I'm sorry.*

The words are Brad's, I know this. But what is he sorry for? I think of the dinner last night, the card he gave me. I don't understand.

And then I do.

I shut off the water and throw Brad's bathrobe around me. It smells like him—musky and spicy and newly showered. I go from room to room, calling for him. The spare room. Our office. Our bedroom. I flip on every light as I go, steeling myself for the illumination of something I don't want to find. I run downstairs into the basement, the steps cold and damp under my feet. I look behind the wall that hides the furnace and along the row of shelves at the far side of the house, but there is no sign of Brad, and for once, I am relieved not to find him.

I am biting my lip, trying to stop the panic that's rolling inside me, like a windstorm gathering and organizing itself into a funnel cloud. Where *is* he?

With a start, I run back up to our bedroom. I pull a shoe box down from the very top of my closet and four more come tumbling down, sandals and peep-toe heels raining down around me. Inside the box in my hands is Brad's gun. I curse myself for not yet getting it to a pawnshop, but I start to breathe easier. Maybe he's out somewhere. Maybe he grew tired of waiting for me to come home for dinner and went to get a sandwich or slice of pizza. Maybe he was bored. Maybe an old friend called and invited him for a beer.

I take a deep breath and shed Brad's bathrobe, pulling on underwear, jeans, a long-sleeved shirt, and a turtleneck sweater. But those words, outlined by the steam on the bathroom mirror, are still nibbling at the back of my mind. And there's one place I haven't yet looked.

I pull on boots over my bare feet and as I approach the back door, I see that it isn't fully closed. Feelings of dread stir in me again. I pull the door closed behind me. And in the thirty or so steps that I take between our house and the old garage behind it that the previous owners converted into a workshop, I hear nothing except the rhythmic pumping of blood in my ears. Woosh. Step. Woosh. Step. Woosh.

The side door to the garage has been layered with so many coats of paint that it's almost grown too big for the frame and it sticks when I try to open it. I have to lean my shoulder in and push. The door gives way with a screech and a groan.

The interior of the garage is dark, and even when my eyes adjust, I can't see a thing. I grope for the switch, and a single bare bulb lights the room.

And there in the middle of it, sitting on an overturned plastic milk crate, is Brad.

He is dressed in his desert fatigues. His hair is shorn within millimeters of his scalp. He raises his eyes, and it's as if he were looking up at me from the bottom of a pool. Above him, from the exposed rafter, hangs an old garden hose that he's formed into a crude noose.

I can't speak. I can't move. We stare at each other. I study him. My mind flips through image after image of Brad—walking me home on that New Year's Eve so many years ago, flipping pancakes in worn jeans the morning after, twirling me around the Monona Terrace's rooftop for our "first dance" on our wedding afternoon—and none of these match the man in front of me. He looks a lot like my husband. But it's not him.

As quietly as I can, I say his name—and then once more. I can hardly hear myself over the pounding of blood in my ears, loud and hollow, like a hammer on tin. He doesn't turn to me. He doesn't answer. But then I see his shoulders sag. I see his body follow suit.

A single tear makes its way down the cheek of this man in front of me and I register a change in his eyes. They cloud with pain, with pleading. My chest constricts. I want to throw myself at him, wrap my arms around him and bury my face in his neck. But I'm afraid. I'm afraid of what he'll do. And of what I'll do. I'm afraid I'll start to beat his chest with my fists for being so stupid, so selfish. I'm afraid that I wouldn't stop.

I step gingerly to him. "I'm going to sit down next to you, okay?" I say. I grab another empty crate nearby, turn it over, and ease myself down onto it. The only movement from Brad is the fluttering of his eyelids and the almost indiscernible rise and fall of his chest as he breathes.

Words swirl in my head, but none take shape. What does one say at a time like this? What can I say? In a flash, though, I think of the card he left for me last night. Of his words, *I'm sorry for being such a burden,* tucked inconspicuously between *Happy Valentine's Day* and *Don't ever forget that you're my whole world.* And I realize that last night wasn't a celebration. It was good-bye.

"You weren't really going to leave me?" I ask him. "Were you? Like this?"

He doesn't look at me.

"Brad, talk to me. Please. Tell me what's going on. Tell me what to do." My voice is hushed. I am sitting as close as I can to him, my knee and hip and arm touching his. I want to be closer.

He starts to cry, silently. Big tears make their way down his face. He shakes his head a couple of times, as though he wants to say something and then thinks better of it.

Finally, he says, "They wouldn't take me back."

I am about to ask "Who?" when I realize what he's telling me: He tried to re-up.

"When?" I whisper.

"Yesterday," he says.

And suddenly, I'm angry—angrier at him than I've ever, ever been. Has coming home to live with me been so awful that his best choice is to head straight back to a desert war halfway around the world? It's as though he's been sucked into the vortex of this god-damn war and forgotten everything else. He's like an amnesiac who doesn't remember who he is, or who I am. Who doesn't remember that he even has a wife, or the great life he had—we had—before all this happened.

"You could have talked to me," I say.

"I don't know how to be here anymore, E. I don't know how to be me here." He closes his eyes, as though trying to block out something that's burrowed into his head, unwelcome—a memory, an image. "I'm tired of being a monster," he says, his voice pleading.

"Oh, Brad. Baby, you're not."

"Over there I'm not," he says. "There, I'm normal. But here, I am."

I watch Brad purposely not looking at me. "Oh, Brad," I say. I go to reach for him and see him flinch. I back away.

"I need you to do something," he says, his tone flat and forceful.

"Anything," I tell him. "I'll do anything."

"Don't tell," he says. He waves a hand feebly in front of him. "About any of this. Please don't tell anyone."

I nod my agreement.

Brad gets up and places the crate he was sitting on near the work-bench, then continues on out the door. I stand and walk to the win-dow, which might as well be oiled paper for all the visibility the dust and grime covering it afford. I watch Brad cross the yard to the house.

I see his shadow dance from window to window inside—first the kitchen, then the bathroom, then our bedroom.

The night is growling outside the garage windows like a wild animal and the light from that single bulb is keeping it at bay. In here, in this room, for now, Brad is safe. We are safe. Right here, in this moment, it is all okay.

Twenty

The next morning, I open my eyes and see Brad next to me in bed. His face is cherubic, like a stubble-faced baby's, and I smile, nearly reaching a hand out to stroke it before I remember: My husband is easily startled. Brad's arm is slung over me, and a part of me wants to revel in this moment, in the simple pleasure of his skin against mine. But I spot the fatigues he's wearing and I remember something else in a flash: My husband took steps to kill himself yesterday.

Slowly, I disentangle myself from Brad. I slide an inch, wait, and listen for his breathing to become regular. Then I do it again, and again, until I am standing next to the bed and he is still sleeping peacefully. I want to kiss his cheek, to snuggle into him, but I can't risk waking him. So I pull on a sweatshirt and sweatpants, and pocket my phone. I tiptoe out of the bedroom and pull the door closed behind me. In the small mudroom at the back of the house, I pull on boots and, as noiselessly as I can, slip outside.

As I dial the number for the firm, the one thought in my head is that I can't leave Brad alone. Jeannie, our receptionist, answers, and I tell her that I won't be able to come in today. She says that Zach has been looking for me, and she will transfer me to his extension.

When he answers, I tell Zach the same thing I told Jeannie. "I'm not going to make it in today," I say.

There's silence on the other end of the line.

"Zach?"

"You stood me up this morning, Sabatto," Zach says.

Shit! I think. Breakfast. *I was supposed to meet Zach this morning.*

"And don't you have a zoning appeal this afternoon? You *really* can't make it in?"

Until now I had forgotten about the zoning case. And one by one, I remember all of the other work obligations waiting for me.

I drop my head into my hand. I haven't thought any of this through. I could stay home with Brad today, but what about tomorrow? What about the next day, and the day after that? How am I supposed to keep him safe and hold down my job? Scratch that. How am I supposed to keep him safe at all? I can hide Brad's gun, but what's stopping him from buying another? And a garden hose? I never could have anticipated that. Mentally, I sort through the items in our house. There are bedsheets, prescription medications, knives, and extension cords. Even if I managed to eradicate all of these potential dangers, a hardware store five blocks away and a drugstore a mile in the other direction could supply him with anything he might decide he needs.

"Sabatto? So you're coming in this afternoon, right? Please tell me I don't have to get someone to cover your zoning case for you."

I think of Brad, sleeping soundly in our bed—for now. And then I think of leaving him to go a mile and a half up the road to work. The thought makes me shiver. I suck in a ragged breath.

"Hello? Sabatto? Is everything all right?"

"Everything's fine," I say. "I'll see you later today."

I end the call and look at the phone in my hand. I know what I need to do.

· · ·

Brad is still sleeping so soundly that I have to watch for the rise and fall of his chest to make sure he's breathing.

His phone is on the bedside table. I take slow, cautious steps, placing weight on only the ball of each foot to seek out any squeaky floorboards, and then pausing to make sure Brad hasn't stirred before continuing. I lean over him and stretch my fingers to reach for the phone. *Please don't wake up,* I think. *Please, please, please.* I slide the phone toward me until I can close my hand around it; then I turn around and step just as gingerly out of the room.

In the front hallway I grab a coat and slip it on. It's Brad's down coat, and it hangs around me like a roomy pillow. I let myself out the front door and close it behind me. Then I sit down on the front steps and scroll through Brad's phone, looking for his dad's name in the address book.

I don't have Mert's phone number in my own phone because I've never needed it. Brad has never been particularly close to his dad, or his older brother, Ricky, for that matter.

The summer after his freshman year in college, Brad took off on a solo trip to hike all of the Colorado Fourteeners. He stepped off the final peak and called home, only to learn that his mother had died two days before from stage-four lung cancer that no one except his dad knew she had. While his dad sat on the front porch, pickling himself with gin, Brad made all the funeral arrangements. He wrote his mother's obituary. He accepted casseroles in Pyrex dishes, labeled and froze them, and later washed and returned each dish. And after it was all over, he lashed out at his dad for not telling him about his mom's prognosis, to which Mert argued that Brad was a self-centered asshole who had gotten too big for his britches. Brad hadn't been back home since then.

Mert answers on the third ring. It's not quite nine o'clock in Marquette, but it sounds like I have woken him up.

"Yeah?" he says.

"Mert, it's Elise."

"Yeah. I know, Princess."

This is not a term of endearment. Brad's father has always believed that I think I'm above people; that I'm too good for him, or his son. I told Brad once that if his father thought a scrawny orphan whose prized possession, aside from her George Foreman grill, was her mother's plain, whip-thin gold wedding band, was looking down her nose at him, then his dad had some serious self-esteem issues.

Jesus, I think, *could you at least try to make this easier on me?* Then again, Mert's never been one to take to the easy path, with anything, at least as long as I've known him. If there's difficulty to be had, Mert will find his way straight to it.

There's silence on the line, and I realize Mert is waiting for me to say something. The problem is, I'm not sure where to start.

"I have a favor to ask," I say.

"Oh yeah?" Mert says. I can sense a note of intrigue in his voice. I have his attention. It's not every day I call asking Mert for favors. In fact, this might be the first time. And the last, I remind myself.

"Well, nothing's wrong or anything," I say, stalling. "It's just that Brad and I could use some help *adjusting*, is all. It's a big change, his being back from over there. He's having a little trouble nailing down a job, and I have this huge case I'm working on, so I'm not around, and I'm not with him as much as I'd like to be. I was thinking that maybe it would be good for him to have something to do—to be with family right now."

"Princess," Mert says, "what the hell are you getting at?"

"I was just wondering if Brad could maybe, well—if he might be able to . . . you know, stay with you for a couple of weeks?"

I spit the last handful of words out like a teenager trying to negotiate a later curfew, and I find myself physically ducking in much the same way a teenager might, anticipating a tirade from her parent.

In response, there's only silence.

"Mert?" I finally ask, unsure if he's still there.

"Well, sure," he says. "If he'll agree to come. That would be fine."

I feel my vision go blurry and my limbs turn weak. *That would be fine*? It seemed far too easy. I sense an ambush, a conspiracy. *When you hear hoofbeats*, I think. It was something my dad was fond of saying: "When you hear hoofbeats, think horses—not zebras." It means that the most obvious scenario is probably the one you're dealing with. Maybe Mert is really a horse. Maybe I just haven't ever given him enough credit. *Me of little faith*.

"He's okay with it," I say, finding my voice. I'm lying openly and fear I'm getting far too good at it. "So, maybe this weekend?" I ask.

"That would be fine," Mert repeats.

"Oh, Mert. Thank you. I really appreciate this. I'll give you a call before we leave town on Saturday."

"Don't mention it, Princess," he says.

As I hang up the phone, I breathe a sigh of relief. But out of the corner of my eye, I still can't help glancing furtively about for the damn zebras.

Brad wakes up midmorning, and I offer to make him eggs and toast. He offers to help. We dance silently and stiffly around each other. I fear having to say what I must say to him, eventually. I know he's embarrassed by all that's happened. I know he's frustrated. I know that everything I feel—powerless, crazy, sad, angry—he feels a hundredfold. And yet.

We are sitting in the living room. The television is on—a daytime show host interviewing some starlet in a too-short skirt that barely reaches her hips when she sits down—but we aren't really watching it. "We need to do something here," I finally manage to spit out.

Brad doesn't look at me. He's staring at the television. But he nods.

"I don't know what to do, Brad," I say. And suddenly I'm fighting back tears. I'm trying to keep my voice from cracking. For the first time in months, I feel how tired I am. It's the kind of tired that can't be cured by rest alone, by one good, solid chunk of sleep. It's the kind of tired that works its way down into you, into every last nook in you, and stays there, aching, for so long that you don't remember what it was like not to ache.

"I'll try harder," Brad says. "I'll find a job." There are notes of hope in his voice that break my resolve. The tears that were smarting at the corners of my eyes spill over onto my cheeks. He thinks I'm punishing him; he thinks I'm blaming him.

It's true—sometimes I do. Sometimes I can't seem to help it. But it's never for long and it's never for good.

"Brad," I say, shaking my head.

"I want to get better, E. I do."

His voice. It's that of an earnest schoolboy trying too hard to please. He's gone from "There's nothing fucking wrong with me" to "I'll try harder." I bite my lip, trying not to dissolve. I don't look right at him. I can't.

I turn the television off and go to where Brad is sitting. I kneel in front of him and take his hands in mine. "Listen to me," I say. "This isn't your fault." Brad is looking up toward the ceiling instead of at me. "Listen, Brad," I repeat, squeezing his hands until I get his attention. Until he focuses on me. "I know you're struggling. And I don't blame you. What you've been through—it's—it's . . ." I trail off, searching for the right word. "Awful" doesn't quite encapsulate all that's happened to my husband—both what I know and what I can only imagine.

"Abhorrent," Brad says.

I smile up at him. "That's a good word," I say. *It's a big word,* I think. Brad doesn't use those kinds of words these days, and I've come to realize that his brain doesn't hold on to—or produce—words like it used to.

He seems to know it, too. "Thank you," he says, smiling a crooked, gap-toothed smile at me.

My God, I love this man, I think. But I don't say it out loud. I need to forge ahead before I lose whatever resolve I've gathered. I figure out where I was in the speech I've been constructing all morning in my head, and I continue. "I can't take care of you like I should. Like I need to. And I know you hate to hear it, but you need taking care of right now. And I'm going to lose my job if all this keeps up. We can't afford for that to happen, and I can't keep this up. I just can't."

I lay my head on Brad's knees and take a deep breath. He twirls a piece of my hair.

"I'm sorry," I say, so softly that I'm unsure if he hears me.

This next thing that I'm about to say needs to come out just right. I straighten up and look at him again, right in the eye.

"How would you feel about going to live with your dad?" I ask.

We both know how big a deal it is for me to ask this of him. I brace myself for his reaction: anger, frustration, outright refusal.

"For how long?" he asks.

I shrug because I don't trust myself to answer him with words. How do you tell your husband that you're tired, that your nerves are frayed because of him—because an injury has made him unrecognizable to you, and to himself? How do you tell him that you're not sure if you can do it anymore? That you need a break—maybe for a few weeks, but possibly forever? How do you explain that you need time to paint a picture of your future that you can live with, that you can survive, and you're not sure if he's in that picture or not?

When I don't answer, Brad says, "Okay." He runs a hand through my hair. I let my head fall back to his lap, wishing I could freeze this moment—the feeling of Brad's fingers working over my scalp, finding a tangle and pulling gently but steadily until it releases, then combing back through the loosened, smoothed strands. "Okay," he says again. And that one word sounds like a white flag, waving.

Twenty-one

The drive to Marquette often seems never ending. Long strings of fast-food restaurants, big-box stores, coffee shops, and gas stations stretch almost continuously from Madison through the Fox Valley, and end abruptly north of Green Bay, as does reliable cell phone service. From that point on, the drive becomes a blur of thick evergreen forests, broken only intermittently by the occasional rest stop or small town or gas station cropping up in the middle of nowhere and advertising cold beer and deer bait on its marquee. In the fall, M-95, which runs from Iron Mountain on the southern border of the Upper Peninsula to Marquette, dips and climbs through foliage as bright as fire. But it's not quite March yet, and that means these parts are still in the throes of winter. The landscape looks cold and wild and foreboding outside the windows of my car.

The only traffic patrols on this stretch are conducted by state troopers, but there's only so much manpower they can throw at such a wide-open area; the chance of speeding tickets is low. So I let my foot press down and then down some more, finally letting it hover as the speedometer reaches seventy-five miles per hour. When I see another car, which is rarely, I ease off the gas until my speed drops, and after I determine it's not a trooper, I pick the pace back up.

Brad has been asleep in the passenger seat since north of Green Bay. Or, I think, he could simply be avoiding having to talk to me. He hasn't said he's angry. But he hasn't said much of anything in the past few days, and so, anger is a distinct possibility. So is medication. I made sure to watch Brad as he dutifully swallowed the pills he'd been prescribed for anxiety when he was discharged and pocketed the rest to take later, an acquiescence so out of his recent character that it made me feel as if I were watching an exotic animal, caged and re-signed, at the zoo.

Before I know it, as if on autopilot, I've made the right-hand turn at Koski's Corner and passed the 41 Steak House and Teal Lake in Negaunee. My body shifts with the curves in the road, and I have the old, familiar sensation of coming home. I haven't been up this way in years—since college. But I've always been drawn to the area in a way I can never accurately describe to the city dwellers I know.

At this point in the drive, you're up above the town right before the road plunges you down into it, and you can see Marquette's quaintness and isolation spread out below. You can see it spill out right up to the edge of Lake Superior, which might as well be an ocean the way it runs off to the horizon. Some days the colors are so vibrant, they almost hurt your eyes—the oranges and reds of the downtown buildings, the glistening black of the water, and the blue, blue, blue sky above it all. Other days, like today, it's a solid wall of gray, as if the whole expanse were encased in dry ice—the dividing lines between town and lake and sky, the shore and horizon, all indiscernible from one another. I used to dread this drive: Marquette isn't exactly easy to get to from anywhere. But right now, I give thanks that it's not. A person should have to do a little work to get to a place this beautiful and remote.

Mert lives past town a good ways, off County Road 550 down a dead-end road that's more like a well-traveled path through the woods. A lot of these dirt roads shoot off from CR 550, almost all unmarked, and I start down two and end up having to back up onto the main road when each one tapers to a single-track path after a quarter mile or so.

Finally, blindly it seems, I pick the right one. The road stays the same width all the way to Mert's house, lit up like a beacon in the blackness. I let myself think that maybe Brad will wake up and tell me that this is all a mistake, that he'll fight a little harder for our life back in Madison—for our life together. But I know better. I know he's all out of fight. I know he doesn't know how to go on any better than I do. And as if to prove that point, he comes to, rubs his eyes, yawns, and exits the car without saying a word. He knows it's what he should do, and so do I. I only wish we didn't have to.

I unload Brad's things from the car along with a few of my own and knock on the front door. Even though Brad is already inside, it doesn't feel right for me to simply walk in. Mert yells for me to come in, and I find him sitting in a ratty green armchair watching the Red Wings and playing solitaire on a metal TV tray in front of him.

"Hiya, Princess," he says, as if my presence here were an everyday occurrence.

I assume Brad has gone up to his room to drop his bags off, and I take the opportunity to talk to Mert, alone.

"I want to thank you, Mert. For letting us do this. For taking Brad in for a while."

Mert flips two cards over and moves a run under the queen of diamonds to its corresponding king. He doesn't acknowledge that I've said anything.

"I know we haven't been up to visit much," I say. This is a lie. We haven't been up to visit at all. Even when, years after his mother's funeral, Brad reached an uneasy peace with his dad, he would stay with friends when he came home, or with me. And when we moved to Madison, his trips north pretty much ceased altogether. I should have done more to encourage Brad to visit his dad, but I didn't. The truth was, celebrating holidays with just the two of us, albeit lonely, was a far better option in my opinion than refereeing gatherings with Mert, Ricky, and Brad.

"Brad always talks about how much he loved growing up here." I pause and wait for Mert to acknowledge me. When he still doesn't, I continue talking anyway. "I've heard all his stories about building jumps on the old railroad tracks and how he and Ricky would try to launch their bikes over, or making two-story snow forts. He sure had a great childhood, thanks to you and Ruth."

Nothing.

I always think that I have done something, apart from being alive, to offend Mert. And inside my head a conversation usually rages in which I wonder what it could possibly be, what I could have said or done in the short, short time that it takes for him to cool on me. Then I think how unfair it is because I haven't done a damn thing, and Mert is simply a grumpy old man, mad at the world and taking it out on anyone who actually seems to have a chance at being happy. But he's a grumpy old man who is the only person I can ask for help. At the moment, he is my lone hope for salvation—a chewed-up, full-of-holes lifesaver attached to a fraying rope.

"Brad was telling me on the drive up about how you used to take him to the Lakeview rink at four a.m. to work on his stick skills before school. He still remembers that, you know. He still talks about it. He was what, seven? Eight?" I look over at Mert, who doesn't so much as raise an eyebrow. Slap, slap, slap. His dealing a new game is my only answer.

"Then he quit. So he could roll around with guys in tights," Mert says after a while.

Perhaps I haven't given Mert a fair shake in the past. Perhaps I've been poisoned by my husband's dejection after almost every interaction he's had with Mert, by the almost palpable hurt that's evident in his voice when he says, "Just once, I wish he'd say he was proud of me." To my knowledge, Mert never has said those words to Brad. He has never told his son that he loves him. And during those times when the gray cloud of Mert settles over Brad, and by extension over me, I can't help but ask God why he chose to take my parents and leave Mert. I was my parents' only child, and they never missed a chance to shower me with love. Where is the fairness in that?

Maybe it's the discomfort of this situation, or the long drive that preceded it, but what comes out next surprises even me: "You know he did this for you, right?" I ask, lowering my voice to an angry whisper. "That he enlisted to prove himself to you? To make you proud. He was blown up by a bomb while trying to make you proud of him, Mert."

Brad never said this, but I saw his face the night he called his dad. I heard the excitement in his voice, the certainty that this would be the time Mert gave him a verbal pat on the back, told him what a great son he was. And I watched Brad's face fall as Mert replied it was good he was finally coming around to taking his patriotism seriously, that Rick had already tried enlisting the day after 9/11 and that he'd still be serving his country if they hadn't turned him away. Mert still claims Rick was rejected because of his eyesight. Brad and I have always had a sneaking suspicion it had more to do with a drug test gone wrong.

"If he was hit by a bomb, he'd be in itty-bitty little pieces all over the desert. He got knocked around by the blast, is all. Got a few pieces of metal in him. That's war. What did he expect—a pony and some cotton candy for his troubles? Besides, it might toughen him up some—might be good for him."

These were all of Mert's complaints about his son rolled up into one neat package: He was too pretty, wasn't macho enough, and didn't have any actual skills past being smart, which didn't hold much water with Mert. Never mind that Brad had almost a perfect score on his SATs and a 4.0 all through college. He was no good with a carburetor, like Rick, who could straighten out the problem of any vehicle— foreign or domestic—blindfolded and with a hand tied behind his back. When Brad called his dad to tell him that he was one of thirty-two people in the country chosen for the Rhodes Scholarship that year, Mert said, "Well, if you get tired of playing grab-ass over there in England, you come on back and help Rick at his shop. It's going gangbusters, you know. He's hired on three mechanics already."

I shake my head. "He's different," I say. "He's like a different person."

Mert squares his shoulders and then his chin. He meets my gaze, boring into me with his eyes. "Princess," he says, "does it ever occur to you that sometimes you don't have a goddamn clue what you're talking about?"

The next day I help Brad settle back into the house he grew up in. Mert hasn't changed a single thing since Brad last walked out. Old wrestling trophies line a few shelves tacked to the wall with no discernible pattern, and crooked to boot. If the house settles any more and in the wrong direction, the shelves will become wooden slides. Varsity letters are pinned haphazardly around a mirror, where there's even a picture of one of Brad's high school girlfriends wedged into a corner. I wonder which one this is—Jocelyn? Cagney? Renée?—and after wondering how Brad never managed to pick a girl with a more normal name like Jennifer or Nicole or some variation thereof, I wonder what this girl in the picture, whatever her name is, is doing now.

I used to be so smug when I would ask about these girls, loving to hear Brad tell me about them, to piece together my husband's life before it intersected with mine. I was always so confident that no matter whom these Girls of Brad's Past had married or how many wonderful children they'd had, they'd swap places with me in a heartbeat if given a chance. Now, as I look at this girl with her long, flaxen hair and pointy chin and earnest smile, I think about what I'm doing here, and a jolt of envy runs through me. Maybe Mert is right: Sometimes I really don't know what the hell I'm talking about.

Given Mert's disinclination for entertaining houseguests, I don't know how long it's been since someone has slept in this bed. It could easily have been years ago, and so I strip the bed even though it's neatly made and I toss the linens into the wash. The quilt I take out back and hang from the porch. I beat the pillows against each other, trying to both rid them of dust and infuse them with cold, fresh air. These are not things men think to do. These are not what they care about. But I will feel better knowing that, at the very least, I've left my husband here with clean sheets, even if he pulls them into a heap on the floor tonight.

It's late afternoon when I finish making the bed, and by the time I kiss Brad good-bye—a subtle, last-minute shift causing my lips to land on the stubble along his cheek instead of his lips—the sun, low and cold in the sky, looks like a worker waiting out the last five minutes of an overtime shift. And by the time Brad, hands in pockets and shoulders squared against being a figure in my rearview mirror, disappears from view, so, too, has the sun.

Part of me feels like I'm dropping a child off at college for the first time. Driving away, I'm bombarded by conflicting emotions: I have an overwhelming urge to turn around and take him home with me, to try again—to try harder. And I feel lighter, freed from the constant worry and supervision of my husband. As I speed down M-95 away from Marquette, Michigan, through a tunnel of evergreen and white, I think that one fact lies at the very root of the problem. I don't actually need to have a child; between the Army and this godforsaken war, one has already been provided for me.

Twenty-two

I pull into the driveway and shift into park. My sole thought is of a warm shower and sleep. As I turn off the car, though, I notice someone sitting on the darkened front steps. Even though she's cloaked in shadows, I can tell it's Sondra: her long, thin limbs; the regal carriage of her head and neck, like a beautiful flower on a slender stem; her hair sculpted into a stunning Afro, like an exotic Japanese tree.

"What are you doing here?" I ask as I walk up the sidewalk.

"I was in the neighborhood," she says. "I sent you a message." And when I check my phone, I see that she did—ten minutes ago.

Sondra gets up as I climb the stairs and steps aside for me to unlock the door. I hold it open for her. "Come on in," I say, though my tone isn't at all hospitable.

I march back to my bedroom to drop my overnight bag and leave Sondra milling around the living room, looking at the photos of me and Brad that adorn the mantel and surrounding shelves. One day while visiting my grandparents—my father's parents—I realized that every photo in the house was of the two of them, and I remember how odd I found that. Everywhere you turned—living room, kitchen, bedroom, bathroom—only my grandmother and grandfather smiled back. Now that I am older, I can see how it happens, because it's starting to happen to me. I don't keep photos of my parents outside of my bedroom, lest it start a conversation about what they did and where they lived, and the awkward, stuttering recovery that people always attempt when I say that they died. I'm not sure Brad even has any family photos, or at least, none that I've ever seen. Neither of us has nieces or nephews to memorialize, and there aren't even pets to dote on. So, it is photos of the two of us or none at all.

I hear Sondra call out, "I want to thank you—for taking care of Antony like you did."

My head snaps up from rifling through my bag for a hair tie. I'm not prepared for the small talk to end so soon. I wonder how she knows that I saw Antony after she left. And then I realize that she's been talking to him.

I let her words linger until I'm back in the living room. "I didn't really do anything," I say.

Sondra is sitting in the recliner, her legs folded under her like a fawn.

"Oh, but you did," she says. "You kept him company, made him feel like he mattered that day. He was in a bad spot. He's grateful for what you did."

I find it hard to believe that I was able to do all that for Antony in the two hours I spent with him, but at least her use of past tense indicates that he's feeling a bit better. Right now, though, I'm livid with Sondra. "It wasn't really my place," I say, "but I suppose someone had to." It's a cutting comment, and I mean it to be.

Sondra gets the dig. I see it register in her eyes. Her smile is sad. "Still angry, I see?"

I shrug. It's hard to be legitimately angry at someone over a very personal choice made about her very personal life. But I can't seem to shake the image of Antony sitting there in his wheelchair, staring out the window and into the sun, with air and bandages where his two arms should be.

"I was going to leave him anyway. You should know that. And not because he was injured. Not his arms, anyway," she says.

"You don't have to explain."

"No," Sondra says, "I feel like I sort of do. Do you have any tequila?"

I shake my head. Brad and I enjoy the occasional beer, but we don't have liquor around because we just don't often drink it. Well, we didn't, anyway. "I can offer you a bottle of beer with an undetermined purchase date or watered-down Jack Daniel's. Bet you're glad you showed up here, huh?"

"You're lucky he doesn't drink it straight."

I look at Sondra. I tip my chin to the side to study her. I didn't say that the Jack was Brad's. I didn't tell her who had watered it down. Yet, she seems to know. "Indeed," I say, still eyeing her. "Just wish I didn't have to."

"Indeed," Sondra says. She chews on her lower lip for a moment and makes an offer. "Why don't we go somewhere—grab a drink? Catch up."

I shake my head. "It's late. Not tonight. Maybe some other time."

Sondra gets up, fetches her boots, and sits back down in the recliner. She pulls one on and zips it, and then the other. Then she grabs my shoes.

"It's ten thirty on a Saturday night. Your husband is gone. I'm in town visiting. And we probably have some talking to do."

I think of the shower I want so badly to take. I think of climbing between the sheets and closing my eyes and forgetting, for a handful of hours, the sight of Brad in my rearview mirror.

I shake my head again. But Sondra holds my shoes out to me and shakes them at me. "One drink," she says. "I promise. After that, you don't ever have to talk to me again."

She shakes my shoes at me again. This time I take them from her. "One drink," I say. I slip on my shoes and grab my keys.

I'm chilled to the bone, which tends to happen when I'm overtired and also when it's winter in Wisconsin, so I pick a cozy Irish pub on the square with a real fireplace and Smithwick's on tap.

In the span of one drink we cover what has brought Sondra to town (work meetings), what she's doing now (sales for a medical record software developer in California, learning to surf), how Darcy is doing (hanging in there, busy with Mia), and how I'm doing (fine, fine).

After the second round of drinks arrives, Sondra takes a sip of her mescal on the rocks. She places the glass back on the table and says, "I'm sorry for leaving you like that."

I take a sip, delaying having to respond, because I don't know what to say. So many thoughts are competing for airtime—that she should be sorry; that she didn't only run out on me that day; and that she's selfish and self-absorbed. I want to ask her if she planned to leave both Antony and me there, and how, in light of my difficult afternoon, she found the strength to point her car westward and drive away. I want to know if she ever looked back.

"It's fine," I tell her. "Really." For a long time, I craved an explanation from her. In the past weeks, though, I've been so fully focused on Brad that I haven't had time or energy to sustain my judgment of Sondra.

We stare at each other. The tone of my voice betrays everything I'm thinking.

Sondra takes another long sip of her drink and shifts in her seat to tuck one leg underneath her.

"This was Antony's third tour. You know, that's almost four years of deployments. Almost four years of the hellish waving good-bye and wondering if he'll be coming back. Four years of learning to live without him, of doing every last damn thing myself, only to then have to turn around and welcome him home and figure out how to live with him all over again. It was exhausting. But I would have done it."

"Except?" I ask.

"Except each time, it was like he left a piece of himself over there. Each time, he was a little less Antony. Until he wasn't really Antony at all—at least not my Antony. Some of them manage not to let the war get to them. Some of them come back like they never left. But not all. And the ones that don't, it's hard. It's real hard."

I nod. Brad hasn't just let the war get to him. He's soaked it in like water to a bone-dry sponge. He's let it infiltrate every last cell of his body, every last thought, every waking moment—and those in his sleep, too. Hard? I think. Calculus is hard. Running five miles is hard. Baking a layer cake with homemade frosting is hard. But this? This is something else altogether.

"You tried to tell me—at Darcy's party, didn't you?"

Sondra nods and again smiles sadly at me. "I did," she says.

"I should have listened."

She shakes her head. "I didn't," she says. "No one does."

"PTSD?" I ask.

Although it's a generic question, Sondra knows exactly what I mean. "Yup—textbook," she says. "Hypervigilance, inability to sleep, flashbacks, disassociation." She laughs. "I sound like a freaking psychology textbook, don't I? They make it sound so clinical. So manageable. But they don't tell you that eating out at a restaurant now means your husband stares past you, constantly surveying all the entrances and exits while you keep up a completely one-sided conversation. They don't tell you that it's going to end up costing two grand to fix the air conditioner that he shot with his pistol when it made a strange noise. Or that you'll never get a birthday, Christmas, or anniversary gift again because malls are nothing more than giant triggers for him."

Sondra's eyes are wet now. She's biting her lip and shaking her head. I'd like to hug her. I'd like to hug us both. But I stay put. I can sense she's not done. I sense she wouldn't necessarily like me to do that anyway. So I offer encouragement in the form of a sympathetic nod.

" 'But not to keep,' " she says softly.

I cock my head, not sure I heard her correctly.

"They give them back," she says, "but not really. It's from a poem: 'And with his eyes he asked her not to ask. They had given him back to her, but not to keep.' "

Not to keep.

"A lot of times, by the time you get to rehab, sometimes before, the doctors won't even talk to the spouses."

"Why?" I ask.

"Because of the washout rate."

"Washout?"

"Divorce. Some ridiculously high percentage of spouses who are there when the soldier gets off the plane on a stretcher have hit the road by the time they're wheeled into rehab. So the docs deal with just the patients from the get-go. Hard to blame them, really."

I tell her then what I haven't been able to tell anyone else. I tell her about the nightmares Brad has, about the one that was so bad I woke up with him straddling me, choking me, and how the next morning he didn't remember doing it. I tell her about how he's slept on the floor since he's been back. I tell her about his tattoo, the smoking, Mrs. Valhalla and the incident at the grocery store, and then finding him in the garage with that noose hanging over him. I tell her that I took him to live with Mert—and that I'm not sure for how long—because I'm afraid to leave my husband alone and I'm afraid to be with him. I tell her how guilty I feel every second of every single day, and how terrified I am that this might never change, that this might be our new normal—my new life.

"You know the first thing Antony said when he got out of surgery?" Sondra asks, none of what I've said seeming to faze her. "First words, honest to God: 'When can I go back?' He said his guys needed him. Never mind that I was his wife and that I was standing right there next to him. Never mind that he didn't even have a hand left for me to hold, or that *I* needed him. No, he wanted to get on the first bird back."

" 'But not to keep,' " I say quietly, noting how the words feel as they form on my tongue.

Sondra stares into her glass as if trying to divine guidance from the liquid inside, to read it like tea leaves. The waiter stops at our table and delivers a new round for each of us.

"We didn't order these," I tell him. I'm instantly angry with Sondra and her stupid one-drink "promise."

"No," the waiter says. "That guy sent them over." He gestures to the end of the bar, where Zach Newsome is sitting with only a sweating glass of stout for company. Zach lifts his hand into a feeble wave.

Sondra looks back and forth between Zach and me. "Do you know him?" she asks.

I nod. "Coworker."

She chews the inside of her cheek. "Good guy?"

"Yeah," I say. "Fantastic attorney."

She looks at me, then at Zach, and then back at me. "Ha!" she laughs. "And what else?"

"I wouldn't know!" I say, mostly in mock offense.

Sondra's face clouds with an unexpected solemnity. "There's no shame in it, you know, Elise. Sometimes you fight the good fight and sometimes the good fight wins. It happens," she says, nodding thoughtfully. "And sometimes, it's for the best."

I'm about to ask her what she means, exactly, when she says, "Why don't you invite him over?" and without waiting for me to respond, she gives Zach a come-hither look and a wave. He wastes no time.

"Ladies," he says, pulling out a chair and sitting down. He's beaming at me in a way that, even if he was angry about being stood up at breakfast last week, says he's long since forgotten it.

"Thank you for the drink," Sondra says, raising her glass.

He clinks his pint against her tumbler. "Thanks for inviting me over."

"Sondra, Zach," I say. "Zach, Sondra. Zach is my go-to guy on all things related to Early, Janssen, and Bradenton," I say to Sondra. "Sondra is—" I stumble, wondering how to introduce her. An old friend? No. A good friend? Nope. A fellow Guard spouse? Not really. "I met Sondra through my friend Darcy," I say, finally. "She's in from sunny California on business."

This delivery is not smooth, but it is effective. Zach asks her what kind of business, and where she lives in California, and the two of them are off and chatting, leaving me to wonder how Brad is and what he's doing right now.

I think about ducking out to call him, when out of nowhere Sondra says, "I read this book by some Harvard psychologist or psychiatrist on the plane ride here whose theory is that we all just need to have lower expectations in order to be happy. That we need to visualize the reality of our situations and not what we'd ideally like to have happen. I think there's something to that."

I look at Sondra, wondering where this non sequitur has come from or if I've missed more of the conversation than I thought I have, but Zach is nonplussed. He shrugs, takes a sip of his Guinness, and dives right in. He loves a good philosophical discussion, I've learned. "I think you're right. I saw something on *20/20* or *60 Minutes* on this very thing. I think Denmark was the happiest country on earth for like the millionth year in a row, and not because it's some sort of tropical paradise—clearly—or has a cure for cancer. People there just have a lower bar as far as what they expect out of life. Garbage picked up? Check. Buses run on time? Check. Population elation? Check."

"That's sad," I say. "That's contentment, not happiness."

"One and the same, no?" Zach says.

I shake my head with vigor. "Absolutely not. It's all practicality. Where's the room for dreams?"

"Do you really need that, though?" Sondra asks. "Aren't you just setting yourself up for disappointment? If you don't have hopes and expectations, contentment can pass for happiness."

I feel my face scrunch and I recoil. "Are you serious? You really want to look back at the end of your days and say that nothing all that bad happened? Or things could've been worse? What kind of life is that? Don't you want more?"

"I do," she says. "Beats the hell out of wishing for things to be different from what they are. But what if you know you'll never get it? If you know you'll never have what you need to be happy?"

"Then I'll keep trying," I say, though I'm not sure I believe myself. If I know that I'm not happy and that nothing is likely to change, will I keep my head down and simply soldier on, hoping for the best? I owe it to Brad to do that, but what about me? Don't I owe it to myself to do what I need to be happy?

"Trying is good, but so is hoping," Zach says. "Being happy isn't too much to hope for if you've got one of the good ones." And as he says this, he places a hand on my knee under the table and lets it linger there.

A waitress arrives and Zach orders Scotch eggs. I'm so thrown by the disconnect between his matter-of-fact order and the warm trail left by his hand on my leg that I don't ask what Scotch eggs are or try to request fries instead. Then he excuses himself to the restroom.

As soon as Zach is out of earshot, Sondra smiles at me with a knowing, sly look. "Someone likes you," she whispers, leaning forward. "So is he?"

"Is he what?" I ask, still annoyed—or reannoyed—with her.

"One of the good ones?"

"We work together," I say. "Zach would flirt with Arnold Schwarzenegger if he were wearing Eau de Estrogen."

"That's not what I asked."

"I don't know," I say. "I think so."

Sondra leans forward. Her face is hard set. "You know you're not going to have it all, right? Your American dream with the kids and the fence? Not with Brad. I'm sure he was a great guy once. But can you look me in the eye and say that you'd leave a baby with him? A toddler? Hell, you said yourself that you can't even trust him alone. Have you thought of how you're going to raise a kid and work full-time and take care of Brad, too? How you're going to keep everyone safe and happy and keep yourself sane, too? It's impossible, Elise. It just is."

I stare back at Sondra, shocked at her directness.

"How do I know all of this? How dare I just put it out there? Because I couldn't do it, either."

I look up to see Zach approaching the table, and behind him, the waitress with our Scotch eggs. I have a nearly full pint in front of me and could use the sustenance of a late-night nosh. But Sondra's words are clanging like cymbals in my head, and I'm suddenly past ready to go home. Scratch that. I'm suddenly past ready to already be between the sheets, fast asleep.

I shrug my coat on and button it. I half expect Sondra to backtrack, to apologize. Instead, she says, "You know I'm right, Elise."

At the same time Zach asks, "You're leaving—already?"

I look at Sondra and nod, and I look at Zach and nod.

"I've had a long day," I say. I fish a hat from my jacket pocket and pull it over my head and ears.

"You shouldn't drive," Sondra says.

Zach jumps up and reaches for his jacket. "I'll give you a ride."

I shake my head and motion to the table. "You have full drinks and eggs to munch on," I say, waving them off. "Stay put. Get to know each other. I need to do some walking."

"It's freezing out," Sondra says. She stands to hug me and when I hold out my arms, she draws me close, rubbing my back. Then she pulls back and lifts my jacket hood over my head. "Bundle up," she says.

I smile at her. She might feel sorry for me right now. Or she might believe she has everything figured out. Maybe she does have everything figured out. But that's her life; it's not mine. And the way she's figured it out, I feel just as sorry for her.

Walking home, though, I can't seem to exorcise her words. They play loud and constant on a loop in my head. There is no PAUSE button, no volume control.

It's snowed since we've been in the pub, and flakes keep falling haphazardly. My footfalls against the concrete sidewalk are muffled, and they remind me of the night I first met Brad so long ago, back in Marquette. The me of that memory seems like a different person altogether, so carefree and certain that there were better days to come.

I walk past a house where someone has forgotten to draw the curtains, and inside I see a man about my age, a few pounds over chubby and wearing flannel pajamas, dancing around the living room with a baby who seems at a glance to be fighting sleep. Its little fists flail at his shoulders and the air. I stop and I stare, and I don't realize that there are tears in my eyes until they spill over, already almost frozen, and onto my cheeks.

I want that man to be Brad. I want that baby to be ours. I can see it clearly: a parallel universe in which that is Brad and I'm up in bed listening to him sway our child to sleep in our darkened living room while snow coats the world outside a striking white. And even as I see it, watch it so clearly, a part of me deep down recognizes that scene for what it is: a mirage.

I hardly remember much of the rest of my walk home, and by the time I reach my driveway, my fingers and toes and cheeks tingle and oh, how I love that feeling. I decided long ago that I would hate to live somewhere warm, where you can't test yourself against the elements like you can in the Midwest. Maybe I'm the only one, but I can't help feeling a sort of accomplishment on nights like tonight when it's cold and the easiest thing to do is to huddle inside, somewhere warm. But when you don't, when you head out into the cold and snow, sometimes you enjoy it. Sometimes it makes you feel more alive than much else probably could. And that's worth a whole lot of being comfortable.

As I climb the steps and fidget my key into the door, I notice a car parked half a block down, idling with its lights off. When I push the door open, the car's lights come on and it eases into the street. It turns the corner just shy of my house and speeds off. Just before it does, I catch sight of the license plate: Nwsom1.

Zach.

One of the good ones.

Twenty-three

The first major snowstorm of the year has picked tonight to hit the Midwest. I have the television on and I watch the hazy white mass on the weather map hover over the upper plains states like a poltergeist as I pack my bag for a short trip to Marquette—up today and back tomorrow—to see Brad.

I like to think that after having spent a handful of years living in Marquette, on the northernmost edge of Michigan's Upper Peninsula, I can handle any snowstorm. After all, Marquette gets upward of 150 inches of snow a year. It starts in October and sometimes keeps up until May, and if the people there were to let every storm dictate their day-to-day activities, they wouldn't leave the house for eight months of the year. After moving to Madison, I quickly learned that the amount of snow that would shut down that city might register only as "heavy flurries" in Marquette, and to take most of the storm warnings with a handful of salt.

But there is something about this particular storm that gives me pause—partially the temperatures hovering right around thirty-two degrees, which means the roads will be either wet or iced over, depending; and partially the fierce winds that are expected to pick up as the snow moves through the area, creating near whiteout conditions in spots according to the concerned meteorologist. Snow alone I can power through, but driving over intermittently icy roads with no visibility is not altogether unlike playing a game of vehicular Russian roulette.

For the better part of a moment I consider not going. But it has been exactly a week since I dropped off my husband to live indefinitely with his father, and today is his birthday.

I knew this storm was coming—it's been featured on every news and radio station for the past twenty-four hours—and a smarter person might have left yesterday. The idea of jumping in my car last night, though, after a full day of meetings and two court appearances, sent me straight to sleep. I lay down on the couch at seven p.m. and woke up this morning just as the sky started to lighten, still dressed in the suit I wore to work.

Over a breakfast of cereal and a diet cola, I sift through yesterday's mail: all junk, with the exception of my school loan payment and a second notice from the plumbing company I had to call when water started leaking out of the wall near the shower. It was a call I wouldn't have had to make had Brad been here, but the fact that I did have to has set us back nearly nine hundred dollars. It's a small company, though, and I know I can delay paying that bill much longer than I can my school loans or credit card payments. I am not proud of this strategy. I originally told myself that Brad was coming home, and would have a job soon. I figured incorrectly.

Not long after the sun has fully taken over, I'm on the road with a thermos of hot coffee in the cup holder and a cake from Brad's favorite bakery on the backseat. The miles, and with them, the hours, tick by, and I negotiate the route by rote. I pass through Iron Mountain, the border town just into Michigan that tells me my trip is nearly over—only an hour and a half to go—without even realizing that I drove through Green Bay. When Brad was arrested after the Margie Valhalla incident, I questioned how truthful he was being. How can a person forget doing something he was fully conscious for? Yet, I just did the same, and I don't have nearly as much on my mind as Brad does. The brain is a funny computer, a prankster.

All week, my brain has been playing with me—teasing me— recalling unbidden, again and again, the memory of Zach's hand resting on my leg.

Also unbidden is the way my stomach continues to flip at the thought of the warm, tingling sensation, the light weight of Zach's palm on my thigh, or the replay of the conversation among Sondra, Zach, and me at the Irish pub that same night that always follows. Sondra's words, especially, have formed a haunting chorus. Will I ever be happy with Brad again? Will I be able to stay with him and not resent him if, because he signed up for war on a whim, our home won't ever be safe enough for me to justify bringing a child into it? Brad and I were perfectly suited for each other. As clichéd as it sounds, there are no other words to say that I married my best friend, my soul mate. But I'm starting to wonder if the man I married didn't die in Iraq. Someone who looks a lot like him came back, but he's not my husband.

I tried calling Brad several times over the last two days, and each time I was put straight into voice mail. I try him again now, hoping to get him on the line, to suss out if he'll be home when I arrive. I'm greeted by his recorded voice. Again.

I imagine that he forgot to charge his phone, which he's prone to doing, and I try to stop imagining other, less innocuous, scenarios that might explain why I can't reach him.

But when I let myself into Mert's house, it's quiet and empty, and Brad's phone is on the kitchen counter, plugged into the charger.

· · ·

I'm no good at waiting, so I rattle around the house, picking up the living room, folding blankets and corralling weeks' worth of the *Mining Journal*, the local source of news, into a sensible pile, and straightening the kitchen. I clean out the refrigerator, tossing bottles of salad dressing and condiments that have lived half a decade beyond their expiration dates. I wipe down refrigerator shelves and drawers with soapy water and then hand dry them. I vacuum and dust and change the bedding in Brad's room. And then I run out of things to clean.

The house makes a noise like settling, and I jump. It's far too quiet in here.

I sit down at the kitchen table and twiddle my thumbs. Relaxation doesn't come easily to me, and although I'd like to be the kind of person who reads books or knits or even naps, I fear I don't have it in me. Every time I try, the exercise lasts only a few handfuls of minutes, and it's like enduring torture instead of enjoying myself. I need motion and purpose to suppress the thoughts that tend to multiply like water-soaked Mogwai. Right now I don't have either.

The front door opens and I jump again. It's Mert.

"Hiya, Princess. He's not here." Mert opens the refrigerator, pulls out a can of beer, and pops it open. I stem the incredulity I feel bubbling up at the fact that it's barely noon and to my knowledge, no one here is on vacation. Then again, this is the person I handpicked as my husband's caretaker. Perhaps my incredulity is misplaced.

"Do you know where he is?" I ask.

Mert walks past me and into the living room, where he turns on the television and tunes it to a Red Wings game in progress.

"Mert?"

He either hasn't heard me or is ignoring me. If I were a betting person, I'd go with the latter. He's yelling at the television now, "Let's go, boys! Get it down the ice!"

"Mert!"

No response. I march over to him, grab the remote, and turn off the television.

"Hey!" Mert yells. "What the—"

I sit on top of the coffee table across from him, among a scattering of ash trays I emptied and just now, wish I also scrubbed down.

"Mert, where is Brad?"

"I'm not his keeper, Princess."

"Come on, Mert," I say. "I'm trying to surprise him for his birthday. You did remember it was his birthday, right?"

"Didn't forget," Mert says. "Just haven't seen him."

A thought occurs to me: What if Mert knows exactly where Brad is and doesn't want to say? What if Brad ran into an old girlfriend he's taken to seeing?

"Is there something you're not telling me?" I ask. I hate the way I sound—needy and suspicious. I don't want to be like that, to feel this way. I hear my mom's voice saying, "You feel how you feel; it's not right or wrong, Leesy," which is what she'd say to me when I told her I didn't want to be scared of the dark.

Mert exhales long and slow. He runs a hand through the mess of gray hair covering his head. He shakes his head, smiling. "For Pete's sake, Princess. He went for a hike yesterday. I don't know where he is right this minute, but I'm sure he's around somewhere. Now can you turn that game back on?"

"Where did he go?"

Mert shrugs, then rolls his eyes as if the answer is to be found somewhere on the ceiling or his forehead. "Dunno," he says. "Hogsback?"

"He went hiking yesterday, and you haven't seen him since then? And you didn't think to go looking for him?"

"Boy's a Marine," Mert says, holding his hand out for the remote. "That's what they train 'em for—to handle the elements and all that."

"He was in the Army, Mert. The fucking Army." I shake my head and toss the remote in Mert's lap as I walk out of the living room and out of the house.

My mind is racing. I can envision Brad out in the woods somewhere, contemplating leaving me again. And in those horrific pictures that cycle through my head, the trigger has already been pulled, the pills swallowed, the noose made taut. In each one, I'm already too late.

I should have been more concerned when I couldn't reach him. I should have called Mert to sound the alarm. But I assumed he was simply angry with me for bringing him up here, and then there was the promise, the only thing Brad asked of me—not to tell anyone what had almost happened. So there was no way for Mert to ever know he should be worried about Brad going out hiking, or not coming back.

Luckily, a bag with boots and snowshoes, winter pants and a vest, and hats and mittens is in my trunk. This is less a result of a Girl Scout level of preparedness and more because I ran out of storage room when we moved into our house. I kept all of this temporarily in my trunk, and temporary turned into permanent residence. I rationalized that it made sense to store these things in my car, that they would come in useful in a roadside emergency. I was thinking of being stuck in a ditch in the dead of winter, not launching a one-person search party for my husband. Regardless, I'm glad it's all with me.

I swap my jeans and sweater for leggings and snow pants, a fleece zip-up, and a vest. I dig out the CamelBak I keep filled with water, and I lace up my Sorels. Then I grab my snowshoes and set out toward an unmarked trail a few hundred feet up the road that will lead me toward Hogsback Mountain.

Although Marquette and its surrounding wilderness are by no means the last frontier, it can get desolate and dangerous up here relatively quickly, and my footsteps speed up as I think of all the other scenarios that could have befallen Brad. Each winter, news reports abound of people falling off trails that they didn't know ended at a cliff or breaking a limb and freezing to death before being found.

There is only one real trailhead to Hogsback and it's unmarked. This is a place the locals like to keep to themselves, unlike Sugarloaf Mountain just down the road, which has a giant parking lot, marked trails with swarms of people hiking them, and at certain points, boardwalks and steps leading to the summit. At Hogsback, you might run across another hiker only once every ten times you go.

Some of the trails here are trails. Others simply resemble trails— paths, beaten down by deer, that end abruptly. And whereas its cousin-mountain, Sugarloaf, makes you climb immediately, always pointing you up, and is flanked on the back side by a cliff that drops into Lake Superior, Hogsback takes its sweet time rising from the landscape, almost all of its six hundred feet of elevation coming in the last quarter of the hike to the summit. This means that a huge expanse lolls gently around the peak in every single direction, and it's unnervingly easy to get turned around—something I've fallen prey to more than once in the past.

What this means, also, is that there is far more searchable area than I can cover. At Hogsback, you're only relegated to certain routes in that last six hundred feet or so. Down here, just off the trailhead? You can take your pick.

I'd forgotten this quality of Hogsback, and recognizing the enormity of the task I've set myself is like being jolted awake. I scan the landscape around me, three hundred and sixty-five degrees of it. It's barely a fraction of the area a person could hike here.

Brad, I realize, could be absolutely anywhere.

With a handful of hours of daylight left, there is no way I can do an effective search. But I have to do something. My other option is to hike back to Mert's to watch the Red Wings and slowly lose my mind with each *thwap* of the cards he deals himself.

I walk without real purpose toward the base of the mountain and call out to my husband. "Brad! Bra-ad!" The wind grabs these words from my mouth and silences them, but I keep going, one foot in front of the other. I keep calling out.

I hike around the north side of Hogsback, calling Brad's name. Each step brings a different sort of panic—what if I'm out here in the middle of nowhere looking for Brad when he's somewhere else entirely? What if he is out here and I don't scan the area closely enough? What if he's too tired or weak or injured to cry out? What will I do if I find his body? What will I do if I don't?

I sit on a downed tree to think. I strain my ear toward every call of a bird, every creek and groan of a tree, every whistle of wind, thinking that it might be Brad. It never is. It's nearly dusk, which means I'm running out of time.

Or—the thought occurs to me—maybe not. If Brad is out here, if he's conscious and wanting to be found, it could actually be easier to find him at night. He'll be able to see the beam of my headlamp dancing through the trees. Maybe he'll be able to signal, and if he has a flashlight or is able to make a fire, that's something easily seen in the dark. I decide to hike back to Mert's, find Brad's brother, Rick, and anyone else he can muster, and head back out when night falls. By the time I reach Mert's and unstrap my snowshoes, I'm practically giddy over the brilliance of my plan.

That giddiness is quickly replaced by dread, when I return to an empty house. I don't know Rick's phone number, and the line to his repair shop rings and rings. Mert doesn't believe in cell phones. I told him once that cell phones are not like God or ghosts; you don't get to say you "don't believe" in them. "Well, I think they're stupid," Mert said. "Why would I want someone to be able to call me anywhere when I don't even like being called here, in my house? That specific enough for ya, Princess?"

My stomach feels like it's mutining on itself, and I realize that I've had nothing to eat since the skimpy bowl of cereal I poured for myself early this morning. I eye the cake on the table. I thought by now we'd all be long finished with dinner, probably burgers or brats on the grill, and would be well on to serenading Brad with "Happy Birthday" and cutting the cake. Instead, I force myself to scrounge Mert's cabinets for some other source of sustenance. I produce bread and peanut butter and make myself a sandwich. And not knowing what else to do, I take up residence with my sandwich on the old metal glider on Mert's porch.

I watch and wait. Wait and watch. For what, I'm not sure. A call, a cry in the night? A thin column of smoke dancing up to meet the sky? I don't want to leave, just in case, though I question how much good it is to sit sentry. Every time I see headlights pass through the trees from cars traveling County Road 550, I strain, listening for the crunch of tires coming up Mert's driveway. But the whoosh of tires against wet asphalt always continues past.

It's nearly pitch-dark when I hear a different kind of crunch—that of a footfall on snow—coming out of the north tree line. I squint, studying the dark, and trying to keep my expectations in check. After all, it could easily be whitetail deer, as prevalent as mosquitoes in these parts, or something smaller like a fox or raccoon. But the image that emerges is one of a person, bulky on top. Carrying something, perhaps. And as that image crystallizes, I recognize the general shape of the person—height and weight and carriage—to be Brad.

I jump off the glider and race across the yard, calling my husband's name. I am not a religious person, but with each footfall, I thank God over and over and over again.

As I near, I can see a dog in Brad's arms. Mangy and tough-looking, it's covered in blood and scrapes, but I don't care. A tsunami of relief that my husband just walked out of the woods on his own volition crashes over me and I go to throw my arms around him, dog and all.

I'm stopped in my tracks by a stern, concentrated growl coming from the animal in Brad's arms. Its lip curls up to reveal white teeth that shine like little blades against the night.

"We need to get her some help," Brad says. "Do you have your car here?"

I nod, afraid to move any other part of my body. It dawns on me that my husband hasn't asked why I'm here, or when I arrived, and he hasn't offered up what he's been doing in the woods for two days or how he came to carry out of those woods a wounded dog that seems to take an instant dislike to me.

"We're going to need some rags and a blanket," Brad says, moving toward the house.

I trail after him. "Do you know how long I've been looking for you?" I yell at him. "Do you have any idea?"

He levels a serious look at me. "Not now, okay?"

I let loose an exasperated grunt and follow him inside the house. He pushes the cake aside with an elbow and sets the dog next to it on the kitchen table. "Watch her," he says to me. Then he goes rummaging through the hallway closet.

The dog smells unholy. It reeks of blood and wet and rot. I cover my nose with the back of my hand, trying not to gag and failing.

Brad returns with an old sleeping bag and shoves it at me. "Here," he says. "Lay this out for me. I'm going to lift her onto it."

I do as I'm told and Brad eases the dog onto the blanket. The animal is nondescript: neither short- nor long-haired, mousy brown, and medium build—maybe fifty pounds or so. Its ears start out sticking up from its head and then fold over. It has a black nose, black-tipped paws, and a white patch on its chest. It looks like a pit bull but not a pure one—its tail is longer, like a Labrador retriever's, and it seems less boxy than the pit bulls I've seen, though that's only on some reality television show about pit bulls and felons; I've never encountered one in person. It might be all pit bull, or it might be mixed with poodle for all I know.

"Run some warm water in the sink, will you?" Brad says, and I oblige this request as well.

I watch as Brad leans down to talk sweetly to the dog, petting its head and stroking its ears. It looks like those dogs on the ASPCA commercials, with the kind of eyes that tell you in no uncertain terms that the creature gave up long ago.

Brad goes back to the closet and appears this time with a fistful of sheet remnants.

"What happened?" I ask him.

"No idea," Brad says.

"So you found it like this?"

Brad smiles. "No," he says. "*She* sort of found me." And then he does something that nearly makes me heave: He leans down and kisses the mangy dog on its mangy snout. The dog closes its eyes.

"She?" I ask. For whatever reason, it's almost impossible for me to think of this animal as a she. Its deplorable condition has seemed to strip any sense of femininity from it, if dogs have such a thing in the first place.

"Jones," Brad says, beaming at me like a proud father.

"But it's a she?" I ask.

"I didn't know it was a she when I named her," he explains. "I was sitting there, in the snow, halfway up Hogsback, and she just wandered up to me out of nowhere, like a ghost."

Brad leans down and buries his face in the dog's scruff. He kisses her ears and her muzzle. It is not lost on me that this is more genuine affection than he's shown me in months.

I take care of calling the veterinarian. I get a recorded message that tells me to call the emergency pager and leave my telephone number. A woman who sounds younger than I do and calls herself Dr. Dickinson—which seems overly formal for a Saturday evening—phones back and asks us to meet her at the office in fifteen minutes. I jot down directions, thank her, and hang up.

"We need to get her into my car," I tell Brad.

Brad starts to form a tight swaddle around the dog. Her eyes follow him, lock on him. If I didn't know better, I would think she trusts him implicitly. When I approach the table to try to help, she bares her teeth at me again, letting loose another low growl. I back away.

I gather my jacket and gloves, and thinking that even if the dog can be saved, it might take a while, I grab my laptop bag as well.

I get in the car and Brad is in the backseat. Jones's head is in his lap. He's cooing to her: "Everything's going to be okay, little girl. We're going to fix you up, good as new. You just hang on. You fight for me, okay?"

I look at the empty passenger seat beside me and can't help but wonder who's going to fight for me. When do I get a turn?

Twenty-four

The veterinarian office is the kind of quiet I haven't experienced in some time. There are no outside sounds—no whirring of machinery or even blowing of heated air through vents. Now and then I can hear Dr. Dickinson moving around in the back room, but out here in the waiting area, it is just Brad and I and our breathing. Brad has leaned his head against the wall and his eyes are closed. When we sat down, he chose to put a chair between us. I wonder if he wanted a more complete view of the room or not to be near me. It's a question to which I can't provide so much as an educated guess.

I am more than tired. I am weary, too. And so I slide over, next to Brad, and lean my head on his shoulder.

I don't know how long I am asleep, but I wake to Dr. Dickinson telling Brad that she was able to stabilize the dog and clean her wounds, but she wants to open her up to check for internal bleeding.

"What are the chances?" Brad asks.

"Hard to say," she says. "But from the looks of her, she's clearly been used for fighting. Who knows what other injuries she might have unless we go in and take a look."

"How much?" I ask.

"How much internal damage?" the veterinarian asks.

"No, how much will the operation cost?" I say.

"Oh," Dr. Dickinson says. "Right. Sorry. It's hard to know, but I would say you're looking at anywhere from one thousand to three thousand dollars, depending. I can work up a detailed estimate for you if you'd like."

I shake my head and turn to Brad. "No. We can't. We can't afford it."

Brad stares at me. "What? Are you serious?"

"As a heart attack, babe. I just had to put more than a grand into my car. The furnace needs to be replaced, and I still haven't paid the plumber." Darcy told me that we were crazy to buy the house we did—at the top end of our price range and with a whole host of problems that I waved off because I had been taken with its charm— the built-in china cabinets in each corner of the dining room, the old stone fireplace in the living room—details that seem so ridiculous now. I only wish I had listened to her. But I didn't, and we really can't afford the care for this dog. "We're out of money, Brad. We can't."

"We have to," he says. "We don't have a choice."

I want so badly for Brad to meet me halfway on this. For him to step up and be an adult. To understand that there's a hierarchy of needs, and this dog, although it's sad and unfortunate, ranks near or at the bottom. But Brad's injuries, it seems, have largely robbed him of that discernment. Instead, I am his executive function, his bookkeeper, his parent. And his wife. Always, it seems, in that order. Angry tears teeter on the edge of my eyes.

Dr. Dickinson looks as though she's watching a tennis match, her head twisting between Brad and me. "I have a few more things I can finish up," she says. "Why don't I give you a few minutes?"

I look at Brad and he stares right back at me. His arms are crossed and I find myself crossing mine as well. "I'm not doing this, Brad. It isn't up for debate. It's just a dog. We'll get you a different one."

"That," he says, his voice quivering, "is not just a dog. Plus, you hate dogs. You wouldn't ever let me get one if I start to live with you again."

I don't understand the attachment Brad has formed to Jones in the hours that he's been gone. Sometimes it's hard to keep up with which Brad I'm dealing with—the TBI-injured, childlike one or this new, caustic, and still-sharp-as-tacks adult. Because he's right. Dogs are dirty and messy. Pets, in any form, make absolutely no sense to me. They require a constant and unrelenting upkeep I can't imagine dedicating myself to willingly. I've made the mistake of mentioning this in the past. I was hoping Brad might have forgotten, that maybe a small portion of his long-term memory pertinent to this very subject might have been wiped out by that IED blast. Apparently I am to have no such luck.

"Where else would you live?" I ask him.

He shrugs. "You tell me," he says, and I wonder if he knows how close to home he's hit, if he knows I've been thinking of leaving him.

I inhale a deep breath, hold it, and breathe out. "I'm going to get some fresh air before I say something I'm going to regret," I say.

I turn and walk out, and Brad doesn't say a word. He doesn't attempt to stop me. And when I complete an out-and-back loop down the road and try to reenter the vet's office, I find out why: He has locked me out, and locked in my wallet holding our emergency credit card.

The final bill comes to $1,080.22. The drive back to Mert's house goes the same as the drive to the vet's office, with me driving and Brad sitting in back with the dog. Jones's head is in Brad's lap and he's talking softly to her, but she's still snowed by the anesthesia and painkillers and seems to be fast asleep.

For all her injuries, the dog, at least at first glance, seems to be in pretty good shape. Dr. Dickinson said she didn't find any internal damage, and that the wounds covering her face and legs—even the ones that needed row after row of stitches—should heal quickly. She is to be kept quiet—no playing fetch, if she even does that sort of thing—for seven to ten days, but otherwise her prognosis is good.

I look at Brad in the rearview mirror. "We need to let the Humane Society know," I say.

"No," Brad says, not meeting my eyes in the mirror.

I check the road ahead and then the mirror again. "Come on, Brad," I say. "This might be someone's pet. She could have run away and gotten those injuries. Maybe she was just *in* a fight and not *used* for fighting. What if some little kid is missing her?"

I'd be lying if I said I'm not hoping against all hope that the dog will turn out to have wonderful owners who love her so much that they will, in turn, reimburse us the money we've sunk into her out of sheer gratitude for saving her life.

"No!" Brad says, and slams a fist against the back of my headrest. I hear the loud slap his hand makes against the vinyl and I feel my seat lurch forward. It's hard to tell if I jump out of surprise or if I am jarred by the indirect action of my husband's fist.

This is not what I had in mind when I set out for Marquette this morning. I realize I haven't yet wished Brad a happy birthday, but I'm not feeling altogether charitable at the moment. I daydream of pulling into Mert's, dropping Brad and his prized dog off, and wishing them all a great goddamn life before I peel out of there and back to Madison.

Mert is waiting for us on the porch. I park and get out, slamming the car door. I head toward the house. Brad can handle the dog.

"Where were you?" Mert says, looking between us.

"Ask your son," I say to Mert, walking past him.

"What is *that*?" Mert asks, referencing the bundle in Brad's arms.

"Her name is Jones, Dad," he says, walking behind me toward the house. He sounds like a proud parent introducing his new baby to the neighbors.

"I don't care what her name is," Mert says. "You're not bringing that thing in my house. She stays in the barn."

The barn is a dilapidated wooden structure that used to house a cow or horse or two. In it are a stall and a few stanchions on the lower level, which is built into a hill, and a hayloft above that's actually at ground level. But that's approximately where its resemblance to an actual barn, as opposed to an overgrown shack, ends. Now it's filled with Mert's tools, an old bike or two, parts of deconstructed cars, and furniture that Brad's mom couldn't bear to part with when she was alive and Mert can't bear to part with now that she's not.

"But Dad—" I can hear Brad arguing from the porch as I shut the door to the house behind me. I agree with him. The barn is no place for a healthy dog, much less a sick one. But at this point, that's far outside the bounds of my current concerns or cares.

I go upstairs to Brad's room and haul the nest he made on the floor down to the washing machine in the basement. A part of me wants to know what is going on with my husband, what he was doing out in the woods for days. But a larger part of me wants—needs—to connect with my husband. I need to know we *can* connect. Otherwise, what am I doing here? What are we doing together? And if we can't connect on his birthday, when can we?

I find clean linens in the hallway closet and as I float and stretch them over the bed, I ignore the thought that this is a fruitless effort—the sheets and blankets will be in a heap on the floor before morning. While I work, I try to calm myself, to put things into perspective. I'll go downstairs and we'll have cake. I'll light candles. We'll sing to my husband and celebrate the fact that he's still here, that he didn't do anything irreparably rash. And maybe we'll end the night by sitting on the glider on the porch, shoulder to shoulder, letting our breath escape in wisps from our lips, heating the night around us.

I take a shower and dress in a fresh pair of jeans and a sweater. I put on a little makeup. I take my time, because we have time. We've been given that much. That gift.

But downstairs, the cake has already been cut, Mert is asleep in his armchair in front of a blaring television, and Brad, once again, is nowhere to be found.

Instinctively, I head toward the barn.

The barn air feels colder than the air outside and it takes my eyes a moment to adjust to the dark. As soon as they do, though, I see a misshapen lump covered by an old sleeping bag in the far corner, tucked in among disintegrating bales of hay.

"Brad?" I say, though I know it's him.

He stirs, as does the lump next to him, curled inside the comma of Brad's body. Jones.

She pokes her head from the blanket and twists it at an unnatural angle, licking at my husband's face.

My husband is lying in a drafty, dirty old barn with a mangy dog instead of in bed—or in the same room at least—with me. The hot tears that smart in my eyes surprise me, as does the sudden surge of anger that swells inside me. *He's safe*, I keep repeating to myself, but it does no good. The swell crashes over me, pinning me in its undertow.

And then I start to cry.

Brad is sitting up now, and I want more than anything for him to stand up and come to me and wrap me in his arms. I need him to do this. Because it will prove that he still loves me. It will prove that he wants to fight for me. For us. It will give *me* something to fight for.

But Brad doesn't get up. His face makes its own shadows and I brace for an outburst from him. Jones, however, apparently has no situational awareness—or the situational awareness typical for a dog. She sits up next to Brad, puts a paw on each of his shoulders, and begins to wash his face with her tongue. His face relaxes, and he buries it in the furry scruff of her neck.

Over the years, I watched several friends' relationships dissolve over infidelity. I saw the anguish they endured after discovering each dalliance. I tried to imagine what I would do if I discovered another woman in Brad's life. I tried to put myself in their places, to feel what they must be feeling. Yet I could never quite get there. I could never seem to adequately contemplate what it would be like to be them.

And here, just standing in this dank barn, I suddenly know. I feel those pangs. I never imagined that the other woman I'd lose my husband to would turn out to be a goddamn dog.

I walk back to the house and up to Brad's room. I peel off my clothes, find a T-shirt of Brad's that's big even for him and a pair of boxers from his dresser, and crawl between the cool sheets. I'm asleep within minutes. The next morning, I wake alone. Brad is still in the barn with Jones, I presume. After a breakfast of birthday cake that I eat off a paper towel while standing over the sink, I'm on the road back to Madison before anyone else has even stirred.

Twenty-five

The college girls of UW-Madison are fully embracing spring today—or, from the looks of it, late summer. The mercury hasn't inched much above fifty degrees and we're not quite into April, but outside my office window they're running and walking every which way in Lycra hip huggers and tank tops. If this is the dress code for these temperatures, I worry that by the time hotter weather rolls around, they'll have left themselves no choice but to go naked.

And while all of Madison seems to be waking up from its winter slumber, I've been hibernating here at Early, Janssen, and Bradenton.

Brad's being gone has freed me to be the kind of lawyer I thought I was when I first took this job. And so, after I returned from Marquette, I disappeared into the bowels of the firm—into the file room, which is not really a room at all but one, long expanse of metal shelves stretching from one end of the building to another. I took with me a long list of cases—nearly twenty in all—that are similar to *Rowland*: wrongful death suits against companies or corporations. I pulled file after file, dissected them, and came up with a comprehensive list of what we'll need for trial.

For two full weeks, I have put out of my mind everything except

Rowland and my job. I spend my days putting together trial binders: contact information for key witnesses and the defense's legal team, an outline of the opening statement, direct and cross-examination questions, the police report, answers to interrogatories, responses to requests for production of documents and deposition summaries, relevant case law, the burden-of-proof chart detailing everything that we need to prove at trial and the mechanism of proof, and experts' CVs, subpoenas, and designations. In three separate binders, I assemble all of the discovery documents, the depositions in full, and all of the pleadings related to the case. Unlike those who prepared a lot of the trial notebooks shelved in the basement, I take care to type up labels instead of hand writing them and I use tabbed inserts instead of sticky notes. I want us to put the very best foot forward in court. And while a clean binder might go unnoticed by our clients, the jury, Judge Cianflone, or opposing counsel, a messy and disorganized binder might make us look the same way, casting aspersions on our abilities.

I subsist on coffee and meal-replacement shakes and energy bars. When I wake in the morning, my toothbrush is still wet and I see the same security guard at the office's front desk as when I left only a handful of hours before. Some nights, instead of going home, I pull two armchairs in my office together to form a tiny makeshift bed and ball up my jacket as a pillow. Other nights I curl up on the floor in the glow of the moon reflected off the Capitol dome. I lose track of hours and days, alerted to their passing only by external cues like the appearance and then disappearance of the lunch carts on the square or the ringing of bells for Sunday services at St. Patrick's.

I decide to try to reach Brad for the first time on a Sunday night. I know this because St. Patrick's bells rang both yesterday at five o'clock and this morning at seven. It's been weeks since I've heard his voice, and I miss it. I miss it in a different way than when I was waiting for him to come home. That was pure longing—longing tinged with the faith of better days to come. This is a hard ache, deep down inside me like a calcified organ.

I've tried hard, these weeks, to give Brad as little thought as possible. I tell myself repeatedly that I've been released from the weight of monitoring him, caring for him, anticipating his blowups and his needs. If I want to be, I'm free. But with that kind of freedom comes all sorts of choices and decisions I'm not ready for, and so it's easier not to think about it. It's easier to think about work. It's easier yet not to think at all.

But thoughts of Brad aren't so easily eradicated. I will be ear-deep in *Rowland*, poring over case law or summarizing depositions or writing briefs, and they just show up, fully formed: silent imaginings playing against the dark walls of my head—of Brad and me pushing a stroller around Capitol Square early on farmers' market Saturdays as the farmers are just setting up, picking out rhubarb, then all different colors of wax beans, and finally, toward fall, bags full of tomatoes for canning and basil for making pesto; smiling at each other, exhausted but so content, at three a.m. when the baby won't go back to sleep; juggling day care drop-off and pickup; scrambling madly each weeknight to get through dinner, bath, and bedtime routines and then sleeping in, three of us to a bed, on Saturday mornings; and later, attending PTA meetings and soccer games. Our lives one long, crazy-but-delightful scheduling exercise until the day sneaks up on us when it's suddenly time to take our child off to college, when we wave goodbye and drive away, teary eyed and astonished that it's all flown by so quickly.

That was how things were supposed to go.

That is not the direction in which Brad and I are now headed. Instead, we are throttling full speed into an entirely different future.

There is no cure for Brad's injuries. They are conditions not unlike building a house on a flood plain: You can try to sandbag and build levees, but now and again, the waters will inevitably rise and spill over; you can try to rebuild and remodel and readjust, but those foundations will never be quite secure.

And so, we're stuck in this stalemate. Brad hasn't called me, and although I pull out my phone and contemplate calling him several times a day, I haven't actually dialed his number. We both seem unwilling to make the hard decisions that need to be made.

When I put the finishing touches on the very last trial binder, it is dark and late enough that there isn't a single soul rambling around the square below my office window. I check my phone to see if I missed a call, even though I know I haven't. It is 3:45 in the morning and I'm bone-tired. The thought of trekking to my house, a little more than a mile away, and working through my bedtime routine of taking vitamins, brushing my teeth, washing my face, and applying moisturizer feels wholly overwhelming. There's a black sweater in my car that I can slip on in the morning to make it look like I've bothered to change outfits, so I curl up under my desk with my coat balled into a pillow. And I think to myself that maybe Brad and I aren't so different after all.

The next afternoon, proud of the hard work I've put in the past handful of days, I shut down my computer for the first time in weeks, fish my coat from under my desk where it was still stashed from the night before, and pack up my laptop and printouts of the two research requests received from Early and Janssen earlier today, to work on at home. I check my phone as I walk out of my office. It is 4:55 p.m. I don't have one missed call, not one voice mail message.

Through the windows of Early, Janssen, and Bradenton, the sky is still a pale blue. It looks warm. Maybe I'll go for a run when I get home.

I am almost to the firm's reception area when Susan emerges abruptly from the office of one of the senior associates and I nearly run into her.

"I'm so sorry, Susan," I say. "I should look where I'm going." Actually, it was she who should have checked to see that the hallway was clear, but it seems like the right thing to say to a partner. Susan doesn't flinch. She doesn't say a word. She looks me up and down, and then back up again for good measure.

"Headed home?" she asks. The question comes out as a sneer.

If there's an easy, obvious lie to tell about why I have my jacket on, briefcase slung over my shoulder, and car keys in hand, it doesn't come to me.

"I—I—," I stammer, thinking of what to say. In any other profession, in other law firms even, leaving work at five o'clock on a Friday would be considered normal, not "already." Early, Janssen, and Bradenton, LLC, though, is a big, meat grinder of a place that thinks highly of itself for giving people the opportunity to work there as opposed to being thankful that it attracts talented, driven people who are willing to do outstanding work around the clock. I remember, as a summer intern, listening to Crane Early complain for weeks that he had "let" one of the junior associates have a Friday and then an "entire weekend" off for her own wedding. At the time, I dismissed it as a row or personality conflict, an isolated situation. I should have seen it for what it was: standard and accepted company practice.

"I've been sleeping here," I squeak. Then I force myself to sound more assertive. "I've been doing trial prep. I've taken it as far as I can until you're both able to give me some feedback on it."

Susan actually rolls her eyes. "Of course you have," she says. "You're on your first big litigation case. I hope you would be. But there's always more work to do."

Susan is a slight woman, shorter and more petite than I am, but you never notice it because she has the uncanny ability to make you feel mere inches tall. I am not easily intimidated or scared off, even by Early and Janssen, but with her sharp tongue, moods that change with a shift in the wind, and beady glare, Susan often terrifies me.

"I'm sorry," I mumble, because I'm not sure what else to say. I am, after all, an adult. The firm contracts with me to do work for it, but it doesn't own me—technically speaking, of course. Susan shakes her head, biting the edge of her lip. It's a disgusted look if I ever saw one.

Then I see what she is holding in her hand along with a manila file folder: last month's billable report, nicknamed "the Rainmaker," which breaks down by attorney, division, and case the hours billed and hours worked, and how much money each attorney has made the firm that month. I haven't seen a copy yet—partners are the very first to receive them—but considering everything that's been going on with Brad for the past couple of months, I don't need to see the report to know what my numbers must look like. Had Susan felt inclined to show me the report, I'd half expect to find a little picture of a desert where my effective rate should be.

I'm not sure how to break out of this little scrum of ours in the hallway. I could ask Susan if there's anything she needs help finishing and tell her I'll do the same with Gordon and Crane, but I'm afraid all that will earn me is a snide look or comment instead of a clear answer as to how she'd prefer I proceed. Or, I could apologize once again and provide an excuse of somewhere I need to be—a dentist or doctor appointment, an outside meeting or board obligation, dinner, or, more plainly, anywhere but here.

And that's precisely when my phone rings. I reach into my bag, pull it out, and see that it's Brad. Or, it's someone calling from a 906 area code—Michigan's Upper Peninsula.

"I'm sorry," I say again. "I need to take this."

As she walks past me, Susan says, "If you managed your professional life as vigilantly as your personal life, you'd be one hell of an attorney, Counselor."

By the time I'm able to answer my phone, it's stopped ringing. And by the time I make it down the elevator to where I get enough reception to call back out, all the phone on the other end does is ring in response.

Twenty-six

As I leave the office, every last nerve in me is on edge.

I started out wanting to be a lawyer because, as a newly orphaned adult, it seemed to offer the best combination of good-paying and interesting work that could, as my mom used to like to say, support me "in the manner to which I have become accustomed." This always made me laugh, because as the daughter of a line worker and a teacher, I hadn't become accustomed to much more than a safe place to live and a new outfit from JCPenney at the start of every school year. I knew that was much more than a lot of other kids in southern Michigan had, but it was still a far cry from a car on my sixteenth birthday or a trust fund set up in my name.

I liked law school well enough (as much as one can like law school) and even my first year at Early, Janssen, and Bradenton. But something has started to change. Now I'm unsure I want Susan's job, and I'm doubly unsure I really want to turn into someone like Susan.

Added to that professional doubt is a future with Brad that's blurry with uncertainty—all of which equals an Elise who is in desperate need of someone to lean on. So I stop at the store just off Capitol Square that specializes in coffee, wine, and chocolate, and I pick out a gourmet candy bar with bacon in it and a highly recommended bottle of cabernet—Darcy's favorite. It's a peace offering of sorts, given that we haven't talked in weeks and haven't seen each other in twice that time.

Darcy's porch light is on and I can see her moving around, a shadow beyond the curtains, as I park in front of her house. Normally I'd walk right up to the door, rap twice, and open it, but I'm out of the routine of coming here. I've been wallowing in my own life, too taxed to take on the problems of someone else's. But as Darcy opens the door, I wish I had set aside a handful of minutes here or there to check in on her. She looks thin and drawn and tired.

She waves me in and asks if I'd like anything. I hold up the bottle of cabernet and the bar of chocolate. "You're a lifesaver," she says, but she doesn't seem to mean it, and I don't believe it, either. One look at Darcy and I feel guilty for coming here to dump my problems onto her, rather than out of concern for her or a pure need to spend time with my friend.

I settle in on the couch as Darcy opens the wine and brings two glasses—mine poured about half as full because she knows it's not really my thing, but that I like to have whatever she's having.

"It got cold out there," she says.

"It was nice before, but yeah, as soon as that sun went down," I say, fake shivering and rubbing each hand on the opposite shoulder. We chat about Mia and how big she's getting and what she does and says now, because it changes by the day. We discuss Darcy's plans to return to teaching in the fall, and the summer trip her whole extended family is taking to Florida. Our stilted conversation strikes me as ridiculous—probably it does Darcy, too. We're out of practice with each other and it shows. But it's like wading into cold water: No one wants the shock that comes with a sudden dunk. Instead, you insert a toe, then a foot, and then let the rest of the leg and torso follow slowly behind.

So that is what we do. After a while, Darcy asks me how work is going. It's a generic, predictable, ace-in-the-hole question. Any other night I'd say that it was fine, that it's keeping me busy, or I'd supply some other rote response.

"I don't know if I can do this, Darce," I say, and to my surprise, I have a sudden urge to cry. My eyes well. I bite my lip to stop them from spilling over.

"Your job?"

I shrug. "Everything, I guess. My job. My life."

I don't know how to come out and reveal what's ricocheting around inside me—all of the thoughts and feelings and second guesses—to Darcy. She doesn't know how scary it is when Brad goes a million miles away and leaves his body here with those black, black eyes. She can't know how it feels to have to tell myself, "He didn't mean it," after he clocks me in the face when I startle him awake; and how saying it doesn't make it all hurt any less. Or how it feels to have sent the man I loved off to war, only to have a different one returned to me. And sitting here, I realize that I can't tell her. For Darcy, even eyes like tar would be better than ones made only of memory. Arms of flesh and bone are easier to wrestle than a ghost's.

"Why? What's wrong?"

I am the wife of a man who went off to war and never came back, I want to tell her. *I am, more or less, just like you—something like a widow.* But looking at Darcy—at the circles under her eyes and the lip that quivers now and then—I know that I am not that, either. I am not a wife, and I am not a widow. And I'm not sure how to play the role in between. That's what's wrong.

Darcy isn't strident with me. She's not accusatory. She just doesn't understand. She can't. From her vantage point, I have a great job, a flesh-and-blood husband, and a future full of possibility. Darcy's own future is chock-full of what-might-have-beens.

So I push everything back down inside and cork it. "No, it's fine," I say, brushing my original volley aside. "Just a bad day at the dough-nut factory is all."

"Everyone has 'em," Darcy says.

I nod. I sip my wine. I think of Susan's cutting comments and Brad curled up with a dog on the floor of his dad's barn, sleeping closer than he has to me in months.

"Everyone does," I say.

"Hey," she says, "how's Brad doing?"

I fix her with a smile. "Oh, he's doing great," I say. "Really good." Because this is what she needs to hear.

The next day, at the weekly status meeting, the partners direct all of their questions on *Rowland* to Susan and Zach while I follow their exchange across the conference table and back like a Ping-Pong match. Zach doesn't even try to loop me into the briefing. Based on a few Fridays I've taken off and a couple months of subpar Rainmakers, it's as though they've already determined that I'm not partner quality. I am as invisible as air.

But I'm the one who has slept, eaten, and breathed *Rowland v. Champion Construction* for the past few weeks. Even if I didn't be-fore, I now know this case better than anyone in this room—perhaps better than anyone in this room and the conference room for the op-posing counsel combined. Nicky Rowland's medical history? That's in the red binder. The history of Champion Construction's inspection violations? Black binder, Tab F. Motion in limine? Blue binder, Tab C. I have even gone so far as to treat Judge Cianflone's law clerk to lunch on my own dime in order to get a read on the propensities, peccadil-loes, and disposition we'll be dealing with in court, and I typed that up, along with summaries and verdicts of similar cases he's heard, into a comprehensive, ten-page memo. All that, and I might as well not even be sitting here.

"What about summary judgment?" Crane Early asks Zach.

Zach starts to talk, but I jump in. "Actually," I say, "we do have a motion on that prepared. I think it's at least worth submitting."

The three partners and Zach all turn to stare at me as though I'm a child who's inserted herself into a conversation at the adult table.

Crane doesn't even acknowledge that I've spoken. "Zach, Susan," he says, "what do *you* think?"

Zach and Susan answer, but I don't hear what they say because my pulse is drumming a hard, angry beat in my ears. My face is hot and, I'm sure, flushed red. I stare out the window and count the columns adorning the Capitol dome, which is a dingy gray in the fading late-afternoon light. It does this—changing color and degrees of brilliance with the weather—as though its surface were the live skin of a chameleon instead of inanimate white granite.

Zach tries to stop me as we file out of the conference room at the meeting's end, but I pretend I don't hear him, and slip ahead of some of the other associates and then into the restroom, where I hide long enough to ensure he isn't lying in wait for me in the hallway. Then I head out.

I cut through the State Capitol building to State Street. My stomach is grumbling and I realize I haven't eaten yet today. One of my favorite eateries—a little Nepalese place that's supposedly one of only a handful of its kind in the country, though that could be local urban legend because it seems like a tough fact to try to substantiate—is still serving lunch.

I duck inside and order chicken palau, which I proceed to push around on the plate with the dal when it arrives, my thoughts on the status meeting, my run-in with Susan, and the number listed under my name and effective rate on the Rainmaker, released to the associates this morning—a paltry twenty-three dollars in comparison with nearly every other associate's rates, most of which fall in the one-hundred- to one-hundred-fifty-dollar range.

I look out at the bustle of State Street. The sun is shining, the air is blowing warm, and energy radiates from college kids walking, biking, and running to and fro. Though this is all nearly enough to convince a person that anything is possible on this fine day, I feel trapped. Stuck. I am a good attorney. I know this. But since yesterday, all of Crane Early's complaints about the junior associate who had the nerve to ask for a Friday and an entire weekend off for her own wedding keep echoing in my head. From what I remember, she was a good attorney, too. And from what I remember, she worked every day up until the hour she quit, trying—and failing—to convince the upper ranks of that.

I look at the crowd streaming in either direction past my table. The college students and young, smartly dressed politicos—mostly Democrats at the moment, though that could easily change come November—heading back and forth from the Capitol and important lunches or afternoon shopping, are only a handful of years removed from where I am now. It might as well be light-years. Their auras drip with possibility. They can still do anything, be anything. Most of them don't have mortgages or spouses or any real responsibility that can't be shrugged off at will. They can quit jobs and boyfriends or girlfriends and take off to work on a cruise ship or teach English in some far-flung country. They are still eligible to try out for *American Idol* or *The Real World*—both of which have an upper age limit that I've already passed.

My BlackBerry buzzes and I check it to find an e-mail from Sondra—her weekly lobbying effort to get me to visit her in California. This one contains only the subject line, *Come clear your head by the sea*, and an attached picture of a clapboard cottage on a sandy beach, saved with the name, *Sondra's_summer_rental_Carlsbad*.

I wish I could take Sondra up on her offer. I wish I could walk away from my life as I could have done ten, even five, years ago. But somewhere along the way, things have gotten complicated. Not so long ago, I was one of these people walking by my table—promise incarnate. Now, I have a job that I feel slipping from me the tighter I try to hang on to it—and a job that I'm not sure I even want to hang on to; a best friend who might not be that anymore; and a husband who is gone in more ways than one.

I feel like I'm being buried under a mountain of snow: Each flake on its own is falling light and fluffy, but taken together, the weight is immense. It blocks out the sun.

I pay my bill and wander out into a brilliant afternoon sun and down State Street. I should be headed in the other direction—up toward the Capitol and back to work. But the need to conserve professional capital pales next to my need to think, really think, about what I am doing here. About what I'm doing with my life.

I'm pleased to discover that it's National Free Cone Day at Ben & Jerry's, and I join the lengthening line. I laugh at this little bit of role reversal: Brad was always the one to stand in line for anything free, no matter how inexpensive the original cost; not me. But today, I have the time.

Though I prefer chocolate ice cream and tend not to enjoy fruit mixed in or even alongside (think banana splits), I choose the Cherry Garcia because the person in front of me does and the girl behind the counter proclaims it a top seller. If so many people have vouched for it, how can I go wrong? Plus, if you're going to take a flyer on something, it might as well be a free something. I receive my cone and take a lick. It's heavenly.

I walk all the way down State Street until I reach campus and take a right toward the Memorial Union. It's early in the season, but the weather has cooperated for once, and chairs in a rainbow of green, yellow, and red are already set up on the Union's giant tiered patio that steps down to Lake Mendota. The outdoor beer gardens haven't yet opened and finals are coming up, so the terrace isn't hosting its usual sea of patrons just yet. But a few small sailboats piloted by Hoofer club members dart back and forth across the horizon, signaling that summer isn't so far off after all.

At the lake's edge, I roll up my pants, kick off my shoes, and sit down, letting my legs dangle in the murky water. It's still winter-cold, though, and my skin smarts from the temperature. I think back to all the times when Brad and I sat right here, our shoulders touching. This is many people's "place," but it's also ours. Was ours? No, *is*, I decide. This place is too infused with Brad in my memories to be anything but.

What about five, ten, twenty years from now, though? If things continue on this way, I might be sitting here on a hot summer day, watching the sun go down over the music and sailboats with someone who isn't Brad. The choice may be that, or eliminating any place that holds memories of Brad and me together from the haunts I frequent. Either way, Brad becomes just someone I used to know.

I'm not ready for that. The thought of relegating him to my past makes my veins feel like they're running with ice water. But then I think of a lifetime married to this man who isn't really Brad anymore, of having to give up every semblance of the life I had dreamed of, and I'm overcome with dread.

What kind of choice is that?

My BlackBerry buzzes incessantly, telling me that I'm missed—or rather, wanted—at work. I roll my eyes skyward. For the past two weeks, I have put every fiber of my being into ensuring that our client doesn't have to compensate the parents of a dead little boy for their negligence. That those efforts appear to be too little, too late as far as Susan and the others are concerned is simply a twist of an already-imbedded knife. And I can't help but wonder what it is I'm doing with my life. I'm on the shore of Lake Mendota, but I might as well be in the middle of those dark waters, trying to thrash my way to shore with a cinder block shackled to my ankle.

I think back, trying to decide if I've ever felt more unmoored than I do now. Perhaps after my parents died, but even then, there was a clear path forward: first with funeral arrangements, and afterward, meetings with estate attorneys and doing the Cohodas shuffle through Northern Michigan University's building of the same name that houses financial aid, admissions, and the registrar's offices. After that it was taking the LSAT and applying to law schools, then getting married and securing a job. There has always been an obvious next step. Until now.

Most of me would love to stay right here in this spot, mesmerized by the lake's rippling surface and the way it seems to lift up, up, up to meet the pale blue sky, far off on the horizon. To not have to think. To stare off and breathe and to just *be*.

But the sun is hanging lower in the sky, and it's time to go. It's time to stop waiting for things to be different, to stop wallowing. No one is going to make these decisions for me. They're not going to happen on their own.

I stand up, unroll my pants, and slip my shoes back on. Then I start to trek back toward the office, having decided what it is, exactly, that I need to do.

Twenty-seven

Back at my desk, there's an e-mail from Zach at the tip-top of my in-box with the subject line, *Sorry.* I delete it.

I stack the trial binders I prepared in alphabetical order on the tiny conference table next to my desk, double check my e-mail one last time to make sure I'm not leaving any loose ends, and send Zach an e-mail with the subject line, *Trial Preparation,* and one simple sentence in the body: . . . *is all but completed and on the table in my office.*

Then I head into Susan's office.

It's difficult not to be nervous while I sit waiting for her to tie up a call that was passed through to her right as I sat down. I remind myself not to fidget, to sit up straight, and to tip my chin up instead of down.

Susan hangs up the phone and looks past me. She nods toward the door behind me. "Do you want to close that?" she says.

I do as I'm asked (told?), then take my original seat across the desk from her. As soon as I'm seated, she launches in.

"Well," she says, "I don't think it can be argued that you've been doing good work lately, Elise. I understand some extenuating personal circumstances have contributed and overflowed into your professional life. I understand that. You've been in a difficult position. But that's put the firm and especially the *Rowland* case in a difficult position and—"

I want to stick up for myself. I want to tell her about the binders and the visual aids and witnesses I've already lined up. I want to tell her what it's been like toiling under the dual, competing pressures of the firm and making sure that my husband, who survived his time in Iraq, is surviving his homecoming. I want to ask her if she understands, even one iota, how gut-wrenching it is to contemplate leaving the man you married because you don't know him anymore and he can't help it.

But I don't.

"Susan," I say, holding up my hand as if to tell her this isn't necessary—we've seen the same Rainmaker report, after all—and then I stop, and so does she. Susan reclines in her chair with a thin-lipped, smug, self-satisfied and condescending smile on her face. I wait another moment, longer than I should. I let silence hang in the air between us for a handful of seconds, just for effect, because right now, for once, I'm the one making her squirm. I haven't yet groveled, or said I was sorry, or even told her why I wanted to meet with her, other than to tell her assistant it was about "my performance." I've interrupted her and asserted myself—two things she's not altogether used to receiving from any junior associate, but especially from me.

And then I tell her that I quit.

"I appreciate all that this firm has done for me—all that you've done for me," I say. "The partners and other associates alike have been nothing but supportive and accommodating, and I know that I've let you down from time to time. I haven't been the kind of lawyer I want to be."

"There's still time for that. You just need to figure out your priorities," Susan says, though her words are flat and rote.

"That's the thing," I say. "There isn't time. I haven't been the kind of attorney I thought I would be—that I wanted to be. And I haven't been the kind of person I'd like to be, either. It's just not a good fit, all the way around. And that's okay."

She leans back in her chair, crossing, then uncrossing her legs. Then she looks out her window, teasing pieces of her bangs to the side. She pulls the hair tight against her scalp and tries to get it to tuck behind her ear, though she has to know it's not long enough. It's a nervous tick—or a tick, at least—that I've watched her do again and again. The knowledge that I won't have to watch her do it much longer makes me smile inside.

"Well," she says. "You will be missed." Susan nods in agreement with herself. "I'll be putting Jaxson on *Rowland* in your place. You'll make sure to brief him?"

She has come up with a replacement for me so quickly that it makes me wonder how much I'm actually going to be missed. I wonder if the plan all along hasn't been to replace me. But that's not my problem to worry about. Not anymore.

"Absolutely," I tell her. "He'll do a great job, I'm sure. I'll make sure to type up memos on all of the other cases I've worked on, too, and I'm bringing Zach up to date on where we are with the trial preparation. I just have one request."

Susan cocks her head to the side and rewraps the multicolored shawl—possibly Italian, definitely expensive—draped around her shoulders. "Yes?"

"I'd like to end my employment effective as soon as I'm able to transfer my caseload and tie up any loose ends," I say. "I'll stay the entire two weeks if you'd like, but I'd prefer a shorter, quicker exit if at all possible."

Susan studies me, then shrugs.

"That should be fine," she says. "Make sure you copy me on any correspondence from here on out, and that you leave a status report of your responsibilities with me, too."

"I can do that. Thank you for working with me on this," I say, standing up and running my palms down my slacks, partly to straighten them and partly to wipe off the sweat I'm surprised to find has accumulated.

Susan doesn't speak. She's staring past me, either lost in thought or debating which thoughts she should give voice to. Then she nods, as if to say, "That will do," and I figure I'm excused.

My hand is on the door handle when she says, "Elise?"

I turn to face her, my hand still on the handle.

"You remind me a lot of myself in some ways," she says.

I've pictured Susan as someone who grew up chewing shredded metal for breakfast, someone who, by the time she was my age, had sacrificed the sacred areas of her life on the altar of her career. A few months ago, I might have reveled in her compliment, but that woman now feels like a stranger. Right now, I could not care less. I even feel sorry for Susan. This is her life—her whole, entire life, after all—and here I am discarding it as easily as an outgrown pair of pants.

But I just nod and smile and say, "Thank you," and then I walk out of Susan's office. Outside her door, I pause and close my eyes. I take a deep breath in and let it out. And then I keep on walking.

Twenty-eight

Zach grabs me as I pass his office. He throws an arm around my shoulders and pulls me in to him.

"You, my girl, are a rock star," he says.

"Yeah?" I give him a sly, sideways smile. "So you like?" I say, knowing he's referring to the binders.

"Oh yeah," he says.

"Good. I'm glad."

"So, I'd like to take you to dinner tonight. Can you knock off early? Say, six thirty?"

"Is this a date?" I ask him in mock seriousness. I am in a light, flirty mood.

"It's a little thank-you for a job well done—totally platonic." The way Zach is looking at me doesn't match what he's saying, and there's a loud voice in my head yelling, "No!" but I tell it to hush up. Until this afternoon, I have tried to do the things I should, to do them right. I have tried to be sensible and loyal and hardworking and selfless and good. But I am tired. I am all out of try.

"Sure," I say. My stomach jumps at the thought of a nice, pseudo-platonic dinner where I don't have to worry if we're seated out of sight line of an exit, or if some trigger will cause us to have to leave the restaurant in a rush, entrées still untouched on our plates. I feel Zach's thumb graze the wispy hairs along the back of my neck, and my stomach jumps again.

"I'll swing by your office, pick you up."

I shake my head and unwrap his arm from my shoulders. "I'll meet you there," I tell him.

He gives me a sideways glance but agrees. "Let's hit up Papavero—that little Italian place on Wilson. I'll see you then," he says, and slaps my hip with the files he's carrying as he walks away, whistling a tune I can't quite finger.

What about Brad? the voice in my head asks.

What about him? I haven't called him, but Brad hasn't called me, either. He chose a stray mutt over me on his birthday. He hasn't said that he wants to come home. He's safe up north. He might even be happy there—or happier than here, with me.

I stop in my office and standing over the computer, pull up Sondra's e-mail with the attached picture of the seaside cottage. I hit "reply," type, *Do I get my own room?* and hit "send" without ever sitting down. Then I power off my computer, put on my coat, and check the time on my cell phone—5:08 p.m.—as I march, unabashedly, past Susan's office.

I have more than an hour before I have to meet Zach for dinner, and it's an hour I don't want to spend in the office. Instead, I wander down to the bike path that loops around the shore of Lake Monona.

If there's one thing you can say about Madison—or, I'm sure, any city in the Midwest for that matter—it's that the people here really know how to welcome the change of seasons. Though it's now more dark than light outside, they whiz by me on foot and bike, invigorated by nothing more than a few extra degrees on the thermometer and the promise of warmer days to come.

As I follow the lakeshore path, just before I reach the intersection with Broom Street, I see a man who, from the back, looks a whole lot like Brad. He's bent over a boy who looks all of three years old, dressed in overalls and a red short-sleeved shirt and wearing a little baseball cap that's riding a little higher than it should on his head. The man's hands are over the boy's, which are wrapped around a miniature fishing pole. I watch as the man guides the boy's arms back, back, back and then snaps them forward, the fishing line streaming out toward the water. The boy beams up at the man, at a job well done, and the man tussles the boy's hat and hair.

But when I let real-life Brad stand in for the Brad look-alike at the water's edge, the whole scene breaks down. In the best scenario, Brad is a younger version of Mert, yelling at the boy with an impatience he didn't used to possess, telling him he's not doing it right. In the worst scenario, Brad isn't there at all. He's sitting on our back steps, glass of Jack in his hand and eyes as black and vacant as two deep holes.

Without warning, the Brad in this mirage morphs into Zach— Zach's slighter build, his floppy hair, the quilted jacket he tends to wear to work on the weekends, the way he laughs with his whole body, throwing his head back almost as though he's howling. And I'm back to thinking about the trail of warmth left by his hand on my knee a few weeks ago, or on my shoulders this afternoon.

Warmth and promise.

My feet find the pavement and I start walking again, away from the man and that boy. But my mind is still with them. An image, a scene, that won't—can't—come to pass. Not with Brad.

Not with Brad.

But with someone else?

I don't want to think about it. I can't. And so, I walk. I walk until the air chills and the sky fades to gray and then to a dark charcoal. I walk past balconies full of college students gathering for the first time outside since the previous fall, the smells wafting from their grills undoubtedly better than the taste of meat cooking on them, but making my stomach rumble nonetheless. I walk back up to and around the Capitol, past sidewalk cafés that have sprung up like flowers overnight and patrons shivering against the chill that's crept into the air since the sun set. I walk until I end up, at six thirty almost on the dot, outside the doors of Osteria Papavero. When I enter, Zach waves to me over a sea of tealight candles from the back corner.

Even though this restaurant feels more like a café than a fine-dining establishment, and even though he himself said this isn't a date, Zach pulls my chair out for me and, once we're seated, orders a bottle of red wine, the name of which I can't pronounce, without asking me what I'd like, which would be to try an Italian 75—a scrumptious-looking concoction of Campari, house-made orangecello, and Prosecco. While we're waiting for the arrival of the wine I didn't want, I try to update him on *Rowland*.

"Elise, let's talk work tomorrow," he says. "Plenty of time for that." He reaches across the table and hooks his pinky with mine. But unlike when he placed his hand on my knee at Brocach all those weeks ago, I feel no fantastic jolt of warm excitement. Quite the opposite, in fact. I pull my hand back and lace its fingers with my opposite hand, placing them squarely in front of me. I am suddenly uncomfortable—and confused. That one simple gesture would have left me reeling and giddy only days ago. Was it Zach's use of my first name? Seeing my pinky locked with someone else's besides Brad's? The absence of our usual banter that felt much more intimate than this forced interaction we're having tonight? It's hard to tell.

Zach is prattling on about the project Gordon Janssen tapped him for help on—a state Supreme Court appeal to overturn the state's medical malpractice caps—but I'm barely paying attention. I want to ask him why this doesn't qualify as work talk, but as we munch our way through an antipasto plate of cured Italian meats and cheeses with melt-in-your-mouth homemade fried bread, I try to decide how to deliver my news.

The waitress has just sent down our entrées—orecchiette with broccoli for me and a wild boar ragout over pappardelle for Zach—and is topping off the wine in each of our glasses when I blurt it out: "I quit today."

Zach gives me a quizzical look and asks, "Quit what?"

I study his face. Surely, he can't be serious. Quit what? "The firm, Zach. I quit. I had just given Susan my notice when you saw me."

Zach sets his fork down, and it clatters against the edge of the bowl. A few heads from surrounding tables turn toward us. Zach opens his mouth and closes it, then opens and closes it again. He looks like a guppy. The thought makes me giggle.

"Is this some sort of joke?" he asks.

"No."

"This isn't funny, Sabatto. And why would you quit? You know how many people would kill to be in your shoes. You know there's a line, right?"

This was not the reaction that I expected from Zach. He'd always been so supportive, so encouraging of my career. Though it's a career I've essentially tossed aside this afternoon in one relatively rash moment.

"I need to get my bearings, Zach. That's all. It's not a big deal," I say, stabbing a piece of broccolini with my fork. Before I bring it to my mouth, I try out a smile on Zach, but it doesn't work. He looks shell-shocked, and irritated. Angry, even.

"No," he says, waving a finger in the air, "what you need is to fix this. And I think it's doable. Here's how we're going to—"

"*We* are not going to do anything," I say. "Zach, *listen* to me." I reach across to pat his hand, which is lying cold and immobile in front of him. "I've thought about this. I can't keep myself chained to that place, day in and day out. Susan has made up her mind about me. They all have. You're the only one who doesn't think I'm a flake, and even that I'm not sure of sometimes." I smile up at him, but the joke falls flat. He is staring at me without registering a hint of emotion, without an inkling of a smile. "Come on, Zach. Don't sit there and act like I'm not right. You've seen the Rainmakers. And don't you remember that junior a few years back who made the mistake of asking for time off so she could get married—the one Early complained about for months?"

"But you're doing great work on *Rowland*. Susan will see that. A few more big projects like that one and you'll—"

"I'll be a dried-out, brittle shell of myself, Zach. I'm doing great work on *Rowland* now, sure. But I haven't slept in weeks. And then"—I inhale sharply—"there's Brad to consider."

"Brad's gone," Zach says, and my eyes snap from my bowl of pasta to lock with his.

"How did you—" I hadn't told Zach that. I hadn't told anyone except Darcy and Sondra.

"Overheard you on the phone a while back," he says. "And if you ask me, you should let him go. He's been holding you back. Christ, just look at you. A year ago you were being fast-tracked for partner. Now you're quitting because of a little extra scrutiny?"

"Wouldn't that be convenient," I say.

"Oh, come on," Zach says. "Smarten up, Sabatto. Do I want to date you? Absofuckinglutely. I wouldn't break up your marriage, but your marriage has been doing a fine job of that all on its own, and I don't think it's any big secret here"—he motions back and forth between the two of us—"that this isn't just a collegial work thing. But that doesn't have a single, goddamn thing to do with the fact that your career is in a tailspin."

"I don't think quitting *one* job to make a fresh start constitutes a tailspin," I say.

"And that's where you'd be wrong." Zach is smug and angry, a bad combination that raises my hackles. I try to lighten the mood.

"What's your dream vacation?" I ask him.

"Vacation?" he asks.

"Yeah. I'm going to have a little time on my hands. I need some ideas."

Brad and I would play this game often over a dinner of pasta and vegetables from a bag, jazzed up with a grilled chicken breast, back when I was in law school. We dreamed of the day we'd be a two-income household that could take its pick of proper vacations instead of getaways that consisted of staying at Super 8 motels within driving distance—Minneapolis, Kansas City, Toledo, Louisville.

Zach is looking at me as though he's wholly unsure what I'm talking about. He shrugs. "I guess I've never been a big vacation guy," he says.

"You're kidding, right?" I ask. How can one not be "big" on vacations? Gardening? Sure. Cycling? I get that—it's expensive and I myself have an unhealthy fear of being run off the road by a truck with monster wheels and a rebel flag in the back window. I see how a person might not like a certain type of vacation. But "vacations" in the general sense? "You really don't like *vacations*?" I ask him.

He shrugs again. "They're a lot of ado about nothing, when you get right down to it. There are all the choices, and the planning. And most of the time it turns out to be one headache after another."

"Headaches?"

"Yeah. Flight delays, taking your shoes off at security. That sort of thing."

"Okay, so no planes. But what about trains or automobiles?"

"Just not for me," he says. "I get antsy. It takes too long."

"Boats?" I try.

"Can't swim. Hate the water."

I see my daydreams of scuba diving in the Cayman Islands or learning to surf in Bora Bora evaporating before my eyes.

"Renting a cottage up north?" I ask.

"Water," Zach says.

"So no vacationing?" I ask.

"I work," he says. "I love what I do. That's not so bad, is it? To love what you do?"

I sense a hint of accusation in his voice, but I don't bite. "What about after?" I ask.

Zach's face is blank.

"After," I say. "After you stop working? You know—retirement?"

"Don't plan to. Why would I?"

Zach's tone has changed. It's reserved, flat, and forceful—a half note off angry.

"You know, I'm a big girl, Zach. I've done pretty well in life, making decisions I thought were in my best interest. I trust what I'm doing."

"And I don't," Zach says.

It dawns on me then, why he's taking this—my quitting the firm—as something directed toward him. I see me from his point of view, as he sees me: someone with a carefree, figure-it-out-as-it-comes attitude, instead of the type-A, driven, and cutthroat attorney I used to be. This new me—the Elise who would rather cut her losses than grovel her way through years and years of scrutiny at the hands of a panel of people waiting for and expecting her to fail—doesn't fit neatly in the box that Zach has created for me. I haven't shifted his expectations; I've blown them to teeny, tiny bits. I don't know how to feel about the way Zach now sees me. I don't know how to feel, period. It's like a multiple-choice question where, depending on how you look at it, none of the answers is correct or all of them are correct.

"Well," I say, "I guess we'll have to agree to disagree."

Zach hands the waitress a credit card before she even drops the guest-check holder on our table. I make a feeble attempt to pay. He waves me off.

I study Zach's face as he tallies the tip and signs his name—his dark curls dipping onto his forehead, his icy blue eyes flashing, his strong jaw outlined with a five o'clock shadow that makes him look rugged instead of unkempt. I think of what his skin, freshly shaven, might feel like against mine. I wonder how good it must smell, right up close. But the air around us has shifted, and I suddenly see this scene differently, as if someone has switched the lens I'm viewing it through. This isn't about Zach—not really. I don't think I'm misreading the chemistry between us, but all this daydreaming, this searching elsewhere, is because of Zach only insofar as he's the embodiment of what could be. He represents my options—the fact that I have some.

We get up from the table and Zach retrieves our jackets from the rack near the door in silence, though not an uncomfortable one. All the tension that's been building between us for all of these years resembles a balloon having been filled with air and it's now been punctured. We're still here, but that *something* between us has disappeared. Deflated.

I notice that outside it has started to drizzle.

Zach is holding my coat for me, and I shrug into it. Then I march out into the fine mist of rain, turning my face up to the cool drops. Zach hangs back, the overhang shielding him. "Maybe we should have a drink," he says. "Wait this out."

I turn to him and laugh. And then I realize that he's serious. "Really?"

"I told you, I don't like water."

"Even water you can't drown in?" I ask.

Zach half shrugs. I can tell by his face, his stooped posture, that he's embarrassed. This guy who isn't afraid of wielding the law to take on bad guys in all their forms is uncomfortable with a heavy mist.

I think back to an afternoon a couple of summers ago. Brad decided to go for a run, and the weather shifted not long after he stepped out the front door and started his usual route out toward Picnic Point and back. I was washing dishes in the kitchen when I felt the temperature drop and the breeze, originally a whisper, turn into an insistent keening against the back door—a wind of serious storms, not simply showers. When the rain started—big intermittent drops that registered a splat when each hit the sidewalk—I jumped in our car to go in search of Brad. By the time I found him on University Bay Drive, my windshield wipers were working at full speed and still hardly keeping up, and Brad was still running. I pulled up alongside him and honked a couple of times in quick succession. Instead of being grateful, he looked surprised to see me. I cracked the passenger side window open and shouted for him to get in. I added a frantic waving of my hand to emphasize why I had come. He stopped running and smiled at me, mimicking my hand gesture.

"You come here!" he said.

I shook my head at him. "You're insane—it's pouring!" I yelled through the barely open window.

"Come on," he said to me. And he looked such a picture standing there—his T-shirt soaked through and clinging to him, showing off the curves of his arms and his chest, rivulets of water running from his flattened hair, that crooked smile of his—that I put the car into park and did as he said. By the time I made it to his side, there wasn't a dry spot on me. Brad took my hand and pulled me to him.

"What are you doing?" I squealed. "Seriously, Brad, Noah's going to float by any minute. Let's go!"

He took my face in his hands. For a second he just looked at me, studying me. Then he kissed me so softly that it was hard to tell his lips from the falling rain.

"I've always wanted to do that," he said.

Zach is holding the restaurant door open, waiting for me to follow him back inside for a nightcap, but my legs aren't moving.

"Zach," I say, shaking my head, "I—I think I'm going to call it a night. Walk home."

He eyes my footwear—black boots that look more uncomfortable than they actually are. His forehead knits together and his eyes cloud with concern. He is ever the chivalrous one.

"I'll be all right," I say.

"Okay, Sabatto," he says. "You sure?"

"I'm sure."

Zach nods then. "All right," he says, his voice soft and husky. "Be safe, you. Good night."

He blows me a playful kiss, and I reach out theatrically to grab it, bringing my fist to my lips and looking to make sure Zach sees me do this. I want to end things this way, infused with all the good-natured, harmless flirting of our past. But he has already let the door close behind him. Tonight, there is no car trailing me as I walk. And tonight, when I reach home, there's no car idling halfway down the block, its occupant checking to make sure I've arrived safely.

Twenty-nine

I spend much of the next week tying up loose ends at work and at home. I decide I will leave once the house is rented, expecting that it could take weeks—or longer. But I have forgotten that we live mere blocks from two hospitals and the university, and within days an incoming internal medicine resident has committed to renting the place, sight unseen and fully furnished, for the next year.

It's a big decision I'm making. And one I'm making all on my own. I'm giving up our home without consulting my husband. I have corresponded with Brad only by text or e-mail in the past weeks because I don't know what to say to him. This is a decision we would have arrived at—or not—jointly in the past. But Brad can't carry this house on the meager stipend he receives from the military or live here alone, and I can't continue to carry on as we were on the off chance that something will improve. Somewhere along the way, our relationship has become an oligarchy.

The house is quiet as I pack my clothes, then Brad's, and then our personal effects—pictures and papers and prized books. I consider playing some music but decide against it. I'm packing up our life, and when I unpack these things, that life may or may not still exist. This is a ceremony that should be performed with some reverence—one deserving of silence.

I realize in the early evening hours of Saturday that the only thing left to do is load all of our things into the car and clean out the refrigerator. I've been here alone for more than a month and there isn't much in it—just some condiments and a jug of sour milk.

I am surrounded by boxes and bins, and as I look around the living room, I wish this job would take longer. I don't want it to be such quick work. I don't want it, period.

Because there's the fireplace that Brad used to have lit and toasty warm by the time I returned home from work on Fridays so we could collapse in front of it and talk the night away, catching up with each other after another chaotic week. The living room that we would sprawl over on Sunday mornings, swapping sections of the *New York Times* and sipping coffee well into the afternoon. There's Brad's empty recliner, and I can almost feel his arms around me as I sat in his lap the night before he shipped out, my head against his chest and legs flung over the armrest, him rocking me like a baby. What am I supposed to do with all of these memories?

I decide I can do this later. I need a break. I also need to tell Darcy that I'm leaving, and I owe her that news in person.

I send her a text to see if she can meet me somewhere for a drink. She writes back that Collin's parents are out of town and she doesn't have a last-minute sitter, but I'm welcome to come over. So I do.

During the drive I rehearse what I will say, how I plan to make her understand. I think of things that will help her see things from my point of view. But by the time I arrive at her street, I can concentrate only on the knots in my stomach. My mind has gone blank.

As I walk up Darcy's front walk, I tell myself that she might not even care. I haven't been the best friend to her lately, after all. I haven't exactly been around. She might not miss me.

I am a terrible liar. Even to myself.

As nice as the weather has been this week, a cold front has moved in tonight and Darcy has a fire going. I settle in on the couch and she brings me a glass of wine, like always. She sits on the love seat and curls her legs beneath her.

"So what's going on, you?" she asks.

I would like to start with small talk. Actually, I would like not to be having this conversation at all. But I don't see that I have a choice.

"I need to tell you something," I say to her, "and I need you to hear me out."

"Everything okay?" she asks.

I shrug. "I don't know. Not now, maybe, but I think it will be."

Darcy leans forward. She's concerned. In a few moments she will be angry. I'd like to stay right here, on this side of that divide. I'm looking into the expanse that's about to open between us, and consider backing away from the edge. But it's too late.

"Elise, what's going on?"

I breathe deeply and jump. "I'm leaving. For a while. I don't know how long. I quit my job and rented my house." I close my eyes like a child.

"You what?"

I look up and meet Darcy's eyes. They're confused, hurt. Not angry.

"It's all happened really quickly, Darce. I know I'm springing this on you, but I'm sort of springing it on myself, too. I've hardly had time to think about it."

"Well," she says, her voice barely audible, "maybe you should. You never even mentioned this possibility."

I knew this would be the rub—that, and what comes next.

"And what about Brad?"

Stuffed into that question are all sorts of micro-questions: Have you thought about him in all this? Are you leaving him? What is he supposed to do? Do you care? And I have one answer for all of them: I don't know.

"He's up with his dad," I say.

"He hates his dad."

"Well," I say, keeping my voice light, "hate's a strong word."

"Elise."

"I know, Darce. It's all messed up. I know I'm complaining to the wrong person and all, which is why I haven't talked to you about it before, even though I should have. I know I should have. But it's bad. Things between us are bad."

"Bad how?"

I picture Brad curled up next to Jones in the barn. A mental slide-show of all that preceded that night plays through my mind, in reverse—right back to the night when I came home to find him standing in our kitchen, spit out by the desert safe and sound. Or so I thought.

I tell Darcy about some of it. Enough to give her a picture of what my life has been like lately. A faint babble wafts from the hallway: "Mum-mum-mum-mum."

"Are you keeping a motorboat in there?" I ask, nodding in the direction of Mia's room. I smile, but Darcy's mouth is thin-set.

"You don't get to do this," she says. Her voice comes out in little more than a whisper now and it's shaky, as if she's on the verge of tears. "You got Brad back. You don't get to leave him. Not now. Not like this."

There are two sentences competing for airtime in my head, lobbying to be said out loud. One is, "I'm not leaving him," which is drowned out by one word "yet." The sentence that should be in contention and isn't, is, "I'm not thinking of leaving him."

Darcy is shaking her head. Her eyes are pressed shut. When she finally opens them, she says, "You didn't have to meet that plane, Elise. You didn't have to see that flag-draped coffin come off it. You can't imagine what that's like. To know that inside that wood box is your husband. To feel your heart lurch twenty-one times during that salute, or feel the weight of that folded flag in your hands. I can say it's awful, but that doesn't come close.

"You didn't have to figure out how to get the deed to your house into your name. You didn't need to access his accounts to make sure there wasn't anything outstanding in any of them. And you don't stay up nights worrying that you won't be able to remember anything to tell your daughter about her dad except generic platitudes like, 'He was such a great guy,' or 'He loved you so much.'"

I know losing Collin has been awful for Darcy. It's been awful for me to see her slogging her way through it all. I know I haven't been around enough, and I know that even if I could have been, there's not a thing I could do to lift the tiny, heavy burdens that keep weighing her down. She's right. I can't imagine what it's been like to be her. But does that exempt me from faltering? Wallowing some? Why do I have to hold it all together and be overjoyed, too, simply because Brad came home?

I want Darcy to know all this, but I look at her and see that her face is still hard. She's deep inside herself, in her own misery, like Brad gets sometimes.

My husband came back and hers did not. There is no purer truth than that. There is nothing I can say to change those facts. And because of them, I will win—or lose—either way, every time.

"He didn't ask for this, Elise. He did what was asked of him."

"I didn't, either," I say. It sounds like whining, when I really only want her to see it from my point of view, too. I want her to understand the pain I feel in knowing that if I stay with this man—this good, good man who is being attacked by his own mind and memories—I will never, ever have the chance to be a mother. Ever. I will never feel truly safe in my own home. I will always be afraid, every time I leave the house, that my husband might not still be alive when I return. I am a strong person. A loyal person. A good person. And yet, I still don't know if I can live that way for the rest of my life. Worse yet, I don't know if I want to.

"I just need some time to clear my head is all," I say.

"So what are you going to do? Where are you going to go?"

"California," I say. "I'm going to stay with Sondra for a while."

Darcy's face hardens. "So you're leaving. Like her."

"You can't judge her."

"I can and I will. This is bullshit, Elise. Sondra I could see, but you? I never expected this of you."

She's lecturing me and it makes me angry. I don't begin to pretend to know what it's been like to be Darcy, to awaken each morning and remember, in a jolt in that first full moment of consciousness, that you're truly alone. That you will never see your husband again. I can only imagine; I can't know. So how is it that Darcy feels so free to assume what my life is like? To criticize me for not skipping merrily along behind Brad with a broom and dustpan so I can pick up the pieces every time he implodes?

"So what's your plan?" she asks. "What are you going to do out there, anyway?"

"I don't know, Darce. Maybe I'll do something totally different— become a real estate agent, get a gig as a tour guide, go to cooking school. The possibilities are endless." I spread my arms wide and grin at her, trying to diffuse my own anger and hers.

Instead, she asks seriously, "Cooking school? Do you have stacks of hundred-dollar bills at home that you're willing to use as kindling?"

"No," I say, confused. "What are you talking about?"

"That would be a better use of your money than your trying to learn to cook."

I set my glass of wine down. "You don't have to be rude," I say. "This isn't the end of the world, you know. It's life. People do this sort of thing all the time—take detours, go off on tangents, figure things out in imperfect ways."

"You don't get it, do you?" Darcy says. She nearly spits her words. "You're living in la-la land. This"—she waves her arm out in front of her from left to right, taking in the contents of the great room and kitchen of her house—"*this* is life. Life is hard. It's hard and it's messy. I have a daughter to raise by myself now, and a house to keep up on my own. I have to scrape together a mortgage payment every month because I can't bring myself to cash Collin's SGLI payout. It's like that money is the sum total of his life—all it's worth—and it feels so wrong to pay for a bunch of wood and plaster with his *life*."

Darcy's face is wet and her top lip is quivering. Her eyes are hard, steely marbles trained on me.

"You think I *wanted* any of this? Nothing has worked out how I wanted, but I don't get to cut and run. No one does—including Brad. But you think you deserve to. You think you're owed something more than the rest of us. Well, you're not."

I am sad and I am angry. I can feel tears smarting at the edges of my own eyes now. What, I want to ask, is so bad about wanting more out of life? About not wanting it to be hard? About trying to be happy? Does that really make me an awful person? Isn't that really, deep down, what everyone wants? And if I have a chance to try, why shouldn't I? But I don't let these questions past my lips because I don't trust myself with words right now.

I stand up and bring my wineglass to the kitchen. I pour the remainder of its contents down the drain, rinse it, and set the glass next to the sink because I know that Darcy never puts her glassware in the dishwasher. I wonder if I will ever perform this simple action here in her kitchen again. It's remarkable how charged with sentiment the simplest acts become when they might be the last.

Darcy is still sitting, still sipping her wine, when I walk back into the living room. It's as though I merely excused myself to use the restroom. As though nothing has happened. As though we didn't exchange the words we just said.

"I was hoping you would be happy for me," I say. "Or that you'd at least try to understand."

Darcy doesn't look at me.

"I'm going to miss you, Darcy," I say. "I'm sorry things are hard for you. They're hard for me, too. I hope you'll forgive me eventually for whatever it is you think I've done."

I hope that at this moment, Darcy will get up and wish me well, or at least hug me. But she remains seated, sipping. She looks past me as if I were not even there.

"Maybe someday, then," I say. I stop at the front door to trace a finger down Collin's packing list for Iraq, still taped to the frame. "Bye, Darce," I say, hoping she won't let me leave. Not like this. She doesn't look up.

I pull the door shut behind me until I hear it click.

The rest of the night I toss and turn, unable to will the sleep that usually comes so readily, and the next morning, I wake before the sun. I consider doing something that signals that I'm leaving this place, of performing some ritual of good-bye. I could stop in to see Zach on my way out, or pick up scones from Lazy Jane's one last time. But I'm afraid of inertia taking over, of noon or four o'clock arriving to find me here, still trying to leave. So, when the early-morning sky is still thin with light, I point my car away from the center of town and steal glances at the Capitol, standing tall on Madison's isthmus and growing smaller and smaller in my rearview mirror. I think about what Darcy said, and our conversation seeps through any space in my thoughts. The car's tires find the highway with little conscious help from their driver. The wheel under my hands and the rumble of my old car feel like an extension of me. I am not thinking about setting the cruise control, or steering, or the traffic I am traveling in. Feeling like this, I could keep driving and driving until I run out of road. Until I end up where I'm supposed to be.

And, maybe, that's precisely what I do.

Thirty

It's late afternoon, and the place is empty when I arrive. I stand in the middle of the kitchen and try to take in what I'm doing here, how I ended up here. But as usual, I haven't eaten yet today, and my questions are too big and tangled for me to try to sort through them on an empty stomach. So I scour the cupboards and find a handful of crackers, and in the refrigerator I unearth the remnants of a block of cheese from beneath something wrapped in tinfoil. Then I find a mug, fill it halfway with milk, and zap it for a minute in the microwave. Just warm enough. It goes down in three, maybe four gulps, soothing the premonitions of heartburn rumbling in my throat.

I sit down at the kitchen table and think first of nothing but eating. I cut a piece of cheese and match it to a cracker—then another, and then another, until the crackers are gone.

I hope that this snack will fuel my synapses, that it will prod them to start firing again. But all it does is make me sleepy. What with the stress of the past week, the tossing and turning I did last night, and getting up at first light to pack the car, I've probably strung together only a few hours of actual sleep. Sitting here at the table, not only can I not seem to think things through; I can't seem to keep my eyes open.

I put away what remains of the cheese and rinse my mug in the sink. Then I drag myself upstairs and down the hall to the last door on the left.

It's exactly as I left it.

The bed is made with my signature, the corners folded to the long sides and the foot of the comforter tucked under (I like my feet to be cozy, to have boundaries, whereas Brad likes his to kick free). This means that no one has slept in this bed for more than a month.

A stab of guilt sinks in. I left my husband up here to withdraw from society, from life, from me. I left him here to sleep in a barn— which is where I assume he is tonight—with no one to watch out for him, to advocate for him. I gave up on him when I should have kept him in Madison, with me.

And where would he be then? a voice inside my head asks. It's a rhetorical question, because the answer is clear. He'd be sleeping on the floor of our bedroom, both of us struggling to get through each day, my rope of sanity becoming increasingly slippery until I could no longer hang on for both of us. Until I couldn't hang on even for myself.

It's better like this, I tell myself. If not now, then it will be eventually. Because what do you do in a situation like the one we've found ourselves in?

I can tell you what you do: You walk away.

I think about how it will work: the disbanding of our marriage, of our life together. Sure, I've thought about leaving Brad before, but it was a theoretical exercise—an idea I tried on for size much the way I tried being with Zach on for size, all of it done in the soft corners of my brain, where I could think certain things and be content in the knowledge that they were only thoughts. I knew all along that I could contemplate leaving Brad and move toward it, in the tiniest ways without making any sort of actual, permanent leap.

And now? Now I am here to tell him that I've rented our house, that his things are in the back of my car, and that I'm headed to California for an indefinite time. Now I'm starting to seriously wonder which attorney to retain or if I'll need one, how we'll divvy up our meager assets, what it will feel like to sign my name to a divorce decree and walk out into the morning or afternoon air when I do. I am considering the fact that this time, there is no safety net. I have no job, no idea what I'm going to do for work, and no best friend to turn to. I have no idea how I could possibly live an entire lifetime with Brad as he is, and no idea how I might ever meet someone who could fill the void that leaving him would create. I have no family to spend holidays with. Brad has always been my family, but once I pay an attorney a few thousand dollars and sign on a dotted line, he will cease to be even that.

In the dark, I lie down on the bed. It's too much thinking. There are too many questions. My brain can't process them all. Not right now. I close my eyes against them. I try to get them to stop their barrage. And when sleep comes, swiftly and unexpectedly, they do.

By the grace of some higher power, I sleep until morning. It's the first solid night's sleep I've had in as long as I can remember—probably since before law school. If that sounds like hyperbole, I have some prescription sleeping pills in my possession and two bags, as black and heavy as steamer luggage, that have taken up permanent residence under my eyes, to say it's not.

Mert is standing at the kitchen sink, looking out a half-raised window. I pour myself the dregs of that morning's coffee and move to stand next to him.

"Didn't know you'd be here, Princess," he says, not looking at me.

"Neither did I."

I follow Mert's gaze and finally see what he's watching so intently.

Brad is standing in the middle of the yard. He has on flip-flops, a gray T-shirt, and worn jeans with a black fleece tied around his waist. His lips are curled into a contented smile and his face is relaxed. He looks like he did on that January morning five years ago, the morning after I first met him. It's a look I love, and the way I picture him in my mind when he's not right there—casual, rugged, self-assured. He is less angular than he was back then, or even a few months ago. And the weight he's put on makes him look softer, happier. There are essential experiences tied to that new softness. There were bridges crossed and baggage hauled and journeys made.

When I was in my early twenties, naïve and not as smart as I thought I was, I would look at couples dragging along a gaggle of kids or making their morning commutes to work, men and women who needed to see their hairdresser or a treadmill or the inside of an apparel store's dressing room more often, and I'd feel profoundly sad for them, even superior to them. I thought they had given up on being a better version of themselves. I thought that their free time and money and energy had been siphoned off by all the pressures of adulthood. I swore I'd never, ever do that. I swore I'd resist life when it tried to wear me down. I'd be vigilant against those changes.

Looking at Brad right now, though, I know better. If I were to see one of those couples now, I'd admire, not pity, them. Brad doesn't look exactly as he used to, but neither do I. We're tethered to all that's happened to each of us, every day of our lives, by a million tiny threads. It's something to wear the passage of time so bravely. There's a quiet beauty in it.

Brad bends over and touches the nose of the dog, Jones, who is sitting attentively in front of him. She looks fit and fatter and healthy. It's hard to reconcile the dog in the yard with the one Brad carried home a handful of weeks ago.

Brad backs up from her a few steps and straightens. He moves around her in a circle, counterclockwise, eventually coming back to his original position. The entire time, that dog doesn't take her eyes off him.

"He does this every day. For hours," Mert says, his gaze focused on man and canine. "It's the damnedest thing."

I'm not sure if Mert means the weird staring contest Brad and this dog are having or that he spends hours working with the dog in general. Brad gives the dog an almost imperceptible nod of his chin and says, "Okay," and Jones breaks her position, spins around twice, and leaps into Brad's waiting arms.

Maybe things have changed, a voice inside me says. *Maybe he's getting better.* But I shake my head, waving it off. I can't afford to keep hoping. Brad needs help and I can't force him to get it. And if that doesn't change, nothing else is going to. Not for long, anyway. Not for good.

I glance sideways at Mert; he's still looking out the window. Brad is walking in a figure eight now, with Jones at his side, the dog following each step Brad takes. The look in her eyes and the carriage of her body convey more than obedience. They communicate total, unconditional devotion. I'm taken aback at Mert's comment, but I try not to show it.

"I know what you think of me," Mert says.

"Right back at ya, Mert," I say.

"I'm not a bad guy, Princess."

"I never said you were, Mert," I say. "I don't think that."

"You think I'm too hard on Brad," he says. "I see the way you look at me."

I shrug. It would be tough to argue with Mert. Then again, it's not really any of my business. "Mert, you don't really have to—"

Mert holds up a hand to stop me. He's still watching Brad. Mert has a softer, wistful look on his face. I see hints of who he must have been long ago—when he was newly married, when his children were babies, when he had his whole life to live.

When he was happy.

"I like that about you, Princess. I always have. You're as loyal to my son as that dog out there."

I suck in a breath. Comparisons like this one feel like the twist of an invisible, serrated knife, especially when, in this case, the dog has me beat fair and square when it comes to winning Brad's affection.

I think about how I spent the last week. I think of Brad's things and my things, packed in separate boxes in the back of my car. I think of how, if not for the heap of guilt Darcy laid on me the other night, I might not be here in person to tell Brad about my decision. As it is, I'm springing it on him with no notice. Those are not the actions of a loyal person. And to think that Mert, of all people, is now going to give me credit for doing the exact opposite of what he thinks I've done. It all makes me feel a little queasy, though coffee on an empty stomach isn't helping matters much.

"Thing is," Mert continues, "Ricky was such a mess. Ran with a tough, fast crowd, that one. Oh sure, he's done fine for himself now, but it could've easily gone another way." Mert is still staring out the window, almost as if talking to himself; yet I get the distinct impression that he's acutely aware of my presence and the level of attention I'm giving him. "But Brad's smart. I didn't want him hanging around here feeling tied to this place because of what happened with his mom—thinking I needed taking care of. I wanted him to go out and do big things. And if that meant hating his old man, then so be it. He always could do just about anything he set his mind to." Mert turns and looks directly at me, raising an eyebrow. "Still can, you know."

I meet Mert's gaze. I wonder what he knows, and if he's insinuating that I knew more than I told him about Brad before dropping him here. But it's hard to tell, and so I just nod. All this time, I assumed

Mert didn't have the faintest idea of what his son was struggling with, when it sounds like maybe he knew better than I realized. But Mert is wrong, too. Brad isn't Brad anymore. Mert might be more observant than I've given him credit for, sure; but he's no North Woods oracle.

And as though he hasn't said a word, Mert turns from the window and pats my shoulder on his way past me. "See if you can get him to bathe that dog," he says, walking away. "She stinks."

I look back out the window at Brad and Jones. He's kneeling next to her, seemingly telling her she's a good girl, though I can only make out the tone of his voice and not the words he's saying.

Brad looks up at the kitchen window where I'm standing. He raises his hand in a tentative wave, and Jones takes the opportunity to give his cheek a lick. Brad doesn't break my gaze and his face erupts into a toothy grin. It's that same earnest smile I first fell in love with, back when I still felt like a young woman. Back when it seemed as though a whole world of possibility was still laid out like a feast in front of us.

I raise my own hand in a feeble return of Brad's wave. *It's a mirage,* I tell myself. Yet I can't help but smile back.

I sit on the back stoop, watching Brad finish his lesson with Jones. By the time he's done, she's panting and there are dark areas of perspiration on his shirt. He releases Jones with a pat on the head and gestures to the yard. "Go on," he tells her. "Good girl."

Jones trots over to a circle of sun at the edge of the grass. She lies on her belly, her stare fixed on Brad. But when he sits next to me, she flops over onto her side, confident that her person isn't going anywhere, and lets her eyes close.

Brad and I sit shoulder to shoulder. He picks at a weed growing defiantly through a crack in the concrete at his feet, peeling each leaf on the coarse stalk one by one. For a long time, neither of us speaks.

"Why are you here?" he asks, finally.

"Where were you yesterday?" I ask, hoping the question comes out loaded with curiosity as opposed to suspicion. It doesn't.

We look at each other, playing a game of visual chicken.

"C'mon, E. Out with it."

"With what?" *I'm not ready to have this conversation.* I want to sit here a little while longer. I want to pretend this isn't happening for a few more minutes. There's something about Brad's carriage, the way he's talking to me so self-assured and relaxed, that makes me want to kiss him. But I can't. We are married and we are sitting right next to each other, but I know that I don't have the right to indulge that impulse now. Two people sitting so close have never been so far apart.

Brad shakes his head. "I know things are a little scrambled up here," he says, pointing to his temple, "but even I know what a packed car looks like, E., and I'm assuming you're not here to move in with me and my old man. So what gives?"

I wonder if the surprise I feel at hearing Brad recognize that his brain isn't working right registers in my eyes. I feel them go wide, but I try not to react. I look down at the weed between Brad's feet and mine, stripped of its foliage and looking bare and vulnerable. I want to slap myself in the forehead. Of course he realizes it. I want to cry for him, for how frustrating it must be to have been counted as among the most accomplished and intelligent young scholars in the country only a handful of years ago, and now—

"I don't blame you," he says. "You should know that."

This is classic Brad: considerate and understanding. But right now, I wouldn't mind a little anger, a little emotion. As I sit here, it suddenly dawns on me why I'm here—why I drove all this way: I want him to fight for me, for us. I want to—need to—know that I still matter to him.

"I don't know what I'm doing," I say. *Talk me out of it* is what I'm really thinking and wanting to say.

"Do any of us?" he asks. He takes my hand in his, and in doing so, notices his watch.

"Shit," he says. "I have to be somewhere. You weren't planning to leave, like, right now, were you?"

I shake my head no.

"Good deal. You can tell me all about it later, then. We'll figure it out."

He stands up and brushes his jeans clean. Then he nods in the direction of Jones, still lounging in her patch of sun. "Keep an eye on that one for me, will you?"

"Sure," I say, though I have no idea what, exactly, he's asking me to do.

I stand and watch in shock as Brad steers Mert's truck down the long driveway. *He's driving. By himself.* I hear the truck turn onto the highway; then, for lack of anything else to do, I sit back down. My normal inclination would be to reach for my BlackBerry, but I turned that in, along with my office key and security card, when I left the firm last week. As sad as it sounds, I feel as if a piece of me is missing. There is no e-mail to read, no voice mail messages to return. Nothing is being asked, or expected, of me.

Instead of liberating, it feels terrible, as if I have no purpose.

I never caught on to reading for entertainment; it always seemed a guilty pleasure—something I could never justify sitting still long enough to enjoy. Right about now, though, I wish I had a book to lose myself in, or some other way to pass a few hours, like knitting or embroidery. The image of me sitting here on Mert's back steps doing counted cross-stitch nearly makes me chortle out loud.

Then again, who am I? I used to be able to answer that: I am an attorney. I am Brad Sabatto's wife. I am going to be partner in a law firm someday and have children and a wonderful, wonderful life. I am blessed and lucky.

Now? I'm not sure.

Jones lifts her head and looks at me. She gets up and sidles over to where I sit. She stops a few feet from me, watching. I remember the way she looked at me, the teeth she bared the first time I saw her, and my whole body tenses. She's an imposing dog, barrel-chested and thick all over, with jaws that look like they could reduce wood to dust. Then her tail starts wagging—slowly at first before picking up speed— and if I didn't know any better, I would think she's smiling. Her long tongue lolls out of her wide-open mouth. She bows down until her head and front legs are touching the ground and her rump is high in the air, tail wagging.

"Hey, million-dollar dog," I say to her, not unkindly. "What's going on?"

And that does it. It's as though I've flipped a switch by acknowledging her. She whirls and spins, bucking like a bronco. In between bucking spurts she crouches again with her front end, looking at me with that grin of hers and wagging her tail. Then she resumes bucking.

I have no idea what I've done to elicit such a response. Maybe there's some command I've given her inadvertently?

It's a beautiful spring day, I have nowhere to be and nothing to do, and I have no idea when Brad will be back.

"How about we go for a walk, girl?" I ask. She looks confused until I enter the house and come out with her leash. I wonder what kind of life she's had that she doesn't even know the word *walk*. Isn't that the one word that every dog in the world hangs on? When I was growing up, our neighbors would try to fool their old golden retriever by calling it, "going for a klaw"—walk, backward. Eventually, the dog caught on to that one, too.

Not only does this dog not seem to know about walks; she also has one of the ugliest, least feminine collar and leash sets I've ever seen. She should have a leash that's brightly colored and girly, with polka dots or a plaid pattern. She should have any leash other than the one Brad has purchased for her: in camouflage to match her black collar. Her name sounds like a male dog's, and now Brad is dressing her like one, too. I make a note to tell him that she needs some new duds, more fitting for her gender.

With that ugly leash in hand, though, I have become the world's most exciting, most wonderful human being. Jones spins around again, tongue hanging from her mouth and eyes bright and wide with anticipation. I hold the leash up, out of her way, and this must be some sort of cue, because she immediately sits square in front of me, trying to hold herself still and succeeding except for the tremors of barely contained enthusiasm that shake her body.

I tell her to stay, and run back inside to pocket some cash, my cell phone, and my car keys. When I return, the dog is still sitting where I left her. I reach a hand out and pat her tentatively on her wide, table-top of a head. I don't lock the door behind me, remembering what Mert said to me years ago when I asked how I'd be able to get in the house without him there, and without a key: "I haven't locked this door since I bought the place in 'seventy-one, Princess. Don't even have a key for it anymore."

I open the passenger-side door to my car and Jones jumps right in, sitting up as a person would, nice and straight. Should I belt her in? I've never had a dog before, and it seems a good idea; dogs aren't any less vulnerable than people in an accident. But I can't figure out how to restrain her, so I leave her free and hope that I haven't violated some basic tenet of dog care.

As we wind our way toward town, past the turnoff for Mead Pond and Hogsback Mountain and then the much more conspicuous Sugarloaf Mountain, I roll the windows down far enough so that the warm-tinged wind musses my hair and Jones can let her head hang out, the very portrait of a happy dog.

We follow County Road 550 until it runs into Presque Isle Avenue just short of the long beach that stretches from Presque Isle Park all the way to the other side of town, and then far beyond. Winter is always slow to leave Marquette, but when it finally does, the local students and residents celebrate with a fervor often reserved only for hockey games. Although I have many memories, my favorite Marquette sight was a group of students on a particularly hot spring day, sunbathing on the beach next to blocks of hard-packed snow and ice floes that had been left behind to melt at their own pace. The students had repurposed them as drink coolers. By the time I had returned with my camera, the kids were nowhere to be found, and now, as I drive past the parts of the beach that are popular with students, I scan for a similar scene, lest I miss capturing it twice.

But Lake Superior, or Gitche Gumee as she's known around here, looks angry—as if she'd rather not have visitors today. Her water is ink black, crashing into the shore and running up the beach, which is completely empty. We can walk and walk and walk the shore without interruption or the worry of bothering anyone.

First, though, I am going to get myself a coffee and the two of us a treat to share. I drive up and then down Third Street and take a right on West Washington Avenue, keeping my eyes peeled for a parking spot. I end up finding one two blocks down. I leave the window partway down for Jones, and I hope she doesn't get any crazy ideas in that little dog brain of hers in the time it's going to take me to run into Babycakes Muffin Company and back to the car.

I wore a baseball cap for our outing because it can be windy near the lake and my hair is too short to pull into a proper ponytail, but as I approach the café's window, I'm glad to be incognito, because sitting there, plain as day, is Brad with some woman.

She is thin, with impossibly long legs and the kind of thick, wavy, strawberry-colored mane that seems to exist only in shampoo commercials. She flips it with her hand twice in the short time I'm stand-ing there. Her teeth are straight and so white that she's either scrubbed the enamel clear off them or that's not coffee in the mug in front of her. She has on a pair of green-rimmed retro-style glasses and a nose ring, both of which suggest that she has a whole other side hidden by that coiffed façade; maybe she's maybe a little edgier than she seems at first glance.

Brad's back is to me. I know I've been seeing versions of him all over the place lately, but this man is wearing the same jeans, T-shirt, and fleece Brad was this morning. And when he stands up from the table, I catch a glimpse of his profile. It is unmistakably, undeniably him.

Thirty-one

Jones and I do not go for our walk along the beach. I grip the steering wheel with shaking hands as I retrace our route straight back through Marquette and out County Road 550 to Mert's house. If Jones is confused about any of this, she doesn't seem to notice. She's just as excited to be going back the way we came.

I think back to this morning, to how Brad acted when he confronted me about leaving. I hadn't thought much of it at the time, but now, in hindsight, I realize that he seemed carefree, some new version of happy, even. And I realize why he seemed inclined to simply let me leave, why he didn't put up any fight. Why he seemed to have so little reaction to my news.

Because he's moving on. Or he moved on—past tense.

I park beside Mert's house, which is still empty and quiet. Before I get out, I unclip Jones's leash from her collar, and she follows me out the driver's-side door instead of waiting for me to come around and get her.

"Go on," I tell her, waving the leash at the shrinking patch of sun she called home earlier this afternoon. But she just stands there, staring at me and looking uncertain. "Go on," I say again. Jones sits, watching me and panting.

"Fine," I say. "Suit yourself."

I head inside the house, hang the leash where I found it, and retrieve my things from upstairs. Then I write a terse note for Brad and leave it on the kitchen table: *Sorry, couldn't stay. I'll call soon. —E.*

In the time it's taken me to do those few things, though, the sun has dropped and the air has cooled. There aren't any pools of warm left for Jones to lie in and she barely has a coat to speak of.

"Come on, girl," I say to her. I pat a staccato beat with my palm against my leg and Jones falls in beside me. The least I can do is bed her down in the barn before I go.

When I enter the lower level, though, I find no sign that Jones—or Brad—has been sleeping there. There are no nests of blankets or straw or hay, no food or water bowls. I shake my head, puzzled. And then my stomach sinks as I think about the woman in the café. *What if*—I start to form the question in my mind and stop myself. Because Brad wouldn't do that. Brad wouldn't be staying with some other woman, not when he's still married—when we're still married. *Would he?*

The dusty, hazy light filtering in through the barn windows swirls around me. I feel dizzy and faint and sick as the pieces fall into place in my mind, like the cams of a combination lock. Brad hasn't called. *Click.* Brad hasn't been sleeping in his room here. *Click.* Brad didn't even seem surprised that I was leaving, or curious as to why, and most of all, he didn't seem to care. *Click.*

How did we get here? I think, as the memories flood in.

I am standing in the airport, seeing Brad off on his second term at Oxford. I've known him for only fifteen days, but it feels like as many years. I don't know when I will see him again, or if. We have kept the past weeks fun and wholly lacking in substance, like three squares of cotton candy a day. For all I know, there will be another version of me waiting to greet him on the other side of the pond when he disembarks, though I don't ask. I want to, but instead I chew on the inside of my cheek, because these are the rules of a fling. He has almost reached the security checkpoint when he turns and walks back to me. "I almost forgot," he says, handing me a folded piece of paper. "Clear the second week of March." He kisses my forehead and then he's gone, swallowed by a swarm of people all moving inch by inch toward destinations scattered across the globe. I am at the stairs leading to the parking ramp before I realize that in my hand is not his itinerary, but one with my name on the top. Unaware of the people clamoring past me, I sink to the stairs right there, so amazed I can't even stand.

I am sitting at the window of my apartment overlooking West Washington Avenue, sipping a beer in the dark—waiting. Bare, sinewy tree branches stretch like veins against the skin of a darkening sky. My heart trips every time a car slows, but most come to a full stop farther down the street, at the Indian restaurant I hadn't realized is so popular. By the time the right headlights slow and then darken, I'm three beers in and feel like I'm coming home instead of the other way around.

Spring. The air is warm and cool all at the same time as it breezes through the car's open windows. I have officially made it through an entire year of law school; I'm a 2L. I've celebrated by having a Snickers Fun Size bar for dinner followed by one-too-many dirty martinis (which would be, approximately, one). I sing along with gusto to "Back in the New York Groove," but I mangle the lyrics, getting them right only on the refrain and making up the rest. Brad is driving and he rolls up the windows. I shoot him a look meant to convey both incredulity and hurt. "Do you not want anyone else to hear?" I ask. "Is that it? You're embarrassed by me?" He takes my hand in his, and without letting his eyes stray from the road, brings it to his lips.

"Baby, you're so good, I just want you all to myself," he says. And I believe him.

Recalling these moments is like having a psychic tell me about past lives I've lived. I know they happened, but I don't feel as if they happened to me.

I can hear Jones's whining. It's constant and insistent, and I follow the sound to the top of a newly repaired stairway at the very back of the barn. The stairs lead up toward the hayloft, and even in the dim light I can see that the steps have been replaced with new wood and the floor joists reinforced. The stairs are steep and the railing on either side has been removed. Images of Jones falling to her death flash through my mind. I imagine that dogs don't have the same ability as cats to land on their feet after falling from great heights, and I wouldn't want to be the one to tell Brad that the dog he so adores died on my watch because of a missing stair rail.

"Get down from there!" I hiss at Jones, but she ignores me. Her snout is pressed into the door at the top of the stairs, her gaze fixed on the handle as if willing it to open.

"Jones!"

Nothing.

"Jones, come!"

Nothing.

"Jones, treat," I say, hoping that if I can't be commanding, perhaps I can entice her with food I don't have to offer.

"Cookie? Goodie? Snausage?"

I don't know that I've ever seen a dog so intent. She hasn't so much as tipped an ear in my direction. I assume there's a rabbit or squirrel or raccoon up there, but the sun is going down and it's getting late. Brad will be back any moment, and I want to be gone when he is.

To be safe, I climb the stairs on all fours. When I reach Jones, I pat her haunches and tell her she's a good girl, which is not my actual opinion of her at the moment. I just don't want to startle her. I hook a finger in her collar and tug it toward me.

"Come on, girl," I say. "Let's go." When that doesn't work, I repeat, "Let's *go!*" She looks at me out of the corners of her eyes, little half-moons glowing in the almost-dark.

I plead with her. Cajole. Pull on her, which is not unlike pulling on a cinder block. Nothing works.

"Fine," I say, exasperated. "Fine! Get it out of your system. Go chase that poor little bunny into the hay bales and then we go."

I turn the knob and fling the door open in front of me, expecting Jones to fly through it. Instead, she walks in and I can hear her nails clip-clipping on wood as she trots and then stops. I hear her lie down with a sigh.

It takes a moment for my eyes to adjust. When they do, I don't see what I expect: the same old stacks of hay bales that long ago molded, the broken floor of the hayloft riddled with holes and loose boards, or chains and tools and decrepit lawn mowers tossed haphazardly about the place.

Instead, in front of me is a giant room with newly laid pine floors and walls, windows with the factory stickers still affixed to the glass, and in the opposite corner from where I'm standing, a wood-burning stove. There is a wrought-iron bed made up with a denim duvet, a braided rug on the floor next to it, and closer to the stove, a desk and chair. Along the opposite wall are cabinets—the start of a kitchen— with space and plumbing roughed out for inserting a stove and refrigerator. It smells new, fresh. It smells something like hope.

I move closer to the desk, and as I do, I see rows and rows of index cards tacked to a bulletin board above it. Some contain lists of directions—*To Town/From Town, To Rick's Shop/From Rick's Shop.* Other cards outline a daily hygiene routine broken down into morning and night; skills to work on with Jones; a list of phone numbers, including one for a Randy Colenso that I don't recognize; and a list of meal options for breakfast, lunch, and dinner. There is a daily schedule of morning, afternoon, and evening routines broken down to the hour and a separate list of medications and the times Brad is supposed to take them.

The cards are bent and worn, and I can picture Brad standing before this bulletin board and selecting which ones he'll need to carry with him that day. It's a bittersweet image—my husband, who could once wax poetic about the political and economic nuances of the Eastern Bloc countries, needs an index card to tell him when to brush his teeth.

I walk to the sink that's been installed in the almost-kitchen. A dirty glass with the remnants of what looks like dried lemonade sits unwashed in it, a juice glass holding one toothbrush and a tube of toothpaste is next to it on the edge of the sink. There's something strange about this space that I'm having a hard time pinpointing until it comes to me. It's not what's there that's odd; it's what isn't. There's no glass of half-drunk Jack on the nightstand. No jug of Jack on the counter. No nest of blankets on the floor next to the bed. And no sign of the woman from the coffee shop.

That woman. The thought of her makes my stomach constrict, makes my blood feel like it's curdling in my veins. And it reminds me that I need to get going. I'll call Brad when I'm well on the road and tell him I left Jones up here, which is where it looks like she belongs, given the fluffy dog bed she's lying on and the full bowl of water next to it.

I take one last look around. Jones watches me with her big brown eyes, and right then, I wish she could talk. She seems wise, and I'm sure she's seen enough to give me a good idea of what Brad has been doing here. Of where I might stand with him. Of where we stand with each other.

"You're just a dog," I say to her, reminding myself of the ridiculousness of this train of thought. "And I'm clearly losing my mind, right girl?"

I bend down and scratch under her chin and down to her chest. I remember reading somewhere that dogs like this much more than being patted on the head, especially since their chest is pretty much the one area they can't reach to groom or scratch themselves. Then I take her big block of a head between my hands. "You be a good girl, and take care of Brad now, okay?"

I pat her head anyway because it's hard not to pat a dog's head, and she squints her eyes closed as I do, either out of contentedness or squeamishness—it's hard to tell just then.

"Who says I need taking care of?"

When I spin around, Brad is standing there, studying me.

Thirty-two

Brad has left the door open, and after trying so very hard to get in here, Jones darts out. I can hear her tearing through the downstairs and out into the oncoming night. I look at Brad, raising an eyebrow, wondering if Jones is okay.

"She probably heard a chipmunk," he says.

"Poor chippy."

Brad walks over to the bed and sits down on it.

"I gotta tell you, that dog is the best thing that ever happened to me," he says, looking wistfully out the door after Jones.

I nod and try to hide my grimace with a smile. He has no idea how cutting that single comment is, because he sweeps an arm wide and asks, "So, what do you think?"

I can tell he's proud of it, but all I'm able to do is nod in approval. Because when I look at him, I see the woman from this afternoon and hear him saying that a dog is the best thing that's ever happened to him, negating, in a flash, every minute of our five years together. I don't have it in me to muster the amazement I felt when I first opened the door to this place.

"You okay?" he asks me.

I nod. "Just tired. Lots going on," I say, tapping a finger against my temple.

Brad stands up and I'm afraid he's going to move toward me. Instead, he slaps both hands on his legs and says, "Okay. I know there are things that need talking about, but here's the thing. I'm starving. It's almost dinnertime and I haven't eaten yet. Let's grab a bite, and we can talk."

I don't know what to think. The man in front of me looks like my husband and now he's even acting like him. He's calm and rational and seems at ease in his own skin. "It's because of her," a voice inside me says. Though I don't want to believe it, that voice, I can't help it. What else has the power to bring about the changes I've seen in Brad? In my experience, only love.

He's holding the door open, waiting for me. "Come on," he says.

I follow Brad out the door, down the steps, and across Mert's expansive backyard toward the car. At the last minute, Brad stops and calls for the dog.

"What are you doing?" I ask Brad.

"Getting Jones."

Jones trots out of the tree line. Brad calls to her: "Come on, girl. Wanna go for a ride?"

I tug on my husband's arm. "Brad, why make her sit in the car?"

He shakes his head no and whistles for Jones, who runs toward him like a cannonball on legs before leaping into the air, confident that Brad will catch her. And I can't help but think, *How nice. How very nice for her.*

Jones rides on the truck's bench seat between us, sitting up and watching the road intently. Well on the other side of town, we pull up outside a dilapidated building with shingles for siding and front steps looking like they could collapse under their own measly weight.

Brad gets out and calls for Jones. Once on the ground, she sits in front of him, her tongue hanging out the side of her mouth. Brad scratches behind her ears and then clips the leash on her. He starts leading her toward the stairs.

"You're bringing her in?" I ask.

Brad nods. "You don't think this is my first choice to take you for dinner, do you?" Then he keeps on walking, forcing me to follow him instead of deciphering what he means.

I expect someone to throw us out as soon as we pass through the door. This is, after all, an establishment that serves food and my husband is leading a pit bull into it. But a graying older man whose belly protrudes well past the rainbow suspenders he's wearing waves to Brad when we enter. There are only four other people in the place—a hard-looking woman who, I would guess, is about my age sitting at the end of the bar; and a table of three—two men and a woman who looks just as hard as the one at the bar, only much older—playing cards. None of them reacts to the dog. Brad heads to a table opposite the bar and sits down, facing the door. Jones collapses at his feet, laying her head on her paws.

The place smells of stale beer and a good time had by all. Patsy Cline is playing on the jukebox. Every wooden surface is covered with carvings—drunken hieroglyphics—and bras of all sizes, styles, and colors hang from the ceiling behind the bar, making it look like a North Woods Coyote Ugly. A hand-drawn sign advertising $.25 *Tappers* is tacked cockeyed on one wall.

The cracked vinyl seat pinches my leg as I slide into it. I'd swap my chair out for another, but by the looks of them, there isn't one in decent shape. Brad catches me eyeing the place. "It's lovely," I tell him, and he smiles.

"Jimbo there served in Korea," Brad says, nodding at the man with the belly and suspenders. "He owns it. And he's cool with Jones. So this is where we come."

A waitress—the younger old-looking woman from the bar—approaches our table and asks if we're ready to order.

"We—ah—we haven't seen a menu yet," I tell her.

She looks at Brad as if I just spoke to her in a foreign language.

"No menu," Brad says. "They've got burgers and then pretty much anything that you can drop in a fryer—curds, onion rings, shrimp, french fries, mushrooms."

"Chili," the woman says to Brad.

"Oh, and chili," he tells me. "Right. It comes with spaghetti. They'll do it without, but it's extra."

I see the waitress wink at him, and I nod, wholly confused. It costs more to *not* get an item? "I'll just have a cheeseburger and onion rings," I say.

"Pickles and ketchup?" She pronounces it katz-sup.

"Sure," I say, afraid that I might get upcharged for not getting either.

Brad orders a double cheeseburger and fries. "You want a beer?" he asks me. I shrug and then nod. "Two Bell's Oberon," he says.

The waitress finishes writing down our order and slips her notepad into her back pocket. She isn't wearing an apron. She smiles out of the corner of her mouth at Brad. "Good to see you back here, Sabby," she says, and something in her tone makes my stomach twist. Something in it convinces me I don't have the slightest clue as to what Brad has been doing up here—or with whom.

Questions swirl. I want to know how he's managed to create a whole apartment for himself and what has him sleeping in a bed again. I want to know if he's better—cured. I want to ask him about the woman in the coffee shop. And I want to know if he's done this for her, because of her. Then again, I don't want to know. Every attorney worth her salt knows that she never, ever asks a question for which she doesn't already have the answer. Sometimes more information isn't always better.

But Brad beats me by talking first.

"Listen, E.," he says. "I don't blame you—for wanting to go. I want you to know that."

I study Brad's face. He looks tired, but content. I wait for the conditional part of that statement, the "but," the part where he says that he doesn't want me to go.

"I know it's been hard on you," he continues. "I know what I'm like. Even when I'm doing some of this stuff, I know. I feel like a monster, sometimes, but I can't seem to help it, to control it. That sounds like an excuse, but it's the God-honest truth, E. I'm just so angry all the time. Not at you—you know that, right?—but I'm still angry, and it can't be easy on you. You deserve more than that."

"I know," I say.

We sit in silence. Perhaps Brad doesn't know what else to say. Perhaps he is fresh out of explanations. He looks at me. He chews his lower lip. I stare past him at a tin Schlitz sign tacked to the wall.

"I was going to take the dog for a walk today," I say. "I stopped at Babycakes. You were there. With a woman. Right?" *Please say no,* I think.

Brad exhales and runs a hand through his hair. He shakes his head.

"Oh man," he says. "E., that's not at all—"

But he doesn't finish because just then, there's a crash behind us and I see a tray with all of our food clatter to the floor.

Before you live with someone suffering from post-traumatic stress, you never notice how many loud noises—how many triggers— make up day-to-day life: buses backfiring, a medivac helicopter whomping overhead, police sirens blaring, doors slamming, the rip and pop of breaking down a cardboard box, neighbors yelling to each other across the street, trays of food and silverware hitting the floor.

After you live with someone with PTSD, you notice. You notice and you anticipate and you prepare. And when you can't prepare, you brace yourself, as I'm doing now.

I have grabbed the table and hunched up against the wall, steeling myself against Brad's reaction. But when I look up, Jones has her front paws on Brad's lap and she's licking his face. Brad's eyes are wild and his breath is quick and ragged, but he's running his hands up and down her back.

Brad breathes deeply, repeatedly, and eventually Jones's licks become fewer and Brad's breathing returns to normal. Jones lies back down on the floor at Brad's feet and in a matter of seconds, falls asleep.

Brad looks at me sheepishly. "Well, that was embarrassing," he says, and it's hard to tell if he's talking about the dropped food or having just made out with his dog right here in the bar.

Jimbo yells his apologies and tells us that lunch is on the house. Brad waves him off. "No need," he says. Then Brad turns back to me. "Anyway, that's what I'm talking about, E. This dog—she's changing my life."

His voice brims with awe—with reverence. It's the same tone he used to use when we'd be cleaning out the dishwasher or raking leaves or reading the Sunday morning paper over coffee, and I'd look up and find him smiling at me; and he'd say, "Out of all the guys in the world, I can't believe I'm the one who got to marry you."

Brad pauses, and I expect him to elaborate, but one of the other card-playing patrons has appeared at our table. She's an older, grandmotherly woman who sets two fresh beers in front of us.

She places a hand on Brad's shoulder, and I see him flinch as if her touch burns.

"Bradley, I don't think you know me," she says. "I'm Janey—Janey Aho. I was a friend of your ma's way back when. We graduated together from Negaunee in—in—well, that's not really important, I guess. It's not why I came over here."

Janey Aho looks nervous—or at the very least, ill at ease—and she still has her hand on Brad's shoulder. He still looks just as uncomfortable.

"I wanted to introduce myself and to tell you how proud I am of you—of your service. We all are. Your ma—I bet she's looking down on you, just beaming. I'm sure she's busting her buttons up there over you."

Janey looks at Brad expectantly, waiting for a smile or a thank-you, for any sign that she has spoken to him. Instead, Brad stares her down with brooding eyes. Janey removes her hand from his shoulder. She doesn't need to say anything for everyone watching this exchange to understand that she's taken aback by Brad's lack of response. I feel the same way. What the hell is wrong with him?

Finally he says, "You must not have known her that well."

My eyes snap to Brad, but he's not looking at Janey or me. I kick his foot under the table, hoping to get his attention or snap him out of whatever funk he's suddenly fallen into. Despite everything that's happened, I've never known Brad to be as downright rude as he's acting right now.

"Well, I know she's been gone awhile," Janey says. "I used to . . ." She trails off, thinking better, it seems, of prolonging this interaction. "Well, anyway, thank you for your service," Janey says, stepping away from our table. "You take care, now."

Well after Janey Aho has settled back at her table, I continue to stare at Brad, who continues to avoid my gaze. Gone is the relaxed, rational guy who greeted me in his apartment this afternoon. Back is sullen, borderline-explosive Brad.

"She was *trying* to be nice, Brad," I say in a hiss.

His face is hard and a single, tiny vein sticks out against his temple. He's gone from zero to irate in a matter of seconds, though I don't understand why. He stands and tugs on Jones's leash and walks out. The dog follows him through the door.

I am still sitting there when the waitress delivers our food. One look at my face, and she offers to box it all up. "Please," I squeak. Then I walk to the bar and lay two twenty-dollar bills on it. Jimbo tells me it's too much.

"Put it toward the new front steps," I say.

The waitress comes out carrying two plastic bags bulging with Styrofoam cartons. I look at Jimbo: "Or give it to her."

On my way out, I stop at Janey Aho's table. "I'm sorry," I say to her. "He's not normally like that. I don't know what—it's just—I'm sorry."

"Oh, that's okay, honey." Janey Aho smiles a sad smile at me.

I should be happy to hand Brad and his problems off to the woman in the coffee shop. I should feel relieved to be free of them. But there was a moment this afternoon—when I saw what Brad had done with the barn, when I saw how relaxed he was—when I thought that maybe I was making a mistake. A moment when I thought that maybe I hadn't given Brad enough credit. Maybe I hadn't believed in his recovery, or in him, enough. There was a moment when I thought that maybe I'd stay. But walking out to the truck with two bags full of burgers and fried food, prepared in a kitchen that probably lacks even a food permit, because that's the only place my husband can take his dog, I see this situation for what it is: unworkable, unfixable.

Thirty-three

We drive in silence nearly the entire way back to Mert's place. Jones
has her head on Brad's shoulder, nuzzled into his neck like a lover. I'm
driving, because Brad was waiting in the passenger side when I
emerged from the restaurant. His driving issues haven't been resolved
after all.

The whole time, I'm thinking of what Brad said to Janey Aho.
What was it that made Brad so angry that he up and left? I'm putting
on the turn signal for Mert's driveway when I get enough gumption
to ask.

"Drop it, E.," he says, staring straight ahead.

"No," I say. "You can't treat people like that, Brad. It's rude. And
she's right; your mom would be proud."

"What the fuck do you know?" he says. He spits the words at me.

"Because I am," I say. And I mean it. I've never been one to dote
on Brad, to tell him he looked handsome and I felt lucky to have him,
even though he usually does and I always did. In that way, I guess I'm
a little like Mert. In the midst of all that we've been struggling
through since Brad's been back, I've never told him I'm proud of him.
My pride got lost amidst all the anger and fear and resentment that

his deployment and return stirred up, but it was always there. I would look at Brad before he left, or think about him as his e-mail rolled in while he was gone, and I would think, *How many guys would join up like he did?* He didn't need to go, but he did, and despite what I told Mert, it wasn't only to court his father's approval. He felt he owed a debt—to his best friend growing up who was killed in a helicopter crash over there, to a country that had given him so many opportunities, and to the rest of the men and women who enlisted. The night before he left, lying in bed next to him, I clutched at Brad so hard that I could feel my nails digging into his skin. I didn't care, though; it meant he was close. I begged him not to leave me. And I knew I shouldn't have. I knew I was only making it harder on him, that I was already failing as a military spouse. He was right there, right next to me, and I was already sick with fear and loneliness.

"If I go, someone else won't have to, E.," he said to me, and my heart swelled with pride then, at what an incredible person Brad was and at this man with whom I got to spend the balance of my life.

I tell him now: "I should have said this before. I should have said it more often, Brad, but you're part of the less than one percent of the people in this country who volunteered to go to Iraq. To help its people rebuild their country. And that's something to be proud of. I don't know what it was like over there, but I know that back here, a lot of people genuinely admire you—your sacrifice and your service. I know because I'm one of them. Your mom would be, too. And when people like Janey come up to you, you need to let them be thankful."

"And you need to shut your fucking mouth," Brad says. He pounds a fist on the dashboard and Jones starts to lick his face, but he pushes her off. "Get off me!" he yells at her. "Get the fuck off!" She keeps trying to lick him, and he keeps pushing her head away so it bumps into my arm. To avoid an accident, I start to pull the truck over, and that's when Brad strikes Jones square in the jaw. I don't know if it was on purpose or an accident, but she yelps and scrambles into my lap. I throw the truck into park and fling my door open, jumping out and pulling Jones with me. I have a hand on her collar and I'm telling her it's okay, but she's trying to wriggle away from me. Then I realize that she's trying to get back in the truck.

Back to Brad.

Brad is punching his fist rhythmically against the dashboard. Punch—punch—punch—punch. The dash doesn't seem to be giving any, but something has to be, and I assume that something is Brad's bones and flesh and ligaments.

"Brad!"

Punch—punch—punch—punch.

"Brad!"

Punch—punch—punch—punch.

I'm afraid he's going to pulverize his hand. But before I can decide how to stop him, Jones wiggles out of her collar and leaps into the truck. I watch, amazed, as she grabs his sleeve in her mouth and bites down, not hard but as if to say, "That's enough, now." A low, guttural growl comes from her, but it's clear to me that she's concerned and not menacing. She tugs backward on his arm until finally he stops hitting the dashboard, until his shoulders slump and start to tremble. Jones lets go of his arm and begins lapping at the tears running down Brad's cheeks. He wraps his arms around her and buries his head in her. I put the keys in the ignition and close the driver's-side door, and I walk the rest of the way up Mert's driveway, feeling once again as if I'm the one at war. I'm shell-shocked from trying and failing to avoid all the land mines Brad brought back with him. I want out. I want to de-enlist.

Stars flicker in the Upper Peninsula's night sky like a bedazzled piece of cloth, and though patches of hard-packed snow and ice stubbornly refuse to melt, there's a note of warmth in the air tonight—a prelude to summer.

I have moved the last of Brad's things from my car onto Mert's porch and am wondering if I should throw a tarp over them for the night, when I see Brad walking toward me across the back lawn.

My arms and back ache from hauling boxes, and my mind aches from the events of the day. It's late and I'm exhausted. So when Brad holds a bottle of beer out to me, I accept. It's our old ritual, only playing out on Mert's porch this time. That, and we're not catching up on our day over a nightcap. I doubt there's much left to say at this point. Even the will to know about the woman from the coffee shop has left me like a spirit. It mattered so much this afternoon. Now, I'm too tired to care.

I sink to the steps, and though I know I'll be sore tomorrow, it feels painfully good to sit down.

"I stacked all of your things over there," I say, nodding to the tower of boxes at the corner of the porch. "Should be everything."

Brad nods. He worries the label on the bottle he's holding, tearing off slivers of wrapper that glow metallic in the moonlight.

"There were these kids over there," he says. His voice is quiet, and if I close my eyes, which I do, it sounds young and husky, like we're teenagers on a date. Like he's winding up to kiss me. "They were all mop-headed and dirty, but they were funny kids. Always laughing. Always hanging around the FOB. We'd give them stuff—pencils, soccer balls. They'd want their pictures taken with us. They loved to pose for pictures, those kids. And there was this one; he was hilarious. Probably nine or ten years old. He liked to work on his English with us. He had picked up all this slang from listening to the Americans. Things were always 'totally' something—'totally rad' or 'totally fucked'—and he was always 'jonesing' for something. He'd come up and say things like, 'Dude, I have had a totally fucked day and I'm jonesing for a Coke. Do you have one, please?' And it was just hilarious—this slang coming from the mouth of a little Iraqi kid with a heavy accent."

I'm not sure where Brad is going with this, but he's talking. He's talking about over there and he's not yelling, so I don't interrupt.

"I started calling him Jones. He came around a lot. A quiet kid, not as pushy as some of them. I liked him—we'd talk. I asked him one day why they're not scared of us—the kids. And he said it was because we were nice to them." Brad chuckles, but it's clear the chuckle comes from a place more regretful than happy.

"I don't think I ever told you this, but I drove the lead truck on patrol a lot of times," he goes on, stopping briefly to take a sip of his beer, which he hasn't touched save for the wrapper since we sat down. "We had orders. We knew what we were supposed to do, but I thought it was an urban war myth or some shit—like it happened to a friend of a guy's sister's brother-in-law's high school buddy." Brad pauses, takes another sip of beer, and shakes his head. "I had guys to think about, you know? Kastor's wife had a little girl the week before that he'd never seen. Patterson's mom had a stroke. There were wives and parents and kids. There were orders." Brad's voice breaks, cracks like thin, brittle paper. "Those motherfucking Hajis started sending kids out in front of patrols, so they could light the whole fucking convoy up when it stopped for them. More bang for their buck, right?"

Brad laughs at his pun, but I can't breathe. I'm holding my breath. I'm holding my breath because I know what's coming and I can't stop myself from hearing it. And I know that for the rest of my life I won't be able to stop picturing it.

Now, I don't want to know why he's like this. Why he's angry and jumpy and not himself. Because what am I supposed to do then? It doesn't change a thing between us. It will only complicate the situation. But I can't stop him. I'm frozen, dreading what he's about to say.

"Brad," I say, my voice hardly audible, "it's okay. You don't have to—"

"I saw him, fucking Jones." Brad is biting his lip. His eyes are closed, but I know that behind those lids, the scene is playing out in vivid detail. "He and this other kid are in the middle of the road, waving their arms. And the CO, in the driver's seat, says, 'Here we go,' and I knew right then that this shit was real. I saw the whites of their eyes. I saw their faces when they realized we weren't going to stop. I felt the fucking wheel jerk."

I shudder. My stomach lurches. I feel like I might be sick. But I have to ask: "Why?" I whisper. "So why Jones? Why her name?"

Brad's eyes are squeezed shut. He looks like he's in physical pain. "Because her—her I could save," he finally whispers.

Brad is crying now—crying and shaking his head back and forth, as if he doesn't want to believe what he's saying. As if he can't comprehend it. He drops his head into his hands. His fingers claw at his hair. "The fucking wheel jerked right out of my hands," he says. "Oh God, they were just kids, E. What were they doing there, those stupid fucking kids?"

Brad looks up at me, his eyes wild, pleading. He's motionless, but his face writhes.

He is waiting for me to judge him. He is waiting for me to recoil from what he's done—to recoil from him.

I pull him to me and hold him as his whole body shakes. My own breath is thick and jagged in my chest. I rock him, saying, "Shhhh. Shhhhh," in his ear. How many times have I done this in the past months? Too many. And this is just one memory—just one day out of the hundreds that he spent there. How many others does he have stored away, tucked into the hard, dark places inside him, guarded with faulty locks?

His hands claw at my shoulders. I drop my nose into his hair. It smells fresh and woodsy, like a copse of ferns after a hard spring rain. Oh, this man I love—this beautiful, broken man. He is my home, my other half. *"Was,"* a voice inside my head says. I shake my head. No, my Brad is in there somewhere, held captive by demon memories of the awful things that he's seen and done. Can I really leave him like this? Can I really leave him at all?

Brad gives in to my arms. His body is limp as he says, "Oh God," over and over again like the saddest prayer you've ever heard.

I rock him until the night air loses its warmth and clouds crawl across the stars. Until his body stops shaking and mine starts to. Until he whispers, "Don't go."

And though I'm not sure if he's asking for right now or for good, I say, "I won't."

Thirty-four

The light inside the little apartment is gray when I wake. Jones raises her head and eyes me with half-raised lids. She slept in a Superman pose between Brad and me last night, staking a claim on her part of the bed, possibly on Brad. This same scene—a husband and wife asleep in bed together, dog between them—has likely played out in hundreds of thousands of homes across the country last night. The normalcy of it overwhelms me.

Brad's arm is draped over me and his breath is warm and rhythmic in my ear. His face is serene. He looks younger and more handsome than I've taken time to notice—the dark waves of hair that roil every which way, his cut jaw, the model-high cheekbones, and those full, full lips of his. I drink him in with those two words, "Don't go," echoing in my ears, and desire ignites in me like a pilot light. The muscles of Brad's arm are lean and defined, and his skin looks faintly sun-kissed. The need to reach out and touch him, to feel that skin under my fingertips and my palms, to run them over his face and down his chest and down, down, down over the rest of him, swells until it almost overtakes me. But he is still Brad, and for fear of startling him awake, I know that I can't touch him. The swell hardens into a dull ache. *There will be time for that. We have time.*

I slip out of bed and walk to the sink for a glass of water. Like Mert's, Brad's kitchen sink is under a window that looks out toward the tree line, and behind it, miles and miles of forest. The sun is just starting to creep up over the treetops and even inside, I can smell the air outside, heavy with moss and pine and all things fresh and new after a long winter. It's a smell unlike anywhere else I've ever lived, the reward—the payoff—in these parts for enduring seven months of cold and more snow than almost any other place in the lower forty-eight states. I had forgotten this smell after so many years in southern Wisconsin, and looking out over the lush landscape outside the window and inhaling a whiff of that freshness, I think to myself how nice it is, this place.

Brad stirs behind me and I'm jolted back into the present, where it feels as though Brad and I are balancing on the thin lip of an overhang. One of us could fall, or the other. Or we could both take a step back from the edge before it's too late.

It's too late for the old us. I know that. The Brad and Elise of those first weeks, those first years—I don't even recognize them. They're like people you knew in high school and can't quite picture anymore. The us that we knew is gone, but could there be a Brad and Elise of the future, too? Two days ago I would have said no. Now, I'm not so sure. And after seeing the effect Jones has on Brad, and the way he opened up to me last night, which felt like some sort of exorcism—an indication that things could someday get better—there's a little voice inside me, which I'm trying hard to ignore, chanting, "Yes! Yes! Yes!"

"You're still here."

I turn to find Brad sitting up in bed, scratching Jones behind the ears. Jones flips over like a fish, offering Brad her belly and wiggling back and forth. He smiles at her, but when he looks back up at me, that smile fades. His question isn't coy or flirtatious. It's as though he really is surprised to see me still standing in his apartment.

"Shouldn't I be?" I ask. As soon as the words leave my mouth I regret letting them free.

"That's your call," he says. His voice is flat. The guard that he let down last night is back up.

I nod, slowly, if only to acknowledge that he said something. My heart constricts in my chest.

"Maybe this is a conversation best saved for after coffee," Brad says. He nudges Jones, who springs to her feet. He pushes the covers back and stands up, pulling on pajama pants that hang low on his hips, abdominal muscles undulating above them. He looks divine, and that hard ache inside me pulses. But when he turns around to fish a sweatshirt from his dresser, I see the jagged pink scars across his back, some as big as candy bars and one as long as a ruler, and the ache tilts toward nausea. I wonder if I'll ever get used to the sight of them. I wonder if I'll have to.

"You could still stand to light that thing at night," I say, nodding at the woodstove.

"I'm going to right now," Brad says. A hint of a smile plays at the corner of his mouth, but something has shifted. I feel as though we've woken up next to each other after a first date—as if we've just met.

Brad feeds a couple of logs into the stove and lights it. Then he places a teakettle on top. While he works—grinding coffee beans, scooping rounded spoonfuls into a French press, and readying two mugs, I dress in the same jeans and shirt I had on yesterday, since all my clothes are still in Brad's other room, in Mert's house. I sit down on the bed. I wrap my lower legs and feet in a blanket that I have to nudge from under Jones, who's still stretched flat out on the bed. I lean back against the headboard and let my eyes fall closed.

When the kettle whistles, Brad pours water over the grounds, waits a few minutes, and presses the plunger on the coffeepot. He brings me a mug, and the coffee inside is black with a glossy sheen of oil on top. It smells strong and smooth all at once. I wrap my hands around it, trying to channel some of its warmth. Brad sits down opposite me, his back against the footboard. Jones settles in next to him, laying her head on his lap.

"So," he says, stroking Jones's ears, "what's your plan?"

I shrug. "I don't know."

"Where are you off to?"

I can't believe how coldly Brad is acting, how clinical he sounds. This isn't a vacation I'm taking—a weekend or two away from him—but no one else would think that if they overheard our exchange.

I shrug.

"You really don't know? You packed up all my things and all your things and you don't have a destination in mind? Just going to start driving, or what?"

"I *was* going to head to California to see Sondra for a while." I emphasize the "was."

"That's good. Real good. Never been to California," Brad says. "You either, right?"

Tell him! my inner voice says to me. *Tell him you want to stay. Tell him you've changed your mind.* But Brad is so cold, so detached. Last night he asked me to stay, and this morning, he's inquiring about my travel plans as if we're strangers seated together on a plane.

I nod.

"Aren't you excited?" he asks. It's like he's playing a game of emotional chicken, my stomach sinking with every syllable he utters.

"Excited?"

"Yeah," he says. "This is a good opportunity. Clear your head a little. Soak up some sun. Relax. You deserve to relax some."

Why is he acting like this? Why is he doing this? Where is the man from last night? Where is the man I've spent the past six years of my life in love with?

He's in love with someone else.

"This is about her, isn't it?" My voice is soft and shaky.

"Her?"

"The woman. In Babycakes."

A sob wells up inside me. Can't I catch one little, tiny break here? I finally come around, and my husband has already found someone else. I choke the tears back down. I'm not going to give him the satisfaction of crying. Not over this.

"Oh, Elise," Brad says, and like a ray of sun breaking through a cloud-soaked sky, there's the faintest hint of feeling in his words. He runs a hand through his already-tousled hair and it spikes from his head in a wave. "That's not at all what it looked like. That was Randy. She's Jones's trainer. She's brilliant with dogs, and she loves this one, doesn't she?" He pats Jones on the top of her head, which is as big and flat as a salad plate. Her tongue lolls out the side of her mouth.

"So you're—you're not—"

"Sleeping with her?" Brad laughs. "No."

I don't appreciate his mirth. And instead of relief, I feel only dread. I suck a deep breath in and blow it back out. The ground is tilting, trembling under me, and I will it to stop. I will it to steady.

"Would you rather I was?" he asks.

I shake my head. I bite my lower lip. I concentrate on my breathing. *I will not cry.*

"Is that what this is about?" Brad asks. "E., it was your idea to leave. This is what you want, right?" The words sound almost flip.

What I want, I think silently, *is for you to give a damn about something besides that dog. For you to want me as your wife, your partner, your lover—not your parent, not your personal police, not your conscience. I want you to make me feel like I matter again. Like I matter to you*. But my voice fails me, and all I can squeak out is, "It's like you don't even care." Then my lip biting and breathing fail me, and I start to cry.

I cry because I had doubted that Brad could get better—not all the way better, which is a place he still might not be able to get to, but at all. I cry because we were so good once, and our relationship has unraveled to the point where I tell him I'm leaving for California and he says, "That's good. Real good." I cry because I want him to want me to stay, and because it seems that what he wants is not me. Not us.

Brad leans forward and grabs my face in his hand. His thumb and forefinger form a vise grip.

He turns my head and holds his forearm in front of me, the tattoo's black letters only inches from my face. "Don't you see this?" he asks, shaking his arm. His voice is husky with anger and frustration. "Didn't you hear anything I said last night?" My teeth hurt from the pressure of his fingers on my cheeks.

I stare into his eyes. They're not vacant, but they're not his, either. He releases his grip and shakes me loose. He moves back on the bed, putting space between us.

"Listen, E.—I don't blame you for doing what you're doing. Don't worry. Things here are actually pretty good."

"What are you saying?" I ask. My fear of voicing that one question, of the answer it might bring, hangs almost tangible in the air between us.

He shrugs. "Up here, my life works. It works better than it has in a while." Brad reaches for my hand and takes it in his. I wonder whether it's cold and stiff and icy, because that's how I feel. I realize I'm holding my breath, and instead of letting it out, I feel it evaporating inside me, my chest constricting. "I don't think it really works with you anymore—nothing personal."

My vision narrows. It's as though Brad has just tossed me into a deep well. As my arms spiral in a panic, trying to grab any available purchase, he's peering calmly down at me, watching me fall.

I think of the life we had in Madison, which already feels thousands of miles and years away. I think of everything I once thought so important there—my career and my cases and our favorite spots and all the memories tied to them—all fading like an old photograph. I think of the man I saw through his living room window, rocking his infant to sleep, and the one teaching his little boy to fish. I think of the heavy and sweet spring air hanging outside these windows and the way Brad looked yesterday morning, working with Jones—jaunty and relaxed—and how Jones calmed him in the truck in a way no one, or nothing, else would or has been able to. I think of the way Brad looked this morning, like his old self, and the feeling that his skin on mine kindled deep inside—a primitive, subconscious part of me recognizing that this is still the man I married. This is still the man I love.

"I don't want to go," I say.

Brad shakes his head. His eyes well, wet and red. "I know, E.," he says. "But if we're honest, really honest with ourselves, I think we both know that you should."

He moves toward me, pulling my hand to him until his arms envelop me. He buries his head in the crook of my neck. I can feel his stubble. I can feel his chest rise and fall against me. And I can smell him—his particular mix of salty and earthy and spicy-sweet. And it smells just like home.

I shake my head no, but he doesn't notice, and our tears mingle like two sad streams in the valley of our necks.

Thirty-five

It's so early, it's barely light out, and Gitche Gumee's waters are still and dark as I walk down West Washington Avenue in Marquette. Morning is my least favorite time of day and early morning even more so, but this was the only meeting time I was offered. Plus, it's not as though I'm working a full day. I tell myself I can always take a nap later.

I order a coffee and a strawberry sour cream muffin. Then I sit and wait. Somehow, I've arrived early. I decide there must be a wrinkle in the time-space continuum for this to have happened. I can't remember the last time I was on time for anything, much less early.

It doesn't take me long to drift off, until I'm lost in my own mind. Is Brad right? Am I that alien to this place—or the other way around? Is he really trying to do what's best for me, or was he not being fully honest with me about his motivations? I belonged here once, and I think I could again. Brad said his life worked better here, without me. Right now, I'm choosing to believe only the first part. What if I can find something to smooth our new, jagged edges so that we fit together better?

What if the answer is already here—right in front of us?

I jump when the chair opposite me scrapes on the wood floor and as if on cue, into it slides the leggy, strawberry-haired woman I first saw here with Brad.

Randy.

"You must be Elise," she says, holding out a hand. She's wearing the same green glasses and a green, worn, short-sleeved shirt that reads PUGS NOT DRUGS over a long-sleeved gray shirt. There isn't a trace of makeup on her face, and her hair is pulled back into an expertly messed ponytail with tendrils hanging in all the right places. I would have to work for hours to conjure up such effortless chic. She might have just walked out of an Urban Outfitters photo shoot. I wonder how she knows that I'm me, and wild scenarios start flooding my mind. Has Brad shown her pictures of me, and how much has he told her about me—about us? But then I look around and realize that I'm the only patron here. I tell myself to settle down already.

I hold out my hand and make sure to grasp hers firmly. It's a handshake I've perfected over the past years as a young, female attorney—one that says, "I might look young and sweet, but you don't want to screw with me."

"It's so nice to meet you," I say.

The barista delivers her a smoothie and a cup of fresh fruit. I had to walk up to the counter for service.

"Thanks, Stef," Randy says, and the barista gives her a little wave. Randy turns back to me, working her straw out of its wrapper, and says, "I can't thank you enough for meeting me this early. I have an insane day, but I really wanted to sit down with you."

She is warm and easygoing, and I would like to hate her. I would at least like to keep my hackles up. After all, this woman has spent countless hours with my husband over the past months, and shared, I imagine, intimate moments along the way; I have only just learned she exists.

But after a few short minutes around her, my edginess dissolves and I'm looking at her as though we're back in junior high and she's the girl who's popular, not because she's commanding or domineering, but because she's just so . . . cool. I want to spend more time with her to see how it is she does it—to absorb a little of whatever is emanating from her, in hopes that it might rub off on me, too.

"Don't thank me," I say, "thank *you*." And I feel as awkward now as I did in junior high.

"So," she says. She smiles at me and nods.

"So," I say. I didn't tell Randy exactly why I wanted to meet, just that I had something to run by her. That's because in my mind it isn't yet clear. I know only that I've seen the effect that Jones has on Brad, and I can't shake the idea that maybe he's not alone. Maybe there are other Joneses and other Brads out there, waiting to find one another. Maybe there's a way to facilitate that process—something Brad and I can do together.

That, and I wanted to meet this woman with whom my husband has been spending so much time.

"So you're a dog trainer," I say. "How long have you been doing that?"

"I grew up showing dogs. My parents were into it. But I always preferred challenging dogs, the tougher projects. So when my husband got a job here—he's a radiologist at Marquette General—and I couldn't find a job, I decided to see if I could make a go of what had been a serious hobby until then."

I nod, feigning interest in her story, but inside I'm thinking, *So, Randy is married. She doesn't wear a ring, but she* is *married.* This revelation slows the thoughts of her and Brad together that have besieged me. I know married people have affairs, but I'm trying to focus on the upside. At least she's not a gorgeous *single* woman with her sights on Brad.

"And?" I ask. "You made a go of it?"

Randy shrugs. "Yes and no. I did some behavioral work with

family dogs, and some sled dogs here and there. But there's not much money in it. Nothing steady enough, anyway."

"You've seen Brad with Jones, though, right?"

"I've seen them work together a lot, absolutely." Randy's tone is polite but flat, as though she expected something out of this conversation that she's already determined isn't going to materialize.

"You didn't know Brad before, but Randy, that dog has changed him. It's changed his life."

"She," Randy corrects me, and I fight the urge to roll my eyes. "And yes, I knew him well enough to see how much she's affected him—all for the better. It's been an amazing thing to watch."

I bristle at her choice of words. Is she trying to one-up me—pointing out that I haven't been here to see Brad's transformation and she has? As true as this might be, it still smarts. I fight the urge to one-up her back and tell her about the incident in the truck only days ago, how Jones with Randy's training hasn't exactly been a cure-all. "Well, that's what I wanted to talk to you about," I say, forcing a smile. "What if there's something to this? Brad can't be alone, right? He's not unique. There are thousands of soldiers like him—struggling with these 'invisible wounds.'" I make quote marks with my fingers.

Randy looks confused. Her brow is furrowed, one eyebrow raised—something, even with practice, that I've never been able to do.

I continue. "What if we could take other dogs—take them and train them and match them up with veterans like Brad?"

"We?" she asks.

I shrug. "Whoever."

Randy fixes me with a sweet, thin smile, as if I were a child who just said that if people around the world would only love one another, we could have world peace. "It's a nice idea, Elise. A really nice idea."

"But?" I ask.

She shakes her head. "But it won't work."

It has to work, I think. This is the only thing I've come up with that might put Brad and me on equal footing, the only thing that would give us both a reason to be here, together.

Only days ago, I was prepared to leave this place, possibly for good. It's no longer what I want. Yet, it seems the most likely scenario, and I have to force myself to swallow, to breathe.

"You think that Jones and Brad are an anomaly?" I ask, my voice cracking. "That it's a fluke, what they have together—how they are together?"

"A fluke? Oh, no. Not at all," Randy says. "There's a stack of research a mile high about the therapeutic benefits of dogs in all sorts of situations. It's pretty common, actually."

"So what's not—common—then? Why won't it work?"

"Years ago, I thought I'd try to contract with some shelters—working with dogs that need rehabbing so they can be placed instead of euthanized. But it was stupid. I was stupid. It didn't work."

"I don't follow," I tell her.

"Euthanasia is cheaper," Randy says. "It all comes down to the bottom line. Last time I checked, I'm not independently wealthy, and neither are you or Brad. It's a nice idea, Elise, but this idea of yours would cost money. A lot of money."

She looks at her watch. "I'm sorry—I have to run. I have an appointment in ten minutes." Randy starts to gather her things to go. "I'm sorry this wasn't what you wanted to hear, Elise. But I am glad to have had the chance to meet you."

She puts on her jacket and turns to leave.

"Wait," I say, desperate for this conversation not to be over. Randy turns back around. "If money wasn't the issue, would it work?" I ask her. I'm pleading with her. "If I could get the money, could we do it? Would it work?"

Randy shrugs. "Theoretically, yes," she says. "But I don't think you realize how big a project you're talking about here. It's a good idea, but there's a gigantic price tag. Depending on how many dogs you'd take in, it could be a million dollars, Elise. Maybe more."

"A million?"

Randy frowns and nods. "By the time you find a training and boarding facility and account for my time, not to mention food and vet bills. Regular service dogs are in the thirty- to fifty-thousand-dollar range. Like I said, it's a good idea, but it costs a lot of money—that none of us has. I'm sorry. Really, I am."

"You don't think we could get sponsors? Donors?"

Randy shrugs, pushing in her chair and turning to go. "I tried that before. This isn't a wealthy area. You might be able to get people to part with some spare change, but that's about it. Not enough to fund the kind of project you're thinking of. Maybe just be happy that it worked for Brad?" Randy gives me a weak smile, full of pity, and then turns once more to leave, the door jingling shut behind her.

After my meeting with Randy I am tired but overcaffeinated—a terrible combination. I walk down to the lakeshore. The air is still crisp, but I warm up enough to strip off my outer layer. I walk southeast, following the bike path until my shoes start to pinch and rub and I have to peel off the long-sleeved shirt I had on under my Windbreaker, leaving myself in only a T-shirt. Eventually, the path gives way to an expanse of sandy beach that snakes along the bay clear across to Harvey. I kick one shoe off and then the other and continue on, the sand cold and delicious between my toes. It's as if I'm on autopilot. I can't think anymore. I can't cry. I don't want to leave, but I can't stay here. Brad isn't going to change his mind, not as things stand. He was so detached. So certain. Something big, something significant would have to happen to get him to see things differently. I thought I could pull off that something; I was wrong.

There's nothing left to do now but leave.

The sun is a small glow high in the sky by the time my stomach starts to rumble with an insistent hunger. I turn around and start to make my way back. Marquette is small, like a model of itself, off in the distance, and I realize how far I've walked—how faraway and how tired and hungry I am. I sit down in the sand and start to cry.

The tears trickle at first, and then stream, until I'm full-on sobbing. A low-grade moan wells up, building into a wail as it escapes. I don't even hear a man's voice ask, "Is everything okay? Ma'am? Are you all right?" until I take a break to breathe, hiccupping as I do.

I look up and see a man slightly older than I am, bent over and peering at me from under his raised sunglasses. He is barefoot, dressed in jeans and a thin fleece pullover.

"Ma'am?"

I rub the tears from my eyes with my forearm and scramble to my feet, waving him off. "I'm fine," I say. "I'm fine."

"Pardon me saying, but you don't look fine, ma'am."

"Really? Do you think calling me 'ma'am' over and over is going to help?" I snap.

He holds both hands up in a conciliatory gesture, and I feel instantly terrible. "I'm sorry," I say. "I'm having a bad day. I didn't mean to take it out on you."

"We all have 'em," he says. "Anything I can do to help?"

I think of Randy and my stomach constricts. She's tall and beautiful and married to a radiologist. She belongs here. She has a connection with my husband that I don't. I'm pretty sure she doesn't have bad days. Not like this.

I shake my head. "No," I say. "Thank you, though."

"You sure?"

Times like these, I wish I lived in New York or Los Angeles, or even Chicago, where people would have gone on their merry way as soon as I said I was fine. Sometimes, upper midwesterners can be annoyingly nice.

"I am. Thank you," I say, and I turn and continue walking. Walking feels good: forward motion without any purpose other than moving forward. That's about as simple a goal as I can handle at the moment.

Not five minutes later, I hear a car horn beeping and tires crunching on the gravel shoulder to my left.

"Ma'am?" a voice calls, and I shudder. Anything, anything but *ma'am*. I glance over and see the man from the beach, leaning over the passenger seat of a red pickup truck. "I'm headed to town. Want a ride?"

I slow to a stop and consider the offer. I don't want a ride. But I don't want to walk all the way back, either. What if he's a serial killer? A creepy stalker? If he is, I decide, his strategy is a piss-poor one. He could've wandered that stretch of beach for hours and not seen another living soul. I decide to take my chances.

I clamber up a short, steep embankment and onto the shoulder. The passenger door swings out toward me. I notice a decal on the back window with the head of an eagle and the word AIRBORNE over it. Suddenly, all the "ma'am" nonsense makes more sense.

"Thanks," I say, catching the door and hauling myself into the truck. The man from the beach nods and waits for me to fasten my seat belt before shifting into drive and easing onto the road.

"So, Army, huh?" I ask.

The man smiles. "Hooah. Twenty years."

"Fucking Army," I say under my breath.

"Not a fan?"

I shake my head and bite my lip. I can feel my eyes smarting with tears again. Marquette is where Brad and I first met. If it weren't for the Army, if it weren't for this war, he would be fine. We would be fine. I have an overwhelming need to rewind time. To go back to that snowy night when he waited for me to get off work, hot cup of coffee in hand. To that kiss. To his standing at my stove the next morning and all the mornings that I woke up next to him until he left for Iraq. I want it all back, and the tighter I hold on, the faster the memories slip through my fingers.

"Neither was my wife," he says. "Can't say I blame her. Hardest job in the military."

I look at him, my eyes brimming. He turns briefly from the road and smiles reassuringly at me. "Your guy overseas?"

I shake my head. "Was."

"So he's back home?"

I nod.

"It'll get better," he says. "Just takes a little time."

We're coming into town, and Mr. Airborne asks where he can drop me off, giving me little opportunity to dwell on the fact that for Brad and me, time seems to have run out.

"The Lower Harbor would be great," I tell him. "Or anywhere near there."

He pulls into Thill's Fish Market, and my hand is on the door before I realize I never introduced myself.

"Thank you," I say. "For the ride. And by the way, I'm Elise."

"Ron," he says. "Elise—that's a beautiful name. You take care now. Sure you're okay?"

"I will be." I hop out of the truck and shut the door. I've forgotten how nice people are here. It's one more reason to make me want to stay, and one more thing that makes my heart sink that I can't.

Ron holds his hand up in a wave, and though he can't see me, I wave back.

I need two things: a shower and a nap. There are decisions to make and good-byes to endure, but I'm having trouble thinking beyond either right now.

There are no cars in Mert's driveway and the yard stretching from his house to the barn is devoid of any activity. The place looks abandoned, and I'm relieved. I don't want to talk to anyone right now. I don't want to pretend anymore that things are fine, that I'm okay.

My legs feel weighted with cement as I climb the stairs to the second floor. Maybe I'll skip the shower and go straight to sleep. When I was little, I never fought naps because my mom would tell me what she had planned for us afterward, and going straight to sleep was, in my young mind, the fastest way to get to the fun afternoon that lay ahead. There's a part of me now that thinks if I can fall asleep, maybe when I wake things will be, if not fun, at least different.

I sit down on the bed to take off my shoes and jeans, and something crinkles underneath me. I reach behind me and pull out a folded piece of notebook paper with my first initial on the front. Inside, Brad's scrawl reads, *Dinner? My place? Six o'clock?*

I wonder why he didn't just call. I wonder why he's inviting me to dinner in the first place. He's prolonging the inevitable, isn't he? There's not much left to say that wasn't said yesterday morning. And after my meeting with Randy, there's nothing much left to do, either. If I weren't so exhausted, I'd consider leaving tonight.

But I am exhausted, and I'm filthy and sweaty from my day at the beach. I look at the clock—it's after five. I have time for a nap or a shower; not both.

In the bathroom, I let the water run colder than I normally do, in hopes that it gives me a brief burst of energy, of alertness. I gasp as I step into the shower and every muscle in my body tenses. But I force myself to stay, to endure the pinpricks of ice cold on my skin. After a few minutes, it starts to feel good, and I relax. By the time I turn off the water, I feel rejuvenated.

I dry my hair and after I'm done, unplug the hair dryer and wind the cord around it. I take it back to my room and pack it into my suitcase. *There,* I think. It's a first step toward leaving, but I don't let myself dwell. I pick out a clean pair of jeans and pull on a light cotton sweater with them, then slip on my sandals. I glance at the clock on the bedside table: ten minutes to six. I have enough time to put on makeup and a spritz of perfume, but tonight I don't see much point. I'm at the very upper border of the Upper Peninsula of Michigan, going to have dinner in a barn with a man I was going to leave, but who is now letting me leave instead. Our situation is beyond anything that Chanel or Burberry could ever hope to overcome.

One look at Brad, though, and I wish I had taken more pains. He's clean-shaven and his hair newly cut. He's wearing an untucked pale blue button-down shirt, dark jeans, and brown slip-on loafers without socks. He looks, in a word, scrumptious. Why were there so many times when I overlooked how handsome he is? So many opportunities that I didn't take to kiss his lips or let myself sink into his arms because I was busy with work or annoyed at some little thing or another that he had done?

He gives me a megawatt smile, but his eyes are sad. "Welcome to Chez Brad," he says, handing me a glass of red wine. A card table is set with a checkered tablecloth and two place settings. The open bottle of wine sits on top of the table, a dish towel wrapped around its neck.

"Thank you," I say. I take a sip, feeling self-conscious and shy around this man I have known and loved for more than five years. I can feel the tears, like musicians waiting just offstage for the encore they know is coming. "So, what's on the menu, Chef?"

"Chicken cacciatore," Brad says. "I wanted to take you to Casa Calabria, but—" He shrugs and turns to the refrigerator, as though he's forgotten something important in there, but I can finish that sentence for him: It's easier for him to hole up here, since he can't bring Jones to a place like the Casa. Here, he's guaranteed to be free of triggers, to sit where he wants, and to control the situation. Here, there are no surprises.

Brad brings a sauté pan to the table and sets it on a trivet. Then he takes a loaf of garlic bread from the oven and breaks it along precut lines, placing each piece in a bowl lined with paper towels, and sets that on the table. "Dinner is served." He shrugs and says, "It's not fancy, but hopefully it tastes that way."

He motions for me to sit down. I place my napkin on my lap and help myself to the chicken cacciatore—the only dish I've ever ordered at the Casa. Brad remembered. That would make me feel special and happy if it didn't make me feel so sad.

Brad and I reach for a piece of garlic bread swimming in butter at the same time and both of us pull our hands back.

"Go ahead," I tell him.

"No," he says. "You first. You go."

I get quiet. It shouldn't be like this—all stiff and awkward. I pull my piece of garlic bread and chew, staring out the window at the moon, framed in it perfectly, like a picture.

"What's up, E.?" Brad asks. "Something interesting out there?"

I shake my head and tell him what I was thinking. "It's all wrong," I say.

"What?" he asks.

"This," I say. "Us. We're like a bad first date on Groundhog Day."

Brad laughs. "It's not that bad, is it?"

I nod. "It is," I say in a whisper.

Brad bites his lip. "E., don't do this, okay? I just wanted us to have a nice dinner together. It's hard enough as it is. You wanted to leave, remember? And I was mad about it at first, but the more I thought about it, the more sense it makes. I need to be here, and if you stayed, I'd always wonder if I was some sort of charity case. That's not a relationship; it's a self-help book waiting to be written."

For the second time today, I try to swallow past the lump in my throat. For the millionth time in the past weeks, I try not to cry.

"Things are different now," he continues. "We're different people, you and me. And that's not good or bad anymore. It just is."

I think of the hopes I had this morning, of how I was sure I had found a solution. There's an alternate reality playing out where a different us is breaking bread and spooning pasta, talking about how wonderful it will be to train more dogs like Jones for more veterans like Brad. Where we're laughing and flirting with the renewed sense that things are going to be okay after all. But I'm not. I'm here, across from a man who can't seem to get rid of me fast enough. I think of Randy's words to me this morning, and Brad's to me now, and combined, they translate into this: It's too late.

After dinner, Brad asks me to stay with him and I decline. "I need to spend a little time alone," I tell him, even though it seems that's all I'll have, soon enough.

He insists on walking me "home," and we stand in the driveway facing each other. A warm wind filtered through a whole forest of pine trees plays like a chorus of whispers in the night. Somewhere, deep in that forest, a lonely dog or coyote or wolf howls. And inside Brad's barn apartment, Jones replies.

Brad pulls me into a hug and his arms feel sure and strong around me. I close my eyes and let myself relax into them. He holds me and I let myself be held, relishing the safe, contented feeling of his arms around me. I don't know how long we stand like this—a minute? More? But suddenly I feel like I'm falling, and I open my eyes to find that I'm standing alone and Brad is already headed back toward the barn, disappearing into the night like a ghost.

Mert's house is dark and I have to fumble for the light switch. I'm not sure if Mert is out playing cards with his buddies at the Third Base or asleep in his room, but he isn't planted in his chair in front of the television as he usually is, so I take his place.

The banal banter of twenty-four-hour news diverts my thoughts. Left to their own devices, those thoughts would dwell on all that went wrong today. As it is, they're tied up in the wall-to-wall coverage of waiting for a plume of white smoke to crawl up from a chimney atop the Vatican.

I curl my knees to my chest and reach behind me for a worn, multicolored crocheted throw that I imagine Brad's mom made. I picture her sitting here, working on it, with younger versions of Brad and Ricky chasing each other through the house, unbound by all that's yet to happen in their lives. I picture a house that feels happy and warm, not mired under the weight of memory and regret as this one is. I would have liked to have been around for that.

As it is, I'd simply like to stay here. I am just all out of ideas as to how to do that.

I could hang out a shingle and build a little practice and make us some money. We could live in the barn apartment and have Mert over for dinner on Sundays. Maybe we'd even become friends with Randy and her husband, or with some of the local attorneys.

But just like the last few years, I'd be the primary breadwinner, only this time without gainful employment for Brad on the horizon. Maybe he'll eventually receive disability payments from the military. And maybe not. He might eventually be able to find a job, but chances are he'll never have a career, because his ability to concentrate, to retain information, to do even the most basic math, to fill out simple forms or think analytically—these essential skills have all abandoned him.

And it would be fine at first. It might even work well. But if I look hard, I can see what Brad sees: a future in which on good days I resent having to bear the weight of our world squarely on my shoulders, and on bad days I resent Brad—what he has become. It's a future in which I inevitably feel like an animal whose pasture is cut by half every year until I'm hemmed in, trapped. And for Brad, it's a future where he will wake up day after day believing he is inadequate and should be someone different from who he is, until he crumples under the futility of trying. It's a future in which being together isn't enough anymore, because simply being with another person never is. Simply existing in the same space, paying homage to a partnership that no longer exists, is a poor substitute.

This idea of mine wasn't simply a nice thing that we could do; it was the only thing.

But Randy is right: None of us is a millionaire. None of us has even a few thousand extra dollars lying around. And what I'm proposing costs a lot of money.

I drop my head into one hand. I twirl the hair behind my ear with the fingers of the other hand. Despite being the one who came here to say good-bye, despite seeing Brad's good sense in accepting my departure, despite knowing that the life I'm holding on to—the husband I'm holding on to—doesn't exist anymore, I still don't want to leave.

While I've been lost in thought, the picture on the television has shifted from views of St. Peter's Square to a senator from Minnesota with wiry hair and jumpy eyes. These guys love to talk, I think; it's just too bad that none are all that big on actually doing anything.

Then the senator mentions Veterans Affairs' health care programs, and my ears perk. "We need to be doing more to help our men and women in uniform," he says. "They've given their all for us. Now it's time we give back to them. We need better reintegration programs, more job training. And you'd better believe I'm going to make sure that happens." A graphic under the politician's name reads *Sen. Bernie Thorne (R-Georgia)*.

I reach for the remote control to rewind, to ensure I heard what I thought I had, but I can't, because along with eschewing all other modern technologies, Mert predictably hasn't invested in DVR as part of his cable package.

Senator Thorne happens to be the ranking member on the Appropriations Committee. Every nerve in me starts to sizzle. My body hums. Why didn't I think of this before?

It's close to midnight, but I walk to the kitchen, pick up the phone, and dial the familiar sequence of numbers, knowing that I'll likely get an answer on the other end. And on the third ring, I do.

"What took you so long, Counselor?" I ask.

"Sabatto? That you?" Zach's voice is husky from disuse and, likely, stress and emotional strain. After a string of false starts, *Rowland* is slated for trial next week. I'd be surprised if Zach has left the office all week for more than food or the occasional cup of coffee.

"It's me," I say, and I feel suddenly shy. I hadn't thought through how this request I was about to make would sound out loud.

"Well, I'll be goddamned. Where are you calling from? Actually, don't answer that. I'd be half tempted to take off and join you on the first plane out."

"Things going that well?" I ask.

I can almost hear Zach shaking his head on the other end. "You might be the smartest one of all of us, Sabatto. I feel like Goose from *Top Gun*, when truck-driving school starts looking like a good career option."

"Hang in there, Counselor," I say, my voice warming at our familiar, comfortable banter.

"So," he says, that one word infused with proposition and temptation, "what can I do for you?"

"Not what you're thinking—or hoping," I tease.

"A little credit, Sabatto. Give me a little credit."

"I do have a favor," I say. I wind the phone cord around my finger, then let it uncoil.

"So this isn't a social call?" Zach asks. "I'm hurt."

"Sorry. Next time—I promise."

"Okay, shoot. Whatchya got?"

I inhale and then exhale. I repeat that breathing once again for good measure. Then I launch in to what I need to ask. "Your family knows Senator Thorne, right?"

"Bernie? Yeah. He and my dad used to golf together way back when. Why?"

"I need to talk to him."

"Sure. I can make that happen," Zach says. "You're not in some kind of federal trouble, though, are you?"

"I'm not in trouble. I just have a question for him. Turns out he's pretty passionate about veterans' issues."

"Everything okay?" he asks. "Things are good?"

I'm not sure, is the only honest answer I can give Zach, but it's late and I can hear the exhaustion in his voice, and that answer would only beget a long conversation about my life choices. So although Zach can't see me, I smile because I want him to believe me when I tell him everything is fine. I had a roommate in college who, when she did phone interviews, would put on a suit and pearls and pumps. She said her prospective employers would be able to hear in her voice that she wasn't loafing around in sweats and a rumpled T-shirt. "Things are good," I say.

"Good. Good," he says, and the line goes silent on his end. I hear Zach breathe in through his nose, as if about to say something. Then there's an audible exhale. "Listen, kiddo," he says finally, "I should jet. Miles to go before I sleep, and all that jazz."

"Bradenton hasn't outlawed sleep yet?"

"Not yet," Zach says. "But I'm sure she's working on it, so I should pack it in while I still can. I'll text you Bernie's cell, and I'll loop back and let him know you'll be calling, okay?"

"Thanks, Zach. I owe you one."

"You owe me more than that, but we can work the details out later." I imagine Zach winking at me on the other end, a mischievous smile playing on his lips. "Night, Sabatto. Sweet dreams."

"Bye," I say, the word escaping my mouth like fog. Zach, the firm, everything that used to make up my life, I now feel tethered to by only the thinnest of threads. And I wonder how long before it snaps.

Two minutes later my phone dings with the sound of an incoming message. When I retrieve it, there's one word, *Bernie*, followed by a series of ten numbers, and then: *Miss you.–Z.*

Thirty-six

I ask Brad if I can borrow Jones and take her into the woods with me.
I need to move, to feel my muscles working and to hear the crunch of
pine needles and leaves underfoot. I need to climb and breathe heavy
and fill myself with the sharp, fragrant scent of this place. I need an
outlet for the energy pulsing through me. I need not to think.

I watch Jones trot along in front of me, her bowling ball of a body
transforming into something lithe and indigenous to the woods. She
works in front of me in arcs, sniffing the ground and chasing scents. I
marvel at how she can look so unlike her wolfish ancestors and yet
know just what to do out here, bounding after squirrels, birds, or the
slightest rustle of leaves. I marvel at her trust, her loyalty—not only to
Brad, but also to me. She doesn't know why we were tromping down
trails. She doesn't know where I'm taking her. For all she knows, it
could be back to the horrific place she came from. Yet she's hunting
and playing and wagging that little whip tail of hers. As happy as she
makes me, I can only imagine the effect she has on Brad.

We hike to the top of Hogsback. I walk to the summit ridge that
faces Lake Superior and dangle my legs over. Jones comes up behind
me, stopping a few feet short and eyeing my perch.

"There's no drop-off," I say, patting the ground next to me. "Come see, girl."

She inches closer, peering around me, and sees that I am right. There are rolls of ledges below, not the steep plummet into nothingness that it looks like from where she had been standing.

Jones settles in beside me, leaning her body against my leg and laying her head on top of it. I soak in the view, losing myself in it. My college roommate—the serious phone interviewer—was also a devout Catholic. She would try to get me to go to Mass at the cathedral every Sunday, but I'd go hiking instead. "Nature is my church," I'd tell her, and in Michigan's Upper Peninsula, this was almost an acceptable reason for not attending Mass. All anyone needed was to experience the view Jones and I have atop Hogsback, still shrouded in mist, to understand.

After a while, Jones lifts her head and looks at me with questioning eyes.

"We're waiting," I tell her. "Not long now, little girl."

She lowers her head and sighs.

The dark of early morning hastens its retreat. I keep my eyes trained straight ahead, and the trees and lake sharpen into focus almost by the second, as if marching toward us out of a fog. Before long, there is a whole rich landscape spread out before us, lit by a soft glow.

The UP doesn't get the kind of brilliant, dramatic sunrises common to seacoast beaches, where you can watch the sun's giant orange globe peek over the horizon and climb until it hangs in the sky like an ornament on fire. The sun here is less showy, more stoic. It has more sky to climb into, colder air to warm. And that makes it all the more special to watch.

"Okay, Jones," I say to her once the sun secures its customary spot and I can feel the sharp, early-morning air burning off in favor of temperatures befitting a brilliant spring day. "Time to go, girl. I'm ready."

. . .

Two hours later, I am standing in Mert's living room, bags packed. Brad takes my luggage out to the car, where he wedges it into the backseat. I wait near the open passenger-side door, and when Brad straightens, we look at each other across the roof of the car. "Ready?" he asks. I toss him the keys and climb in beside him.

At the airport, Brad steers to the curb outside the departure gates. "You sure about this?" he asks.

I nod.

He leans over to kiss me and as he does, places a hand softly against my left cheek. I feel something else, wet and warm against the other side of my face. I open one eye and see Jones and her flat pink tongue. Brad and I laugh, our lips still touching, and she licks us both with one slurpy swipe. She's good for us, this dog.

I lean into the backseat and take Jones's head between my hands. She struggles forward, still trying to work my face with her tongue, and I hold her in place. I wonder if she's really this fond of me or if my makeup tastes good to her. I secretly hope it's the former.

"You take care of him, okay little girl?" I say, pressing my forehead to hers. She stops struggling and quiets, as though trying to read my thoughts. I kiss her between the eyes. Her fur smells faintly sweet, like cupcakes. I pat her where my lips had just been. "You keep him safe."

There's so much I want to say to him, but there isn't time. I have a plane to catch. I have a future to fly into.

Then, afraid that if I don't leave right then I won't ever, I scramble from the car.

I stand at the curb as Brad steers away from it and I blow him a kiss. I see his hand reach out as if to catch it, and the last I see of him is that same hand held fast over his heart.

My heels click a staccato beat toward the ticket counter and my stomach turns in on itself. I want to call Brad and tell him to turn around, that I don't want to do this. I want to tell him to come and get me and we'll figure something else out. But the ticket agent is already asking for my identification.

"Do you have bags to check?" she asks.

I shake my head.

"All right then," she says, handing me a small paper folder with my ticket. "Gate A-Four. You'll be boarding in ten minutes. You're all checked through to Washington, D.C. Enjoy your flight, ma'am."

Thirty-seven

Senator Thorne looks older in person, and his office is smaller than I expected, but maybe that's because it's chock-full of dead animals. They're hanging from every available wall space (antelope, deer, moose, large-mouth bass), sitting on shelves (fox, loon, and a two-headed squirrel), and hanging out in the corners (black bear on its hind legs and opposite, as if getting ready for a boxing match; a coyote in full howl). Dotting one wall is a series of small wooden plaques on which I can only assume are mounted the testicles of various animals. I don't go close enough to verify this, but only two things lead me to believe this man is not a lunatic: He's a friend of Zach's family and he has held his office for close to thirty years.

"So," he says, then stops to stifle a yawn. "So you're Zach's girl, huh?"

"No, Senator," I say. "Zach is a friend and colleague of mine." Even though neither one seems exactly right, it's easier than explaining.

"And it says here—" He flips through some papers on his desk. "It says here—" He does more flipping. "Well, it seems as though I can't find where it says why you're here, Ms.—?"

"Sabatto," I offer. "Elise Sabatto. I'd like to talk to you about your support of veterans. Specifically—"

Senator Thorne slaps a hand down on the desk in front of him. "Yes!" he says. "Of course. Now I remember. Well, you know, I'm a very big supporter of our boys."

"Our troops, you mean?" I phrase it as a question in hopes that he'll recognize on his own the error in what he just said.

Senator Thorne knits his brows together. "Yes, troops, of course. That's not what I said? In any case, you've come to the right place, young lady. If you know me, you know that I'd do damn near anything for our boys. If they're in harm's way, then we'd better be using everything in our financial arsenal back here to keep them safe. That's why I've personally gotten more than a billion dollars in earmarks passed over the years to upgrade military facilities. I signed onto the post-9/11 GI bill, I sponsored an amendment encouraging companies to employ our veterans as part of the Tax Reconciliation Act last year, and I've supported an increase in TRICARE fees for retirees and reservists."

He leans back in his chair, his fingers laced together and resting on top of his desk. He looks very pleased with himself. I've just been on the receiving end of his "Working for Veterans" list of talking points, but he is right—this does seem to be the right place. Or, rather, he seems to be the right person to talk to.

"That's an impressive list, Senator," I say. "And I think—I hope— you'll be interested in what I want to talk to you about today. You see, I'm married to a—"

"Deborah! Deb-or-ah!" The senator, who a moment ago seemed poised to listen to my pitch and take notes, interrupts me as if I haven't started talking. His assistant pokes her head inside the door and he waves a green pen at her. "I need a new one. This is all out of ink."

Deborah's body catches up to her head, and the whole of her enters the room and takes the pen from the senator. "Thanks, dear," he says to her. To me he says, "I can only write in green ink. Don't know what it is, but I just get these mental blocks when it's any other color. It's gotta be green." He shakes his head, this peccadillo seemingly a heavy burden to bear, and he tips his chin at me to continue. Silently, I repeat, *Zach's family friend, thirty years.*

"Well, as you probably know, Senator, our troops face significant challenges when they return from theater. They—"

There's a knock at the door and Deborah reappears with a handful of green pens. Senator Thorne turns from me and says, "Thanks, doll. Listen, can you also get me Mike Deaver's cell? We talked about trying to fit a round in this week." He turns back to me. "Now, where were we?"

I smile at the senator and launch back in: "I was about to say that when our troops return from theater, as you know, they often have a hard time adjusting to life stateside—and so do their families. From depression to PTSD to the new signature of this war, Traumatic Brain Injuries, or TBIs, these returning soldiers are . . ." I trail off. Senator Thorne is doodling on a legal pad in front of him. Nesting stars, to be exact, each one slightly smaller than the one that surrounds it. His lines are straight and even and precise. And I gather that he hasn't listened to one word I've said.

"Senator?" I say. "I think that—"

I'm interrupted by yet another knock at the door, and without looking up, Senator Thorne waves the person in. This time it's not Deborah, but a boy who looks approximately twelve years old and as if he dressed for work in his father's closet. His suit bags at the shoulders and in the arms, and the pants are too long.

"Sir, I just wanted to drop off the one-pager you requested for your Appropriations subcommittee meeting tomorrow," he says. The senator takes the paper from him, smiles, and thanks him. As the boy leaves, easing the door closed behind him, I expect Senator Thorne to set the one-pager aside and return to our conversation. Instead, he continues reading. Then, he starts to take a green pen to it.

It has taken me far too long to realize what is happening. Senator Thorne has no real interest in me or in the project I'm here to pitch to him. The only reason I got an appointment with the senator himself was because I was able to drop Zach's last name and his scheduler or a staffer recognized it and deemed me important enough.

I stare at Senator Thorne and his green pen, scribbling furiously on a document that has nothing to do with me or this meeting, and I seethe. I have spent money we don't have to fly all the way out here. I have prepared a sheet of facts, figures, and statistics and a compelling pitch. I have staked everything on this meeting going well. And given Zach's connections and the senator's repeated insistence, at least in the media spotlight, that he'd do "anything and everything for our boys," I had no reason to think that it wouldn't.

It appears I thought wrong.

And now what? I told Brad about this meeting the night before I flew out, as we lay awake next to each other, Jones between us. Without saying a word, he picked up my hand and brought it to his lips. Then he pressed my hand against his cheek and held it there. That was when I knew that we would be all right and that things between us could be patched and made whole again.

But all of that hinges on this meeting—on Senator Thorne's buy-in. And now I realize that this meeting is a formality, but not in the way I expected.

I pick up my briefcase and pull a packet of papers from it—my own one-pager on our program along with a memo summarizing current research on the therapeutic benefits of psychiatric service dogs—and float it onto the senator's desk. I took the time to type it up; I figure I might as well leave the document here with him. Then I close the briefcase and fasten the clasp on it before standing and folding my coat over my arm.

"I'd thank you for your time, Senator, but I don't know if that's appropriate in this case."

Senator Thorne looks up at me, surprised, as though I've awoken him from a nap.

He nods and smiles. "Sure thing, Elaine. You let me know if there's anything else I can do for you, now, okay? And tell your guy Zach I said hello."

I stare at him. I'm so amazed by his brazenness, his complete disregard for the time and effort I've taken to be here, that I actually have to tell myself to close my mouth. But it opens right back up again.

"You say you've done so much for our veterans, Senator," I say, "but you won't even take one whole minute to listen to something real and effective that's actually able to help some of them. Not if it won't get you on television or credit with your constituents, right?"

Senator Thorne's writing slows, and then stops.

"I'm sure you know that PTSD is currently the fourth-highest service-related injury and that thirty-three percent of all combat-related injuries and sixty percent of the patients with blast-related injuries seen at Walter Reed Army Medical Center have sustained a TBI. I'm sure I'm not telling you anything new when I say that more than half a million veterans suffer from PTSD or traumatic brain injuries—sometimes both—and that there's no cure for either one."

Senator Thorne sets his pen down and laces his fingers once again. He's listening.

"I'm guessing you're very well aware of how hard it is to even get diagnosed with TBI or PTSD, and as a result, how hard it is to get treatment. Or, once you finally are, how long it takes to get an appointment scheduled.

"Do you know that every day, four or five veterans commit suicide? That there are a thousand suicide attempts a month—and those are only the ones we know about, who are under VA care? How about the fact that more than a hundred and fifty thousand veterans are living on the streets? And that a lot of that can be traced back to the diagnosis and treatment issues?"

I'm incapable of stopping myself. In full lawyer mode, I fire off fact after fact and, because the senator hasn't tried to talk yet, I keep firing. It occurs to me that I'm filibustering the senator in his own office. I smile inwardly.

"Senator, it's great that you've thrown some money at bases and put your name on a few veteran-related bills—it really is. I'm not discounting those efforts, but behind every one of those numbers I just quoted is a soldier or family suffering out there with real problems that need solving. And no one's doing a damn thing about it. Mostly because no one knows what *to* do about it."

I take a breath and Senator Thorne takes advantage. "And you do?" he asks.

"I believe I do, sir."

He leans back in his chair and groans, lacing his hands behind his head. He buzzes Deborah. "What's my two o'clock?" he asks her.

"Ramey, at the State Department, sir," Deborah says.

"Great. See if he'll push it back until three." Thorne presses a button and cuts Deborah off. Then he stands up and pockets his cell phone.

"Care to take a walk?" he asks.

We stroll down the National Mall. It's hot and muggy, and I don't need a suit jacket, much less an overcoat. Both are draped over my shoulder bag, leaving my bone white arms to stick out of the sleeveless shirt I have on. These arms haven't been touched by sun in months, and with D.C. far ahead of Michigan in seasons, their translucence looks misplaced here among the green grass and blooming flowers.

My flats kick up small clouds of dust on the dirt path, and I'm thankful that I thought to stow a pair of walking shoes in my bag. A hike like this in heels might have crippled me.

The path stretches out in front of us, straight and seemingly endless, but Senator Thorne, still fully dressed in his business best, chats amicably about his memories of Zach and how much things have changed here since 9/11. When it seems that he's run out of small talk, he says, "So how did you get involved in all this, anyway?"

"All this?" I ask.

"Veterans stuff."

I tell him, then, about our project—Pets and Warriors, or PAWs for short. I tell him about how Jones has completely transformed Brad. I tell him that psychiatric service dogs have been used to treat bipolar disorder and schizophrenia, obsessive-compulsive disorder and general anxiety. "There's conclusive research showing that dogs have helped members of the general population with PTSD. If it works for them and if it's worked for Brad, I believe there's no reason this can't work for other soldiers, too."

Without my realizing it, Senator Thorne has led us to the Vietnam Memorial and I stop talking. There's something about this wall of polished black that commands silence. He slows, examining a panel, and then stops. He leans forward and with one finger traces the names down, down, and down until he stops even with his hip on the name Davis Smith. He finds the name quickly and efficiently. It's clear this isn't his first time at this memorial, in this spot.

"I knew this guy," Senator Thorne says, turning only his head toward me. "Hell, I knew too many of these guys. But this poor son of a bitch, I don't think I'll ever forget. Not as long as I live."

He taps Davis Smith's name twice with the tip of his finger. Then he traces it like a line of Braille and starts walking again.

"Davis Smith," he says, shaking his head. "He was a tunnel rat. Know what that was?"

"No," I say.

Senator Thorne shakes his head harder, as if trying to jar something loose. "Worst job in Vietnam, and that's a pretty low bar. Viet Cong built tunnels all over that hellhole, and tunnel rats would go in after them with a couple of hand grenades, a pistol, and a flashlight. That's what Smith did for back-to-back tours, even though they weren't supposed to do the tunnels for more than a handful of months at a time. Man had nerves of steel, until one day he didn't. Started talking to himself, seeing things, stringing VC ears on a necklace— all the shit you think Hollywood makes up for their movies. It was awful to watch. But what were we all supposed to do? Then, one day, he solved the problem for us. Walked out into a clearing in the middle of a firefight as if sauntering onto a dance floor. And that was that."

I look at Senator Thorne, who glances out the corner of his eye at me, still facing straight ahead and still walking at a good clip. "No dog was going to save Davis Smith," he says after a few strides. "War is hell. A dog's a dog. It's not a miracle worker."

"With all due respect, Senator, I disagree."

"How do you know?" he asks.

I think of Brad nuzzling Jones. The way his body relaxes when she's near him, touching him. The way she can snap him out of one of his spells the way nothing else can. "Because I've seen it," I say.

The senator stops this time and turns to face me. "It's one dog," he says. "One guy."

It's my turn to shake my head.

"My husband was the love of my life. He's the only family I have. And I almost left him. I was afraid all the time. I was afraid when I was with him and I was afraid of what he'd do if I wasn't. And then came this dog."

Senator Thorne turns, leading us off the mall and onto a sidewalk.

"This can work, Senator. It works with the elderly and the infirm and the disabled, and it works with soldiers like Brad."

"But it's not been proven," the senator says.

"Nothing's been proven," I say. I am trying not to raise my voice, but for an elected official who seems so enthralled with the idea of helping veterans when the cameras are rolling, he sure isn't now. "There aren't any cut-and-dried treatments for any of these problems. You want to support our troops—really support them? Then do something more than talk about it."

We come to Twenty-first Street, where Senator Thorne has to turn off for his meeting. "And what, exactly, young lady, do you propose I do?"

"You're the Appropriations chair. You could direct the VA to work with nonprofits that train service dogs to pair their dogs with veterans, fund that program, and then direct additional funds for research."

"And how much funding would you propose I throw at this little project of yours?" he asks.

Senator Thorne has a bulbous nose that looks like raw meat, and I have an urge to squeeze it. Hard. *Little* project? What an ass!

I repeat Randy's quote to me, substantiated by a fair amount of research on my part. "Fifty thousand dollars per dog—give or take," I say, flinching. It sounds so much bigger, more impossible, to say it out loud.

Senator Thorne chuckles, and I instantly wonder if I should have quoted something more reasonable.

"You have to train the dog and the dog-soldier combination," I continue, by way of explanation. "Then there are vet bills and overhead, and transportation costs. A lot goes into these dogs, sir, but I can tell you that they're worth it. They let these vets live a normal life."

"You mean they let *your* guy live a normal life." I picture squeezing that nose again. *Honk, honk.* The senator offers me his hand. "I like a girl with enthusiasm," he says. "And I appreciate what you're trying to do."

My stomach clinches. It hasn't worked. I've tried, but it isn't enough.

I take Senator Thorne's outstretched hand, making sure to get a good grip on it. I can feel my eyes well, but I smile, willing the tears to stay put a few moments longer. He pumps my hand once, twice, three times, four.

"Well, you know, I'm not big on earmarks." The senator releases my hand, and he winks at me. Then, turning on his heel, he walks away, whistling "Yankee Doodle."

Thirty-eight

August 2006

A late-summer sun beats down, teasing drops of sweat from our pores. My skin feels as crisp as a baked chicken. Even my hair is hot.

Today, it's all hands on deck: Ricky; Randy and her husband, Kevin; Mert; and Brad and I. A chorus of ringing thuds fills the afternoon as we all work to put the finishing touches on the place—nailing freshly painted siding on the barn and planting some shrubs and flowers. Tomorrow, three soldiers will arrive: two veterans of Operation Iraqi Freedom and one from Operation Enduring Freedom. They will each be paired with a dog that will help them to live in their own skin again, that will help them piece the broken parts of their lives back together.

I hold a board in place, pressing my body against the rough grain to make sure it doesn't move while Brad and Mert secure it on either end. Sweat stings my eyes, and I bring my shoulder and face together to try to wipe them clean. When I look up, I see Brad pause, his hammer in midstrike, and smile out the corner of his mouth at Mert. Father and son. Each taps a nail a few more times, and it's done; the last board is in place. Mert steps back and wipes his hands on the front of his jeans, then takes out a handkerchief from his pocket and wipes the sweat from his face. He nods in acknowledgment, his eyes beady and serious, and he says, "This is good. Real good."

The smell of hamburgers wafts from the grill, and we rehang shovels and put tools away before our collective hunger leads all of us to the picnic table. Ricky's new girlfriend, Coreen—a lovely woman who adores Rick and spends her days cashiering at Walmart and her nights caring for her Alzheimer's-stricken mother—sets out platters of burgers, salads, and fruit, and we eat in near silence born of contentment and pride. Four of us, save for Randy's husband and Coreen, squish together on the side of the picnic table facing the barn so we can admire our work while we eat.

Our chorus of hammering has been replaced by the yipping and happy growling of our newest dogs at play: exuberant and lovable Bama, beautifully brindled and kind-eyed Orlando, and puppylike Monchichi—all pit bulls, all rescued from fighting rings, and all now destined for a gentler, more purposeful life.

As I watch the three of them along with Jones wrestle and play, I feel an arm slip around my shoulders, and I'm surprised to find that it's Randy.

"You should be proud of this," she says.

"We all should be," I tell her.

Randy shakes her head. She gives my shoulder a squeeze. "Maybe, but you most of all. You had the most to lose. You're the one who made it happen."

"I didn't have anything left to lose. Either Senator Thorne said yes, or he said no. It was the only thing I could have done. I had to ask."

In the months that followed our meeting, the senator introduced legislation that created a program pairing psychiatric service dogs with veterans. Brad and I attended the bill signing, where he and

Jones were mobbed by the media. Pictures of Jones—looking like she was mugging for the cameras, with her big tongue hanging out the side of her mouth, and my husband, looking handsome in a navy blue suit, sans tie, with a smile to match Jones's, ran on every station. Anderson Cooper interviewed him on CNN. The ladies of *The View* asked him to stop by. He and Jones joined Matt Lauer on *Today*. Donations started to pour in, and though the senator's legislation hadn't yet taken effect, we had enough funding within a month of the bill's passage to start our operation.

"Well," Randy says, stopping to take a sip from the glass of pink lemonade sweating in front of her, "I'm just glad you thought to do it. I never would have. Not in a million years."

"It was luck, as much as anything. I feel like we've won the lottery."

Randy puts her hand over mine. "We have," she says. "We all have." She scissors her legs over the bench and extricates herself from the table. She stands and stretches her arms toward the sky, grimacing. "That's going to hurt tomorrow," she says. Then she turns to Kevin. "Ready to go? We've got a big day coming up."

She's right. Tomorrow, Second Lieutenant Kit Fritz, Specialist Ryan Evers, and Corporal Jose Soto will arrive for ten days of intense training before being sent home with their new service dogs.

We're all exhausted from the day, and with Randy's announcement as cover, Rick and Coreen get up, too. Most of the table is strewn with paper plates and plastic cups, which everyone helps to clear, and Coreen and Randy make quick work of the rest of the dishes, stacking them and transporting them to the kitchen. By the time Randy's and Rick's trucks disappear down the driveway in a thin haze of dust, Mert is asleep in his recliner and Brad has gone to work, feeding and watering the dogs.

Inside our apartment, I sink into Brad's ratty old armchair that I moved up here from Madison. Three camouflage vests hang by the door, each bearing a patch that reads PETS AND WARRIORS SERVICE DOG.

One day, a handful of months ago, Brad and I tried to board a bus with Jones and Bama, but the driver stopped us.

"No dogs," he said.

"They're service animals," I told him.

"Service dogs have a handle to hold on to," the driver said. "They don't got a handle."

"They're not *guide* dogs. These are *service* dogs," I said. I could see Brad tensing, his face hardening. I saw Jones move closer to him and nudge his leg with her snout. She could often sense one of his attacks coming on long before I, or even he, could.

"Why you got a service dog? What's wrong with you? You don't got a missing leg. You don't look blind."

"By law, we're not required to answer that," I said, smiling. "You can legally ask two questions: 'Is the dog required for assistance because of a disability?' and 'What tasks or work has this dog been trained to do for you?' But you can't ask what disability someone might have, and you can't request proof that the dog is a service dog." I reached into the bus to hand the driver a postcard I'd had printed up regarding rights and responsibilities related to service dogs under the Americans with Disabilities Act. He scanned it, then handed it back to me. "So we can board now?" I smiled at the driver, trying to win him over, even though inside I wanted to wring his ignorant neck.

The driver shook his head and started to close the doors. "I said no dogs. Not on my bus. Especially when you sure don't look crippled." He reached for the doors and pulled the lever to close them.

"And you don't look stupid!" I yelled at him as they hissed shut.

I turned around to find Brad, his eyes wide, trying to stifle a laugh. "Hooah!" he said. "My little lady is fi-red up."

I rolled my eyes at him. I wanted to remain indignant, but a giggle escaped, and before long we were both doubled over on the sidewalk, laughing.

"Little lady?" I said, as Brad and I finally calmed ourselves and started walking down the street.

He shrugged. "I guess not. If I had a choice between taking on this one"—he drops a hand to scratch Bama's neck—"and you, I think I'd take the pit bull."

That night I dug my mother-in-law's sewing machine out of the basement and set to work on making Jones a proper vest out of Brad's fatigues, still stiff with desert sand and his sweat. On one side I sewed a patch I had ordered that read OPERATION IRAQI FREEDOM/INJURED VETERAN/SERVICE DOG, and on the other, the triple bars of a sergeant insignia—one step above Brad's rank. ("She's in charge," he said. "She should outrank me.") When we accept a soldier into the program now, I ask if he'd like me to do the same for his dog's vest.

Almost two years have passed since Brad returned. Sometimes it seems like yesterday. But most of the time, it feels like decades have gone by, not months. Our work together, our life here, feels so right, so natural, that it's hard to believe there was ever a choice to make at all, or that we so nearly made a different one. I try to imagine a version of me somewhere in California right now, one dating someone like Zach—or maybe Zach himself—but the vision won't crystallize. It's as difficult as trying to imagine the harsh bite of snow while lounging on a tropical beach and baking under a hot sun.

In the past year I've become the fundraising, lobbying, and legal arm of our operation. I've made weekly trips to Washington, D.C., to court potential donors and politicians. We have built kennels, bought food and bowls and cots and paid vet bills, and brought Randy on full-time. She has created a stable of reliable interns from nearby

Northern Michigan University. We're still waiting for the senator's legislation—the federal funding—to kick in, and for a couple of grants to come through, but we're doing well enough to have rescued eleven pit bulls or pit bull mixes from local shelters. Three—Bama, Orlando, and Monchichi—are ready to be placed, while the rest are in various stages of rehabilitation and training.

We've done all that in only a year. And now, I'm looking at those vests, and the sight of them hanging there in a row makes me a little wistful. Tomorrow, we give the dogs new homes where we can't be absolutely certain they'll be taken care of and loved as we've cared for them. These dogs have become our family. I've come to accept that they may be the closest thing to children I'll ever have. Brad's made great gains, but I'm not sure a baby, a child, is something Brad will ever be able to handle. A few weeks ago, Darcy came for a visit with Mia, and Brad wouldn't—couldn't—hold her. That night, lying in bed, I heard him say, "Those eyes." I could sense him shaking his head. "Every kid has those same goddamn eyes." For him, the equation is that simple. That tragic. That haunting.

The door to our apartment opens and Jones bounds in, all muscle and exuberance, a linebacker at a tea party. Brad follows her and catches me eyeing the vests.

"You tired?" he asks.

I nod.

"Me too." Brad hunches down onto his heels. Jones bounds back to Brad and bucks in circles around him. She doesn't slow down enough for him to even pet her. "Let's go for a walk," he says to me.

I raise an eyebrow at him and stuff myself deeper into the chair. "I thought you said you were tired."

"I am," he says, "but I want a little time with you."

He's right—the next two weeks are going to be round-the-clock work. And something in the way he looks at me stops me from protesting and makes me want to go along with him. It's equal parts pleading and kind. It's Brad—my Brad.

"Okay," I acquiesce.

We drive along County Road 550 with all the windows down and two dogs hanging their heads out of either side of the car, the wind flapping their jowls like flags. I drop my hand out of my window and meditate on this moment—the wind and the warmth and Brad's hand resting on my leg.

Brad turns right onto a dirt road that spits us out almost on the beach, where white sand is lit by a burning, setting sun. We each open a back door to let the dogs spill out and charge ahead to water that has only recently warmed enough to wade in, at least for me.

Brad shoulders a backpack and I ask him what it's for. "Just in case," he says, but the dogs are bounding out into the lake, happy and carefree, and the sun is hovering low and orange and beautiful over the water, so I don't press him. If he feels the need to be overprepared, so be it.

"Come here," Brad says, twining his fingers with mine as we reach the beach. His skin is soft and warm, and his touch makes me tingle. Still. After everything we've weathered, I feel so alive in this moment that suddenly I'm nearly brought to my knees with gratitude.

The dogs give chase up and down the beach, juking one another like running backs on the football field. Sand sprays under their feet. Tongues hang from their mouths, relaxed into playful grimaces as each tries to outrun the others. I watch them, amazed at their capacity to trust, to heal. Monchichi was found downstate, chained to an old car axle on a leash so short she couldn't lie down, starving and freezing to death. Bama and Orlando were rescued from a dog-fighting ring. Bama escaped the worst of it, but the first time I saw Orlando, his face resembled crusted raw hamburger. It was impossible, really, to tell if he still had a face. And yet, he crawled right into my lap, licked my cheek once, circled, and fell asleep.

When I asked Randy if it was really the best idea to have a kennel full of pit bulls, she was sitting cross-legged on the ground with Monchichi belly-up on her lap. Her answer was immediate and un-equivocal. "If this operation is really going to be about saving lives, then we need to help those who most need it," she said, explaining that most people are afraid of pit bulls, so most shelters can't adopt them out and end up euthanizing them. "These guys are so willing that when you tell them to fight until they die, they do it. Imagine what they'll do with a little love and positive motivation. You just wait."

She was right. Running on the beach in front of me is the proof.

This is the last time they'll be together like this—their little fur family—and I'm sad for them. But when I think of where they've been, where they're going doesn't seem so bad at all. They'll have one person to dote on them, care for them, snuggle them; they'll have one person who needs them, who will honor them, who is de-serving of their unconditional trust and love. Each will have a new life—a new normal.

The sun dips below the horizon, and despite this afternoon's swel-tering heat, the air takes on a sudden sharpness. Marquette's weather is interesting—as a rule, only in July do the days and nights seem to belong to the same month. By August, even the hottest summer day gives way to a night better suited to fall. I shiver and run my hands up and down my arms to ignite some spark of warmth. It doesn't work. It never does, that move.

Like Brad, I should have prepared. But I have a sweatshirt in the truck that I can grab. When I turn my attention from the dogs, though, I see a blanket spread on the sand and sitting on top of it, Brad with a toothy smile so warm it makes me forget all about the chill. He pats the space next to him. I smile back and walk to the blanket's edge. "What's this?" I ask, lowering myself beside him. "You're like a Boy Scout."

"Nah," Brad says. "I'm not nearly as good at fire building and I have a lot more facial hair."

I shake my head and roll my eyes. Out in front of us, Gitche Gumee is transforming in the almost-moonlight from ink black to a sheet of liquid silver. The dogs have slowed, shifting from play to quiet exploration. Monchichi and Jones are wading through the shallow water near shore. Orlando is rolling in the sand, flipping back and forth on his back like a beached fish. Bama is teasing a stick the size of a small tree from the edge of the woods. Brad and I are sitting shoulder to shoulder on a blanket on a beach in Michigan's wild Upper Peninsula. Tonight we'll curl against each other in a bed in an apartment fashioned out of a barn and over a pack of dogs with whom we live.

Each of these statements is true, strange though they seem. Yet living it, this life we've built, feels like the second best thing I've ever done.

"Give me your hand," Brad says, but he doesn't wait for me to comply. He takes my hand in his and opens it, palm up. I am looking to see if I can spot Bama, if he's sticking around, when I feel something cold and sharp in my palm. Brad closes my fingers around it.

I look down and open my hand, and in it lies a gold heart affixed to a purple ribbon—a Purple Heart medal. I look at Brad.

"This is yours," he says.

I think about the scars crisscrossing his body, about the pieces of metal, sharp and jagged, hibernating inside him, about his brain that doesn't work quite right anymore, and probably never will—not as it used to, anyway. I think of what he had to do for this medal. I think of that little Iraqi boy called Jones.

I shake my head. I hold the medal out to Brad. "I can't—"

He closes my fingers around it again. "It's yours, Elise. I want you to have it."

"But I didn't do anything," I tell him.

"You stayed," he says, and his voice cracks.

I reach for his arm and push up the sleeve covering it. I trace the letters, inked into his skin in black, following each bend they make. I am trying to understand. This body of his has a new topography that I need to learn. When I get to the tail of the last letter, "a," I let my finger fall from his arm and replace it with my lips, closing my eyes and letting them follow the same trail. Brad holds still, watching me.

Then he reaches for me and presses my head to his chest. I can hear the faint thud of his heart. I close my eyes and lose myself in its rhythm. I want to be this close to him. I want to be his, always.

A truck backfires on the road above us, and I tense and pull back, anticipating Brad's reaction. Jones has the same idea, because she bolts up to us. She licks Brad's face hard, three times, and when Brad tousles her ears, she must sense that she's not needed, because she pivots and runs back down to the water's edge.

Brad still goes away sometimes. His eyes get small and hard, his face goes blank, and his body stiffens. Mine does, too, then. But not Jones's. That's when she springs into action, leaning into Brad or putting her paws in his lap and licking his face with a fervor most dogs reserve for peanut-butter-covered toys. Sometimes she'll yip at him, too, when he needs a little extra coaxing, when she needs to be extra assertive. Regardless of how she does it, she always brings him back.

She always brings him back to me.

Acknowledgments

No book gets to the shelf without a whole team of people dedicated to making that happen, and I've got quite the team, if I do say so myself. Thank you to Andrea Somberg for championing this book; to Ellen Edwards for being the editorial mastermind that she is; and to Kara Welsh for believing in this project. Thanks to my beloved Inwellians—Aaron, Ann, Carrie, Erika, Maggie, Marysa, and Trish. Thanks to Jason and Nicki, and Brian and Georgett, for your invaluable feedback and input, and for your selfless service. To Angela, for being the best beta reader a girl could ever ask for, and to Anne for your double checks on law firm life. To my friends for their unending patience with phone calls slowly returned and social outings skipped. To Mary and Dean—if this project were a pair of pants, you'd be the suspenders; I can't even begin to tell you how appreciative I am of your constant willingness to watch over, occupy, and love the Wee One, no matter what deadline was looming. Always, to my big, extended family—*all* of you—who have believed in, encouraged, loved, and supported me, then and now. To my little family—ADO and the Wee Z; you are my whole life. And finally, to all those who have served: thank you, thank you, thank you for your dedication and your sacrifice. It does not go unnoticed. It will not be forgotten.

Erin Celello was born in Michigan's Upper Peninsula, where she earned an MFA in fiction from Northern University. She now lives in Madison, Wisconsin, with her husband, son, and two unruly vizslas. She teaches writing at the University of Wisconsin-Whitewater.

CONNECT ONLINE

www.erincelello.com
facebook.com/ecelello
twitter.com/erincelello

LEARNING TO STAY

ERIN CELELLO

This Conversation Guide is intended to enrich
the individual reading experience, as well as encourage us
to explore these topics together—because books,
and life, are meant for sharing.

A Conversation
with Erin Celello

Q. *It took you ten years to write your first novel and you were determined to write this second one faster. How long did it take?*

A. This book took me a year to write, and another year to rewrite and polish for publication. I think part of the reason that the writing went more quickly is because I learned so much in the process of crafting *Miracle Beach*. But another reason, equally important, is that I learned to be a much more dedicated writer. I used to wait for my muse to announce her presence before I would sit down to write. Now I'm better at stealing scraps of time to write whenever and wherever I can. I had a full-time job while writing *Learning to Stay* and learned to be disciplined about writing on my lunch hours and for another hour or two either before or after work—sometimes both. That kind of schedule can mean a diminished social life at times, but it's so worth it to see the finished book hit the shelves.

Q. *This novel is quite a departure from* Miracle Beach. *What inspired you to write it?*

A. It is definitely a departure, but a journey I was excited to take. Years ago, I read *Where Is the Mango Princess?*, Cathy Crimmins's brilliant memoir about her struggle to come to terms with her husband's traumatic brain injury. The story stuck with me, as did the central question it posed: What do you do when the person you married is no longer the person you're married to? I knew I'd eventually play with that same question in the realm of fiction, but I didn't know how—partially because Crimmins's story was so powerful. But during the years that followed, I started to see and hear stories about TBIs everywhere. I had an opportunity to edit a PhD thesis on students with TBI intersecting with community colleges, which gave me a deeper understanding of that injury. Then, when TBI, along with post-traumatic stress, started to be termed the "signature" injuries of Operation Iraqi Freedom (OIF) and Operation Enduring Freedom (OEF), I realized I had a backdrop as powerful as Crimmins's in which to explore the central question she raised as well as these ancillary issues.

Q. What kind of research did you do?

A. I don't come from a military family, nor have I served in the military, so I had a steep learning curve. I started by reading anything and everything I could find about OIF and OEF, as well as books about traumatic brain injury (a comprehensive reading list follows this guide). I also watched endless hours of documentaries and films about the wars in an attempt to take in the details that I hoped would make this story compelling and real. I also relied heavily on blogs. One huge benefit of writing *Learning to Stay* when I did, as opposed to five or ten years earlier, is the access I had to veterans and their families who have chosen to publicly record their thoughts and feelings through blogging. Even if I were to have interviewed as many veterans or spouses as I could find, my knowledge would not have been as thorough and informative as it became by reading these on-line journals.

Finally, I gave drafts of the book to a few veterans I knew for feedback, to ensure that each and every detail was as accurate as possible. Their input was invaluable. Any remaining errors are mine and mine alone.

Q. *There aren't many novels available about military veterans of recent wars, and their families. Why do you think that is?*

A. Honestly, I'm not sure, though I suspect the reasons are many.

Part of the reason might be that it's just still too new. The United States has been at war for more than a decade, but OIF ended only about a year ago and OEF is ongoing. I think it often takes society a long time to gain the perspective necessary to put events like these in context so that they can begin to be analyzed and explained. I also suspect that maybe people who haven't been on the front lines of the war, so to speak—whether veterans or their families—are hesitant to tackle some of these issues before veterans themselves have had a chance to. Often, throughout the writing of this book, I feared that it was an audacious endeavor—one that I had no business undertaking because I hadn't personally experienced any of the issues facing Brad and Elise, and because I didn't have much more than a passing familiarity with the military. But many veterans who read drafts of the book, and others to whom I gave my elevator pitch, expressed gratitude for my effort to do their struggles justice. I don't know if I succeeded or not, but dang, did I ever try.

I hope I'm wrong about the final possible reason for the dearth of stories about veterans of recent wars: that the American public has been slow to come to terms with the fact that we've actually been at war for the past ten years. It's been easy to dismiss OIF and OEF as something happening clear across the globe from us, as something that only takes place on cable news, because only one-half of one percent of the U.S. population has fought these two wars on behalf of the rest of the ninety-nine-point-five percent of us. It's important to remember the very real sacrifices made by each and every one of our service members. Many have made the ultimate sacrifice, and many have come home with a range of physical and psychological injuries. The sacrifice is great even for those whose service does not take them into war zones. Enduring constant relocations due to deployments, suffering disconnects between civilian and military life, and juggling the demands of military service with family commitments—these are all daunting challenges that the men and women of the armed forces face every day.

Q. *What do you most hope readers will take away from reading* Learning to Stay?

A. I hope that this book gives readers a glimpse into the very real difficulties faced by so many veterans and their families. Many situations are not as extreme as Brad and Elise's, but some are even more overwhelming. There is no average or typical experience for a returning veteran and his or her family. Our efforts as a country to support our troops need to go far beyond tying yellow ribbons on trees or sticking a picture on a car bumper.

Q. What can we do to help veterans who are readjusting to life state-side?

A. If you live near a military base, you can reach out to the base's Family Resource Center, or contact your state National Guard's Family Readiness Group for ways that you can help. First Lady Michelle Obama and Dr. Jill Biden's initiative, Joining Forces (www.white-house.gov/joiningforces), is also a wonderful clearing house for volunteer opportunities. Employment and mental health services for returning veterans are in great demand and homelessness among veterans remains a serious problem. Widely varied programs aim at helping veterans secure the services they need, and the organizations that run these programs welcome volunteers. Efforts can be as simple as donating magazines or board games to VA hospitals, to as complex as volunteering for veterans' suicide prevention hotlines. (According to a 2012 *New York Times* article, more than 6,500 veterans commit suicide every year—that's more than the total number of soldiers killed in Afghanistan and Iraq *combined* since the beginning of those wars.) Chances are, whatever unique talents or interests you might have, there's a way to parlay that into providing help for our nation's veterans.

However, there are two very simple and direct steps that each and every one of us can take. Making ourselves more aware of the circumstances facing returning veterans is one of the most basic tools we have at our disposal. A 2011 PEW Research Center study found that eighty-four percent of returning veterans feel that their fellow Americans do not understand the myriad problems they have had to face, including long separations, physical and psychological injuries, and stress. The better understanding we all have, the better position we will be in to help.

The second thing each of us can do is to express gratitude when we see a service member in uniform, or one who has identified him- or herself as a veteran. It might seem awkward to approach a stranger in an airport or restaurant, but a simple, "Thank you for your service," can mean a great deal. It lets the service member or veteran know that his service is not forgotten, that his efforts are appreciated, and that the difficulties that so often accompany those efforts are understood and acknowledged.

Q. *Your personal life has changed significantly since you wrote* Miracle Beach. *Did those changes have an impact on the writing of* Learning to Stay?

A. While writing *Miracle Beach*, I had similar reservations as I had during the writing of *Learning to Stay*—mainly, the question of how in the world do I think I have any business writing about this? With the first novel, I was a single twenty-something, fresh out of graduate school, tackling in fiction the inner workings of two complicated marriages and the death of a spouse and child. Since then, I've married and had my first child, and those life changes did help in gleaning some of the subject matter for *Learning to Stay*, but the book was still a stretch for me. However, that's less problematic, I think, than it sounds. I've never ascribed much to the old adage of "write what you know." Instead, I'm a proponent of starting with what you know and then pushing your limits as a person and as a writer. That kind of writing is more interesting for me, and I hope by extension, for the reader.

I also firmly believe that no two stories are alike, which is a re-markably freeing belief. I was often asked how I could have written *Miracle Beach* without ever having personally experienced the loss of a spouse or child, but by the time you immerse yourself in the lives of your characters enough to get their story on the page, it's not about you anymore. It's not about what you've experienced or the choices you've made. It's about what they choose to do, who they are as people, and the hopes and dreams they have. I often reminded myself of that in the course of writing *Learning to Stay* when doubt started to creep in: Even if I had been a veteran or had lived a similar experience to the characters in the book, their unique story would still have evolved, and even among real-life veterans and their fami-lies, there is no typical or average story. Each is unique. So, too, is Elise and Brad's story.

Q. Is using service dogs to help veterans an actual idea or program? Does something like PAWs exist?

A. Yes and yes. I originally got the idea for the PAWs program after watching a *60 Minutes* program about dogs trained by inmates to help those suffering from PTSD. I was surprised, and heartened, to find a whole host of programs that match therapy dogs with return-ing veterans.

As it turns out, Senator Bernie Thorne of *Learning to Stay* was a little ahead of his time. In 2009, real-life Senators Al Franken (D-MN) and Johnny Isakson (R-GA) cosponsored a bill—the Service Dogs for Veterans Act, which was part of the Defense Authorization of 2010—that helped provide disabled veterans with service dogs to "help keep America's promise to returning soldiers and improve their quality of life after service." As a result of senators Franken and Isakson's efforts, programs helping to train dogs and match them with physically and mentally wounded veterans have recently cropped up around the country. Psychiatric service dogs help veterans overcome their social isolation simply by needing to be walked outside, forcing many veterans to venture out into public. The benefits they provide in reducing the fear and anxiety of many veterans suffering from issues such as PTSD has been well chronicled, and programs pairing dogs with veterans continue to crop up across the country.

Q. What's next for you?

A. That's a great question! Veterans' issues remain very top-of-mind for me. I'm hard at work designing a veterans-specific English composition course at the University of Wisconsin-Whitewater, where I am an assistant professor. I am also in the very early stages of working on a nonfiction project about a Marine who returned home from Iraq with a severe TBI and the horribly difficult decision his wife had to make in order to honor his end-of-life wishes. And in all of the spare time remaining after those endeavors, and after chasing around my now-mobile (and incredibly active) son, I've been tinkering with the beginning of a third novel as well.

Questions for Discussion

1. What was your general reaction to reading *Learning to Stay*?

2. Did you know anything about post-traumatic stress syndrome and traumatic brain injury before reading the book? What did you learn that most surprised or shocked you?

3. Discuss the company culture and expectations at Elise's job at the law firm, within the context of the novel and from your own job experience. Are they unrealistic expectations, or necessary ones? Do they exact too high a price? Is it a price you would be willing to pay, especially during this time of high unemployment?

4. Discuss Elise's efforts to get Brad help. Does she do enough, or does she pack him off to his dad too soon? Not soon enough? Would you have handled the situation differently?

5. Should more tax dollars go to supporting U.S. veterans? Have you seen indications that more services are being made available? What additional programs would you like to see?

6. *Learning to Stay* is, at heart, about a marriage in crisis. Is it fair to say that the marriage is saved by the dog Jones?

7. Animals can perform amazing services for humans. Discuss the stories you've heard, or personally experienced, in which an animal enriched, or even saved, a human life.

8. Darcy thinks Elise should stand by Brad no matter what. Sondra urges her to leave him. If you were in Elise's situation, what would you do?

9. Do you think Elise should go ahead and have a child with Brad? What kinds of questions should a couple consider when deciding whether to have a child?

10. Compare the life Elise might have had with Brad if he hadn't gone to Iraq versus the life she expects to have with him at the end of the novel.

FOR FURTHER READING

Memoirs on TBI

Where Is the Mango Princess? by Cathy Crimmins, Vintage Books, 2000.

In an Instant by Lee and Bob Woodruff, Random House, 2007.

A Three Dog Life by Abigail Thomas, Harcourt, 2007.

Non-Fiction about the Iraq and Afghanistan Wars

Black Hearts: One Platoon's Descent into Madness in Iraq's Triangle of Death by Jim Frederick, Broadway, 2010.

Where Men Win Glory: The Odyssey of Pat Tillman by Jon Krakauer, Anchor Books, 2010.

The Looming Tower: Al Qaeda and the Road to 9/11 by Lawrence Wright, Vintage Books, 2007.

The Unforgiving Minute: A Soldier's Education by Craig Mullaney, Penguin, 2010.

Generation Kill by Evan Wright, Berkley Publishing Group, 2004.

War by Sebastian Junger, Twelve, 2004.

Here, Bullet (2005) and *Phantom Noise* (2010) by Brian Turner, Alice James Books.

Black Hawk Down: A Story of Modern War by Mark Bowden, Transworld Paperbacks, 2002.

The Good Soldiers by David Finkel, Sarah Crichton Books, 2009.

Lone Survivor: The Eyewitness Account of Operation Redwing and the Lost Heroes of Seal Team 10 by Marcus Luttrell, Little, Brown, and Company, 2009.